How a Scot Surrenders to a Lady

Highlander Vows: Entangled Hearts, Book Five

by
Julie Johnstone

How a Scot Surrenders to a Lady
Copyright © 2017 by Julie Johnstone
Cover Design by The Midnight Muse
Editing by Double Vision Editorial and Victory Editing

All rights reserved. No part of this book may be reproduced in any form by any electronic or mechanical means—except in the case of brief quotations embodied in critical articles or reviews—without written permission.

The characters and events portrayed in this book are fictitious. Any similarity to real persons, living or dead, is purely coincidental and not intended by the author.

The best way to stay in touch is to subscribe to my newsletter. Go to www.juliejohnstoneauthor.com and subscribe in the box at the top of the page that says Newsletter. If you don't hear from me once a month, please check your spam filter and set up your email to allow my messages through to you so you don't miss the opportunity to win great prizes or hear about appearances.

Dedication

For all the readers who have written to me to tell me how much they love my *Highlander Vows: Entangled Hearts* series. Your letters mean the world to me!

Author's Note

Dear Readers,

I have taken great pains to make sure the words I used in writing this story were as historically accurate as possible. However, given that I am writing to a modern audience, there are some instances when I chose to use a word that was not in existence in the fourteenth century, as they simply did not have a word at that time to correctly convey the meaning of the sentence.

If you're interested in when my books go on sale, or want to be one of the first to know about my new releases, please follow me on BookBub! You'll get quick book notifications every time there's a new pre-order, book on sale, or new release with an easy click of your mouse to follow me. You can follow me on BookBub here:
www.bookbub.com/authors/julie-johnstone

All the best,
Julie

Prologue

1352
Isle of Skye, Scotland

Cameron MacLeod paused at the top of the seagate stairs to strip off his clothing, leaving on only his braies, which were hanging low on his hips.

"What are ye doing?" his older brother Graham demanded from behind him, his voice rising sharply above the music of the pipers from the shore below.

Cameron ignored Graham for a moment. His brothers were always questioning him—what he did, why he did it, why he *didn't* do something, what was he thinking when he'd done a particular something. It made him so angry!

An all-too-familiar tic began in Cameron's jaw. He clenched his teeth as he stared down at the torches that littered the shore. They flickered bright orange in the slowly descending night sky. Thoughts of the past stirred on the salty breeze that blew off the loch, cooling his sweat-slicked skin after hours of target practice. His father's voice, harsh and razor-sharp, hummed in his mind, making the twitch grow worse: *Ye'll nae ever be the warrior that yer brothers are.*

"Brother," Graham growled. "Did ye hear me?"

Cameron nodded absently. How was it that his father's critical voice could still be so loud from the grave?

Attempting to shake the memories, he looked out at the

thick throng of revelers who'd traveled from near and far to join in the MacLeod clan's annual St. John's Eve celebration. His father had died right before the same celebration two years prior. The recollections were always strong this night. Father was gone, yet Cameron still expected to see him, eyes narrowed and mouth twisted with disappointment.

He's nae here, Cameron reminded himself. *And ye are worthy.*

Below, on the shore that surrounded one side of his and his brothers' home, Dunvegan Castle, rings of fire blazed in perfect lines, as if an army of flame advanced from the loch to attack. It was a sight to behold and conjured memories that his older brothers Iain, Lachlan, and even Graham had told Cameron about going into battle. His brothers had risked their lives to protect others, but he had not. He'd asked—repeatedly—when scrimmages had arisen, but Iain, as the eldest brother and the MacLeod laird, had denied him each time, insisting fifteen summers was too young to fight.

But Iain had lied. Cameron knew this to be true because his brother had been in battle by fifteen summers himself. Their father had often bragged that one as young as Iain had been a fiercer warrior than men who were much older than he was. Iain simply didn't think Cameron ready. That desperate feeling to prove himself—and prove everyone else wrong—flushed him like a fever.

"Are ye dallying here in hopes of missing the dagger-throwing competition?" Graham asked, his goading tone snapping Cameron to attention. He opened his mouth to answer, but Graham spoke again. "Do ye fear ye will nae win? I staked my horse, who ye ken I love more than ye, against Archibald MacLean's boastful claim that he would beat ye so soundly ye'd be ashamed to hold yer head up."

Cameron smiled grimly. Archibald MacLean, cousin to

Alex MacLean—the laird of the MacLean clan and friend to all the MacLeod brothers—thought too much of his own skills. "Dunnae fret, Brother," Cameron said. "I'll send Archibald home without yer destrier and with a much-needed reminder that I'm the best dagger thrower in Scotland."

Graham whistled. "'Tis quite an assertion."

Cameron shrugged. "'Tis a fact. Iain and Lachlan are the best at hand-to-hand combat," he started, "ye are the greatest hunter, and I've the most skill with forging weapons, throwing daggers, and charming the lasses."

Graham smacked Cameron in the head with a grunt. "If ye spent less time wooing the lasses, ye'd have more time to focus on becoming a better warrior."

Cameron's skin prickled with irritation, but he shoved the anger away. It did no good. For years, he'd been vexed at his father for making him feel unworthy to be a MacLeod, and it had not changed his father's opinion. Besides, he *was* focused—merely on the lasses. He still trained diligently, as he'd done when their father was alive, but now he refused to walk around like a dog begging for recognition.

"If training to be a warrior was half as enjoyable as charming the lasses, then I'd dedicate myself to the task body and soul," Cameron replied, falling into the familiar habit of cloaking himself in indifference. Lately, apathy hadn't been coming easily, though.

As the words left his mouth, his gaze fastened on Mary, a household servant with a sweet smile and kind disposition, with whom he'd often flirted. She ascended the seagate stairs, and when she saw him, a smile transformed the look of deep focus on her face to one of pleasure. "Talking of lasses…"

A grunt came from Graham. "Ye're wasting yer potential by dividing yer attention between training and the lasses." His rebuking tone, so similar to their father's, caused Cameron's jaw to immediately lock, sending a sharp pain shooting along the edge.

His irritation increased, yet he knew well that showing it was pointless. Instead, he snorted and said, "If ye believe time spent with lasses is a waste, ye have simply nae met the right lass."

"Apparently ye have nae, either," Graham drawled. "Every time I turn around, ye are with a different lass."

Cameron winked at his brother, though his tic now beat a rapid tattoo along his jaw. "All the lasses I give my attention to are the right lasses for my purposes."

"Ye have a purpose, then, do ye?" Graham asked, arching his eyebrows.

Cameron flinched. Devil take his brother for getting to him. "Aye. Enjoyment of life. There are four of us. *Four* MacLeod brothers." Sometimes they seemed to forget he was one of them, as if he didn't belong. "I suppose the duty of enjoying life falls to me since the lot of ye will nae give me another."

For the love of God, where had that come from?

Graham's eyes widened, and pity appeared in his brother's gaze. "Cameron—"

"Iain is the oldest, he's laird, and he's married," Cameron rushed out, his throat tightening even as he spoke, as if he were struggling to hold in a truth. "There is nae a chance he can enjoy life, the poor man, what with his duties as laird and husband to Catriona."

Graham frowned at him. "Cameron—"

Cameron cut him off again, that tightening feeling in his throat causing him to swallow hard. "Lachlan is too busy fighting battles or training to fight battles. The pitiable wee devil barely takes time to enjoy the sun on his face, let alone a lass."

Deep lines appeared between Graham's brows. Cameron didn't know whether it was because he still hadn't let Graham speak or because of Graham and Lachlan's contentious relationship. To say the two brothers were not close was not strong enough. Cameron may only have been fifteen summers, but he saw the things his brothers tried to hide. He suspected much of the problem between Lachlan and Graham was that Graham was jealous of Lachlan. But it was not Cameron's problem to sort out.

"And ye…" He speared Graham with a knowing look. "I ken ye only have eyes for one lass, though ye dunnae ever seem to make any progress with her." Cameron was boldly alluding to his suspicion that Graham was smitten with Bridgette MacLean, Alex MacLean's sister.

Graham's face turned red, and he opened his mouth—likely to deny it—but Cameron pushed forward again, glad to have the focus off himself. "Dunnae bother crying false. I will nae tell yer secret." He continued toward the shore but had not gotten more than five steps when he met with Mary, who was slow to climb the stairs with the jugs of ale she was carrying.

She paused directly in front of him and gave him a saucy look. "If ye win the dagger-throwing contest, I'll give ye a kiss."

Out of habit, Cameron winked at the lass, though he felt no desire to woo anyone at the moment. "Then I must be sure to win," he replied smoothly, ignoring the derisive noise that came from Graham.

"Come find me in the kitchens when it's over, aye?" she asked, stepping around him.

She had already walked past him when he replied, "Aye, I'll do that."

He continued at a faster pace down the stairs, wanting to reach the shore before Graham might speak of his purpose in life again. Lillianna, a curly-headed brunette one year his senior, came quickly up the stairs toward them.

The daughter of the stable master paused in the middle of the steps to smile up at him, and he slowed to a stop. "I've been looking for ye, Cameron," Lillianna said.

"Have ye now, lass?" he teased. Lasses and humor usually helped to keep the empty feeling away. "What is it ye be needing from me?"

"I've collected fern seeds for ye to rub on yer eyelids so ye can see the fairies that come out tonight during the celebration," she replied with a flirtatious smile.

He barely repressed the urge to shudder, which would likely offend her. He had as deep a belief in fairies and in seers as any man or woman in his clan, but that did not mean he wanted to see the magical creatures. Before his father had died, he had told Cameron about a time he had sought out Eolande, the seer who lived at the Fairy Pools on Skye and was thought to be of fairy blood. Long ago, Eolande had gifted one of his forefathers with a charmed Fairy Flag to be used to save his clan in a time of dire need, so when the seer had foretold his father's death, Father had believed her. Not a day had passed that Father hadn't regretted the burden of the knowledge.

No thanks. He didn't want to see fairies, or seers, or the seer-fairy of Skye and learn some dire foretelling of his own life. Still, he'd take the seeds so as not to hurt Lillianna, and he would toss them away. He held out his hand. "That was verra sweet of ye to collect seeds for me, Lillianna."

"Close yer eyes," she commanded, surprising him.

"What for?" he asked with a frown.

"So I can rub the fern seeds on yer eyelids, of course," she answered.

Behind him, Graham shifted from foot to foot, and Cameron could imagine the restless, irritated expression his brother likely wore. It no doubt resembled the one his father had worn for years whenever he had looked at Cameron.

His stomach tightened. He was stuck. But he'd not appear fearful now. "Dunnae fash yerself, lass. I'll do it."

Did his voice sound panicky, or was that his imagination? He studied Lillianna's face for signs that she might have noticed his hesitation.

She smirked at him. "Dunnae tell me ye're suddenly afraid to let a woman touch ye?"

"Aye," came Graham's laughter-choked voice. He shoved Cameron in the shoulder. "Are ye scairt to let the lass put the fern seeds on yer eyelids?"

Cameron's tic returned with the force of a hit to his jaw. He inhaled sharply, his nostrils flaring. His brother knew good and damned well that he had no interest in seeing any magical creatures. Graham was the one person to whom Cameron had long ago confessed his wariness.

Lillianna gave him an expectant look, and then her lips parted. "Are ye fearful of the fairies, the seers, or both?" Surprise muffled her tone.

"Nae either," he said as decisively as he could manage and promptly closed his eyes. "Just eager to reach the dagger-throwing contest. Be quick about it, aye?"

"To be certain, I will," she responded before her cool, smooth fingertips touched his lids and gently rubbed the fern seeds on them. Unease stirred deep within him, but he held himself perfectly still. Suddenly her touch was gone, and he opened his eyes to find her face a hairsbreadth from his. "Do ye ken what I have under my gown tonight, Cameron?"

He gave her a wolfish smile. He knew well the tradition of wearing nothing under one's outer clothing on St. John's Eve. Legend had it that young, unmarried folk would divine lovers for the night, or perchance even find their future spouses. He had no interest in a spouse, but a lass to dally with…? He started to raise his hand to run it down Lillianna's rosy cheek when his brother clasped his shoulder.

"Time to go," Graham barked. Stepping to Cameron's side without releasing his hold, he propelled him down the stairs.

For the space of a breath, Cameron considered resisting, but he did need to get to the dagger-throwing competition. Still, he glanced over his shoulder and winked at Lillianna. "Wish me luck."

Lillianna blew him a kiss. "Come find me in the great hall when ye're done."

He nodded even as Graham snorted loudly beside him. As they continued their descent, Graham spoke. "How do ye plan to meet with two lasses at once?"

Cameron blinked in confusion until he recalled his promise to Mary. "Simple. I'll meet Mary first and then Lillianna," he said with a grin.

Graham scowled at him. "One day, Brother, ye will meet a lass who will make things confusing."

"And I'll wish her farewell faster than she can take a breath," Cameron replied, not liking how much his brother's glare reminded him of their father's. The past was haunting him tonight, and he felt out of sorts. "I dunnae want one lass," he continued, but the feeling of being confused—or rather, on the verge of something important—grew. "Especially a confusing one." His voice had become quieter, and his mind whirred as if a storm had slipped into his head. "I want nothing more than to be a warrior." The truth came out before he could stop it.

His brother's eyes widened a fraction, and he sighed. "I suspected." Graham clasped him on the shoulder. "Dunnae be yer own worst enemy, then."

Cameron frowned. "I'm nae. I train as much as anyone else, but Iain dunnae seem to see, nor care."

"Iain sees everything. Dunnae ever forget that. He sees that ye have given up; we all do. Iain is testing ye, waiting to see if ye will rise up and become the man we all ken ye can be. Presently, ye're failing Iain's test. Dunnae continue to be a clot-heid. If ye truly wish to be seen as an equal, ye must pursue that desire with utter determination."

Their eyes locked, and Cameron realized with a start that what his brother had said made sense. He *had* given up, had settled on being the reckless brother.

He clasped Graham's shoulder. "Thank ye, Brother. I'll nae give up."

Graham nodded as they moved onto the shore from the stairs, and the noise of the assembled crowd swallowed them. They weaved through clansmen and strangers, and in and out of bonfires that had been lit to ward off evil spirits. Near where all the contestants were lined up side-by-side for the dagger-throwing competition, Cameron halted as a group of barefooted children raced in front of him, giggling and waving sticks as they pretended to battle one another. Once they were past, Cameron strode toward Iain and Catriona, who leaned against her husband, looking pale as the moon and fragile as a newborn babe.

Cameron's throat tightened at his sister-in-law's sickly state. Her difficulty breathing and horrid coughing spells seemed to be worsening by the day, but he'd not utter the thought aloud. To do so would bring his brother's wrath down upon him. If a body could be saved from death by the love of another, then Cameron had no doubt Catriona would regain her health, as his brother loved her mightily.

When Cameron moved to his place in the line of competitors, Iain gave him a narrow-eyed look that conveyed, without doubt or words, his vexation with Cameron for being late. His older brother was almost always irritated with him, just as their father had always been, but maybe it was a test, as Graham had said.

Cameron was about to apologize for his delay when Archibald looked at him and spoke. "We were all beginning to wonder if ye were scairt to face me in competition."

"I dunnae fear ye, Archibald," Cameron drawled as he donned his plaid once more. "Yer aim is about as impressive as this day is short." He twisted his mouth in a smirk.

Archibald furrowed his brow. "'Tis one of the longest days of the year…"

"Aye," Cameron said with a chuckle, then tapped the man on the side of the head. "The day is nae short, and yer aim is nae impressive."

Guffaws rang out down the line of twelve men.

Archibald smacked Cameron's arm away. "I'll show ye how impressive my aim is," the man thundered, swinging a punch at Cameron.

As Cameron ducked, a hand shot out in front of his face to stop Archibald's fist.

Alex appeared seemingly out of the mist. Archibald's cousin towered over him, dark and grimacing. "Keep yer temper and yer wits about ye, or ye're certain to be bested as ye were the other day by my wee sister."

Bridgette MacLean tossed her long red hair over her

shoulder before offering a smirk from where she stood with the other women. Her green eyes danced with mirth. Knowing Bridgette, she'd much rather be in the competition than watching it, but her brother had refused to let her participate.

"She did nae best me," Archibald grumbled. "I let her win."

"Ye're lying to save yerself the mortification," Bridgette replied matter-of-factly. "I told ye then, and I'll tell ye now—women are better at dagger throwing because we've more patience."

"Step up in line and prove it," Hugo, the Earl of Ross's son, jeered.

Cameron grimaced. He'd never liked the grasping bastard son of the earl, and it had nothing to do with Hugo being the result of an illicit affair between the earl and his wife's sister. Cameron didn't give a saint's sniff about the shame that others said was attached to Hugo. What Cameron did care about was that Hugo had used the fact that his father was cousin to King David to attain land he did not deserve. But as of late, fate had taken care of Hugo and the earl, as both seemed to be falling out of favor with the King of Scots, who was presently imprisoned in England.

"What's the matter, Bridgette?" Hugo taunted. "Are ye fearful ye'll shame yerself if ye throw with the men?"

Cameron glanced swiftly at Graham, wondering if his brother was going to finally make known his feelings for Bridgette by coming to her defense. His jaw was set and his sword drawn, but as he stepped forward, Bridgette snorted and waved a dismissive hand at him. "Och, if my brother would let me throw, ye'd be the one shamed, Hugo."

Iain raised his hands for silence, and a hush fell over the

assembled crowd. "Ye all ken the rules, but they bear repeating. The dagger closest to the target wins. Twelve men stand ready to compete and have offered up the necessary purse of coin. The winner takes all twelve purses."

Iain quickly called out the clans present, as well as one lone competitor. The man had no plaid on to indicate he was part of any clan, so Cameron assumed the stranger was a *Ceàrdannan*. He wasn't overly taken aback to see a Summer Walker at Dunvegan for the festival, but he hadn't expected to see one competing. The clanless land travelers usually did not partake in such things.

Cameron studied the man at the end of the line. His build was unimpressive—slight, really, almost like that of a lass. The stranger's hands looked smooth, his fingers long and thin, but he displayed amazing skill as he stood there flipping his dagger repeatedly. He twisted it over his wrist and then under it, clearly adept and comfortable with the weapon. The competitor wore a cloak with a hood pulled low. Cameron's gaze trailed up to the warrior's face, but all he could see was the tip of the stranger's chin. Cameron would have thought that odd enough to confront the man, but Summer Walkers were known for disregarding convention, so he let it go and began his own exercises to warm up his throwing hand.

He took a long, slow breath in preparation to throw and moved his gaze across the crowd and down the long center of the twenty blazing circles of fire. The small target was fastened to a post at the end of the circles.

He gasped at the sight of Eolande suddenly standing in front of the target, her dark hair billowing around her shoulders, though the wind was not strong enough to cause such a thing. His gut clenched as he felt the coldness of her violet gaze land on him. The white léine she was wearing seemed to shimmer like jewels upon her as she raised a hand and motioned in his direction. Was she beckoning him? He glanced around at the others, but no one else seemed to notice her.

Cameron rubbed his eyes, unsure of his own mind. When he brought his hands away, all he saw was the fire and the shadows cast in the darkening sky. Relief washed over him, and he raised his hand just in time for Iain's signal to throw the daggers.

The knives swished through the air, numerous thuds resounding in rapid succession, almost simultaneously meeting their marks. The men whooped in hopeful triumph, and Cameron's blood rushed through his veins in his own expectation of victory. He took one step out of line toward the target with the surety that he was the winner, but as he moved, a dagger whistled through the air and hit the target hard, sending a vibration through the now-silent crowd. A collective gasp sounded from the spectators, and Cameron glanced at the man who had thrown his dagger well after everyone else—the Summer Walker.

His first inclination was to cry foul, but he kept his mouth shut. No rule had been made that all contestants had to throw their daggers at the same time. The only thing this man had done was make a clever choice to wait. Cameron clenched his teeth in anger, but it was at himself. All the competitors, save himself and the Summer Walker, rushed toward the target, and most of the crowd that had been watching did so as well.

Cameron looked from the stranger to the target. His gut told him he'd lost. His dagger had a black hilt, and from here, it looked like a dagger with a light-colored hilt was lodged in the center of the target. He turned to study the man once again. The Summer Walker stood perfectly still except for his slender hands, which were twined together as he tapped his thumbs in a frenzy. The man was nervous. But why?

"'Twas clever of ye to see the advantage of waiting to throw and taking it," said the man—well, he was nearly a man—standing beside her.

Sorcha Stewart sucked in a sharp breath at the warrior's admission. As she looked at the man who was studying her, it was hard to think upon her plan, upon anything other than him. He was tall and surprisingly thick with muscles for a man with such a young face. He looked to be a year, maybe two, ahead of her fifteen summers. His gaze was probing, like that of someone much older, and it was locked upon her. It felt as if his will alone could move her hood to reveal her face. She nervously tugged the material farther down, though she knew very well it was impossible for someone to move something without touching it.

The man—Cameron, she'd heard him called—tracked her movements, and she had to force herself not to fidget. His expression had become one of fixation, as if he was trying to figure something out—likely her—but there was a friendliness to his face that made her want to smile at him.

Down near the target, a cacophony of shouts exploded in the semi-silence. A deep, angry male voice sounded above the others.

She tensed as she glanced toward the target. She had to flee now before she was caught. She took a step to do so, but Cameron clasped her shoulder. It took only a breath to realize fighting him would be futile. She jerked away twice, and his grip tightened, unrelenting.

"Are ye nae going to speak to me?" he asked, his voice gravelly. His eyebrows, thick and golden like his hair, rose into a high arch.

She shook her head. She prided herself on her ability to judge people the minute she met them. It was a skill she'd acquired when quite young and living in a house where everyone had secrets. She considered herself quite adept at forming quick conclusions on the make of a man—or woman, for that matter. This warrior before her was clever and curious; it was in his searching, twinkling eyes. He'd hear her voice and know immediately that she was not a man, and then she'd be found out. And her father would learn she'd not stayed in the tent as he had told her to do, which would be a very bad thing. Father had ordered her twin brother, Finn, to stand guard at her tent, but Finn had left to chase a lass the minute Father had departed. So if it was discovered that she had departed the tent, Finn would pay dearly, and she didn't want that.

Devil take her faults! If only Hugo had not bested her by cheating when they had thrown daggers yesterday, then she would not have felt the need to best him today in an honest competition. He was such a braggart, and she detested the way he tried to make her feel inferior and weak every time he and his father came to visit her father. He did it to Finn, as well, and she could never fight the urge to protect her brother. Yet, it did seem that lately he was resentful of and irritated by her need to watch out for him. She intended to tell Hugo what she had done later and happily watch his face drain of color. There was no worry Hugo would reveal her secret either, as he would rather have his eye stabbed out than let it be known that a lass—especially one three years younger than he was—had bested him.

"That man used tricks to win!" someone bellowed from near the target.

Sorcha flinched, and her heart jumped from her chest to her throat. Pinpricks raced across her skin as her stomach tightened. Now she was done for. If they dragged her down to the targets to quarrel about if she had won fairly, they may demand she pull back her hood, and then they would discover she was a girl and not a man at all. Of course, Hugo would be humiliated, but risking her father's temper wasn't worth the public shaming.

"Cameron!" called a deep male voice from the target. "Get yer arse down here now and bring the Summer Walker with ye. The man needs to defend his win."

A fleeting spark of pride filled her, but it died quickly, smothered by worry.

"Ye heard my brother," Cameron said. "It seems ye've won, and though it pains me to be outwitted I'll take it like a man… unlike some others." Releasing her, he glanced toward the crowd gathered in the distance. "Shall we?" he asked, his head still turned.

Her answer was to run.

She quickly turned and sprinted in the opposite direction of the laird and the other competitors. Behind her, Cameron's footsteps thudded as he raced to ride up to her. Her breath rang in her ears, the puffs coming in a rhythm of one in, two out. He called to her, his voice seeming closer now. She dashed in front of a cart, and a woman yelped and threw a pitcher, which Sorcha ducked under just before it thumped to the ground.

She pushed her legs harder, her hood falling away, and her hair flew out to flap against her shoulders as she twisted through the crowd. She made for the thick rows of tents beyond the rocks. If she could reach them, she felt sure she could lose Cameron and make it back to her own tent before anyone was the wiser.

A group of children ran in front of her waving sticks and laughing, and she had to come to a shuddering stop to keep from trampling them.

"Part!" a high, melodic voice commanded. The children gasped as one and quickly obeyed, leaving an opening for Sorcha to run through.

She didn't question it nor hesitate to flee. She glanced over her shoulder only to see how close Cameron was, and her jaw dropped as their eyes locked. Even from a distance, she could feel his gaze burrowing into her, memorizing the details of her face. Thanks be to God that Cameron had been stopped by the children and a woman with long, flowing black hair.

A relieved laugh escaped her, and she boldly raised her hand, waving farewell to the warrior she'd bested. But the woman beside him caught Sorcha's notice. Her gaze probed Sorcha, causing unease to prickle across her skin. Though it was impossible to hear the woman say anything given the distance between them, Sorcha was certain that the woman was talking about her.

"Allow the lass to flee," Eolande said.

"And why should I do that?" Cameron demanded, stepping to move around the seer and frowning when she shifted to stay in his way.

"'Tis not yer time to meet her."

"Well," he said, "considering I've already met her, I'd say it *is* my time. It seems—" He stopped talking as he stared in amused shock at the slip of a lass with long golden hair. She paused in her flight, turned toward him, and grinning, waved a farewell before turning her back to him once more. He started toward the lass, her smile as blindingly beautiful as the now-full moon, but Eolande put up a hand. Before he could move away, she grasped him.

His entire body went rigid as she curled her long fingers around his arm. He could have broken free if he'd had the ability to move, but that was the thing he had always heard about seers: once they touched ye, they stole yer capacity to move as they saw into your future. His feet felt heavy as stones as Eolande's nails dug into his skin and her violet eyes speared him.

"'Tis nae time yet," she pressed.

"Why?" he demanded.

Eolande hissed between her teeth, her breath coming out in white circles as if it were freezing cold out, not as warm as it was. Wariness stirred deep within him as she spoke. "Because it is too soon. She will come to ye again, but this time in battle, bathed in blood and marked by a heart."

"What do ye mean she will come to me?" he found himself asking, even though he had never wanted to know his future.

Eolande didn't seem to hear his question. She looked through him as if he was not there. "To yer knees she will bring ye, and for her, ye will betray everything ye hold dear."

Cameron jerked, his denial surging through his veins. "I'd nae ever do such a thing."

"Ye will," Eolande said flatly in a voice so eerily certain that his gut twisted. "Ye will betray yer king, yer family, the very honor ye cloak yerself with."

The tic from earlier began to pound in his jaw. "I'd nae

ever do these things for a lass, nor any other," he growled.

Eolande's mouth pulled into a thin smile. "I only tell ye what I have seen."

"Yer vision is cloudy, then, Seer," he ground out.

"Perchance," she said with a shrug that contradicted the surety of her tone. "But I dunnae believe so. She is the mate of yer heart and the enemy of yer clan. With her comes life and death born of yer choices."

He looked past the seer toward where the lass had disappeared. The powerful urge to search for her, despite what he'd just heard, swept over him, leaving him vexed. He locked gazes with Eolande once more. "I will always put my family, my king, and my honor above all else."

"So says the blind man," Eolande replied, releasing him. "Yer eyes have just begun to be opened to lasses."

He could not help but laugh at that. "I assure ye, Seer, I have seen lasses for a good while."

"Nay. Ye have used lasses to cope with the loneliness ye bring to yerself."

Her words struck so close to the truth that a knot formed in his chest.

"That lass"—she pointed to where the girl had last been—"will catch ye like a fly in a web of longing. Kenning her will lead ye all the way out of the prison ye have created by allowing yer past to overshadow yer future."

"Enough," he snapped, not wishing to hear one more word about a future he'd never let come to pass. "I bid ye a good night," he growled and moved away.

Behind him, Eolande chuckled. "Ye kinnae run from yer future."

"Who's running from it?" he called back without stopping his flight. "I'm racing toward it. There are two lovely lasses waiting for me, and I intend to see them both. What say ye to that?"

She laughed. "I say it will be amusing to watch a blind man stumble in the dark."

"Blind man," he muttered, ignoring the curious gazes of the people he passed. "She's the one who has lost her sight."

Yes, that was it. He was certain of it. Because the future she foretold was simply not possible. Even on the slightest chance that it was, he knew of it now, and he would not allow himself to become so attached to a lass that he was willing to sacrifice honor, family, or king. He was worthy of the MacLeod name, and he'd never do anything to confirm otherwise.

One

1360
Abernathy, Scotland

Sorcha was supposed to be asleep, but her father's yelling had awakened her. Of course, she could have stayed abed, which was what she knew she *should* do, as it was not yet even dawn, but she'd always had trouble doing what she was supposed to do. Her mother, God rest her soul, had said it was because Sorcha had needed to battle her way into this world, turned the wrong way as she had been in her mother's stomach, and then she'd been born sickly and had to struggle to stay alive. Mother had always said Sorcha was a natural-born fighter.

Unfortunately, that is not the accepted thing for a lady to be, Mother had always added with a sigh.

Hearing her brother Finn's voice rise up in protest to something Father was saying, Sorcha quickly donned a gown and slippers and crept down the stairs, staying low. Her legs trembled from both her nerves and her crouched position. If Father caught her, she feared he'd marry her off in a fit of anger, as he had done to her sister, Constance, several months prior, not even a fortnight after Mother had died. Poor Constance had never even been disobedient like Sorcha, not until the day Father caught her in the arms of one of his commanders. Father had yelled that the Earl of

Angus's daughter was not supposed to waste her worth on a mere commander. All the years of Constance's meek, obedient behavior had not saved her from Father's anger.

It had taken only a sennight after the discovery of the kiss and Constance was gone, married off to the Earl of Mar, who had shamelessly arrived to collect Constance with his mistress on his arm. The earl had informed her sister in front of a room full of people, Sorcha included, that he expected an heir immediately or Constance could anticipate the same treatment his first wife had received. If the cook's whispers were correct, the earl's first wife had met with her death in a most suspicious manner. Sorcha knew by Constance's letters that she was absolutely miserable. The earl was a cruel, selfish man who kept his mistress in the room across the hall from Constance.

Directly after Father had married Constance off, he had told Sorcha in plain terms that if she disobeyed him one more time, he'd find a husband for her that made the Earl of Mar seem saintly. She didn't doubt him for a breath. He'd threatened it several times in the past few weeks, too, and she had spent many a sleepless night worried about to whom he might marry her.

When her mother had been alive, Sorcha had kept the slightest hope that she might one day have the good fortune of marrying a man she cared for, as Mother had often managed to influence Father's choices and treatment of them without him seeming to realize it. It was one of the great secrets Sorcha and her siblings knew but never dared to utter aloud. Thanks to Mother, Sorcha had been allowed to learn to read and write, Constance had not been married off at fifteen as Father had wanted, merely so he could gain land, and Finn had been able to avoid going to war after Mother had convinced Father that Finn's talents were needed at home. Her brother had a quick mind for arguments but no skills as a warrior, a fact Mother and Sorcha had often done their best to help Finn disguise. Yet Father knew and was cruel to Finn because of it.

Mother had managed to protect him for a bit, but not one day after her death, Father had demanded Finn go to battle. And it had only taken that one battle for him to realize the full extent of how his son, his *heir*, was not the man he hoped. Now Father was determined to make Finn a warrior.

Sorcha peered over the top of the stairs toward the open door of the great hall. She could see Finn's profile as he stood just inside the door. The man next to him was much taller and broader, but all she could see was a wide expanse of shoulders. With care, she moved down one step and then another until she could see curly dark hair, a chin covered with dark stubble, and the side of a square jaw. Her stomach twisted with recognition—Hugo, the Earl of Ross's son. His arms were crossed in his usual arrogant and annoying manner.

She nearly groaned. What was he doing here? She narrowed her gaze on Hugo. The man had absolutely no compassion for others, which was only one of the reasons she did not care for him.

She shimmied down another three steps, craned her neck to see if anyone had turned toward her, and dashed off the steps and to the left, where she could see fully into the room.

Her brother's and Hugo's backs were now to her, and upon the dais sat her father, Hugo's father, and two men she did not recognize. She instantly knew they were wealthy, however, by the richness of their cloaks and the many men hovering about them. She glanced over her shoulder toward the stairs and the direction of her bedchamber. If she were wise, she would go back to bed and keep doing her best to go unnoticed by her father. She prayed that at the upcoming feast, she might finally meet a man that truly stirred her and that, God willing, the meeting would lead to a love match that Father would accept. Or one that she would be willing to defy him to secure.

Her stomach flipped at the prospect of marrying a virtual stranger, but her stomach turned to hard knots at the thought of being forced to marry someone like the Earl of Mar, who would treat her like a brood mare, or Hugo, who would forever think himself better than her simply because he was a man. She wished to have a marriage like the one her aunt, Blanche, Baroness Wake of Layton, had found. Blanche had disobeyed her and mother's father's wishes long ago by running off into the night with an Englishman she had met at a tournament and had truly loved.

So far, Sorcha had only met men with whom she didn't care to be in the same room, let alone spend the rest of her life.

"Finn!" Her father's booming voice made her flinch. "Ye've failed me again!"

Sorcha winced, and her heart clenched for her brother, imagining how their father's cruel words likely made him feel. Finn had once been a happy child, but over the years, he had become an angry man, and Sorcha suspected it was because he could not please Father. She didn't know for certain, because he no longer confided in her. It seemed the more she tried to help, the more scornful he became. It didn't improve the matter that Father had often pointed out to Finn that she had more skill as a warrior than he did.

She could sense his resentment when he was around her, but he was her brother, her twin, and she loved him still. Because of this, she found herself creeping to the alcove under the stairs so she could see and hear better.

She watched as Father moved off the dais and advanced toward Finn, whose shoulders visibly stiffened at their father's approach. Father's boots thudded against the floor as he strode across the room and stopped directly in front of Finn. "Ye had one simple task," he snarled. "Kill Katherine Mortimer."

Sorcha's breath caught deep in her throat, and she found herself pressing as far back into the shadowy, dusty alcove as she could. Her back met with the wall, and she inhaled a long breath of the musty air, trying to calm her suddenly racing heart. Father had ordered a woman's death? Sorcha had long ago lost the notion that her father was a good man, yet to order a woman to be killed? And who was Katherine Mortimer?

Finn turned his head, and even from the cobwebbed alcove, she could see the side of his jaw set in anger. "The king's mistress was heavily guarded."

Gooseflesh prickled across Sorcha's entire body, and her scalp tingled with fear. Father had ordered the king's mistress killed?

Treason! Her father had committed treason and drawn Finn into it with him!

But why? Why?

She bit her lip, fearing she knew the answer. The king had been steadily stripping the nobles—her father included—of power, and the nobles were starting to rebel. She wrapped her arms around her waist, her heart pounding nearly out of her chest.

"Ye should have planned for guards!" Father rebuked, jabbing his finger into Finn's chest. "King David would guard his mistress well! Anyone who is nae a clot-heid would ken this. He is obsessed with the woman, which is precisely why I ordered ye to kill her!" Father shot out a gloved hand and smacked Finn so hard that her brother stumbled into Hugo. A disdainful look swept across Hugo's face as he shoved Finn away from him.

Sorcha pressed farther into the alcove, but there was nowhere to go. The wall blocked any retreat. For a moment, she wished desperately that she had stayed abed and had not heard this exchange, but with a squeeze of her eyes and another long breath, she pushed the thought away. Mother had always told her that everyone had secrets. Some would kill you slowly with the keeping, some would kill you quickly when revealed, and others would shape who you were. Secrets could make you better or worse, depending on if you learned from them. The trick was to know which was which. This was most definitely a secret that could get them *all* killed if King David learned of it. Thank God above that her brother had failed to murder the king's mistress.

Finn straightened his shoulders and stood tall, his eyes glittering dangerously. Sorcha sucked in a breath, certain he was about to finally make a stand against Father. "I'll hunt her down," he said instead, causing bile to rise in Sorcha's throat. "Even if I die in the process, I vow I'll nae fail ye again."

Sorcha trembled even as her father snorted. "If only yer vow held the weight of a capable warrior."

Finn seemed to grow smaller before Sorcha's eyes. His shoulders hunched, and his head dipped forward as if in shame. Usually, she would feel his woe at being dismissed so by their father, but all she could feel was horror. Finn intended to kill a woman because Father had commanded it; her brother was further gone than she had realized.

Feeling powerless to stop it or to help him, she dug her nails into her palms, the edges cutting into her sensitive flesh.

"All is nae lost," Hugo said. His strong confident voice rang of secrets that wielded power. "I ken where Katherine's party is going and the path they are taking."

Her father's eyebrows shot up. "And how did ye come by such information?"

Hugo turned to speak to her father, and she could see that one side of his mouth had pulled into a pompous smile. "I joined with one of Katherine's maids two days ago in Edinburgh. Once I learned who she was, it occurred to me I could get information out of the wench that might aid our cause."

Her father chuckled. "What a sacrifice ye've made, Hugo."

Now Hugo chuckled. The sound of his mirth at the dastardly thing he had done made Sorcha cringe. "I've nae a doubt I can overcome Katherine's party and kill her," Hugo said. "They are headed through the Caledonian Forest on the westernmost side, following the trail of the Marching Oaks."

Sorcha's stomach roiled at Hugo's offer. The man never did anything that he did not think would benefit him somehow, and she had a horrible suspicion…

"What would ye wish in return for completing the mission that was assigned to Finn by myself and the others?" Sorcha's father asked, waving a hand toward the two men who still sat at the dais.

Other rich nobles, she presumed, angry that King David was taking their land and giving it to commoners he thought more loyal. Of course, he was right. Her father and these "others" were not devoted to King David. In truth, they detested him because he would not let them influence the way he ruled.

Hugo turned to face the dais. "I would do anything to aid ye," he said and glanced to her father before looking back at the dais, "and my lords Stewart and March in your quest."

It was just like Hugo to avoid a direct question. He had to want something quite important to show such reluctance to reveal what it was until he felt certain of her father's answer. Sorcha did not miss how Hugo's gaze flicked to his father, the Earl of Ross, nor how the earl gave an almost imperceptible nod of approval at his son's words. The churning in her stomach turned so violent that she doubled over a bit, feeling sick.

"Of course ye would, Hugo," Sorcha's father said lazily. "We all ken ye want what's best for Scotland, as each of us certainly does. The king surely does, as well, though he seems to have forgotten that having us, the nobles, work with him to rule *is* what's best for Scotland."

Sorcha barely resisted the urge to grunt her disgust. Now that she knew who the noblemen in attendance in the room were, it was undeniable that each of them—from her father to King David's own nephew, the Steward—were not gathered here out of concern for Scotland. They were here to ensure they kept their power, just as she had guessed. Apparently, they had decided to strike at King David through his mistress to show the king they could hurt him despite the fact that he was king.

"Still," her father spoke again, "for risking yer life to help us tell David that without us by his side nae even his beloved mistress is safe, we—" her father waved a hand behind him to the men who sat silently on the dais "—would wish to reward ye for yer aid. Tell me, what sort of reward would ye care for?" It was a command more than a question; he was clearly weary of Hugo's stalling.

"If it pleases ye, my lord, I'd like to marry yer daughter," Hugo responded, finally revealing what he had been after.

A gasp escaped Sorcha, and she slapped a trembling hand over her mouth. Her pulse raced when Hugo's gaze shifted in her direction. For one long moment, she felt his eyes searching the darkness, and she feared greatly that somehow he could see her. She held her breath, but he looked at her father again. She exhaled, placing her palms flat against the walls to either side of her because her legs felt as if they might buckle beneath her.

"That certainly pleases me," her father replied so easily that tears instantly pricked Sorcha's eyes. He knew she did not wish to marry Hugo, did not even care for him, but none of that mattered to her father. *She* did not matter to him. He had bartered her away without so much as blinking.

Her throat tightened as the tears blurred her vision then slid down her cheeks in twin paths of warm, wet betrayal. She swiped angrily at them. She had understood for many years that Father considered her and her sister possessions to be used for gain, but she had never feared greatly what might come to pass because she believed Mother would somehow influence him. Sorcha had foolishly relied upon that knowledge for her future. But Mother was gone. Constance was gone.

Father clapped Hugo on the shoulder. "Once the deed is done, return to me and Sorcha will be yers, along with Blair Castle, which I will give to her as a wedding gift."

"Father!" Finn burst out.

Sorcha flinched, fearing what was to come, and within a breath, Finn's head jerked violently to the right when the back of their father's hand struck his cheek.

"Ye're nae worthy to command Blair Castle," Father snarled.

She cringed at the words. Blair Castle had been given to him by King David when he had helped negotiate the king's release from captivity in England just three years earlier. Father had promised the castle to Finn when he finally proved himself a worthy warrior.

She glanced to her brother and bit her lip, hoping he would not do or say anything that would make the situation worse. Finn turned so that she had a direct view of his face, and much to her relief, he pressed his lips into a thin white line as his cheeks turned a blotchy red. His hands curled into fists at his sides, but he did not speak.

She started to exhale a relieved breath when Father spoke. "Ye are nae worthy of the Stewart name, Finn. So help me, I will make a warrior out of ye if it kills me. Ye will ride with Hugo to hunt Katherine's party, ye will watch how a real warrior completes a mission, and then ye will return and serve as guard to yer sister as she makes her way to Blair Castle to rule it by Hugo's side." He paused. "And when Hugo deems ye to finally be a true warrior, ye may return to me and command my men, and someday, when I die, you may rule this castle. But if ye're never deemed worthy, as God is my witness, I'll give this castle and all others to the children Sorcha bears Hugo."

She cut her gaze to Hugo, who was struggling not to smirk. Panic swept through her at what was unfolding. If Hugo was successful and she did nothing to stop him, she would be a party to murder, not to mention she would become the man's wife. She could not live with herself if she did not try to prevent an innocent woman from being murdered, and she certainly did not want to be chained to

Hugo forever. Yet, if he wasn't successful and he was captured, or worse, Finn was captured, they may well all hang by the king's command once he traced the order back to the lords in this room.

She ground her teeth. She knew where the trail of the Marching Oaks was, and if she fled now, she had a very good chance of reaching Katherine before Hugo, Finn, and the others. She thanked heaven that her uncle Brom had secretly taught her how to ride a horse. She was an excellent rider, but if she did this, there might very well be no returning home if her betrayal was discovered by Hugo or his men. They'd tell her father and he'd brand her a traitor, and she shivered to think how Father might punish her. Marriage to Hugo surely would seem a blessing.

She pushed the fear out of her mind. She had to save the king's mistress, not to mention herself from Hugo and her brother from doing something so dreadful as to be party to the murder of the king's mistress.

Taking a deep breath, she crept out of the shadowy alcove and raced out of the castle. She had intended to take the most direct path to the stables, but to her horror, Hugo's men were already gathered in the courtyard, dressed battle-ready like Hugo and mounted on their destriers, as if waiting to depart as quickly as possible when the order came. She ducked back into the castle and made her way quickly to the rear door that led to the gardens.

Running now, she raced through the gardens toward the stables. She burst through the door, not at all surprised to see her uncle sitting on a stump talking to the horses. Brom was more comfortable around animals than he was around most people, so he was in the stables much of the time. He turned toward her, a childlike smile pulling at his lips. His eyes had always reminded her of Father's, but

Brom's were kind, unlike his brother's. His gaze darted all around her, yet never settled on her. Her throat tightened with emotion. She could flee to her aunt Blanche's home if her betrayal was discovered, but Brom and Finn were the two reasons she had not done so after her mother had died and Constance had been married off so callously by Father.

Brom had the big, burly body of a strong warrior but the mind of a child, and Finn had the mind of a man but not the will of a fighter, nor the spine to stand against Father. She feared what would become of both of them if she left. Sorcha was the only one other than Mother who had ever been able to calm Brom when he was agitated and could get him to talk at all. Her fears for Finn were entirely different but just as real. There was a desperation in him that had grown more and more each year, fed by Father's criticism and the pressure to become a coldhearted warrior—and man. She feared he was becoming just that, and she could not idly watch it happen.

She walked slowly toward Brom, though the urge to hurry swirled inside her. She had no idea how long she had before her brother, Hugo, and his men departed, but approaching Brom quickly had always been a sure way to agitate him. She paused close enough that she could get him to look at her but not so close that he would strike her if he became fearful and swung out. Brom would never intentionally hurt her, but when he was fearful, he became crazed.

"Brom," she said firmly, clapping her hands to get his attention.

His gaze flittered over her, then came back to her and settled. The small smile on Brom's face grew huge. "Sissy," he crooned.

She'd told Brom more times than she could remember

that she was his niece, but in his mind, he always thought of her as his sister. "Brom, I need to ride out quickly. Will you help me ready Summerset?"

He glanced to the door behind her, and a crease appeared between his brows, causing his smile to disappear. "Dark now," he said, his sparse words heralding his brewing agitation. Brom loved routine and hated anything that disrupted it.

"Brom," she said, making her voice stern. "I must ride out now. Someone needs my help. Ready Summerset."

Her uncle shook his head violently, his shaggy hair whipping from side to side. "Dark now," he repeated. "Dangerous and dark."

Sorcha looked toward the castle. Her time to gain a lead was quickly disappearing. "A woman's life is in danger. I must save her."

"Dark and dangerous. Dark and dangerous," Brom sang, his deep voice rising in volume and reverberating through the stables, causing the horse in front of him to neigh and dance.

Sorcha blew out a frustrated breath. She had not anticipated Brom's response to her request, and she knew that if she tried to charge past him, he would likely swoop her up and march her straight to the castle. She saw no other way to get to Summerset than to trick him, as much as she hated it.

"Aye, I suppose ye're correct," she lied. "'Tis too dark to ride now. I'd like to sit with ye a spell though. Will ye fetch my stump from under the oak?"

Brom's eyebrows dipped together, and she knew he was trying to decide if her sitting here at this hour was too much of a change from what usually occurred, so she hurriedly added, "Please, Brom. Father is in a mood."

A fearful look swept across Brom's face. Her uncle may have the mind of a child, but even children could remember what happened when a parent was angry. "The switch hurts."

Her throat tightened. Brom well knew the switch hurt, as Father had used it on him many times. On Finn, as well, but never on her, Constance, or Mother. Still, she nodded so he'd do as she'd asked. "Aye." The word caught in her throat with anger and sadness. "The switch does hurt. Will ye get the stump so I may sit with ye until Father's mood passes?"

He nodded, rose to his towering height of nearly six and a half feet, and started toward the door as he chanted, "Get stump. Get stump. Brom get stump for Sissy." She hated to leave Brom to deal with Father's wrath, but there was no choice. He was too unpredictable to take with her.

The second he rounded out of sight, she raced to Summerset's stall, threw open the door, saddled and bridled the beast, and then led the horse outside. Immediately, voices assaulted her ears. Pinpricks raced across her skin as the flickering of torches lit up the night.

"We ride fast and hard and on my command," Hugo said to his men, alerting her to the fact that he had come outside fast on her own flight from the castle.

Sorcha didn't wait to hear more. She swung onto Summerset's back and turned her away from the oncoming party and toward the woods that would lead them to the trail of the Marching Oaks. The sound of her breath and her thundering heart filled her ears, but as she entered the woods, a high, keening pitch broke through her fear.

"Sissy! Sissy!" Brom called.

Her heart ached at having to leave her uncle, but she would come back for him, no matter what. She stole one glance over her shoulder and met Hugo's shocked stare before righting herself, nudging Summerset into a gallop, and racing into the forest. She was fast on a horse but so was Hugo. And unlike her, he was accustomed to riding in the dark. She could only pray she would reach the king's mistress before Hugo did.

※

Cameron's senses were on alert as he guided his horse, Winthrop, slowly through the black woods that would take them back home. He rode at the front of the party tasked with guarding King David's mistress, Katherine Mortimer, as they traveled to Dunvegan to be reunited with the king. Being in the lead meant that he was the first to see signs of danger and warn the others, and he was the first to take any arrows that may be shot at them if he failed to recognize a threat. He welcomed the challenge. For five years, he had worked tirelessly to prove he was worthy of such responsibility and equal to his legendary brothers. This was his chance to attain all he had long desired. That knowledge had been with him since a fortnight ago when they had first left Dunvegan, and it was with him now on the last leg of the journey home.

The darkness penetrated almost everything now that they had entered the thickest part of the forest, yet it did not cause him fear. After years of hunting and tracking through this area, he could travel the land in his sleep. He could not see the roots growing up from the mossy forest floor, yet he knew they were there, so he took care to keep his pace slow. He knew just ahead was the trail of the Marching Oaks because they had traversed four hills, rounded six corners, and crossed two streams. With the Marching Oaks would come such blackness it would feel to those who were not used to it that it swallowed their very soul. The gnarled tree branches would rise on either side of them, the thick leaves blocking all light. But to him, the darkness meant greater protection from ambush, which is why he had chosen this route.

Just before the start of the trail lay a stream, and its trickling water whispered against his ear. He stopped and reached out to his right, brushing his fingertips along the rough branch of the first oak, and then he turned his attention to listening for any sound that was not natural to the forest. The wind whistled, and behind him, leaves crunched and twigs snapped as the men in his party brought their horses to a stop, obeying his silent command. The majority of the men were MacLeod-born, and of those who were not, two of them served King David and the other two served Alex MacLean. It meant that on this mission they served him, the leader, without question.

As if Alex could sense that Cameron had thought of him, the MacLean laird brought his horse up beside Cameron's. The slow, steady breath of the beasts filled the silence, but there was something else in the air—a low hum that reminded him of the vibrating sound of many galloping horses. "Do ye hear the hum?" Cameron asked Alex in a low voice.

Alex's brow furrowed as he cocked his head to listen. "I kinnae say for certain. What does it sound like to ye?"

"Horses galloping," Cameron replied, scrubbing a hand across his chin. The softness gave him pause, until he recalled he had shaved his beard before they left for home.

They sat in silence listening, but he could no longer hear the sound. Maybe he'd imagined it, or maybe the whistling wind merely now disguised it... His gut tightened as he strained to hear, and his muscles twitched in anticipation of what might be coming. An uneasy feeling swirled inside him. In the past several years of strife among the Scottish clans, he'd learned to trust his instincts. And after Graham had almost died defending Iain's and Lachlan's wives two years prior, Cameron also learned that in order to be the best warrior he could be, he had to rid himself of the fear that he would never match the skill of his brothers. He still wanted to be as skilled as they were, but he no longer worried that he would not be. Instead, he worked tirelessly so that he would.

"I hear only the normal night sounds of the forest now," he said in a low voice, "but I feel unsettled."

"I trust yer instincts," Alex replied, wiping rain from his face as the light mist had suddenly become heavier. "What do ye wish to do?"

Behind them, Katherine Mortimer's whiny tone filtered through the dark and grated against Cameron's ears. He found himself clenching his teeth. He could not wait to be rid of the lady. She had no care for her own safety or the directives he'd given her. He'd explained carefully that they must travel stealthily and in silence, and yet she complained continuously, seemingly oblivious to the noise she made.

The rain began to fall more heavily, making him keenly aware that if someone was to approach, the attackers would now be even more difficult to hear. He drew his sword, and without having to command it, he heard the swish of all weapons behind him being drawn.

"Let us make haste down the trail of the Marching Oaks," he said. To go around would waste too much time.

"Lord MacLeod!" Katherine Mortimer bellowed. Cameron winced as birds flew out from branches in fright of the woman's screeching. "Lord MacLeod, why have we stopped? I'm eager to get back to the king."

He hissed between his teeth at her folly. If an enemy *was* waiting for them, her yelling certainly announced their presence. He turned and whistled softly to Rory Mac, a council member of the MacLeod clan and loyal friend, who was one horse behind him and Alex.

Rory Mac quickly answered the call, bringing his horse near. "Aye, *my lord?*"

The emphasis on the words *my lord* was not lost on Cameron. Rory Mac was not used to answering to him. The man was much like an older brother to Cameron. Rory Mac had seen him at his most foolish and angry, and when he spent entirely too much time wooing countless lasses to fill the loneliness that keeping his brothers at a distance had caused. Cameron had learned slowly to allow them closer and not to always expect that they would belittle him as their father had done. The need to still prove himself worthy burned inside him, but differently now. He wanted to be trusted to help protect the clan, not for glory or praise. This was his chance to show his brothers that he was capable of a commanding role so they would rely on him as fully as they did one another.

He would not fail.

Cameron glanced in Rory Mac's direction but could not see his face in the darkness. The awkward feeling of the reversal of positions could not be allowed to inhibit his command. He'd asked the king for this assignment, and he could ill afford to have any mishaps. The king had been leery about acquiescing to Cameron's request, but he'd done so after Iain had spoken up and said he believed Cameron was ready for the position. The support had shocked Cameron. Knowing that his brother may actually finally believe in him had moved something within. It was a foreign feeling, but one he was glad to experience. He prayed his brother's faith was not ill bestowed.

"Go explain to Lady Mortimer that her yelling in the forest when we are trying to travel in stealth could be the verra thing that gets her killed," Cameron clipped out.

"Aye, my lord," Rory Mac said once more. "Being a commander seems to come naturally to ye," he added with gruffness before doing as he had been ordered.

The words made Cameron smile, despite his tension. They were as close to a compliment as the Scot had ever given him.

He stared in the direction of the trail of the Marching Oaks. Darkness was both his enemy and friend right now, as was the rain. He would need to be ready for anything. Taking a deep breath, he let out an owl call, alerting his men to advance.

Two

Sorcha saw Hugo before she heard him, but only because he was carrying a torch. His horse bolted from between two trees, and when he glimpsed her and extinguished the torch, the blackness swallowed him whole. Yet she knew he was still there, in spite of the fact that she could not hear his horse's hooves because of the pouring rain. Hugo was not the sort of man to give up on something simply because a problem—her—had arisen. She glanced toward the trail, obscured in darkness and then toward where Hugo had been. She started to give the order for her horse to flee when the reins were snatched from her hands. *Hugo!* He yanked back hard. Summerset whinnied loudly and reared back her head.

"What the devil are ye doing?" Hugo demanded in a voice just fierce enough to be heard over the rain. The darkness may have concealed his features, but the anger in his tone was easily discernible.

Her mind raced, and before she could think of an answer, she felt motion to her left. A horse brushed her leg and a hand gripped her by the arm. Fingers dug mercilessly into her flesh. "Answer now, Sorcha," came her brother's voice, his words cold as ice.

Her heart hammered so hard she feared she could not form words, let alone a believable lie. "I overheard Father speaking with the two of ye, and I wanted to help," she replied truthfully.

"Ye wish to help kill the king's mistress?" Hugo asked, his disbelief evident in his tone.

She nodded, barely containing her sigh of relief that Hugo had drawn such an erroneous but beneficial conclusion.

"Damn yer eyes," Finn snarled. "Ye betray me—yer own brother."

Sorcha sucked in a sharp breath at the barely contained anger in his voice. She could see how he'd think that, given Father had said he would give Blair Castle to her as a wedding present after Hugo killed Katherine.

"Finn, nay! 'Tis nae what ye think!" But she could not explain more. Not now. Not with Hugo listening.

"Hugo," a man hissed from behind her, making her jump. She had not even heard anyone else approach. "Someone is coming!"

Before she knew what was occurring, Finn had released his hold and her horse was being turned. "Wait by yer sister," Hugo commanded. "Keep my future wife safe."

Finn muttered his disgust but led her through the darkness until she felt a branch brush against her cheek. "Dunnae move." He spoke so near to her that she jerked. His warm breath washed over her. "That castle is mine, Sorcha. I'll be killing the mistress. Nae ye and nae that damnable Hugo."

The air swished around her as he moved away, but she blindly reached out and grasped his arm. "Finn, nay," she whispered furiously hoping no one else could hear. "Ye must nae do this!"

"I am soaked to the bone!" a woman cried out.

Sorcha released Finn and moved her horse toward the

voice, filled with the certainty that the woman had just sealed her own death. "Lady Katherine!" she screamed.

Lightning slashed across the black sky, illuminating it long enough to see a fair-haired man at the front of a group of warriors. Their gazes locked before the night closed around them again. Thunder boomed, as did Sorcha's heart. Then the clank of swords meeting resounded around her.

Blindly, she urged her horse forward toward the woman's whimpering voice. A second voice, deep and male, demanded the woman's silence, but her cries grew louder. Thunder shook the earth again, and lightning once more slashed across the sky to illuminate the melee. All around her, men battled one another. To her right, the whimpering woman was on horseback, three guards surrounding her. One of Hugo's men struck down the man closest to the king's mistress, then a couple of arrows sliced before Sorcha's face. She stared in horror as the arrows hit Katherine's two remaining defenders.

A war cry came from the darkness that once again blanketed them all, and thunder and lightning crashed. When she could see again, she screamed at the sight of Hugo beside her, bow raised and arrow aimed at the king's mistress. Hugo released it as the fair-haired man she'd seen a moment ago cut down two of Hugo's men to get to the woman. But it was too late. Hugo's arrow struck with a *thunk*, straight into the woman's heart.

"Flee!" Hugo roared.

Before Sorcha could decide what to do, a hand slapped Summerset on the flank, and her horse took off so suddenly that she nearly toppled from the back of the beast. Fear raced through her as she reached out, searching for the reins that had been snatched from her. Branches whipped across her face, leaving a trail of stinging skin and warm, trickling blood. Tree limbs snagged her sides, cut her legs, and caught the sleeves of her gown, ripping the material as Summerset surged forward, too terrified to heed Sorcha's commands to slow.

The jolting ride rattled her teeth, and sharp pain shot up from her bottom and along her spine. Her head pounded as she leaned farther down over the horse, feeling around frantically for the reins now. Finally, her fingers grazed the rough leads, and she began to sob, grasping them and sitting up as she pulled back. Relief flooded her, but it was fleeting as Summerset neighed loudly and something knocked Sorcha in the middle of her forehead. A horrified scream was ripped from her as she flew off the back of her destrier and landed hard on the ground. Her head smacked against a rock that robbed her of all thought.

Cameron found he could kill just as easily blinded as with sight. Sound guided his movements, and rage made him quick and deadly. He cut down a man to his right and struck two to his left. Then, as a sword sliced behind him whispering death in his ear, he whipped around, lunged forward, and sliced his blade through soft flesh and hard bone. With a grunt, he yanked his sword from his enemy's torso and whirled around to face another foe. Lightning illuminated the area where he stood as rain pelted him. In the brief flash of light, he saw that Katherine was lying upon the ground unmoving. Kieran MacLeod and two of the king's men were lying near her, also unmoving, and their attackers were fleeing.

"After them! All of ye!" he ordered, even as he dismounted to help the king's mistress and the injured men. At least he hoped they were merely injured.

Stark terror mingled with rage as he strode through the darkness. Guided by memory, he moved toward where he had seen Katherine and the men. His boot had touched a body before he realized he was upon one. He kneeled, his knees hitting the now-soggy ground and sinking into the muck. He strained to see, sweeping his gaze first over Kieran and then one of the king's men. Both were dead, killed by well-aimed arrows to the head. The storm lit the sky once more, showing the other king's guard with a slit throat, open eyes, and an open mouth.

Cameron moved instinctively toward Katherine. His heart thudded heavily as he slid his hands up her body with care, feeling for injury. The silk of her gown was wet, whether from the rain or from blood he wasn't sure. When lightning split the sky once more, it illuminated her long enough for him to see the crimson soaking her gown, upon his hands, and on her face where he had slid his hand to find her neck and cradle it.

"Katherine?" He pulled her close, and the metallic smell of blood filled his nostrils. With trembling hands, he found her nose. He placed one hand on her chest to feel for her heartbeat and one hand below her nose, hoping her breath would tickle his fingers. Nothing. No beat, no breath, just eternal stillness. Death hung over her, and guilt cloaked him.

You are unworthy, his father's long-ago voice whispered in his head. There would be grave consequences for Katherine's death, but not now, not while his men were pursuing the attackers.

He whistled loudly for Winthrop, and when the horse nuzzled Cameron in the shoulder, he swung onto the beast's back and sent out a loud sea hawk call. Immediately, calls came back from his men, letting him know the directions in which they had scattered to give chase to the enemies who had fled like cowards. Blessedly, the rain stopped, and he stilled for a moment, listening. Horse hooves pounded somewhere from the left. He turned Winthrop and raced toward the sound. As he rode out of the thickest part of the woods, a small measure of light from above guided him.

He sent the call out again, then following it, he drove Winthrop over a crest and down a steep, rocky embankment before crossing a stream into a much less dense part of the forest. As he galloped toward the answering sound of his call, his mind swung to the woman with the long, pale hair who he had seen just before the battle had begun. What in God's name was a lass doing in a party of murdering men? Had she been taken by them, or was she with them voluntarily?

Early-morning light trickled through the branches in this part of the forest. He blinked, his thoughts abandoning the unexpected woman as his eyes adjusted and fixed on Alex battling two men in the distance. Cameron tapped Winthrop's flanks with his heels, urging his destrier into a faster pace. He drew his sword high as he surged toward the man on Alex's left. He struck a blow to the man's sword arm, but he surprised Cameron by ducking and slashing his sword at Winthrop. Cameron jerked his horse back and dismounted in a flash, sending Winthrop to safety while whirling to face the man who was charging him.

The enemy attempted to hit him from the left, but Cameron easily defended the attack, rid the man of his sword, and felled him with a quick, savage cut of his blade to the man's chest. The enemy gripped himself and fell sideways to join his comrade, who Alex had killed.

"How many?" Alex demanded, light from the rising sun washing over his face as he wiped the sweat and blood running down his forehead and into his right eye.

"How many left, or how many dead?" Cameron asked.

"Dead by yer sword?"

"Five including this one," Cameron responded, gesturing to the man on the ground.

Alex jerked his head in a nod. "I killed two," he bit out.

"Both men?" Cameron asked, thinking once again of the pale-haired lass.

"Ye saw her, too? I thought I imagined it."

"Nay," Cameron said with a frown. "What ye saw was real." The woman's presence was a puzzle, but it was one that would have to wait. He let out another owl's call, and one came back loud and from the right.

Quickly moving toward the dead men, he glanced down, dismissing the first almost immediately. He didn't recognize the man, and the stranger had no distinguishable characteristics that might aid them in discovering who had attacked them. But the second man's eyes were wide in death and quickly caught Cameron's attention.

"Do ye recognize him?" he asked Alex.

"Nay. Do ye?"

Cameron shook his head and kneeled, then bent closer so his face was right up to the man's. He hissed in a breath. "He has one green eye and one blue eye. And look at the scar on his cheek." It was shaped like a bolt of lightning.

"Shall we take him with us?" Alex asked, leaning in beside Cameron.

"Nay. We can ill afford to be slowed with enemies still lurking. He'll be easy enough to recall. I dunnae imagine there is another man with two such colored eyes and that sort of marking on his cheek," Cameron replied. He stood abruptly and whistled for Winthrop. He trotted over, as did Alex's destrier. Once they had both mounted their horses, they rode fast in the direction of the answering call from moments before. He released two more calls to guide him to his men.

They crested a hill, and in the distance, he saw his men gathered. He counted them quickly and cursed, searching the men to see who had fallen. Who was not there? As he rode closer, his gut twisted with the realization that there was a body slumped over the front of a horse manned by another rider.

His and Alex's men stood silently watching their approach. Cameron stopped in front of Broch, his second-in-command after Rory Mac, and with a nod of acknowledgment to the man, he moved closer to Rory Mac, who was slumped over the front of Broch's horse. By the horse's feet lay a dead enemy. Cameron touched Rory Mac's shoulder, but he did not otherwise move. With a grunt and help from Broch, they shifted Rory Mac into an upright position as gently as possible. He winced when he saw the deep wound at Rory Mac's midsection. It was a blessing the man had passed out. With care, he probed the wound to judge its severity.

Fear threaded through him. This was a killing wound. There was nothing he could do now except get Rory Mac to Dunvegan Castle and to Marion, Iain's second wife and a woman with great knowledge of the healing arts. "Can ye ride with him?" he asked Broch. Rory Mac was not a small man.

Broch's hard stare met Cameron's. "Aye." He slid an arm around Rory Mac's midsection and together they leaned the man back against Broch. "I'll watch over him. I vow it."

Cameron gave a brief nod before sweeping his gaze over his men.

"I counted ten enemies," Cameron said. Nods of agreement came from the others. "Two have escaped us?" he asked. He presumed it was so, but he wanted confirmation.

Again, the men nodded, some looking down in shame, others' faces twisting with anger, and still others looking at him with questioning expressions. They were awaiting his orders. He knew it, but his mind was going over every choice he had made, wondering if each had been the right one. It prevented him from speaking. Where had he misjudged? He could not see the exact moment in his mind, which worried him. For so long he had wanted to prove he was worthy to lead, and he had proven the opposite. He had failed Iain. He had failed Katherine. And he failed the king's dead men and Rory Mac.

Cameron's throat tightened painfully. What to do? Pursue the attackers or save Rory Mac?

There was no question.

"Ride fast and hard to Dunvegan," Cameron ordered, meeting every man's gaze. "I'll collect Katherine's body and nae be far behind."

All the men nodded and immediately started to move to obey, except Alex. "Cameron, a word?"

"Hold," Cameron commanded to the men as he moved his destrier away from the group along with Alex.

"The king will nae be pleased at the choice to put Rory Mac before pursuing the attackers," Alex said when they were far enough away for discretion.

"The king will likely want my head for Katherine's life; it dunnae matter what I do now," Cameron bit out. "So I dunnae give a damn at this moment if my saving Rory Mac angers him more. Nae that I would have made the choice differently under other circumstances."

Alex clasped Cameron on the shoulder. "I agree. I just wanted to ensure ye had thought about his response."

"Aye," Cameron replied grimly, "I have."

Alex eyed Cameron. "I'll ride with ye. And dunnae attempt to argue."

"I dunnae fear that the attackers have lingered, Alex. Ye ken as well as I do, they were after Katherine. And since they succeeded..."

Alex nodded. "They've likely fled. I dunnae stay with ye because of them. I remain with ye because of David."

Cameron let out a derisive chuckle. "Yer presence by my side will nae stop the king from taking my life on sight if he wishes, and it may get ye killed as well for simply being with me when I deliver Katherine to the king."

"I'll take that chance," Alex replied, determination lacing his tone.

Cameron nodded. He knew it was futile to argue with the man, who was as stubborn as Iain. It meant a great deal to him that Alex would willingly risk his life for him, but it would not come to that. He'd have to ensure that Alex was not by his side when the king found out about Katherine. Precisely how he was going to achieve that eluded him now, but he had the journey back to Dunvegan to formulate a plan.

"Broch," Cameron called, getting the man's swift attention. "Ye're in charge. Alex will remain with me. Ride swiftly and save Rory Mac."

"Aye. Ye can trust me, Cameron," Broch replied, already turning to depart for Dunvegan.

Cameron watched long enough to see the men follow, and then he silently guided Winthrop in the direction he had left Katherine and set out to collect the king's dead mistress.

Just as he pressed his heels into his destrier to signal a gallop, Alex said, "Her death was nae yer fault."

Cameron involuntarily jerked at the words spoken aloud, words that completely contradicted what he knew to be true. In pulling backward, he slowed Winthrop, whom he'd just set into a gallop. The horse threw his head back at the opposing order but settled when Cameron rubbed a soothing hand down the back of his neck.

"It was," Cameron replied, his tone as desolate as he felt inside.

Alex shook his head. "It was her own damn fault for speaking when she was told nae to. If she had nae opened her mouth, the arrows would nae have found her in the darkness."

"It was my responsibility to ensure she understood the consequence of disobeying my orders, and to be ready for the possibility that she might. I failed on both accounts."

"My God, Cameron." Alex's tone held frustration and sympathy. "Nae even the keenest leader could have been ready for Katherine's foolish actions. The standards ye are holding yerself to are nae attainable."

"They are the standards required of a leader of the MacLeod clan," Cameron snapped.

"I dunnae believe yer brothers expect ye to be faultless," Alex declared.

"I expect it," Cameron growled, setting Winthrop to a gallop.

They made their way back across the stream and started through the thick brush and under overhanging branches. When a snake fell from the trees above them, Cameron threw off the slimy thing with a hiss, spooking Winthrop.

The horse reared up on his hind legs and tossed his head back with a snort.

"Settle, ye wild beastie," Cameron ordered as he and Alex searched the ground for the snake. He glanced above them to ensure there were no more surprises to come.

When he deemed it clear, he looked again to the path, more vigilant now as he watched for anything amiss. Winthrop hadn't moved two steps before Cameron yanked up on the horse's reins when he spotted something pale and slender on the ground. His first thought was that it was another snake, but he dismissed the insensible notion as he'd never seen a snake such a color. He moved Winthrop a step closer and let out a slow breath. An arm. He was staring at an arm.

"Och!" he swore, pointing at it. "Do ye see that?" he asked Alex as he dismounted.

"Aye," Alex replied, the thud of his feet landing on the ground resounding behind Cameron.

He drew his sword, preparing for an ambush, but as he drew near the body, his lips parted and he lowered his sword. "By God," he muttered and put away his weapon.

Alex gave a sharp intake of breath from beside Cameron as they stared down at the woman. This was the flaxen-haired lass he'd glimpsed earlier. She was lying still, her delicate features bathed in the early-morning sunlight and her forehead covered with blood. He dropped to his knees in the cold, hard dirt. Rocks dug into his skin as memories sliced through his mind like sharp daggers, shredding his control.

He saw the St. John's Eve festival of five years before and the lass turning to wave a mocking farewell after she had bested him in dagger throwing and dashing away. He recalled Eolande's violet eyes penetrating him as she foretold his future. A shudder ran through him as the seer's words echoed in his head.

She will come to ye again, but this time in battle, bathed in blood and marked by a heart. To yer knees she will bring ye, and for her, ye will betray everything ye hold dear.

His heart began to pound a fearful beat as he stared at the lass. Long, dark lashes rested against her pale skin. Her cheekbones were high, lips full, and nose pert. Her thick hair fanned out around her, stark light against the dark dirt. A deep, dark gash of dried blood ran across her forehead. She must have bled a great deal, for the blood had run down the side of her face and matted in her hair by her shoulders. She smelled floral, like bell heather, and he immediately thought of sunshine as his gaze passed over her blond hair and moved to her hands. A dagger rested against her palm, and by the way her fingers had folded open, he knew she'd been clutching it when she had been knocked from her horse. It was obvious what had happened by the long cut across her head and the branch above her.

Alex elbowed Cameron. "Do ye fear she's dead?"

"Do ye?" Cameron growled, his response so violently strong at the possibility that it made him almost nervous to touch her. He waited for her to take a breath. When it came, slow and shallow, he exhaled an odd feeling of relief. "She lives," he announced. When his fingers grazed her cool skin, his body responded by tightening all over. It took great will not to release her immediately. He gave her a small shake, and when she did not respond but remained motionless with her eyes still closed, he raked his gaze over her, searching for the heart the seer had spoken of while fighting back a sense of dread.

No heart was readily seen, but it gave him little comfort as she was fully clothed and there could well be the marking

Eolande had referred to in a place he could not see. His fingers twitched with the desire to explore, but his wariness at actually discovering the mark stilled him. He wanted to reject the seer's prophecy, but how could he if this lass was marked by the symbol of which Eolande had spoken? He clenched his teeth. She may have had a heart, but he was no betrayer of family and king.

"Shall I gather her and ye go for Katherine?" Alex asked.

It was a reasonable suggestion. Actually, it was what Cameron would have insisted upon to ensure the king did not take his anger out on Alex if he were to arrive with the king's dead mistress on his horse. Yet knowing it was the sound thing to do did not stop the sudden flare of possessiveness that arose in Cameron. That feeling—that strange, inexplicable emotion for a woman he did not know—jolted him to his feet and sent him skittering back a few steps, his blood surging through his veins.

Alex frowned at him. "What's amiss?"

Eolande's damnable prophecy throbbed in his head, and even without seeing the heart upon the lass's body, Cameron was somehow certain it was there. And if it was there, despite believing he'd never betray his family nor his king, concern twisted through him at the strange feelings the lass had caused. He didn't want to be anywhere near her, yet he did. And because he did, despite knowing the prophecy, he needed to keep a safe distance. "I'll go gather Katherine and meet ye here."

Alex grasped him by the arm just as Cameron was turning away. "Are ye fashed about the king? Is that what has ye behaving suddenly so oddly?"

Cameron nodded, though he had hardly given thought to the king's response to Katherine since they had come upon the lass. "Aye," he forced out, shrugged out of his friend's hold, and then mounted his destrier and rode away. He wanted to look back and certify that Alex had gathered the lass upon his horse, but Cameron compelled himself to keep his gaze ahead of him. As he rode through the woods, the lie he'd told his friend lingered like ash on his tongue. He never lied, yet he had just now. Honor and truth were one, yet he had just broken the bind. Eolande's words roared even louder until they drowned out the sound of Winthrop's galloping.

For her, ye will betray everything ye hold dear.

"God above," he muttered. Where was his control?

He inhaled a ragged breath. All his life, he had wanted nothing more than to rectify his mistakes and prove he was worthy to fight by his brothers' sides.

And no lass was going interfere with that.

Three

It was nearly nightfall, and Cameron and Alex continued to ride in silence toward Dunvegan Castle, each carrying a woman across his lap. As they exited the thick woods, the outer bailey, which was lit with hundreds of torches, came into view.

"They await our return," Alex said, his voice grave.

"Aye," Cameron replied, his own tone heavy with tension. "I supposed they would, once the men gave word of the ambush."

Cameron glanced at Katherine's lifeless form. He could no longer see her injuries clearly due to the darkness, but he had stared at them long enough during the journey that they were seared into his memory. The deep crimson that had stained her gown when the arrow had pierced her flesh had spread across the fabric, and the metallic smell of blood still wafted from her. Bile rose in his throat, as it had done when he had first gathered her off the forest floor and into his arms. Death was not foreign to him. He'd been in a few battles and killed men who had intended to kill him, but he had never seen a helpless woman shot down, and never had he held a dead woman in his arms.

The wrongness of it struck him to the core. The pain, which had been piercing at first, then faded to a dull ache as the day had worn into night, became sharp once more, stabbing his belly as if he had swallowed knives. The need to obtain justice for Katherine throbbed within him, and the shame of his failure roiled in his gut.

As they drew closer to the castle, the distinct sound of many voices raised in a song for the injured floated to him. He tensed, knowing the refrain had to be for Rory Mac. His gaze slid to the mysterious lass in Alex's arms. She slept as if she were dead, yet she lived. He knew it to be so because he had made Alex check repeatedly on the journey.

"The king will be waiting," Cameron said, solemnly.

"Aye," Alex agreed.

"He'll want blood," Cameron continued. "And it dunnae need to be yers as well as mine."

Alex opened his mouth as if to argue, but Cameron held up a staying hand. He'd thought about what to say to persuade Alex to break away from him and let him face the king alone, and he believed he knew what words to use. "Please. The king will be unreasonable. We both ken this. Grief and rage may drive him to have the lass in yer arms immediately killed before we even ken if she is our enemy. Will ye help me prevent it?"

"Ye're too swift of mind for yer own good," Alex grumbled. "Ye thought of exactly what to say to get me to do yer bidding without argument, did ye nae?"

"I did," Cameron replied, relief that Alex would aid him gliding over him. But it did not linger under the dark sureness of the dire situation he faced and the knowledge of those gone and injured because of his mistakes. "Since we are agreed, go on and be quick about it. Take the seagate stairs up to the castle and seek out Marion to tend to the lass. If I manage to keep my head, I'll come to ye as soon as I can."

"I'll see ye soon," Alex replied before turning his horse

to leave.

Cameron watched Alex depart until he disappeared into the darkness, then he rode forth toward the growing light and noise. The voices, he realized, as he neared the front of the castle, were coming from within. A call went up, announcing he had been spotted, and the castle doors immediately opened. Out streamed King David, his cloak billowing behind him. On the king's heels were two of his guards and behind them were Iain, Lachlan, Broch, Ragnar MacLeod—one of their fiercest warriors, and Father Murdock, who was the MacLeod priest. His brother Graham would have been among the group, Cameron well knew, if Graham had still lived at Dunvegan, but he did not. He was at his new home with his new wife, and Cameron was glad of that. It was bad enough to drag Iain and Lachlan into this mess. At least one brother was well away and safe from the king's anger.

The castle door slammed shut with an ominous *thud*. Cameron studied the approaching group, very aware that his brothers had surrounded themselves with two of the fiercest MacLeod warriors. Not only that but they all had their weapons. Cameron's gut twisted with the realization that his brothers meant to defy the king if David ordered his death. Gratitude tightened his throat and shame burned his chest at the show of fealty from his brothers, both in blood and not. He did not deserve it, and he could not allow a war to commence over his mistake. His mind raced with what to say to maintain the peace and keep his life as he pulled his destrier to a halt at the first glowing torches. He carefully dismounted and released the binds that secured Katherine to his horse and drew her limp body into his arms. As her head lolled back, an anguished cry came from the king, who broke away from the men behind him and hurried forward, not stopping until he stood in front of Cameron.

"Give her to me," King David commanded, his face a twisted mask of pain and his voice gruff and laden with sorrow. He gesticulated rapidly at Cameron as he held out his hands.

Cameron passed Katherine to the king as gently as he could, then stepped back as the rest of the party approached. Immediately, his brothers and the MacLeod warriors came to flank him and face the king and his men.

King David walked away from the group, Father Murdock trailing behind him. As the king reentered the castle and the door closed once again, Iain motioned Cameron, Lachlan, and the other MacLeods away from the king's men. Once they were standing in a circle with their backs to David's guards, Iain said, "Dunnae speak when David returns. Let me talk for ye."

"Nay," Cameron replied.

Iain's dark brows drew together, and his eyes narrowed. "Nay? Do ye forget I'm yer laird as well as yer brother?"

A tic started in Cameron's jaw. "I did nae forget either, but ye will nae shield me this night. Nor ye," he quickly added, spearing Lachlan with a warning look. "Ye have both kept me safe from harm my whole life. This is my error, and I alone will carry the blame for it."

"We ken it was nae yer fault, Cameron. The men told us how Katherine disobeyed ye," Lachlan growled.

Cameron shook his head. "I was the leader, so it is my fault."

"We dunnae have time to argue fault now," Iain bit out. He turned his steely blue eyes on Cameron. "Dunnae say a word."

"I kinnae obey ye in this," Cameron said.

A murderous look crossed Iain's face, followed swiftly

by what looked to be fear and frustration. He clutched Cameron by the arm. "If ye kinnae keep yer mouth shut, then beg for yer life."

"Nay!" Cameron shrugged out of Iain's hold. "Why is it that ye would instruct me to beg when ye ken well ye would nae ever do so?"

"Ye are the youngest," Iain flung out as he jerked a hand through his hair and motioned between himself and Lachlan. "Ye are in need of our help!"

Cameron flinched, feeling his brother's words like hard hits to his gut. If they had faith in him, truly, they'd not think he needed help.

"Ye could lose yer life if the king becomes unreasonable," Lachlan said, staring hard at Cameron. "Ye kinnae ask us to stand by and do nothing."

"Think of yer wives and bairns," Cameron replied, knowing he was striking where both men were vulnerable. They loved their wives above all else. Cameron didn't claim to understand it, as he had never loved a woman in such a way, but he accepted it, and now he used it. "Would ye risk their lives for mine?"

Before either brother could answer, the castle door banged open once more, and David stormed outside. In his hands, he now held a sword that shone in the moonlight and the flames of the torches. "Kneel!" he thundered as he made his way toward them.

Cameron had no doubt the king was talking straight to him. He took a purposeful step away from his brothers and dropped to his knees.

"Seize his weapon," the king ordered his guards.

Cameron saw both his brothers' and the MacLeod guards' hands go to the hilt of their weapons, so he gave a subtle shake of his head, hoping to dissuade any action. The king brought the point of his sword to Cameron's throat. The tip dug into the flesh, and a stinging pain came directly before warm blood trickled down his neck.

"Tell me," the king demanded, his voice vibrating with fierce anger, "why should I nae take yer head right now for failing me so grievously?"

Cameron looked up to meet the king's glare. "I kinnae say ye should nae," he replied, his voice calm but his pulse racing.

"Cameron!" Iain rebuked, but Cameron ignored his brother.

"I was responsible for Katherine's life; therefore, her death is my responsibility."

"Aye," David agreed in a menacing tone. "It is. Shall we move forward with yer death, then?"

"Ye may choose that, Sire," he said slowly, considering how he would feel and what he would want to happen if he were the king. Revenge would be utmost in his mind if the woman he loved had been killed. "But I vow to ye, if ye allow me to live, there is nae a man alive who will be as relentless as I in hunting down Lady Mortimer's killers and exacting revenge. I pledge it to ye."

The king moved his sword and pointed it toward the ground before leaning close to Cameron. "It is fortunate for ye that I believe ye." The rage simmering inside him was unmistakable in his brittle tone. "And it's only because of this belief that I will spare yer life…for now."

Cameron did not allow himself the exhale of relief he felt. He was glad he didn't, as he realized the king was carefully watching him.

The king took a long, slow breath and spoke again. "I will have a head for this crime, and if ye dunnae give me one, it will be yers. Ye have until the leaves turn to bring me those who conspired to kill my Katherine."

Cameron nodded. That gave him the rest of the summer, which was not long but was more time than he could have hoped for. "I'll find them."

"Ye best," the king replied, his voice thrashing in intensity. "But," he added, drawing the word out, as his eyes flashed bright, "I require something more."

Cameron gritted his teeth. Of course there was more. King David had not managed to keep his throne for the twelve years he was in prison and then come out such a strong, ruthless leader merely by chance. The man was as calculating as he was clever.

"What more do ye wish, Sire?"

"I want ye to learn the names of every lord conspiring to overthrow me—and bring me proof of their treason—so I may quash them like the bugs they are. I've nary a doubt that killing Katherine was a blow by the lords who wish to show me they still have the power to control me."

God only knew how long it would take to discover each name and gather the proof, but if he wanted to keep his head...

Cameron nodded. "Ye have my pledge."

"Excellent." The king bared his teeth in some semblance of a smile. "Now tell me exactly what happened."

As he had no intention of relaying the tale on his knees, he got to his feet and told the king of the attack and the man with the scar and two different colored eyes. Then he paused as the weight of what—or rather *whom*—he had yet to mention pressed down upon him.

He flinched with the realization that his first instinct was to keep the lass's presence a secret. Eolande's words of betraying the king rang in his ears. The king seemed more reasonable now, so Cameron felt safer revealing her. "There was a lass with the men who attacked, and we have her," he said.

"The king's eyes narrowed to slits. "Ye captured her?"

"Nae exactly," Cameron admitted. "Alex and I came across her when we were riding to collect Katherine."

"Where is the lass?" the king bellowed. "Why did ye nae bring her to me immediately?"

"Because she's nae awake. She was felled from her horse by a branch across the forehead, and though we attempted to awaken her, she still sleeps as if she's dead."

"She will be shortly," the king snarled. "Where is she?"

The instinct to lie to the king and say the lass was not an enemy, even though Cameron had no notion whether that was true or not, was so strong that it astounded him. "I asked Alex to take her to Marion to see if she could awaken her."

When the king turned away and started for the castle door, Cameron bolted after him, as did the king's guards. A sense of urgency gripped him as he bypassed David's guards and fell into step beside the king. "Sire, the lass may well be able to tell us who led the attack. I dunnae believe killing her is the best course of action."

"I will be the one who decides that," King David growled before stalking into the castle.

Servants and MacLeods alike scurried away when faced with the sight of their king's livid face. But Cameron could still hear Iain's, Lachlan's, and the other warriors' heavy steps behind him. He met the king's rapid pace step for step, and it didn't take long to reach the healing room. When they arrived, the king didn't pause to knock on the closed door. Instead, he threw it open, causing Marion and Cameron's sister, Lena, to gasp.

Alex's sword was already drawn as he shoved both

women behind him. A murderous look flitted across his face, but as his gaze skittered first over the king, then Cameron, and then everyone behind him, Alex's gaze widened, and he slowly lowered his sword.

"Sire," he said, waving a hand toward the cot where the lass was lying. As the king brushed past Alex and the women to get to her, Marion darted toward the king. Cameron grasped her arm as she started by him and pulled her back, yet even as he did, Iain was by his side, taking his wife by the arm and giving her a warning look.

Marion was a kindhearted lass, which was miraculous since she was half-English and half-Scottish and had been born and raised in England by a man with no honor or love for his daughter. Yet, somehow she had become a woman who never wavered in risking her life for others. And by the determined look upon her face now, that included the mysterious, sleeping lass.

David looked down at the lass and then back at Marion. "Has she woken?"

"No," Marion answered in her perfect English accent, which never failed to make the king frown. She gave her husband a pleading look, and Iain reluctantly let go of her. He had been overprotective of her since the very moment he met her, after King David had asked—or rather subtly demanded—Iain marry her almost three years prior.

Still, as Marion moved to the king's side, Iain and Cameron went with her and Lachlan came up behind her. "She's taken a terrible injury to the head," Marion explained. "It could be days before she awakens. If she ever awakens..."

The king turned to face them all, a vicious smile twisting his lips. "Even in sleep I can see she is a rare beauty."

Disquiet stirred within Cameron. The king had a mind to use people to suit his needs, and it sounded like he had decided upon a use for the lass. Cameron had the pressing need to look at her, but he forced himself to remain still with his gaze locked on the king, who was spearing him with dark, unmerciful eyes.

"If she awakens and proves to be embroiled with those who killed my Katherine, I have just the man to sell the lass to. If she also proves to be unmarried and of worthy stock, of course, he will be the perfect match for her." The unease within Cameron increased as the king's smile twisted further. "And she will wish every day that I had ordered her death."

Cameron could feel himself frowning. He struggled to straighten his features, but the king's words battered at him. *Married?* He'd not once considered that the lass could be married, given Eolande's foretelling, yet the seer had not mentioned it.

Aware that David was staring at him expectantly, Cameron nodded. "As ye wish, Sire." Even as he gave his promise, unwillingness swirled within him.

The king pointed at him. "Until the leaves turn. Dunnae forget it," he warned. "And keep me informed."

"Ye've my word, Sire," he said, doing all he could to infuse his voice with fervor.

"I've had that before, and it did nae prove worth having," David snapped.

Cameron flinched as the king brushed past him. He rested his gaze briefly on his brothers and Alex who had drawn together and were speaking low.

The king paused at the door. "Iain. Alex. I wish a moment in private."

Both men quickly followed the king out the door. The moment it closed behind Alex, the king, and his guards, Cameron's gaze swept past his sister Lena, who stood near the cot the lass was on. Lena scowled down at the lass and then at him, but his attention had been drawn from his sister to the lass. He burned to ask questions about her, but first...

"How is Rory Mac faring?" Cameron asked as concern flooded him.

Marion nibbled on her lip. "Fever has set in already, but Alanna and I bathed him, and made him as comfortable as possible in his own bed. I was able to clean his wound satisfactorily, so I have hope that he will bear it and live to be as stubborn as ever."

Relief moved through Cameron. It seemed that Marion and Rory Mac's wife had done well; only time would heal him now. Cameron focused on the still unmoving lass. "Have ye ever tended to a body who did nae awaken from such an injury?"

"Aye," Marion replied. "But only one. The others awoke, some disoriented and some actually not recalling the day or other such memories. One even forgot his name for a bit."

He disliked the sudden lump of dread that settled in his belly. He wanted to believe the dismay was simply because he needed to question the lass, but as his gaze landed on her delicately sculpted face, then moved lower to her long neck, and lower still to her slender, creamy shoulders, shock stole his next breath. Her gown had been tugged down over the curve of her shoulders to the top of her arms, and there, on her right shoulder, was an unmistakable heart-shaped mark.

There could be no denying Eolande's words regarding the lass now.

He moved toward her, aware of the door opening, Iain entering the room alone, several pairs of eyes drilling into his back and his sister's gaze searching his from the front, yet he did not meet her questioning eyes or turn to meet those of his brother's and Marion. He reached down and traced his fingers over the mark. It was smooth, her skin silky and warm.

"Cameron?" Iain asked.

He heard his brother, but he could not seem to answer or turn from the lass. His breathing and heartbeat became ragged as her eyelids began to flutter. It felt as if she had raised a hand and slipped it around the back of his neck to pull him closer. He leaned toward her until her body heat touched him, her smell surrounded him, the whisper of her breath sent jolts through him.

"She's waking," he murmured, unable and unwilling to say more.

"Move back, ye clot-heid," Lachlan growled. "Ye'll scare the lass."

Cameron nodded, yet he stayed where he was. He couldn't have moved even if he wanted to, for in truth, he had never felt so drawn, so compelled to be close to someone in his life.

Her dark lashes fluttered slightly, and a soft moan came from between her rosy lips. Behind him, his family pressed nearer, too near for his liking. He wanted to be alone with her, yet that was likely dangerous. No matter what, he had to remember Eolande's words and not allow any connection to the lass to form. With that in mind, he dug within himself to find the determination to pull back and put physical distance between them, just as her eyelashes fluttered once more and her lids opened.

Bright, silvery-gray eyes met his. Unmistakable desire claimed him as her gleaming gaze widened, and she frowned. "Do I—" she croaked and then started to cough.

Immediately, a mug appeared by his right shoulder.

"Give her this," Marion commanded.

He took the mug and offered it to her as coughs racked her throat.

Slowly, she sat up, reached out, and grasped the mug. Her fingers grazed his, and the shock of her touch caused the stirring longing within him to blaze. He pulled back when he was certain she had a grip, and he watched, fascinated, as she took a long drink, cleared her throat, and handed the mug back to him. He accepted it without question while she pressed her fingers to her temple.

"What have ye done to me?" she asked, her voice low and husky, likely from lack of use.

"We've nae done a thing to ye," Lena muttered.

Ignoring his sister who he would try to reason with later, Cameron set the mug on the table beside the bed to gain a moment to compose a response. The real question, he thought as he turned to face the compelling lass before him, was what could she do to him if he was not careful enough?

Her mind spun as she waited for the large warrior—was he a warrior?—in front of her to answer. She didn't know him, did she? Slowly, she swept her gaze over him, hoping for recognition. Something within her seemed to register a memory of him, but it was muddled and she could not grasp it. She stared, sensing the rudeness of her actions, but she could not make herself look away. And either he could not care less for manners or he was just as confused as she was, because he matched her stare. Grass-green eyes penetrated her, making her shiver.

As she did, he frowned and, bending toward the foot of

the bed, grasped what she saw was a blanket. Murmurs and grunts came from behind him as he handed it to her. Doubt about whether to accept the offer or not assailed her, but when she looked into his eyes once again, she saw kindness there. She reached out and took the blanket, as her gaze strayed to the swell of muscles in his arms. Scanning the length of his body, she could see instantly that he was honed for battle.

"Ye could present yerself," came a man's half-irritated, half-amused voice from behind the warrior.

She snapped her gaze to the voice's owner. Guarded blue eyes met hers. She took in the black-haired giant of a man. His expression was intense, yet his stance relaxed. A contradiction that she felt certain was purposeful. Another shiver took her, even as the petite, blond woman beside him smiled. The warmth of the woman's smile eased the fear a bit, yet tension still built inside her. Pulling the soft blanket around her shoulders, she glanced around the room, passing her gaze over the myriad people gaping at her.

A woman with long, russet hair and wary blue eyes stood by a man who resembled her greatly, with the same color hair that touched his shoulders; however, his green eyes were very similar to the possibly familiar warrior. A thought struck, and she quickly studied the russet-haired man and woman, the golden-haired man in front of her, and the dark-haired man. Their eyes all had the same shape. They had to be related. But the blond woman? No. She looked out of place, yet at ease—a contradiction like the dark-haired man who hovered, obviously protectively, beside her.

She pulled the blanket tighter around her with a sudden need to hide herself, yet she was fully aware she was still very much exposed. Who were they? A quick perusal of the other occupants in the room confirmed that she could not recall any of them. There was only that slight niggling of recognition for the man who had handed her a blanket. Worry twisted in her belly.

"I dunnae ken ye," she murmured, but before anyone could answer, she added, "Do I?"

She sought the answer in her mind, but it was like a dark, black, soundless room. What was wrong with her?

"There's something out of sorts with me," she said, tapping the side of her throbbing head. A hundred thoughts tumbled around in her mind but not one would crystallize. A hot shaft of pain shot through her skull, and she moaned and drew her knees up to press her head against them. By all that was holy, her head felt as if it would burst like a berry that was being squashed underfoot. "What's wrong with me?" she whispered, hearing the fear in her own voice.

A heavy hand, warm and reassuring, came to her shoulder. "A branch felled ye from yer horse." The deep voice rumbled from above her.

Slowly, she glanced up to find the muscled warrior kneeling. "I fell?" she asked, raising her hand to her head and gasping when her fingers met a soft cloth bandage.

A crease appeared between his brows, and he glanced back at the blond woman, who gave him a quick nod. He met her gaze once more. A gentleness was there, but a guardedness, as well. "Dunnae ye ken what happened?" he asked.

She started to shake her head, but then she hissed with the pain and stilled. "I dunnae ken anything of how I was hurt." She searched her muddled thoughts, and fright filled her as she realized she had no memories. None! Not of her fall, nor before it, nor after. "I kinnae remember!" she cried out, instinctively grasped his hand, afraid this moment, this memory she was making and the drifting one of this man, she could not quite form into a picture would disappear.

A startled look came to his face as he glanced at their intertwined hands, then back to her. For one breath, she thought he might attempt to pull away, so she curled her fingers tighter and gripped harder. "Please," she whispered, embarrassed yet the fear overrode it. "Dunnae leave me. I dunnae ken these people. Ye are the only one who seems at all familiar."

He flinched at her declaration, making her feel foolish, but she pressed on. "I dunnae ken what happened to me."

Doubt flickered across his face, and tears blurred her vision. A strong desire not to cry took her, so she blinked repeatedly as he watched her.

"What do ye ken?" the russet-haired woman snapped.

Before there was time to answer, the blond woman said, "Don't mind her." She motioned to the woman. "Do you not recall anything?"

She met the woman's large eyes. The vast emptiness of her memories caused a hopelessness to blossom in her chest. Knots twisted in her stomach, and her scalp tingled. "Nae a thing," she pushed out, having to blink rapidly now to fight the tears. "Nae a thing," she repeated, hearing the desperation in her own voice. She didn't care. She *was* desperate! "The only thing I ken is this man here," she whispered in a half sob, lifting the hand that was still intertwined with the blond man's.

When she turned her eyes to his once more she could see the astonishment on his face. "Who are you?" She asked the question as a plea for knowledge, as well as a demand that he answer and help her. When his lips parted and he simply stared at her, her frustration at not remembering spilled over. She jerked her hand from his and glared at him.

"Who are ye?" Her voice pitched higher as her despair mounted. "Who are ye to me?"

She felt all eyes in the room upon them. The Scot's eyes became veiled, as if a mist had descended to hide his feelings. "I dunnae ken ye, nae really. I met ye once—"

She exhaled on a rush, feeling as if she were reaching out and grasping an invisible rope that would keep her from disappearing into a black void.

"What?" the dark-haired man bellowed from behind them.

Irritation flickered across the blond Scot's face. "Years ago," he said, without turning to look at the other man. Instead, he kept his gaze steady on her, but the gaze became seeking. "Ye were dressed as a lad and bested me in a dagger-throwing competition at our annual St. John's Eve festival."

She stilled, waiting with hopeful expectation that the revelation would shed light on the darkness clouding her mind, but no light came. Tears pricked her eyes and tightened her throat. She bit hard on her lip to stop herself from crying. "I dunnae remember it," she said in a shaky voice.

"What is yer name?" demanded the dark-haired warrior as he strode closer to tower over her.

She opened her mouth to answer but simply stared at him, feeling her mouth agape like a dead fish. Panic rioted within her, twisting and turning, and she gripped the light-haired Scot so hard, she felt him jerk. "I dunnae ken," she blurted, trying to hold back the rampaging terror.

"What's her name?" the gruff man demanded of the Scot.

The Scot swept his emerald gaze over her. "Ye did nae ever say, and ye ran off before I could find out."

"Ye must ken *something* about me?" she cried out. The room seemed to be spinning to her.

"All I ken about ye, lass," he said slowly, softly, as if he sensed her growing fright, "is that ye were amongst a party of men who attacked my men as we were bringing the king's mistress back to him."

She felt the hard stare of all eyes in the room upon her, especially the Scot before her. He looked at her expectantly, as if he wanted her to explain her presence there, which angered her since she could not remember anything. "I dunnae ken why I was with those men since I dunnae remember anything! Where is the king's mistress?" she gasped, her fear escalating. "Please," she almost begged. "May I see her?"

"She'd dead," the russet-haired woman replied flatly, watching her with obvious wariness.

Dear God above! Did they think she was a party to murder? She swept her gaze over the occupants of the room, coming back to the Scot before her. "Ye kinnae think I had something to do with it," she bit out, but even as the words left her mouth, her lack of memories taunted her. Had she had something to do with it?

"We dunnae truly ken yer part, if any, yet, do we?" the dark-haired man replied.

Four

"Might I talk to ye alone?" Cameron demanded more than asked Iain. His brother's jaw tensed. Cameron suspected Iain's ire had more to do with worry for him should he not find Katherine's killer than anger at the lass who shook like a leaf and who had fear swimming in the fathomless pools of her eyes.

"We can talk here, in front of—" Iain's words faltered "—the nameless one," he growled, locking his disbelieving glare on her.

A protective instinct flared within Cameron. "Dunnae call her that," he ground out as he moved to shield the lass from Iain. Cameron had seen grown men piss themselves from the force of his brother's glare, and he'd be damned if he was going to stand here and let Iain intimidate the lass.

His brother's eyes widened and his nostrils flared. "What would ye have me call her, then, since she claims she dunnae ken her own name."

"It's likely true," Marion inserted, putting her small hand on Iain's arm and giving him a chiding look. Cameron knew well if anyone had the power to calm Iain and make him see reason, it was his gentle but stubborn wife. And sure enough, Iain relaxed his rigid stance a bit as he gave his wife a skeptical look and a hint of a smile.

"Ye're too trusting, Wife," he said.

A scowl crossed her face, and she set her hands to her hips. "I trust when my heart and head tell me to, as I once did for you when you asked me to do so. Were my instincts wrong, Husband?"

"Nay, but that was me." He offered a cocky grin.

"And this is now," Marion replied sternly. "Speak with your brother outside and let me examine…" Marion shot an apologetic glance toward the lass, who was looking back with a mixture of awe and skepticism. "I fear we will have to simply give you a name until we learn your true one." Marion tilted her head. "How about Marna?"

"Nay," Cameron blurted. The lass was definitely not a Marna.

Lachlan, Iain, and Lena all gave him incredulous looks. He was sure they were wondering why he even cared what they called her. He would have been wondering about it himself if not for Eolande's prophecy. He knew why he cared, and he knew why he should force himself not to since she presented a danger to him, and yet this one thing seemed harmless yet important.

"What the devil do ye wish to call her, then?" Lena demanded, making him grimace with her snarly tone.

Cameron turned to look at the *her* in question. She shifted on the bed, slipped her feet to the ground, and slowly stood. She was a tall, graceful creature. At first glance, one would almost judge her fragile with such fine bones, yet she held her backbone straight with her shoulders squared and her chin tilted up. She had obviously taken control of the fear that had cloaked her moments before. Her thick, pale hair looked tousled, as if she had just enjoyed a good tumble in a bed, and her glittering eyes reminded him of the way the water in the loch looked when the sun hit it, like shiny bits of glass. She was so beautiful she looked like a princess or a queen.

"Serene," he blurted, knowing the name to mean *princess*.

Lena made a derisive noise, which he ignored.

Slowly, the lass nodded. "That seems acceptable. What do I call each of ye?"

Iain was the first to answer with one, gruff word. "Laird."

After Iain's reply, Marion, Lachlan, Broch and Ragnar offered their name. Lena's lips pressed into a thin line, as if she would not give the lass her name, but when Marion nudged Lena in the side, she muttered her name. Cameron sighed inwardly at his sister's unwelcoming behavior. He knew it stemmed from protectiveness of him.

Cameron was the last to speak. He met Serene's questioning eyes. "I'm Cameron," he said simply.

"Ye," she said, coming toward him and stopping near, so near that he could once again feel the heat of her and smell her intoxicating scent. Slowly, she reached for his hands, and when he realized she intended to grasp them, he shifted away. He wanted too greatly to hold her close. His irrational desire for the woman was a thing to fear.

"I've a memory of ye," she murmured, "that is like the mist. It's swirling in my head, but it will nae form a picture."

"In this memory," Lachlan drawled, humor in his voice, "were ye flat on yer back in a bed or possibly upon hay with my brother hovering over ye?"

"Shut yer mouth," Cameron growled as a deep crimson blush covered Serene's cheeks.

She focused on Lachlan, a scowl now marring her lovely face. "My memory is of his hands."

"That about suits what I'm saying," Lachlan replied with a chuckle.

"Brother," Cameron warned at the same moment Iain did.

Serene set her hands on her hips. "My memory is of his hands on a dagger."

Lachlan's smile turned into a smirk. "Some lasses would say—"

"That's enough," Cameron barked, clutched his older brother by the arm, and fairly dragged him toward the door. He stormed out with Iain on his heels.

The door slammed shut behind Iain, and both Iain and Cameron glared at Lachlan as they stood in the hallway. "What's the matter with ye?" Cameron growled. "Ye kinnae speak of my past to that lass."

"Yer past?" Lachlan remarked, cocking an eyebrow. He had a smug look on his face as he slid his gaze to Iain. "I told ye."

Cameron frowned. "Ye told him what?"

"Ye did tell me," Iain remarked, studying Cameron.

"What in the name of God are ye two speaking of?" Cameron demanded.

"Lachlan whispered to me in there"—Iain motioned to the healing room—"that ye were behaving out of sorts."

Cameron tensed, and Iain clamped a hand on his shoulder. "Ye kinnae get under the skirts of that lass."

Cameron narrowed his eyes on his brothers, but before he could respond, Lachlan spoke. "She's bonny, to be certain, but she may verra well be our enemy, and even if she's nae, the king has other plans for her."

"I ken," Cameron growled, though his chest tightened with the knowledge.

"We've already defied the king once," Iain added, referring to when they thwarted the king's order to send their sister, Lena, back to her abusive husband. The king did not know of their outright failure to obey, but it was obvious from comments he'd made that he suspected it. The MacLeod clan had always been a strong supporter of David, particularly since Iain and David had grown up together, but the king's insistence on reuniting Lena with her husband had put a strain on the relationship they had with the king.

"I dunnae have plans to seduce the lass," Cameron muttered.

"Then why did ye nae want her to ken of yer reputation with the ladies?" Lachlan asked.

"And why do ye keep defending her?" Iain added.

Cameron sighed and glanced at the door that separated him from Serene. It was a good thing to have space. A relief almost. Ever since he had beheld her face in the forest and recognized her, he had felt drawn to her, and his feelings were growing and changing at a rapid pace. She was a stranger, yet his instinct was to protect her as if he had known her all his life. He had not wanted to tell his brothers of Eolande's prophecy, but now he felt obligated to do so. "Ye ken how I said I met her at one of the St. John's Eve festivals?"

"Aye," came the immediate response from both Iain and Lachlan.

"Eolande stopped me from chasing Serene that night after she bested me and the others in the dagger-throwing contest. 'Tis why she got away and I never learned her real name."

Iain frowned, but Lachlan's face turned dark and wary. Cameron understood why. The seer had prophesized that Lachlan and Bridgette's love would drive a wedge between Lachlan and Graham, who had at one time wanted Bridgette for his own out of a need to best Lachlan. Eolande had foretold that one brother would end up dead as a result. This prophecy had kept Lachlan and Bridgette from acting upon their feelings, and it had nearly destroyed any chance for them and almost cost Bridgette her life. Lachlan had ended up pursuing Bridgette despite the curse, but most of what Eolande had prophesized had come true.

"I dunnae allow that seer's prophecy to rule the choices of my life," Lachlan said in a steely tone.

"I dunnae, either," Iain added, "but I dunnae dismiss it. Most of what she says comes true. So if there's a way to do what she tells ye, I believe it's wise."

Cameron noted that Lachlan did not disagree. Instead, he jerked his head in a nod. "I suppose I agree, but for me, I would have rather faced the worst of what she prophesized than live a life without Bridgette, so I pursued her. Ye ken the rest." He grinned. He often smiled when speaking of his wife.

"What did Eolande say to ye?" Iain asked Cameron.

Cameron's skin prickled with the recollection. He hesitated to speak aloud what she had predicted, yet he felt compelled to, given his intense response to Serene. "She told me that I would forsake everything I hold dear for the lass. King David." Cameron swallowed and forced himself not to glance away from his brothers. "The family." Iain's eyes went wide, and Lachlan's nostrils flared. Cameron curled his hands into fists. "And my honor," he added in a flat tone. He turned his face away for a moment, shamed by the foretelling of his weakness. "She said that the lass was the mate of my heart and enemy of our clan." He had to force the last words out. "And that with her comes life and death born of my choices," he finished, turning to look at his brothers once more.

"Stay away from the lass," Iain pronounced without

hesitation.

Cameron glanced at Lachlan, expecting him to mock Iain for his obvious fear of the seer's words or, at the very least, to disagree. Instead, Lachlan shifted from foot to foot, an uneasy look on his face. "Avoiding the lass seems the best course to me, as well. There's nae any sense taking chances that any part of Eolande's prophecy will come true."

"How am I to avoid her?" he demanded, truly questioning it but also keenly aware that he wished to unravel her secrets, not avoid her. "My life hangs precariously in the balance," he said, first eyeing Iain, then Lachlan. "I need to learn everything about this woman, because one small detail may verra well help me discover who she is and what she kens about Katherine's murder."

"Ye're assuming she is nae lying about nae remembering, and that she will share what she kens with ye," Lachlan pointed out.

"I dunnae believe she's lying," Cameron said, though he had questioned it at the very first.

"Dunnae be led by lust!" Lachlan spat.

Cameron inhaled slowly, working to control his temper. Was he being led by lust? He didn't think so. It was more a feeling in his gut that had grown as he talked to her. Still, he would need to tread carefully. "I'm nae such a clotheid to allow lust to rule me," he growled, willing it to be true.

"Use yer head, Brother," Iain said, clutching Cameron's shoulder as he faced him. "If she is telling the truth—"

Cameron made a derisive noise from his throat. It was more of the same—his beliefs being questioned because his brothers did not think his instincts could be as sharp as theirs.

Iain held up a hand. "Hold yer temper. I'm also inclined to believe she is telling the truth, especially given what Marion told us about treating others with the same such injury."

Cameron remained silent, recognizing the need to allow Iain to speak, though the ire that simmered within made him want to walk away from his brother.

Iain took a deep breath. "If she dunnae recall anything, what good does it do for ye to be around her?"

"She may say things without realizing it that might provide clues to who she is or what her part was in the attack, if she even had one," Cameron explained.

"Lachlan and I can listen for such things just as well as ye could," Iain insisted. "And we will order Broch and Ragnar to guard her when we are nae with her. Yer time will be better spent scouring the countryside for information on the man with the mismatched eyes and the scar."

The desire to argue his brother's logic burned through Cameron's body, which is exactly why he merely nodded. He was not ruled by lust, no matter what his brothers thought. His desire to be around her was great, it was true, so he'd do the opposite. The less time he spent with the lass, the less time for him to do something foolish that would make Eolande's foretelling a reality.

Iain cleared his throat. "I ken why ye feel as ye do about being to blame for Katherine's death, but ken this, I will nae let ye die because of it."

"*We* will nae let ye," Lachlan added. "Dunnae fear that if ye kinnae find her murderers that we will stand by and allow the king to kill ye. It is our brotherhood that makes us invincible. Only alone are we weak."

Cameron's chest tightened in gratitude, but the frustration that they were in this situation because of him still boiled below the surface.

"We defend one another always," Iain added so fiercely that it almost seemed as if he could read Cameron's thoughts. Iain held out his forearms to be clasped, as they always did as a symbol of unity before separating for battle.

Aware of his brothers' expectant looks, Cameron stuck out his own forearms to be clasped as he gripped theirs.

"Agreed?" they asked.

"Aye," he replied, though guilt and shame made him want to disagree. He'd set out to prove he was their equal, and instead, he had dragged them—devil take it, he'd dragged the entire clan—into a dangerous situation. Self-loathing filled him. He wanted their respect, and the only way to earn it was to show them he deserved it.

"I've nae a doubt that the attack on Katherine was meant as a direct attack against the king," Iain said.

Lachlan and Cameron both nodded, and Lachlan said, "The king has many enemies."

"Aye," Iain agreed, then looked to Cameron. "Ye have always been very astute when it comes to matters of Scotland, the king, and the other clans and nobles all vying for power. Do ye have any thoughts as to who could have ambushed ye?"

Cameron considered the question for a long moment, thinking on all the men, most especially the nobles, who were vexed—no, that word was not strong enough—*disgusted* with the king. "The Earl of Ross, as the king stripped him of one of his castles recently, and the Campbells possibly because of their recently failed attempt to manipulate the king. They likely have not given up the idea that they should have a measure of control in ruling Scotland."

Both his brothers nodded and gave him almost matching expectant looks. That they sought his opinion and seemed to trust it made his chest feel full. "Possibly the Earl of March."

Lachlan nodded. "Aye, I agree. I kinnae think of any good reason why he attempted to marry his son to Graham's wife, Isobel, other than to gain her castle so he could control the sea entry to the Isles. We all ken that whoever controls the entry to the Isles holds a powerful position that could remove David from the throne if enough forces rise against him."

"Aye," Iain added. "And March did it all secretly, trying to keep the king in the dark. I dunnae trust him at all."

"Aye," Lachlan and Cameron agreed.

"Since ye mentioned Isobel and Graham," Iain said, referring to their other brother who now lived at Brigid Castle with his wife, "we need to send word to him about what has occurred. Who should we task with it?"

"I'll go," Cameron replied. "I intended to make my way to the largest castles to see if anyone kens anything about the man with the scar. If I can learn what clan he belongs to, we will ken who ordered him to act. And as Brigid is near the Earl of Ross's home, it will be easy for me to stop and see Graham and warn him of the trouble stirring."

"Wait to depart until the king does, Brother. This way he kinnae send men behind ye to track yer every move," Iain said.

"Ye speak wisely," Cameron agreed. "Did he share his plans?"

Iain nodded. "He intends to go to the MacDonald hold and to make his way to the Steward's home from there."

Cameron frowned. "Is that wise to go to his nephew, given the king's suspicions that he is involved in the plot to force him from the throne? After all, the Steward did block

David's release from captivity by the English twice, and he seemed well pleased to sit on the throne in David's absence for all the years of the king's imprisonment."

Iain smiled grimly. "I believe David finally feels he has enough power to punish his nephew for his part in keeping David imprisoned and for what he believes are the Steward's attempts to rally other noblemen to rise against David so that the Steward can take the throne."

"Does the king mean to publicly declare the Steward a traitor?" Lachlan asked, voicing what Cameron also wanted to know.

"Aye," Iain replied, his voice vibrating anger. "The war for the throne is beginning, brothers. Pray to God we all come out alive."

It felt like days had passed, but Serene knew by the moon rising in the night it had not been that long. She stood surrounded by a bevy of chattering women in the bedchamber she had been escorted to when she was allowed to leave the healing room, yet she felt very alone. Though the laird's wife, Marion, was friendly enough, the other three women wore varying expressions that ranged from wariness to barely concealed hostility as they poked her to assess the fit for fashioning her some gowns. She looked toward the door once more, hoping Cameron, the only person who felt familiar to her, would appear. But the door to the bedchamber remained stubbornly closed, just as the door to the healing room had.

Cameron's sister, Lena, caught Serene's gaze as she looked toward the door.

The woman scowled at Serene. "My brother has more

important things to do than attend to ye, so ye can quit staring at the door," she snapped.

"Lena!" Marion and the other woman, Bridgette—who was rocking a swaddled babe in her arms—shouted as one. When the infant started to wail, Bridgette cooed, "Hush, my darling Magnus. I've ye safe in my arms." When she looked up from her babe, she glared at Lena.

Serene's cheeks flamed with astonished embarrassment at Lena's words. She quickly looked away from the door to the gown that Marion had been holding up but was now crumbled against her hip. Marion frowned at Lena. "Don't be cruel. It's only natural that she is looking for Cameron since he is the only person, or even thing, she recalls of her past. You are being too protective!"

Lena's fierce glare did not indicate that she agreed with Marion.

Serene touched her fingertips to the bandage around her head. The panic, which she had managed to keep under control thus far, stirred at the mention of her memory loss.

Lena tsked. "I dunnae ken the lot of ye. She says she dunnae recall anything, and ye all believe her without question."

Serene's spine stiffened at the woman's angry tone and the accusing glare she fixed on Serene.

Lena pointed at her. "I dunnae believe ye," she growled. "I'll be more than happy to be proven wrong, but for now, I'll be watching ye."

"Lena," Marion said on a gasp as she bent down and picked up the young child tugging on her skirts. "You are being rude," she said, standing and settling the black-haired boy on her hip. He grinned as he began to play with her hair.

"Nay," Lena disagreed. "I'm being truthful. I'll nae

mince words in this instance, nor force myself to pretty manners. My gut tells me ye will bring great strife to my brother, and I kinnae sit back and allow it to happen. I will defend him."

"Yer brother is a grown man, and a warrior at that," Serene said, trying not to be antagonistic but rather placating.

Lena narrowed her eyes into slits, and Serene rushed through the rest of what she wanted to say. "But I understand yer desire to keep him safe from harm, *as it should be*. He is yer brother, and even fierce men are nae invincible. If I had a brother—" Her heart squeezed within her chest, and she halted her words. Wrinkling her brow, she cleared her throat and started again. "If I had a brother—"

There! There it was again. That same tightening in her chest.

"What's troubling you?" Marion asked, concern lacing her tone. The child on Marion's hip stared at Serene with large blue eyes for a moment before he started playing with Marion's hair once more.

Serene rubbed at the tension in her chest. "I believe I have a brother," she said in almost a whisper.

"Do ye remember him?" Lena asked, the wary look she had been wearing replaced by a dubious one.

"Nay, but it's a feeling I have here." She pressed her fingers to her heart.

Bridgette nodded. "Aye, I understand what ye mean. When I think of my brother, I get a warm feeling of happiness in my chest."

The blue-eyed, brown-haired woman called Marsaili, kneeling at Serene's feet suddenly stopped pinning the gown they had demanded Serene put on to replace her bloody and torn one. Marsaili stood as a dark look swept across the woman's features. "When I think of my brothers, Colin and Findlay, I feel gladness that the murdering devils are dead. But when I think of Graham, Iain, Lachlan, and Cameron, I feel hope."

Serene must have worn a confused expression, because Marsaili said, "I only recently discovered I am half sister to the MacLeod brothers—and Lena, of course."

"What do ye feel?" Lena demanded, studying Serene.

Serene thought about it for a moment. Beyond the tightness, her belly felt hollow, and a sense of dread and worry prickled her skin. "I dunnae feel happiness," she admitted.

"That might be because yer brother killed the king's mistress," Lena bit out.

Serene recoiled at the suggestion. "Nay!" she blurted, but the worry within her blossomed into fear.

She struggled not to show it on her face, but Lena leaned in close and said, "Ye look guilty."

"Let her be," Marion snapped. To Serene, Lena's gaze seemed less friendly than it had moments before, which meant Lena now looked like she could cheerfully shoot an arrow through Serene's heart.

Bridgette quirked her mouth, then spoke. "Perchance her brother is like Colin and Findlay were. That would explain why she looks terrified."

Serene quickly pressed her hands to her cheeks. She looked terrified?

"Aye, that would explain it," Marsaili added. "She looks the way I felt about my brothers."

All four women stared at her as if trying to determine whether she was friend or foe.

But even she didn't know! Not truly, and the realization made her throat ache terribly with the need to cry. "Might I rest before supper?" she asked. She was weary and her head ached horribly, but mostly, if she was going to weep like a babe, she'd rather not have an audience.

"Certainly," Marion replied, giving the other three women a stern look. They filed out with barely a backward glance, except for Marion, who paused at the door.

She smiled hesitantly. "I'm certain you had nothing to do with killing Katherine. You have kind eyes, and people with kind eyes are not murderers."

Serene laughed, despite how dreadful she felt. "I'm nae positive that's correct, but I thank ye for trying to make me feel better."

"Food will make you feel better, as well."

The young boy on Marion's hip said, "Me eat!"

Marion chuckled as she ruffled the child's curls. "Yes, Royce. Mummy is going to feed you." Marion glanced to Serene once more. "I'll come fetch you for supper in a little while, and I'll bring a fresh gown with me, but ye can don this one until then. She handed Serene the wrinkled gown she had been holding."

Serene was certain neither food nor a fresh gown would make her feel better. Only her memory had the potential to do that. Or it's possible that remembering would make her feel worse... Either way, she kept the thoughts to herself, took the gown that Marion extended, and then shut the door behind Marion once she had exited the room. Serene leaned against the door, pressing her pounding head into the hard wood. On the other side, she could hear the women speaking.

"Ye're too trusting," someone cautioned, surely to Marion as no one else appeared to trust her.

"Would you have me judge her our enemy without any proof?"

"Aye. She *is* our enemy until she proves otherwise."

"Aye," came a chorus of agreements that made Serene's heart squeeze. Not only was she in a foreign place but she was a stranger to herself, unsure of the sort of person she really was. And now it seemed the one potential friend she had would likely not be a friend anymore.

She shoved away from the door, took off the gown the women had been pinning, made her way to the bed, and fell backward to stare up at the ceiling, wondering if she was good or evil. In her heart, she felt she was good, but perchance everyone felt that way about themselves. She had to recall her past, and it seemed to her she needed to remember sooner rather than later. But how? She had one memory, if one could call the recollection of Cameron MacLeod's hands on a dagger a memory. But it was all she had, so lying there, in the chilly room in the growing darkness, she pictured his long, strong fingers, which had wrapped easily around the dagger. And then she pictured his face and focused hard on it. Something niggled in her mind. It was a muddled image of a younger man smiling a teasing smile.

His features were not defined, but somehow she knew it to be Cameron. She closed her eyes and searched through the mist in her head until another memory appeared. Cameron stood beside a woman with long, dark hair and eyes that seemed to pierce the distance between Serene and the two of them. Serene laughed and was startled by the noise. She had been laughing! In her memory she had been laughing and breathless, and then she had been filled with trepidation.

Determination filled Serene. She needed to find Cameron and question him about what she had remembered. She stood abruptly and started toward the door, but paused as her hand touched the latch. She had no notion where Cameron might be, and she doubted any of the women would be willing to tell her. But perchance she would come across an unsuspecting man and she could persuade him.

She glanced around the room, saw a bucket, and walked over to it. She twisted her hair into a knot, then set about washing her neck, arms, and face. When her fingers brushed the bandage on her head, she winced. She doubted it made her appear very fetching, but she'd have to leave it. Releasing her hair, she picked up the comb that was lying on the vanity and tried as best she could to get out the tangles. Then she tugged on the gown that Marion had handed her. It was too tight and too long, but so was the one the women had been working on, and since her old gown was in tatters, this one would have to do. She took a breath for courage, and her breasts very nearly spilled out of the top of her gown. She heaved it up once more and made her way to the door. She slowly opened it and poked her head out just enough to see who, if anyone, was in the passageway.

A tall, wiry man with red hair and a hawklike nose, made all the more prominent by his square jaw and ruddy complexion, stood opposite her door. Beside him was a rotund man in the black robes of a priest. The two men immediately stopped talking, and the priest offered a smile that reached his brown eyes. He dipped his head to her in greeting, showing a shiny, bald spot at the crown, which surprised her given the relative thickness of his mop of faded-brown hair. "Ye're the wee lass found in the woods," he said, his words slow as if she were of simple mind.

The man beside him elbowed him. "I told ye she lost her memory, not that she was a clot-heid."

Splotches of red appeared on the priest's cheeks. "Begging yer pardon."

She waved a hand at him. "Dunnae fash yerself."

"I'm Angus," the red-haired man said. "Yer guard." He eyed her pointedly.

She felt suddenly the way she imagined a thief or murderer who'd been caught would feel. Did that mean she was a murderer, or a thief, or both?

"I'm Father Murdock," the big Scot said in a jolly tone. "Dunnae mind Angus. He's always rather churlish."

She smiled at the friendly banter between them and the relief she was feeling. Surely a man of God would help her. She dipped into a quick curtsy. "I'm—" She paused at the name Cameron had bestowed on her. It wasn't the right name, but she didn't know what was. "They're calling me Serene," she said, lamely.

Angus tilted his head at her, eyeing her. "The clan is calling ye Serene the Slayer."

She flinched at the new information, then anger burst within her. How dare they judge her treacherous before they even knew for certain! Yet, could she blame them? She had no notion if she could be trusted, so how could she expect them to? A very large lump suddenly clogged her throat, and she felt a sudden prick of tears in her eyes, which she determinedly blinked away.

Father Murdock glared at Angus. "Now why did ye go telling her that?"

Angus hooked his thumbs into his plaid as he stared at her. "Because I wanted to see how she responded."

"And what do ye judge from my response?" she snipped.

"Ye seemed hurt," he replied, and her cheeks flamed with the truth of his words. He stared at her expectantly. She could lie, but no matter what she had been in the past, she'd not be a liar presently, nor would she be in the future.

"I suppose I am hurt," she murmured. "I dunnae believe—" she hesitated, searching her heart and trying to listen to and judge how the words she wanted to say made her feel "—that I had a hand in killing the king's mistress."

"But ye dunnae ken for certain, do ye?" Angus demanded.

"Nay," she admitted reluctantly. "I dunnae ken for certain, but I feel I am not a murderess."

Father Murdock surprised her by slipping an arm around her shoulders and squeezing her before releasing her. "Take heart, lass. God is merciful even to the worst sinners, if ye will just beg forgiveness."

"I dunnae believe I can beg forgiveness for something I'm nae certain I did, Father."

He scratched a hand over his cheeks. "Ye make a good point. As soon as ye remember ye must come see me. Now, what brings ye out here into the passage?"

"Looking te kill someone else?" Angus asked, narrowing his eyes on her.

"Oh aye," she drawled. "Since ye asked, that is just what I'm doing. If ye'll be so kind as to slip yer neck into my hands—" she held her hands up as if she was preparing to strangle someone "—I'll just choke ye, and Father Murdock here can look on until I'm ready to kill him, as well." She bit the inside of her cheek on saying more, but she suspected the damage was already done by her loose tongue and hot temper.

"Ye're a sharp-witted lass," Angus said slowly. "The question is, have ye used those wits for evil?"

"I can nae honestly say," she replied.

Angus's eyes widened, and his mouth opened and closed like a fish on a line. Beside him, the priest burst out laughing.

"I've never seen anyone strike Angus speechless, lass. That's quite an accomplishment."

Angus glared at them both. "Ye should return to yer bedchamber."

She quirked her mouth, wanting to say something snippy again but judging it imprudent. "I would like to see Cameron. Do ye ken where he is?"

"I may," the man retorted, "but Cameron has more important things to do than to be bothered with ye."

She scowled at the man, but showing her irritation would likely not sway him to her cause. She relaxed her features as best she could. "If ye would be so kind as to take me to him, he can be the judge of that, I'm certain."

"And why would I take ye to him?" Angus demanded.

"Because it may be that I am having memories that could help him unravel the king's mistress's murder." It wasn't technically a lie. She *could* have memories come to her that would help Cameron if she was around him.

Father Murdock cleared his throat. "Angus, ye dunnae want to be the reason the lass dunnae get her memory back, now do ye?"

Angus looked as if he were about to argue that statement, but instead, he clamped his jaw shut, then growled, "Follow me."

The man set such a pace that poor Father Murdock could not keep up. Serene stayed by the priest's side, preferring his friendlier company to that of the snarly Angus. The man trod a good distance ahead of them, looking back at them every now and then to give her an accusing look, as if he suspected she was doing something sinful as she walked with Father Murdock.

"Dunnae mind him, aye," Father Murdock said between

huge huffs of breath. "He has a kind heart but a gruff exterior."

She nodded, the simple words making her feel a bit better. "Do ye ken where Cameron is?"

Father Murdock nodded. "Since it's close to the supper hour, he'll be down at the loch taking a swim. He does so every night before dinner. It dunnae matter if it be winter or summer."

"But the waters must be freezing in the winter!" she exclaimed.

"Aye," Father Murdock said with a chuckle, "they are. But the man has something to prove, I reckon."

She frowned. Why would a man so powerful looking and so seemingly in control need to prove anything to anyone? She thought upon earlier in the healing room. Had there been a strain between him and his brothers? It hadn't seemed so, truly, but there may have been a slight awareness of something. "To his brothers?" she hazarded a guess.

"Nay," replied Father Murdock, his brow dipping into a frown. "To himself, lass. To himself. He just dunnae ken it yet."

Not long later, as the loch came into view, Serene paused in her flight down the seagate stairs and stared in amazement at the vast expanse of water. Her response was so strong it made her think she'd never seen such a large body of water. She swept her gaze across the gently lapping water in search of Cameron but did not see him.

Angus had stopped also and was looking toward the right side of the castle. He turned to her and Father Murdock. "He'll be swimming around that bend. He likes his solitude."

She nodded, expecting him to continue, but the man surprised her by stepping toward her, and saying, "Raise yer arms."

"What for?" she asked.

"I'll be checking that ye dunnae have a weapon ye're planning to use."

Her jaw dropped open at his words.

"For the love of God!" Father Murdock bellowed. "Do ye truly believe that Iain and the others would nae have already checked her for weapons?"

Angus pressed his lips together. "I suppose." His gaze lingered as if he was still considering searching her, but then he snorted. "I'll offer my apologies now because I ken this will anger ye, but...," he said, moving to her once more and running his hands quickly and lightly over her legs, waist, and ankles.

Her anger was so great she nearly choked as she glared at him. Beside her, Father Murdock shook his head and murmured, "Ye're a suspicious old fool."

"Say what ye will," Angus growled, finished, and moved away from her, "but being suspicious has kept me alive all these years. Ye can go see Cameron now," Angus pronounced.

"Are ye certain?" she asked, making her voice syrupy sweet while narrowing her eyes on the Scot. "Perchance my hands are weapons." She raised her hands in the air in front of her. "Perchance I can break a man's neck with one twist!" She clucked her tongue, and Angus made a derisive noise from his throat.

"Ye'd nae even be able to get yer hands around Cameron's neck. He's that much taller than ye. And I feel sure he's faster and certainly stronger."

The man irritated her, yet she did understand his feelings, which frustrated her and made her want to scream. Instead, she turned and marched in the direction the man had said she would find Cameron. She'd gone ten steps before she remembered her manners for the priest. She swung back around to find both men staring at her. She grasped her skirts and dipped another curtsy. "I hope to see ye again soon, Father Murdock." To Angus she simply grimaced, to which the priest chuckled.

"Ye best hurry," he said. "Supper will be soon, and Iain dunnae abide stragglers to the great hall, especially Cameron, as captain of the guard."

Nodding, she hastened her steps down the rest of the narrow stairway, making sure to watch where she was placing her feet. The passage was windy and slick with mist, and when she reached the bottom the ground was covered with rocks. She imagined falling down these stairs could well mean one's death. She rushed across the rocky shore, struggling to keep her hair out of her eyes as the wind whipped it in her face. A quick glance up showed dark, gathering clouds. A storm was coming.

The instant the thought left her head, rain fell from the sky as if she had unleashed it. She trudged along the craggy land, her head pounding with each step. Following the shoreline around the bend, the land narrowed, and a hidden alcove of water came into view. Above her and to the right, thick woods loomed from sharp rock. As she drew closer to the water's edge, she raised her hand to shield her eyes from the rain so she could see better. She gasped at the sight of Cameron MacLeod emerging from the water without a stitch of clothing on his body. Now she knew why he wished for solitude. She had no doubt that Angus had known, too. The man could have told her!

Her anger fled under her curiosity. She gaped at Cameron. Slabs of muscle on his stomach formed into a vee. There was not an inch of extra flesh on the man. Every part of him was honed for combat, from his thick arms to his Viking legs.

She was well aware that she should look away, yet she could not. She feasted on him, staring in awe. He moved with swiftness, full of grace and emanating a palpable virility. Her belly tightened with awareness as he came closer, his muscles rippling with each step. She inhaled a sharp breath as he stopped in front of her, shock clear in his eyes. Without a word, he bent down, picked up the plaid she had not even realized was at her feet, and quickly donned it. He slicked back the wet hair from his face, which emphasized the rugged masculinity of his sculpted cheekbones and square jaw.

Her heart sped at his nearness. He overwhelmed her with his height, muscled build, and the intensity that seemed to radiate from him. Surely, she had been around men before, but she felt certain she had never been affected by one the way she was by this man. She didn't believe anyone could ever forget such a heady feeling.

"Ye're beautiful," she blurted out. She gasped at her own brazenness.

His eyebrows drew together, and he looked almost agonized by what she had said. Heat burned her cheeks, neck, and chest, despite the cool rain that was now steadily pelting her. She tried to think of something to say, since she had made herself look so foolish and he clearly was uncomfortable. But then his brow softened, setting into a straight line before a defeated look swept across his face.

With an audible sigh, he said, "So are ye, lass."

Thunder boomed in the sky, and lightning slashed

across it in a brilliant show of blinding color. The very air around them seemed to crackle with danger, yet she stood unmoving, feeling protected just by his nearness. When he raked his gaze slowly from her feet to her face and their eyes met, she shivered at the voraciousness gleaming in the green depths. He desired her! It was both shocking and compelling at once. Her lips parted, and she sucked in a sharp breath to steady her pulse. When heat consumed her, she reached behind her head to lift her heavy hair with one hand and she fanned her face with the other.

Cameron groaned, and she could see a tic start at his jawline. He tilted his face toward the sky for a moment, and she stood entranced at the sight of the rain showering the glorious warrior. When he glanced at her once more, the hunger in his eyes was gone. In its place was undeniable indifference.

"What are ye doing out here?" he demanded, his cold voice slicing through her composure like a serrated dagger.

She worried her lower lip. She had vowed to speak the truth. Though there was a large part of her that suddenly did not want to admit that she felt they must be entwined somehow, since her only memories were of him, she could ill afford to speak lies simply to protect her pride.

"I've only two memories," she said, blinking the rain out of her eyes. "Both are of ye." Lightning slashed through the sky again, this time so close that she flinched, the hair on the back of her neck prickling.

Wariness flickered in his eyes, making her discomfort grow, but determination to get answers from him, answers she felt he had, coursed through her. She shoved her sopping hair back, and his eyes fastened on her forehead. "Does it hurt?" he asked.

"Aye," she replied, "but it does nae cause me half as

much pain as having nary a notion of who I am. What do ye ken about me?"

Uneasiness danced across his face. "Nae a thing," he said slowly, "besides the fact that ye were with the group of men who ambushed me and my men and killed Katherine."

"I dunnae believe ye," she growled, then rushed to say more before he interrupted her. "My other memory is of ye standing beside a woman with long, dark hair." She swallowed hard, shivering with the recollection of the all-knowing eyes. "The woman had eyes that seemed to see into my verra soul, as if she knew a dark secret about me."

The only indication that Cameron heard her was a subtle shift of his body away from her. He seemed almost scared of her.

Icy fear of what his response might mean twisted into her. Dear God above! A hundred possibilities battered her mind at once. "Did we," she said in a broken whisper, "conspire together to kill the king's mistress?"

Five

Cameron felt his eyes widen and his lips part. Either the lass was the most accomplished liar he had ever met or she truly had lost her memory. His gut told him she was not lying, but he realized his gut might be misleading him, with such strong lust coursing through him.

"I met ye only once, Serene, and that was the night of the St. John's Eve festival eight years ago, as I already said. Ye were dressed as a lad, and ye won the competition with cunning. If I wanted to strike at the king, which I dunnae," he said, vehemently, "I would nae kill a helpless woman to do so. So, nay, I did nae conspire with ye. But it seems, upon thinking about it now, that ye have a history of lying."

Such hurt flashed across her face that the wish to be able to take back his words filled him. She opened her mouth to say something, but a blur in the sky alarmed him, and he shoved her behind him as an arrow came flying from the woods and blew by them so near that it whistled in his ear. Furious, he glanced toward the overhanging rock ledge that would provide protection for Serene while he chased down the intruder. He lunged for his sword and dagger, both of which he thankfully had laid close to his plaid. But neither would protect them from arrows. He had to get Serene to shelter.

"Come," he hissed. He grabbed her by the hand, and

taking care to keep his body in front of hers, he fairly dragged her over the rocky embankment as she struggled to keep pace.

Another arrow flew toward them, and he almost failed to get them both out of the way in time.

As the rain poured from the sky, partially blinding him, he raced toward the rocks while looking up high past the woods to the watchtower where Roland, the loch guard, was set up to spot and warn them of any attacks. But the man was too far away, and the noise from the rain too great to try to call to him and alert him to sound the horn telling the others that there was an intruder on Dunvegan's grounds.

"Watch out!" Serene screamed, snapping Cameron's attention back in the direction of the woods. He saw the arrow too late to move out of the path, so he threw up his arm to deflect it. The arrowhead skidded the length of his forearm, slicing the skin with stinging precision but mercifully not causing grave harm.

Finally, they reached the rock ledge, and he shoved Serene into the shelter. "Stay here!" he commanded.

"Nay!" she retorted. "I'll nae sit here like a helpless bairn while ye chase after the attacker."

"Unless yer aim is to get me killed by distracting me with yer presence, dunnae move. Do ye ken me?"

"I ken ye," she grumbled, her eyes flashing her ire. "I dunnae wish to get ye killed presently, but that may change, given how churlish ye are."

Laughter bubbled in his chest, despite the dire circumstances. He held his dagger out to her. "If the enemy should reach ye..." He didn't finish because she was already nodding, indicating that she understood.

He turned away and dashed out of the cave, glancing

back only once to ensure she was following his orders. She glared back. Many a lass would be crying, distraught, after being shot at, especially when still facing mortal danger, but not Serene. Admiration filled him as he moved along the rock, staying as flat as he could make himself against it. Shortly, the overhanging ledge would end. He'd no longer be sheltered from view, but it wouldn't matter. The thick woods met the shore where the ledge ended, and there, he'd be able to move through the cover of trees to move up to where the arrows had been shot from. Then, if the intruder was still there, he would capture the attacker.

He quickly reached the end of the overhang, and he shoved his way past gnarled branches and sticker bushes to climb the steep hill that led to the ledge overhanging the shore below.

Through the gray haze of the storm, he saw a lone figure standing with a flapping cloak on, arm drawn back, and arrow nocked. The rain had lessened as Cameron climbed and now drizzled into nothingness. The man moved suddenly, swiveling his body toward the right, and Cameron was filled with the certainty and the fear that Serene had come out of the cave. He flew across the distance separating him from the attacker and launched himself at the hooded man with a roar, crashing into him as the stranger let loose his arrow. Cameron swung his arm out and knocked the man to the ground before stealing a glance down to the shore. A shadow raced across the rocky ground toward him, skirts flying and hair flapping. God's teeth! She was damned lucky she'd not been—

The hit atop his head sent him to his knees and made his teeth jar together. Pain exploded in his head, but he rolled forward, coming up on his right knee and swinging his sword in front of him to defend himself. His blade sliced across the attacker's cloak, and with a gasp, the man stumbled backward.

"Cameron!" Serene screamed from the rocks below. Cameron did not have time to spare a glance. He scrambled to his feet, but the ground immediately swayed underneath him and he stumbled forward onto his knees once more as he watched the attacker turn to flee.

"Devil take ye!" he roared, shoving up to his feet and swiping at the blood dripping from a fresh cut above his right eye.

His thoughts were muddled, and his feet moved slower than he wanted as he started to pursue the attacker. Still, he pressed on through the gathering shadows in search of the man who had tried to kill him. No, that wasn't right. The intruder had been here to kill *Serene*, which likely meant whoever it was thought she knew something about Katherine's murder.

He shoved through the thick brush, ignoring the cuts to his feet and hacking at the branches with his sword as he went. His speed gained as his balance did, but he had lost precious time. If the attacker was smart, he would head deep into the woods where trees, plants, and caves provided numerous places to hide. There, if he was not discovered, he could wait, biding his time for the next opportunity to attack Serene. A chill shot up Cameron's spine at the thought, and he pushed on, up hills, over rocks, through streams, but the forest was vast and he needed aid.

Cursing, he turned and raced back the way he had come, and as the shadows turned to darkness, he moved by moonlight and memory.

"Cameron!" shouted Serene's voice again, followed by a bellow that sounded like Angus, close and to the left.

Cameron opened his mouth to give an answering call,

but suddenly Angus and Serene crested a hill. Serene raced past Angus, dagger in hand, and over to Cameron, panting as she placed her free hand on his chest. "Are ye injured?"

The genuine concern in her voice struck him like an arrow to the heart. He liked the concern. He wanted it, even. He gritted his teeth against the emotions for her, but the need to keep her from harm rushed through him, thicker than blood. He moved closer to her and pulled her to his side, telling himself it was for her protection, *only* for her protection.

"I told ye nae to leave the cave," he yelled, his fear for her making his words harsh. She tensed and tilted her chin up in defiance. "Come," he ordered, slinging his arm over her shoulder to keep her close.

Angus fell in step with him on Serene's other side. Cameron didn't think she realized they had formed a human shield to protect her.

As they strode through the woods toward the shore, he growled, "Ye did nae heed my orders."

She huffed. "I could nae verra well sit helpless and let ye possibly be killed."

He looked at her, awed. Risking her safety for him had not given her pause. These were not the actions of a woman with evil intent. He stored the knowledge away to consider later, when all was safe.

Glancing past her to Angus, he said, "How did ye come to be out here?"

"I led the lass to ye earlier," Angus said. "I stayed near in case she proved treacherous." He shrugged, almost apologetically, and looked toward Serene. "I heard her scream, and I came running. I misjudged ye, lass," Angus admitted, remorse in his tone.

A short laugh escaped Serene. "I kinnae rightly be cross

given how I came to ye. I forgive ye," she said simply.

Cameron was struck with how gracious and brave she seemed to be, and his mind swirled with it as they returned to the castle.

The thoughts were still in his head when they entered the great hall, all three of them sopping wet. The hall hummed with the normal sounds of supper, the inhabitants of his clan oblivious to the danger in the woods. Cameron strode up to the dais, his hand firmly grasping Serene's, where Iain sat with Marion, Lachlan, Bridgette, and Lena, among others. Iain stopped talking to gape at him, and Lachlan spit out a mouthful of wine as they approached.

"Sound the alarm," Cameron said without preamble. "An enemy is lurking."

<hr />

Serene felt very out of place with Cameron's entire family staring at her from the dais, especially when his sister, Lena, turned an icy stare on Serene at the word *enemy*. She tried to disentangle her hand from Cameron's and move to a corner out of view, but he curled his fingers tightly around hers, his hold like a vise. He pressed her closer to him.

At first, she thought he might be questioning her, too, but when he moved slightly in front of her as if to guard her from his sister's anger, she realized he was trying to defend her. Shock caused her to inhale sharply, and when Cameron's gaze landed on her briefly and she saw the concern in his eyes, her knees suddenly felt weak. The sense of being an unwelcome intruder lessened instantly.

It struck her as rather odd—and a bit frightening—that a man she hardly knew seemed to have such sway over her emotions. Surely, it was because currently he was all she knew, even if it was precious little. Before she could ponder it, a flurry of activity commenced. Supper abruptly stopped, the castle horns announcing an enemy sounded, and the men left the hall with such speed that Serene would have believed none had ever been there if it was not for Cameron, who lingered for a moment, along with Marion and Lena. The other women, Bridgette, and Marsaili, left the great hall as the men did.

Cameron's hand came to the small of Serene's back, warm and reassuring, as he guided her to Marion and Lena. "Watch out for her," he said to them both.

Marion nodded and smiled, but Lena scowled.

"I'll watch her," she growled. "Already she brings trouble to our door, and—"

Before Lena could finish her sentence, Cameron took her by the arm and dragged her across the room. Serene shifted from foot to foot, uncomfortably aware that Cameron's problem with his sister was because of her.

Marion patted Serene's shoulder. "She doesn't hate you truly."

Serene snorted. "It certainly seems that way."

Marion nibbled on her lip with her head cocked for a moment, as if trying to decide something. Finally, she whispered, "I cannot explain it all now, but Lena was taken from here as a young child, which meant she was denied the opportunity to be a doting sister to her brothers as they grew from boys to men. And as Cameron was the youngest, she would have had the role of protecting him as his older sister, and that was also taken from her." She gave Serene a tight, sad smile. "She only recently returned, and all the brothers except for Cameron now have wives to care for them. I do believe she is trying to be the older sister that she was not able to be earlier in life. Unfortunately, I also think it may seem to her that none of her brothers need her."

Serene thought about what Marion had just revealed as she watched the exchange between Cameron and Lena. He was speaking and waving his hands in the air, but when Lena's shoulders sagged and she bit her lip, Cameron suddenly stopped talking and pulled his sister into a hug. Serene's chest tightened at the display of brotherly love, and Marion sighed.

When Serene looked at Marion, she was smiling. "Cameron is especially sensitive to Lena's feelings," Marion explained. "Likely because most of her attention is focused on him. He watches over her, as well, but in a more reasonable manner."

When Serene looked back toward Cameron, he was leaving the room with Lena. He turned at the last moment, and his gaze found Serene's. He stared at her for the space of a breath, making her heartbeat quicken before he departed.

"Well," Marion replied, linking an arm with Serene's as she stared toward where Cameron had disappeared. "It seems you have made quite the mark on Cameron's mind."

He'd made quite the one on hers, too—years before, earlier, just now—but she intended to keep that to herself until she could figure it all out.

Six

As the first light of morning broke and the mist that covered the land started to dissipate, Cameron rode between Lachlan and Iain as they left the woods and headed toward Dunvegan Castle. The night had been long and full of tension as they had combed the woods for the invader, but to no avail. Between himself and two hundred other MacLeod warriors, they had been unable to find a trace of the man or the direction in which he may have gone. Whoever had shot the arrows at him and Serene was skilled at disappearing.

Steering Winthrop toward the courtyard, which had just come into view, Cameron glanced at Iain. They'd tracked in almost complete silence so as not to give away their position, but now Cameron felt he could talk. "Whoever it is out there," he said, glancing back toward the woods they had just left, "is intent on killing Serene. They were shooting at her even when I was nae anywhere near her, and when the man had the chance to kill me, he did nae take it. Instead, he fled."

Lachlan's eyes narrowed. "Why did the attacker ever gain an opportunity to kill ye?"

Cameron heated with embarrassment at the question. His jaw twitched as he opened his mouth to answer honestly. "I turned my back to him for one moment."

"Why the devil did ye do that?" Iain roared.

"Brother," Lachlan said, in a stern tone, "ye ken better than that. Ye are smarter than such folly and well versed on the ways of fighting."

Cameron nodded, unable to argue with his brothers or soothe their anger, which came, he understood, from concern. "I needed to see that she was still safe. I'd left her below in a cave, thinking to keep her from harm. I told her nae to move…" He let his words trail off at the mixed looks of incredulity and surprising understanding on his brothers' faces.

"They never stay," Iain said with a sigh. "At least Marion never stays when I tell her to."

"Bridgette dunnae ever stay, either," Lachlan added, a frown furrowing his brow.

Cameron's brothers exchanged a long look, then both focused their steely gazes on him. "Strong women dunnae ever remain, Brother," Iain said as Lachlan nodded his agreement.

"I would have looked, too," Lachlan said, "if I feared for Bridgette's safety. I may have been just as reckless."

Cameron felt his lips part on his brother's astonishing admission.

Iain scowled. "I would have seen that Marion was safe by keeping one eye on my enemy and turning one toward her."

"That would be quite the trick," Lachlan drawled.

"I'm laird," Iain said in a blunt tone. "I can do anything I say. That is but one benefit of being laird. Ye dunnae get to question me," he added with a pointed look at Lachlan. Then he gave the same look to Cameron. "It dunnae bode well, considering Eolande's prophecy, that ye compromised yer own safety for a lass that dunnae mean a thing to ye. Ye just met her."

Iain's words were all true, but his saying them irritated Cameron, nonetheless. "Ye married yer wife after kenning her for less than a day," he growled.

Iain's faced darkened, showing a bit of the temper he usually kept so well restrained. "Ye ken well that I married her by edict of her king and mine."

"I ken it," Cameron said slowly, "but nary a king ordered ye to care for her as quickly as ye did. It just was in ye."

Iain's jaw fell open. After a breath, he snapped it shut, grunted, and said, "Are ye telling me—"

"Us," Lachlan corrected.

Iain flicked his gaze to Lachlan before settling it on Cameron once more. "Are ye telling us ye care for the lass?"

"Nay," he answered immediately. "Nae in the way the two of ye care for Bridgette and Marion, but I feel—" What did he feel? As they drew to the entry of the courtyard, he paused his destrier while he struggled to find the words to describe what he himself did not understand.

A crowd was gathered at the entry to greet them, and Serene stood off to the side, alone. She had on the same gown she had worn the previous day when she had come to talk to him, the one that showed too much of her enticing breasts. It heated him to recall just how very well he could see the rounded mounds and her hard nubs straining against the wet, gossamer material. Desire roiled through him in unstoppable waves. His muscles tightened with blossoming, aching need. He wanted her. He barely knew her, but it didn't matter. He wanted her like he'd never wanted another.

Her gaze locked on his, and relief swept across her face as she picked up her skirts, called his name, and raced toward him, heedless of the stares she was drawing.

"Bound," he finally said to Iain and Lachlan. The husky word held a ring of finality that worried him. It felt unstoppable, as if despite whatever he did, he would still fall under her spell. "Bound," he said again at his brothers' puzzled looks. "To her, I feel bound."

※

She wasn't quite sure what response she expected from Cameron, but dismounting his horse, taking her by the hand, and leading her away from his brothers and the many warriors who had just come up behind them took her by complete surprise. Yet, she did not worry, nor feel she needed to question or fight him. He gave her a look to calm her, then his fingers curled firmly around hers, causing her to suck in a sharp breath. Desire jolted through her, sparking a fire in her veins.

It was only when she realized he was leading her back to the seagate stairs, toward the shore where they had been attacked, that she hesitated. "Is it safe?"

"Aye," he assured her with such confidence that she did not doubt him. He paused on the steps and turned to her, his vibrant gaze holding her captive. "Iain tripled the watchtower guards and set men to defend the woods in sections, along with the entire perimeter of the castle and land surrounding the loch. "Nae a single enemy will get through this day again."

She exhaled a relieved breath. "What of all the other days? The men kinnae be kept away from their families day after day."

"They are warriors, and they will do as commanded to keep ye safe. Now you, however…" His eyes narrowed. "I told ye nae to leave the cave, and ye vowed ye would nae. Does yer vow nae mean a thing?"

Her first instinct was to be angry, but she quickly realized he was worried for her and that realization stole her anger. "Aye. It means something," she growled. "If ye intend to yell at me, though, I prefer ye do it where yer entire clan kinnae hear ye. Nae anyone but Marion likes me, and I'm nae sure she truly likes me, either. I fear it's more that the lady is just too nice to be cruel to anyone, even someone suspected of killing the king's mistress."

Cameron gave her a pensive look, and she suspected he was making his mind up what to do. When he finally turned toward the loch again, took her hand, and continued down the stairs, she exhaled. At least the entire MacLeod clan would not hear him yelling at her.

Once they reached the shore, he led her to some rocks and guided her gently down, then sat beside her. He leaned forward and rested his forearms on his knees, and she could not help but notice how the muscles of his back and arms coiled, as if prepared to fight.

After a long silent spell, he faced her, yet did not sit up. His golden hair just touched his right shoulder as he tilted his strong face to her. She didn't think there was likely a more compelling warrior on the Isle of Skye. "Do ye have a lass?" she blurted. She slapped her hand over her mouth in embarrassment.

When he frowned at her, she forced her hand down and mumbled, "I'm sorry. I dunnae ken why I asked that. It's nae any of my concern. I dunnae ken what is the matter with me. Ye affect me oddly. I cannot say for certain why, though, since I kinnae remember my past." She wrinkled her nose at how greatly she had managed to mess up the apology and make herself look like a fool.

A smile tugged at the corner of his lips, making her heart squeeze. "I dunnae claim a lass as my own." The smile that had been curling his lips disappeared abruptly. "I wonder if a man has a claim on ye."

The displeasure that the thought brought to him was apparent in the tightening of his jaw and his hard, clipped words. She was startled by the jolt of pleasure his jealousy gave her. She may not know what had been in her mind in the past, but right now, Cameron MacLeod possessed her thoughts.

"I dunnae feel claimed," she mumbled, heat burning her cheeks. "I feel adrift, except when I am near ye. I think it must be because my only memories are of ye and the woman with the dark hair. Who is she? Is she someone special to ye? Did I meet her?"

He let out a jagged sigh, then shoved his hands through his hair before cradling his head between his palms. "She's a seer, and nay, ye did nae meet her, as far as I ken." She watched as his fingers dug into his thick locks. Something was weighing very heavy on his mind. Hesitantly, she touched a hand to his bare, muscled shoulder. He flinched, and a low growl sounded from him, but he did not move her hand away, nor did she. The contact with his warm skin made her feel safe.

"This—" He waved a hand between her and himself but did not raise his head. "Ye, we"—another growl came from him, but this one was filled with frustration—"*our* circumstances are much more confusing than I anticipated."

"Our circumstances?" she asked, fascinated by the vein that visibly pulsed at his left temple.

He inhaled a long breath, making the slabs of muscle on his back ripple. "Someone is trying to kill ye."

"Aye," she replied, a hard knot forming in her chest. "I

still dunnae ken what ye mean by *our circumstances*, though."

His hands slid through his hair to the back of his neck. He linked his fingers together, lifting his head to look straight ahead. "Ye risked yer life leaving the shelter of the rock to aid me." His head whipped in her direction, eyes so bright that she sucked in a sharp breath. "Why?" he demanded, the word harsh and aching. "Why would ye risk yer life to help a stranger? Especially one who ye ken suspected ye to be guilty of murder?"

Why? It was a good question, and not one she had paused to ask herself yet. Her hand fluttered to her hair, catching a silky strand, and winding it around her finger. The action soothed her and seemed to help her think. "Suspected?" she asked, curious if he no longer thought her a part of the plot to kill Katherine and wishing to gain time to give him an answer to his question.

He nodded. "Aye. I kinnae make sense of why someone would be trying to kill ye if ye are working with them."

"Perchance they want to silence me," she said in a hushed tone, voicing her fear.

"Perchance, but my gut tells me nay, so unless I discover otherwise, ye are nae my enemy. Now, do ye intend to tell me why ye risked yer life for me?"

She shifted, assessed her heart and her mind. "I kinnae say for certain, except I…I feel as if our paths are somehow intertwined."

Tension crossed his face, and then a look of understanding filled his eyes. She exhaled a breath she had not even realized she had been holding. "Do ye—do ye feel so, as well?"

His mouth twisted as if he wanted to deny it, but he nodded, shoulders sagging. "I do."

It seemed to her there was more there he wanted to say, but when he remained silent, she spoke. "Ye sound as if that is the worst thing in the world," she said in as light a voice as she could muster when her feelings had been trampled upon.

He stood swiftly. "I fear it may well be," he replied, looked as if he might say more, but he clenched his teeth and abruptly turned away.

Seven

After Marion collected Serene from her bedchamber the next morning, she took her to the great hall, and the first person they encountered was Cameron. Faster than Serene knew what was occurring, Marion was handing her over to Cameron and striding away. For a long moment, he simply stared at her with an uneasy look on his face before he took her by the arm, and then he led her to a table and deposited her for the morning meal without a word. From the pitying looks the curly redheaded woman beside her gave her and the sympathy-filled blue eyes Marsaili turned upon her, Serene was certain it was as obvious that Cameron wanted nothing more than to put distance between them. She swallowed hard as she listened to him order the giant warrior sitting beside Marsaili to guard her.

When the man acknowledged his duty, Cameron turned away and strode toward the dais. Confusion churned in her belly. He'd said he did not consider her his enemy, but the moment she had confessed that she thought their lives were meant to intertwine somehow, he'd become cold. Feeling her throat tighten with all the emotions bottled inside her and her vision blur with unshed tears, she reached blindly for the goblet in front of her, desperate for some way to quell the tide within. Her fingers brushed someone else's, and she pulled back quickly while glancing to her right. Dark, assessing eyes framed by long, dark lashes met hers.

"I'm Alanna," the woman said in a serious voice while shoving a mass of red curls over her shoulder. "I'm Rory Mac's wife."

When Serene frowned, the woman's mouth pressed into a grim line. "Rory Mac is the warrior who was gravely injured in the attack that killed the king's mistress."

"Oh!" Serene gasped. "How does he fare?"

"His fever has broken," Alanna said, her tone anything but friendly.

Serene got the feeling Alanna blamed her for Rory Mac's injuries. "I'm glad to hear his fever broke," she said, choosing her words with care. "I hope he makes a swift recovery. I wish I could remember the attack so that I could help find who ambushed yer husband and the others."

Alanna raised a skeptical eyebrow. "Just because ye dunnae have a memory of doing evil, dunnae mean ye did nae do it." The woman stood. "I'll nae break my fast beside ye."

Serene clenched her teeth for a moment. Anger coursed through her, but understanding did, too. "That's yer choice," she said quietly. "Though I hope to prove to ye and everyone else that I'm a good person."

Alanna pursed her lips, and then she let out a rattling sigh. "I hope ye prove that, as well."

Her departure and the words she'd spoken left the table in absolute silence. Marsaili quietly stood next, causing Serene's breath to catch. Were they all going to leave the table one by one? How humiliating that would be!

Much to her surprise, Marsaili moved to the empty space Alanna had left on her departure. Marsaili turned to her. "I ken well how it feels to be an outcast here. I dunnae believe ye would have bothered to try to aid Cameron last night, if ye were a willing partner in the attack against Katherine."

"I dunnae believe so, either," said the large warrior Cameron had assigned as her guard. The man swiped a hunk of bread through the thick sauce on his plate, wiped his hands on his plaid, and grinned at her as he leaned his elbows on the table. "I'm Broch, and it will be my pleasure to keep watch over ye." With those surprising words, he winked at her.

An older gentleman with red hair and nubs for ears leaned around Broch to look at her. He eyed her for a long moment before thumping Broch on the head. "Dunnae let lust for a beautiful lass rule ye. Ye see that Cameron dunnae lose his good judgment simply because the lass is bonny. She may have tried to aid him," the man said, directing his steely gaze at Marsaili, "but let none of us forget she dunnae remember who she is. When she does…" His eyes narrowed.

Heat singed Serene's cheeks, and she opened her mouth to defend herself, though she did not have much of a defense since she did not recall the truth. Before she could speak, Marsaili slammed her hand on the table, rattling the trenchers. "Ye are a grumpy old man, Neil," she bit out. "Ye have decided she's guilty of the worst without any proof."

"I'm nae the only one," the man named Neil sputtered. "Clearly Cameron has decided so, as well, and Alanna. I am certain everyone in this room is wary of her but ye, Broch, and Marion. We all ken Marion is too nice and too trusting, and as for Broch…" He waved a hand at the warrior. "We all ken his brain is nae leading him in this."

The heat in Serene's cheeks spread down her neck and to her chest.

Grunts of agreement sounded from all around the table, and Neil said, "Broch turns into a clot-heid whenever a bonny lass smiles at him."

"Aye," everyone at the table besides Marsaili said.

"Ye're the clot-heid, Neil!" Marsaili said with such force that people from the nearby tables turned to look at them.

Desperate to quiet the rising argument, Serene said in a low but firm voice, "If I am guilty of conspiring to kill the king's mistress, I will willingly give my life."

"Ye'll be giving something anyway," someone to her left snarled.

She turned to ask them what they meant and blinked in surprise at the sight of Cameron standing there. Fury was etched into his features and burned in his eyes. He jerked the younger man out of his seat and yanked him forward until their faces were a hairsbreadth apart.

"Keep yer filthy mouth shut, Cormac," Cameron growled.

The man scowled. "We all ken what the king has planned for her. Why do ye defend this woman who may well have murdered our king's mistress?" His words were like thunder, reverberating around the now-silent great hall.

Serene wished she could disappear, but she forced herself to sit tall.

"I find I've the same question as young Cormac," a deep voice said from the direction of the dais.

Serene turned to find a man standing. His brown hair and beard were both impeccably kept. He wore a long, ruby-red cloak trimmed in gold; the material was thick and obviously rich. He was tall and of lean build, and he had a long, patrician nose and prominent cheekbones.

"Dunnae ye have an answer for yer king?" he asked in a quiet, yet powerful voice that managed to send chills racing down Serene's back. "If ye dunnae, perchance I should rid us all this very hour of this woman who trouble seems to haunt."

Terror clawed at Serene, but she forced herself to sit perfectly still, except her gaze, which she cast furtively at Cameron, who shoved the man he'd been gripping back into his seat. Cameron did not look the least concerned with the king's question. In truth, the expression on his face almost bordered on anger. But it seemed to disappear before her very eyes, as if he had slid a magic shield in place that was to leave whoever was staring at him baffled and confused.

"Because, Yer Grace," he said in an easy, casual tone, "Serene recalled a new memory that further points to her innocence. I simply have nae yet had a private moment to share it with ye nor Iain."

Shock bolted through her at his lie. She barely managed to keep her lips together, but as his gaze settled on her, his shields dropped down, and in the depths of his mesmerizing eyes, a warning dwelled. He was warning her to stay silent! Her heart thudded heavily as she tilted her head ever so slightly.

Footsteps resounded in the silent hall, and without turning to see who approached, Serene knew it to be the king. He appeared beside Cameron. The king was a bit shorter and his build not near as commanding; nevertheless, he had a presence about him that commanded attention.

"Do tell," he said in a tone that was low enough that the whole room could not hear but not so hushed that everyone at the table did not lean forward to listen. Serene found herself leaning forward, as well, unsure what he was going to say or why he would boldly lie to his king for her. She was both terrified and so grateful that she wanted to weep.

"She recalled that she had been taken by force from land near her home," he said smoothly.

Serene felt her lips part, but she immediately pressed them shut and looked down at her hands. She feared she would give away his falsehood, and she would rather cut out her tongue than betray this man who had just deceived his king for her.

"What else do ye remember, my lady?" the king demanded in a harsh voice that made her twitch.

Slowly, she looked up and met the king's probing gaze. Her blood roared in her ears as she licked her lips and swallowed hard. "Nae anything else, I'm afraid, Sire."

His eyes narrowed, and he offered a tilt of his head. "I'm certain if ye are now recalling things, ye will soon remember more that will help Cameron in his search for my Katherine's killers."

She wiped her suddenly sweaty palms against her skirts. "Aye, Sire," she started, but had to clear a catch in her throat. "I'm certain I will recall more that shall shed light." Pray God it would prove innocence when she did finally remember.

The king strolled over to her and motioned for her to stand. She did so on trembling legs. He quirked his finger in commandment for her to come to him. She took a deep breath to quell her quaking nerves as she walked to the king. When he gripped her by the chin, she bit her lip on her cry of protest. His grip was not punishing but firm, and seemed to hint that punishment would come if she were to move.

Behind the king, Cameron tensed, and his hands curl into fists by his side. Suddenly his brothers Iain and Lachlan were flanking him. Her attention was diverted back to the king when he turned her face sharply to the left, then the right.

He smiled, the brittleness increasing her fears. "I'm pleased to hear it is unlikely that ye are a traitor," he offered, turning her face directly to his. "I've designs for ye, my lady, but first..." He squeezed her chin with such force that she winced. The king shifted, and she could once again see Cameron. Both his brothers had a hand on each of his arms. The king released her as suddenly as he'd grabbed her, and she rubbed her aching chin. "First, I think it wise if ye go with Cameron on his search for Katherine's killers."

Relief at the king's proclamation nearly sent her to her knees. She did not want to be left at Dunvegan Castle without Cameron. She looked to him, afraid he'd argue that she'd slow him down in his quest, but he was already striding toward the king.

"An excellent idea, Sire," Cameron replied. "I can use any information Serene may recall."

The king's mouth twisted into a smug smile. "Just be sure to keep her unscathed," he drawled, raking his gaze over her so she had to back up a step. "I want her returned just as lovely appearing as she is now, to use as I see fit."

Serene shuddered inwardly at what the king was implying. She yearned to flee the great hall and keep running, but she had no notion where she would even go.

With those ominous words, the king turned toward the silent great hall, held up his hands, and announced, "I'm away to my home in a short while. Let us finish breaking our fast before my departure." The hall once again erupted into chatter as the king strode back to the dais.

Serene stood face-to-face with Cameron, her heart racing as he stared into her eyes.

"Brother," Iain said, coming up behind Cameron. He

studied Serene before he spoke once more. "Come back to the dais and break yer fast. We will discuss Serene and what's to be done after the king has departed."

She stilled, wishing fervently that Cameron would not leave her once more, and when he shook his head, she could not hold back the exhalation of relief that he planned, perchance to keep her near. His eyes widened, and wariness flickered within them. "I'll be down to the loch for the king's departure, but I've nae an appetite for food."

"As ye wish," Iain replied, though he looked anything but happy about relenting.

He passed by her, as did Lachlan, both of them seeming guarded, as if she could somehow harm them. She didn't have time to question it as Cameron stepped closer and took her by the elbow. His fingers curled tightly around her arm, and he started to pull her closer when a startled look crossed his face. He dropped her elbow as though it burned him. She swallowed. He hadn't meant to touch her. She knew it was unreasonable to be bothered by it, but it was like he had taken a chunk of her pride and smashed it with his fists.

His eyes had an almost hungry look as he stared at her. "Try nae to cause any more trouble as ye break yer fast."

She flinched at his words as disappointment that he had every intention of leaving her filled her chest. She clenched her teeth at her continued foolishness. Given the way he was acting toward her, it was obvious that, despite his earlier words, the man detested her. Embarrassment mingled with sorrow and confusion. She shouldn't care. She didn't even know him, not really; the little she remembered of him was all she knew. But whether she should or not, the simple fact was that she did care.

She forced out a steady response. "I did nae cause the

trouble," she said, frustrated that her voice was not as strong as she had liked. Devil take it, she sounded weary, defeated, almost wounded. "Yer clan hates me," she whispered furiously so only he could hear, though as the words left her mouth she could have kicked herself. Now she sounded wounded and like a weepy child. She vowed in that moment not to say anything else that would make her seem weak or foolish.

He looked as if he was about to argue, but then he clamped his jaw shut and raked a hand through his hair, making her wonder what it would feel like to run her fingers through his thick locks. How appalling! Apparently she was weak *and* wicked.

"Dunnae move," he growled.

She nodded, and he strode purposely around her toward Cormac. His eyes widened at Cameron's approach. She noted with self-satisfaction, which was likely sinful, that the man was not so full of bluster now.

"My lord," he began, but Cameron interrupted him by holding his palm up. The man fell silent, and when Cameron leaned over him to talk—she supposed so no one else would hear—all the color leeched from Cormac's face. When Cameron stood up straight again, the other warrior slunk low in his chair, hunching his shoulders and casting his gaze down. The men around him jeered openly at him, calling him a clot-heid.

Though the young warrior had made her angry, her heart ached for him, and she felt a twinge of familiarity, as if she too had been humiliated before. Cormac's gaze darted to her for a moment, and she vowed she saw remorse there, but he turned his eyes quickly down before she could offer an understanding smile.

Cameron grabbed two hunks of bread, cheese, and a

carafe of wine before striding back to her. "Come," he said gruffly, making her certain he didn't really want her to but that he felt he must offer.

"Ye dunnae have to snap at me," she grumbled.

His lips parted, then twisted into a smirk as a dangerous gleam filled his eyes. "If it pleases ye, *come now.*" The paltry *please* he'd added did nothing to disguise the order that was still there. She ground her teeth at his high-handed treatment and folded her arms across her chest, tilting her chin up stubbornly.

He grunted. "I did nae ken ye wished to stay and break yer fast amongst my clansmen who dunnae like ye." he said in a low tone. "I'm nae one to stand in the way of a lass's desire." He swiveled on his heel and started for the door. She was sure he'd turn back, so when he got to the door and started out of it, she raced after him, catching up just as he rounded the corner out of sight.

Cameron felt horrible treating Serene as he had—as he *must*—but it would be better for both of them if he behaved that way. There had to be a wall between them. He had to be cold and measured, getting only as close to her as he needed to glean as much information as she could remember. He'd not intended to take her with him as he searched for the attackers, but there'd be no choice now that the king had commanded it. The relief he had felt when David had given the order worried Cameron. How easy it would be to allow desire for her to overcome good choices.

His brothers would never do such a thing. When Marion had been stolen by English swine, Iain had not rushed off to rescue her, overcome by emotions for the woman he loved. His brother had methodically planned out the attack, gathered his forces, and then went to reclaim his wife and conquer his enemies. Cameron wanted to be that logical, that controlled. His father had often accused him of lacking the required control needed to be a legendary MacLeod warrior, and his father had been right.

Cameron clenched his jaw as he led Serene to the solar in silence, the memories clamoring in his head. He'd been an impetuous child, often doing things without thinking, which had often resulted in injuries to himself and sometimes others. He could still recall climbing a tree he'd been told not to climb and Lena coming up after him. She had fallen from the tree and broken her arm. Luckily, she had healed and retained the use of her arm, but that did not change that the accident had been his fault. His father had never for a moment let him forget it, just as he hadn't let him forget the countless other thoughtless things he'd done. Cameron had tried to think before doing something, but he had always forgotten. It wasn't until he had reached thirteen summers that he could recall stopping to ask himself if he should do something just because he wanted to. It was too late to change how his father saw him; no matter how he'd tried, it had not changed. But it was not too late to prove himself to his brothers, to be a true protector of Lena as a brother should, and to prove his worth to his clan.

He entered the empty solar and led Serene to the window seat. He deposited the food and wine on a nearby table. He imagined she'd want to talk first. He'd known it would likely be empty in here, and it was the best place to ensure no one overheard them. It occurred to him then, as he stood there, that some people might whisper it was untoward for them to be alone in here. No one had seen them come in so he felt it was fairly safe.

Sunshine streamed through the windows, bathing Serene in its golden rays. It glistened over her, making her hair and skin shimmer. Desire strummed through him, and he struggled to keep control of it. If there had been any doubt in his mind that this woman posed a danger to him, there was none anymore.

His mind still whirled with the astonishment of what he had done. Lying to the king was a crime punishable by death. Given that his life was already in danger, his actions appalled him not only for the dishonor but the idiocy. Yet no matter how hard he thought back to the moment, he could not see that there had been any choice. There had been real fear in him when the king had threatened to be rid of her. Not for himself, nor that he'd no longer have her to learn anything she may remember. The stark, all-consuming fear had been for her safety.

He thought back to the sequence of events that had led up to this moment, examining his memories once more for places he could have made a better choice. He'd recognized his desire for her immediately when she had entered the great hall with Marion. That's why he had not spoken to her and left her at the table at the far end of the great hall, away from him.

But distance had not stopped his gaze from finding her. The moment anger and then misery had swept across her face, it had been as if a spirit possessed him. He'd risen, heard Lachlan demanding to know what he was doing, and seen the king and Iain give him questioning looks, but he'd ignored them all to go to her aid. He'd sensed in his bones that the argument had to do with her. And when Cormac had made the crude reference to the king's intention to give her to an ally, Cameron had known well the man had meant what she would be giving, willing or not, was her body.

The king also had made the threat to rid himself of Serene, and something inside Cameron had come unhinged. Reason had fled him. There was no other explaining it. Rage had consumed his thoughts for Cormac's words, true or not, as well as a strong desire to deny that another man would ever touch her. What was the matter with him?

He stole a glance at her, and she gazed back steadily with those passionate gray eyes. He wanted to lose himself in her eyes, her arms, her body. The thought made him groan, and he gripped his head, battling to gain the control he needed to have. He had to guard himself from her, as well as guard her from others, yet he was keenly aware he was failing miserably on both counts. The effect she had on him was as unstoppable as the gales of a fierce storm, yet he had to stop it.

"Cameron?" she asked, her voice a tentative whisper.

"Aye?" He couldn't look at her yet. If he did, he feared he'd seal his mouth over hers.

Her hand settled on his arm, her warm, silken touch like lightning through his veins. "Why did ye lie to the king and to yer clan?"

He slid his teeth back and forth, listening to the grinding in his ears and feeling the scrape between them. A war raged within him—the need to speak the truth versus the need to lie. His honor had to bow down now to save it and his clan from what he might be led to do in the future. He swallowed the metallic taste down. "I could nae allow the king to rid himself and us of ye before I glean all the information ye have to give me."

Her sharp intake of breath gutted him. He had to curl his hands into fists and conjure all his restraint to keep from telling her the truth. He had simply not been able to stand the thought of her being killed or sold off to a cruel man at the king's whim. He could not allow her to be hurt. But eventually, he would have to stand by and allow her to depart. He was acutely aware of that fact dangling sometime in the future.

"I'm sorry I dunnae remember any more yet," she offered tentatively, like a peace offering one was unsure would be accepted. "Hopefully, I will soon, and then ye can rid yerself of me."

He shouldn't look at her. He shouldn't. Yet he rose, turned, and when he saw her eyes shining bright with unshed tears, his will unraveled as if someone had yanked a loose string on a blanket and destroyed it in the blink of an eye. He scrambled to gather the remains of his control, but she sucked her lower lip between her teeth. A sharp ache to snag her lip and suck it into his own mouth gripped him. He cursed inwardly as he battled the rising tide of his desire for her. She dashed a hand at a tear that fell down her cheek, while quickly turning her face to hide her actions. But she was not fast enough.

He'd seen the misery he was causing her with his callous words and cold treatment. His insides twisted like an ancient vine twined upon itself. He wanted to undo it. His body trembled as he raised his hand, gripped her chin softly, and turned her face toward him. Her eyes rounded as he sealed his mouth over hers, and then something primal took over. The need to possess her blazed through him like a wild fire. He slid his hands into her silky hair, capturing her moan with his mouth, and demanding with his tongue that she open for him. And when she did, oh God, it was heaven. She tasted like honey stolen from a beehive that sat in the heat of the summer sun. He wanted to plunder all that she had to give.

He swirled his tongue around hers, and when hers hesitantly touched his, he encouraged her to boldness with his growls. She gave a sweet, low moan, and her hands swept up his back, over his arms, and down his chest, finally resting on his thighs, where her fingers kneaded his burning flesh. She had the power to destroy him if he was not careful, and in this moment, he was but a foolish lamb racing to the slaughter. He moved his mouth over hers, devouring its softness. She matched his hunger, sliding her tongue over the crease of his lips and then circling her tongue around his enticingly. Her response would have brought him to his knees had he been standing. She writhed in his arms, her nails digging into his thighs, causing biting, pleasurable pain. With a thundering heart, he tore his mouth from hers, trying to gather the will to stop, but her eyes gleamed, and he knew then that her desire equaled his.

A groan of submission escaped his lips. He kissed the pulsing hollow between her collarbones, then her neck, and finally low on her chest where the too-tight gown exposed her breasts. She pressed her mouth to his chest and his throat, and traced her soft lips along the edge of his jaw. Desire so acute took him that he feared he would not stop until it was too late for both of them. He wrenched away, jerked to his feet, and stormed to the other side of the room to a window overlooking the loch. His blood pumped viciously through his veins as he lifted his hands to the wall and pressed his palms against the cool surface, struggling to calm what raged within.

The loch shimmered in the distance. He knew his men would now be on the shore, waiting on him to train them and lead them, and here he was doing what he had vowed he would not do. He cursed and turned to face her. She looked as disheveled as he felt with her mussed hair, swollen mouth, flushed cheeks, and bright eyes. Confusion swam in their depths, and her lips had tugged into a small frown. He wanted to go to her once more, and this time kiss her with tenderness. He hardened himself slowly from the inside out until it felt as if ice had replaced the blood in his veins. If he could not rely upon his will alone, he needed hers, as well.

"I will hurt ye if ye let me, Serene," he growled, striding toward the door. "I need ye to remember that for both our sakes. I have to leave." He didn't want to hurt her more by telling her that he needed space from her. "I'll send someone to fetch ye."

With those parting words, the door slammed behind him, separating him from her physically. But she was in his head now, and he was unsure how to get her out.

Eight

Her name was not Serene. The knowledge swept over her and made her gasp.

Sorcha! Her name was Sorcha!

She stood, full of excitement to tell Cameron, but she paused halfway to the door out of which he had just stormed and much of her joy drained away. Confusion buffeted her mind as she raised a trembling hand to her swollen lips. She could still feel his kiss, still taste him. He tasted of wine, intoxicating and warming. She pressed her fingers to her ravaged lips, and her belly clenched with the memory of how he had lit her body on fire. She was positive she had never felt such desire in her life. What Cameron had just made her feel was seared into her memory as well as her lips.

She was sure she'd never been kissed before because it felt strange but wonderful. All her fear and confusion had disappeared while he had held her in his passionate embrace, but it all rushed back now. What did he mean that he would hurt her if she let him? Was he saying he was not good or just not good for her? Or perchance it was because he knew all he wanted from her was to join with her?

For a moment, she debated running after him, but he'd looked irritated enough that she feared what might happen if she did. Not to mention that her thoughts and heart raced, and she needed time to calm down. She walked back to the window seat and sat. What had just happened? No, the better question was, what was happening between them? Something was, but she didn't understand what. One minute the man was warm and kind, and the next he was cold and distant. Then he'd looked at her after she'd apologized, and his eyes had smoldered with desire.

The thought had her wrapping her arms around her midriff. Her body had responded eagerly to his touch, almost wantonly. Yet, she truly did not think she was a woman of questionable morals. Maybe she had simply not yet met a man who she would abandon her morals for until Cameron.

She ground her teeth, and when her stomach growled, she stomped over to the table and snatched up a hunk of cheese and bread. She took a bite and tried to calm her chaotic thoughts, but her heart still beat too fast from Cameron's touch. She bent down and picked up the wine carafe, lifted it to her lips, and took a large gulp. She winced at its strength, nearly spitting it out. A cough racked her body once she swallowed the liquid, and when she was done, her belly felt pleasantly warm. The wine seemed to be working to ease her tension. She took another sip, but this time she exercised care with how fast and how much she drank.

The second drink made her feel even better than the first. Taking the wine, bread, and cheese, she made her way back to the window seat and sat for a long while, drinking and thinking about what had occurred with Cameron. She went to take another sip from the carafe and was startled to find it empty. Hiccupping, she plunked it onto the ground. She had sat and waited long enough for Cameron to send someone to fetch her. She'd make her own way back to her bedchamber.

She strode to the door, threw it open, and blinked in surprise when she saw Broch. He consumed all the space of the doorway.

"My lady," he said with a gentle smile. "Cameron instructed me to see ye to Lady Marion in the healing room. She wants to look at yer head."

Sorcha ran her fingers over the bandage that was still wrapped around her head. She'd forgotten it was there. She nodded at Broch, then gratefully took the elbow he extended to her. The room seemed to be spinning a bit, though, and when he started to lead her out of the solar, she realized just how wobbly she was and had to clutch onto him so she wouldn't sway.

He frowned at her and paused at the stairs. "Is something the matter, Lady Serene?"

"My name is Sorcha," she replied, immediately correcting him.

"My apologies," he said. "Cameron referred to ye as Serene still."

"That's because he dunnae ken that I recalled my true name. I only did so after he'd left the solar."

Raced away from her was more like it, but this man didn't need to know that.

"Ah," Broch replied. "I'll tell him immediately. We've been instructed to relay any information ye recall to him the moment ye recall it."

"I'm certain ye have," she replied, feeling sour at the reminder that the only reason Cameron had lied to the king about her was so he could glean what she might remember.

"Are ye feeling unwell, Lady Sorcha?"

Broch looked at her with genuine concern. Couple that with the fact that he'd not agreed with everyone earlier in the great hall when they said she wasn't to be trusted, and she decided that she liked him. She took a deep breath and said, "I believe I've drunk too much wine." With that, she promptly hiccupped once again, and they both burst out laughing.

Once the laughter died, he tightened his grip on her arm. "If ye need to lean into me more as we walk, ye may."

"That's verra kind of ye," she said, doing just that as he started them down the stairs.

She debated for a moment asking him to explain what the man in the great hall had said about her. The worst Broch could do was refuse to tell her, but maybe he would reveal something she needed to hear, and then she would know for certain what awaited her in the future. She had a niggling suspicion what the king likely intended, but she prayed she was wrong. Her stomach knotted as she wet her lips and gathered her courage. "Do ye ken what the man in the great hall meant when he said the king had plans for me?"

A disgusted look swept across Broch's face. "I ken what he meant, but if Cameron has nae told ye, I dunnae believe that he will wish me to do so."

She scowled at that. "Dunnae I have a right to ken my own future?" she demanded, her words coming out in sharp breaths.

His blue eyes widened. "Ye do. I kinnae argue that. However, 'tis doubtful ye'll find the kenning pleasant. Are ye ready for that?" he asked as he led her out a door and into the courtyard. The day was gray and misty, which seemed rather appropriate for their conversation.

She nodded. "I'd rather ken my future and be ready than nae ken a thing."

"Spoken like a lass with a braw heart," he replied. He

shifted from foot to foot and sighed. "I kinnae deny ye the right to ken what the king intends, so I'll tell ye."

She understood that the man may well be putting himself at risk for being punished by telling her. Despite how much she wanted to know, she could not ask this man to do something that would cause him harm. She set a hand to his arm to still his progress across the courtyard. He stopped immediately and turned to her.

"Dunnae tell me," she said. "I could nae abide it if harm came to ye for my sake."

Both his eyebrows arched high, and he surprised her by taking the hand that was tucked into his arm, raising her fingertips to his lips, and kissing them.

"Why did ye do that?" she asked, feeling only confusion and not the rush of desire she had when Cameron had touched her.

"Because ye are beautiful, compelling, and kind," he said with a sly smile.

Irritation flared in her chest. Was he trying to lure her to him?

"Perchance I did nae wish ye to do that. Did ye nae consider asking first?" she demanded.

He grinned. "Nay. I've nae ever met a lass who complains when I kiss or touch her."

Sorcha gaped at Broch for a moment. "Are all MacLeod men this arrogant?"

Broch cocked his head and scratched at his beard for a moment. "Only those of us who ken we are great warriors and nae too terrible to look upon." He winked at her, and she could not help but laugh, to which he responded by kissing her hand again.

This time, she jerked her hand away and gave him a stern look. "Dunnae kiss my hand again!" she insisted.

He frowned, looking so truly perplexed that she almost laughed again, but she held it in, not wishing to give him any reason to try to kiss her once more.

"Am I nae pleasing to look upon to ye?" he asked.

"Ye're made less pleasing by yer boastful nature," she chided.

He threw his head back and laughed, and when his laughter died, he kissed her on the cheek before she even realized what he was going to do.

She placed her palm against his chest to stop him from kissing her again. "I dunnae wish ye to kiss me, Broch. I dunnae mean to be hurtful, but I—It's just—"

He cocked an eyebrow. "Ye're a lady?"

"I may nae be," she grumbled, irked that she could not remember. "I honestly kinnae say for certain."

He grinned at her. "Ye seem quite the lady to me, and it makes me want to kiss ye more." She opened her mouth to protest, but he held up a staying hand. "I'll nae tonight, but I will nae vow that I won't try to sway ye to let me kiss ye again in the future."

She shook her head in dismay. She could not very well tell him that she feared her interest was stuck upon Cameron, and she was glad she did not have to, because the truth would suffice just fine. "The king has designs for me, remember."

"Aye, if ye be of worthy stock and unmarried he intends to either marry ye or sell ye."

"I told ye nae to tell me," she whispered as her heart squeezed with worry over her worsts fears being confirmed and ones she had not imagined being announced.

He shrugged. "Ye did, and I ken ye were trying in yer way to protect me, which pleases me mightily."

"I would have done that for any honorable man," she

said emphatically, her thoughts whirling around what she had just learned. She had suspected marriage might be on the king's mind. She may not have her memories, but she didn't need them to know men used women for their own gain. But to sell her? She inhaled a shaky breath. "Do ye ken when this is to occur?"

"I suspect soon. Cameron's needing ye for information secured ye some time, but as soon as ye remember yer past…"

"The king will marry me or sell me according to what I remember?" she asked, her tone as shaky as her body.

"Aye," he replied, his mouth thinning into a grim line. "If ye be a traitor, he'll sell ye to the worst possible sort of man."

Her scalp prickled at Broch's words.

"But if ye be an ally," he went on, "he'll reward ye by using ye in marriage."

"Aye, 'tis quite the reward," she growled. "Dunnae he care if I am innocent for this marriage? Perchance I'm nae," she muttered, bitterness edging her tone.

Broch sighed as he shook his head. "Yer innocence will nae matter to any man the king would give ye to," he said gently. "Though I'm certain the king will wish to ken if ye are innocent or nae. If ye're nae, a simple reward of land to make up for yer coming to the marriage without yer innocence will do for most men when they look upon yer beauty."

Broch's words infuriated her. She was not angry at him, but furious that women were used so. "Ye men seem to think that women should have as much choice in their future as a newborn bairn does," she bit out.

Broch smiled gently down at her. "Nae me. I believe women should have choices. If ye wish to join with a man ye desire before ye are married or sold to a man ye dunnae want, I'm happy to oblige ye," he offered with a grin.

It was hard to get cross with a man who was grinning so happily at her. But that did not mean she didn't need him to understand her. "I dunnae believe I'll accept that offer, but I thank ye."

"Ye're certain?" he asked, his grin still on his face. "The king will likely wed ye to some crotchety clot-heid, nae a warrior." Broch cocked his eyebrows at her again, and she did laugh then.

"Ye dunnae relent do ye?"

"Nae when I see something I want," he said, his tone serious.

She had to discourage this man somehow. For even if she decided she wanted to join with a man before marriage, as Broch had so crudely put it, the man that came to her mind was Cameron. "Perchance I'm already married," she said, hoping that would dissuade him.

A troubled look crossed Broch's face. "I had nae thought of that, but if ye are, dunnae ye find it odd ye kinnae even remember yer husband? If he be a good one, dunnae ye believe ye would recall him?"

If she liked her husband, she would think she'd remember him. Perchance she did not care for him, then. Not willing to voice her private concerns, she shrugged nonchalantly. "I would have thought I would recall a great many important things, such as my own name, but I did nae at first. I'm sure I'll remember soon," she said with much more conviction than she felt.

※

Cameron stood at the window in the library and looked

down into the courtyard where Serene faced Broch with her hand upon his chest. He still tasted the honey that was her, and when he breathed in, her scent tantalized his senses and heated his blood. His fingers still tingled with the feel of her soft skin and silky tresses, and his body hardened with the memory of her moans when he had kissed her and the urgency of her response to his ravishment of her mouth. By God, the lass had caused him to temporarily lose his mind, and even now, separated as they were, she battered his self-control. Jealousy—the emotion was so strong there was no point denying it—coursed through him. His brothers and Alex were behind him, gathered at a table arguing about the best way to find those responsible for Katherine's death.

"Cameron, are ye going to offer input into this?" Lachlan demanded. "'Tis yer life at stake."

Cameron jerked his head in a nod, though he did not move from his position at the window. Whatever Broch and Serene were talking about in the courtyard, the conversation seemed very intense from the looks on their faces, but then suddenly, Serene said something and Broch threw his head back and laughed, as did she. The smile that lit her face made the jealousy within Cameron multiply, and when Broch drew Serene's hand to his lips and kissed the tips of her fingertips, Cameron growled.

"What is it, Brother?" Lachlan asked, now directly behind him.

Cameron faced his brother, realizing he'd been so mesmerized with Serene he'd not even been aware that Lachlan had approached him. "Nae anything of import," he quickly replied, moving away from the window and hoping Lachlan would follow. He'd rather his brother not know he had been staring at Serene and Broch. Instead of following suit, though, Lachlan stepped closer to the window, and after a second said, "Ah. I see now exactly what it is. I suppose such a scene would anger any man who was drawn to the woman involved."

Cameron was back at the window before he considered how it might look if he'd come so quickly, lured by Lachlan's words. He glanced back down into the courtyard and ground his teeth. "Devil take Broch!" Cameron spat under his breath, for the warrior had Serene's hands to his lips once more. "He's supposed to be watching her, nae wooing her. The king will nae like this!" he added. It was true, but Cameron had mostly said it because he couldn't voice that *he* did not like it.

Lachlan gave him a knowing look. "I'd say *ye* dunnae like what *ye* see. In truth, I'd say ye seem jealous that Broch is wooing her." Lachlan looked at him suspiciously.

"I'm nae," Cameron lied.

"Good. Because if ye already feel the tug of possession for a woman ye have kenned for only two days, then I'd fear ye dunnae have a hope of withstanding yer desire for her."

"I thought ye said ye dunnae hold living yer life by what Eolande said," Cameron bit out, his frustration with himself making his words short.

"I did nae hold mine with her dire prophecy for myself and Bridgette because Bridgette was mine." Lachlan's voice was fierce, and his eyes blazed. He leaned close to Cameron and dropped his voice to a whisper. "I'll tell ye something I have nae ever told anyone, except Bridgette… From the moment I first claimed her mouth, she claimed me completely. So ye see, by the time Eolande spoke her prophecy, it was too late for me to turn away from Bridgette. My advice is dunnae kiss Serene. Nae matter how much ye want to, dunnae chance it. If she is the mate of yer soul, even one kiss could bind ye."

"Too late," Cameron said flatly, meeting his brother's eyes.

"Ye giant clot-heid," Lachlan groaned. With a shake of his head, he added, "Well? Do ye feel changed?"

"Aye," Cameron admitted, but when concern swept Lachlan's face he added, "Dunnae worry. I will resist the pull to her. I will nae put my family in peril for a woman I lust after."

"Lust, ye say?" Lachlan replied, and incredulous look twisting his features. "Ye're a fool if ye believe a man feels changed by mere lust. There's nae hope for ye now."

"I'm stronger than ye give me credit for," Cameron ground out.

"I give ye more credit than ye recognize," Lachlan said. "Much more than ye give yerself. 'Tis nae a matter of strength, though. It takes more strength to claim yer heart's desire when it may hurt others ye care for than it does to turn away from what ye long for."

"Join us, if it pleases ye two gossiping lasses," Iain barked from where he stood by the table.

Cameron quickly relented, not even answering Lachlan or seeing if his brother had more to say. He welcomed the reprieve that plotting his scheme could offer. Iain pointed at the drawing on the table. "Alex and I agree that ye should go to see Graham first and tell him what is happening. With the king making his way to the Steward's home, if David names his nephew a traitor, Graham will need to ready Brigid Castle to defend the sea passage to the Isles."

"I agree, and I can question some of the people in the Earl of March's town. Those who will nae recognize me but who may ken something about the men we seek."

"Agreed," everyone around the table said.

"Since ye will be searching for traitors in enemy territory, anonymity is required," Iain said.

"Aye," Cameron agreed.

"The fewer men ye take, the easier it will be to achieve that," Lachlan added.

Cameron nodded. "Of course."

"Ye need to take men that are experts at moving in the shadows but who are also skilled fighters," Iain said.

"I'll go," Alex immediately offered.

Cameron raised an eyebrow at his friend. Alex was definitely an extremely skilled fighter who could move unseen, but he also was laird of the MacLean clan and had already risked his life many times to help not only Cameron but the whole MacLeod clan. Cameron shook his head. "I kinnae ask ye to risk yer life for me yet again."

"Ye did nae ask," he said matter-of-factly. "I offered. Besides," he added in a rush as Cameron opened his mouth to protest, "I dunnae do it simply for ye. I offered because a betrayal of the king is a betrayal of all those who support him, including my clan."

Nods of agreement came from Iain and Lachlan.

Alex's words were true enough. Though King David had done several things lately that made Cameron and his brothers question if they would be able to continue to support David in the future, he was still their king. If the day came that they could not offer fealty any longer, they would tell David, as was honorable, before breaking away.

Cameron clapped Alex on the shoulder. "I welcome ye by my side."

"Ye should take Broch, too," Lachlan said. "The man moves through the shadows with the ease of a blind man."

Cameron's first instinct was to say no, but it was jealousy from earlier, and he well knew it. "Aye. I'll take Broch. I wish Rory Mac were well, though. I'd take him if I could,"

Cameron said, feeling the weight of guilt that his friend had been injured at all.

"Aye," Lachlan agreed. "Thanks be to God that the fool is nae dead," he added, smiling briefly, as they all did now that their friend's fever had broken.

"What about Grant Macaulay?" Cameron suggested. "If he agreed to go it would be a great help. He was held prisoner at March's castle and kens it well."

"Not to mention it was March's own servants who helped Grant escape," Alex added.

"Aye, Grant would be an asset," Lachlan said.

"It would mean a delay in leaving here in order to get word to Grant and await his reply," Cameron said, "but I believe it would be worth the delay. The men who ambushed us had one intent—to kill Katherine, so that the king might bend to their wills. They will wait now, I believe, and see what the king will do. Do ye all feel the same?"

"Aye," came a chorus of replies.

"Then 'tis agreed," Cameron said, filled with relief. Here, it would be easier to avoid her, until he could build up a better resistance.

"If ye'll all pardon me," Iain said, "I need to attend to a tenant who was attacked by a wolf. I'll likely be gone the night."

"I'll go with ye," Cameron offered, glad for an excuse to put distance between himself and Serene."

Iain arched his eyebrows. "Ye need to train with Alex, Broch, and even Serene. Ye must all work as a smooth unit, and ye need to teach the lass to defend herself. Like it or nae, she'll be with ye and will be either an asset or liability."

"Lachlan can train her," Cameron said, feeling uneasy about being with her.

Iain's eyes narrowed. "Do ye feel ye kinnae control yerself around her?"

He knew his brother asked only out of concern, but the question made Cameron feel weak, lesser than his brothers. "Nay. I'll stay and train her." He would maintain iron control over his feelings even if it killed him to do so.

Sorcha entered the healing room, looking warily around for Bridgette and Lena, who she knew well distrusted and disliked her.

Marion emerged from a smaller inner room and smiled at first Sorcha and then Broch. She waved a hand to Broch. "You can leave."

"My lady, Cameron ordered me to stay with her at all times."

"I'm well aware," Marion said with a sweet smile, "but I vow I'll not let her out of my sight."

When Broch did not move, she scowled at him. "Oh, fine! At least wait outside, if you will."

Broch looked immediately to Sorcha, giving her an unmistakable questioning look. His concern warmed and worried her at the same time. She had tried to dissuade him, but she was not sure she'd done very well. When she gave a slight nod of the head, he immediately left. She watched him go, thinking upon how he was indeed a fine-looking man, but he did not stir her blood in the least. That was a relief, because the way Cameron had made her feel with his kisses had left her a little fearful that she had the heart of a wanton woman. Now she was sure her body seemed to want to be wanton for only one man.

When the door closed she faced Marion, surprised to

find the woman carefully watching her. Marion set down the herbs she had been holding, wiped her hands, and then motioned to a chair. Sorcha sat, and Marion did the same, her steady probing gaze never moving away from Sorcha.

"It seems," Marion said, "that ye have an admirer in Broch."

The slowness of Marion's words reminded Sorcha of the care one might take in testing water to see if it were too cold to swim in. Did Marion think there was something more there? Surely not! Hot embarrassment swept over Sorcha's face and neck. She cleared her throat. "I tried to make clear to him that I did nae wish for his attention."

A choked laugh escaped Marion. "Knowing Broch, that will only make him pursue you with more zealousness."

"I ken that well enough now," Sorcha muttered. Marion's eyes narrowed and a pucker appeared between her brows. "Are you sure nothing has occurred between you and Broch?"

She bit her lip, considering if she should tell Marion that Broch had kissed her. She needed someone to confide in, and get advice from, and Marion was her best, really her only, option. "He kissed my hand twice," she said, a hot flush spreading to her chest. "I told him nae to, and then he kissed my cheek. I had to be verra firm and warn him quite sternly nae to do such a thing again."

Marion scowled. "I'll have Cameron talk to him for you."

"Nay!" Sorcha gasped.

Marion quirked her mouth. "Why ever not? I assure you that Cameron would not like—"

"I'm afraid Cameron would think I encouraged Broch to steal the kisses," Sorcha blurted, her blood pounding as her entire face, neck, and chest grew even hotter with her humiliation.

"Why would he think that?" Marion asked, her tone filled with confusion.

Sorcha was embarrassed to share her kiss, but her confusion and need for a confidant overrode her embarrassment. "Cameron kissed me, and I could nae stop myself from responding rather eagerly, so ye see—" She halted abruptly at Marion's gaping mouth but decided she best rush through the rest in hopes that Marion would understand how lost she felt and not judge her too harshly.

"Cameron may think I willingly receive kisses from any man, but I assure ye, his kiss was the only one that I could nae help but return. It… Well, it stole my senses." And so Marion would not think she was blaming Cameron, Sorcha added, "But I have to admit I liked having them stolen by Cameron. *Only* Cameron."

She fidgeted as Marion stared open-mouthed at her, and the need to keep talking now that someone she hoped she could trust was listening filled her. She took a deep breath. "I remembered my real name after Cameron kissed me, but he fled me before I could say anything. Yer brother-in-law is so confusing!" She gulped a breath and let more words rush out. "One moment he's nice and then he's nae, but his kisses lit a fire inside me. That is, until he said he'd hurt me." She frowned in remembrance. "It was as if he threw a bucket of cold water upon my head. Do ye ken what I mean?"

Marion snapped her jaw shut and nodded, which made Sorcha feel better about continuing. "I ken the king has plans for me that dunnae include Cameron or any man I even ken. I'm a pawn to be moved at the king's whim. Perchance I deserve it for my past, but perchance I dunnae." She sucked in another quick breath. "I dunnae ken what I deserve! I dunnae even ken if I'm already married!" She clutched Marion's hand. "I need help. I need a friend."

Sorcha's heart raced so quickly the beat of it roared in her ears. Her entire body now felt flushed, and her head pounded. She reached a trembling hand to her head and pressed it to her temple, but on a hiss of pain, she quickly drew her fingers away from the wound she'd forgotten about once more.

Marion frowned and patted Sorcha on the arm. "Shh, now," she said in the softest, most soothing voice. "It will all be fine. Put your worries in God's hands."

The words were like a shot to Sorcha's head that lodged in her brain and loosened another memory. She gasped and then grinned. "My mother used to say something similar! I have the loveliest feeling in my chest when I recall my mother," she finished, blinking rapidly to keep the tears filling her eyes from spilling over.

Marion squeezed Sorcha's hand. "Let's start by taking a look at your head, and we'll work our way to your heart," she said with a wink that immediately put Sorcha at ease.

Sorcha merely nodded.

Marion leaned forward and raised her hands. "I'm going to check your wound." Sorcha nodded again as Marion unwound the bandage, then gingerly examined Sorcha's head. "It's healing nicely. Has it been hurting much?"

Sorcha shook her head. "Nay, though I do feel as if I've something stuffed in it," she said on a hiccup.

Marion frowned. "Did ye drink wine when ye broke yer fast?"

"Aye," Sorcha replied, her stomach roiling in protest of the wine still in it. "An entire carafe."

"Oh dear!" Marion exclaimed. "Be more careful with the wine. The MacLeods make especially strong wine. I'm shocked a carafe did not put you to sleep."

Sorcha yawned at the mention of sleep. "In truth, I *am* verra tired."

Marion nodded. "It could be the injury or the wine. Either way, you need to make sure to get plenty of rest tonight. Now," she said, sitting once again as she set the bandage that had been wrapped around Sorcha's head down beside her chair. "What is your real name?" She quirked an eyebrow and offered a smile.

"It's Sorcha," she said.

"Sorcha," Marion repeated but much slower as she cocked her head. "Yes," she murmured. "That suits you perfectly. I happen to know your name means *brightness*, and you are that." Marion chuckled, sweeping her gaze over Sorcha's blond hair and then meeting her eyes once again. "Have you recalled anything else? Like what clan you belong to?"

Sorcha shook her head, her thoughts seeming to slosh around like water. "Nay, but surely more will come soon?"

Marion's nod of agreement sent relief surging through Sorcha. She hoped remembering her past would be a good thing, but even if what she remembered was bad, it would be better than not knowing.

"So," Marion said, her mouth pulling into a teasing smile, "Cameron kissed ye."

"Aye," Sorcha said, unable to keep the glumness from her tone. She hiccupped again. "And then he fled me as if a fire was nipping at his plaid, but nae before he made sure to tell me he would hurt me if I let him."

A contemplative expression came over Marion's face. "That's not overly astonishing. Things do seem rather tangled, and I'm sure it's weighing heavily on his mind."

"What do ye mean? My memory loss?"

Marion sighed. "I imagine your lack of memory is part of it. And the king's intentions for you are likely another part."

"I ken what the king wants to do with me," Sorcha blurted, wanting to hear what Marion had to say about it.

Marion's brows shot up. "Did Cameron tell you?"

"Nay." Sorcha didn't want to keep secrets from Marion when she was asking for the woman to be her friend, but she also did not want to put Broch in a position to be disciplined.

"It matters little who told you," Marion said, giving her a look of understanding. "My husband says David is a good man at heart, but even good men sometimes lose their way."

Sorcha was surprised Marion would share such a thing with her but heartened that she had. It showed trust, and Sorcha did not intend to betray it. "Whether he is good at heart or nae dunnae make a difference in the end if he forces me into a marriage I dunnae want. What if I'm already married?" Sorcha asked, voicing one of her biggest concerns.

Marion blinked at her. "Do you think you are?"

Sorcha shook her head. "Nay. I truly dunnae. I've had nae any memories of any man but Cameron. It seems to me that if I was married, I would recall my husband, whether I loved him or nae, before a man I'd only met once and whose name I did nae even ken."

Marion nodded. "It would seem that way to me, as well. What about when Cameron kissed you? Did it feel as if you had done such a thing before?"

"Nay." Sorcha's cheeks burned. "It seemed strange and foreign, as if I had nae ever experienced such a thing, but—" she took a deep breath, determined to forge ahead despite her embarrassment "—it was strange in a wonderful way." She paused and worried her lower lip, nervous to voice what she was thinking next. "Marion, is there any way for a woman to ken if she is still an innocent?"

Color immediately blossomed on Marion's cheeks as she nodded. "There is," she said on an uneasy laugh. "Why?"

"Because if I'm still innocent, then I kinnae be a man's true wife."

Understanding dawned in Marion's gaze. "I warn you that the process is quite, um, familiar. But it may be wise for us to know immediately if you are married, because if you are, that at least will stay the king's hand in marrying you to another. Not to mention that you just kissed a man," she said grinning.

"He kissed me," Sorcha protested. She bit her lip on a wave of guilt. "Of course, I did kiss him back."

Marion chuckled. "Yer secret will remain just that. Now, if you are truly married—that is, if a man has joined with you and made you his true wife—I can learn from a simple exam. Again, it's quite familiar, but I assure you, it is painless. Do you wish for me to examine you?"

Of course she did not *wish* for an intimate examination, but she did not wish to remain in the dark about whether she was married or not, either. She chewed on her lip for a moment, considering. "I do," she said hesitantly, "but—"

"Before you tell me you'll be embarrassed, I assure you that you don't have any parts I myself don't have, and I feel certain you would be far more embarrassed without a carafe of wine in your belly."

Sorcha chuckled. "Ye are verra good at arguing yer points."

Marion winked. "That's because I have had much practice striving to get my way with my husband." A fond smile came to her lips that made Sorcha wonder what her own face would look like when she spoke of her own husband one day. Would it be miserable or happy? Unbidden, Cameron's image floated in her thoughts, and she sighed. One very exceptional kiss and she already was imagining the man as her husband? She hardly knew him! And regardless, the likelihood of such a future was almost nonexistent.

"So then," Marion chirped, breaking into Sorcha's thoughts. "You will need to take off your underclothes and lie on the bed." Marion indicated a small bed in the far corner.

Sorcha frowned. "Why do I need to take off my underclothes?"

Marion's face turned as red as an apple. "Have you never been in a household where a marriage takes place and the men watch the joining to ensure it has actually occurred?"

Sorcha faced burned. "I dunnae ken. I kinnae remember," she said emphatically. But as she thought of what Marion was saying, more memories flooded her mind. She saw herself standing in a stable watching two horses mate—more accurately she was gaping at the stallion, shocked at what she saw. The same shock swirled through her now. "Ye wish to see if I've been mounted?" she exclaimed.

Marion's brow furrowed. "What?" Understanding dawned on her face. "Oh, well, er, yes, that's the way of it. If you've been mount—er, joined with, then there is a small barrier inside you that will not be there any longer. I will simply feel for the barrier with my fingers."

"Ye will nae!" Sorcha cried.

Marion gave her a stern look. "I will have to if you wish to know for certain if you are someone's true wife."

Sorcha stood there for a moment, torn between her desire to know and the embarrassment of allowing Marion to do such a thing. Finally, she jerked her head in a nod. "Be quick about it, aye?"

"I assure you, I've no intention of taking my time," Marion said, her lips twisting in a comical smile. She quickly went to the bucket, cleaned her hands, and waited patiently with her back turned for Sorcha to say she was ready.

By the time she took her underclothes off, lay back on the bed, and called for Marion, she had worked herself into such a nervous state that her legs trembled when Marion asked her to spread them. She took five deep breaths as Marion had instructed in a low, soothing voice, and just as the shock of what was occurring hit her, it was over.

"All done," Marion said, sitting up. She smiled at Sorcha. "You are not the proper wife to any man."

"Thank God!" Sorcha declared, not realizing just how much she had dreaded hearing she may be married.

Marion smirked at her. "Is that relief I hear in your voice because of Cameron's kiss?"

"Nay!" Sorcha protested, though the memory of his kiss made her stomach flutter. "I barely ken him. But I kinnae deny I feel much better that I did nae play a husband false, nor nae even remember a husband when I remembered Cameron." She quickly donned her underclothes and faced Marion once more. "Although," she said, worry suddenly knotting her belly, "this does mean that there is nae a marriage to prevent the king from marrying me to a stranger."

"Yes," Marion replied solemnly. "It does mean that. I propose we keep the knowledge of your innocence to ourselves for now. That way the king may not act as soon on his desire to use you for gain if he is unsure who he may be crossing."

Sorcha's eyes widened. "Ye'd do that for me?"

Marion walked over to Sorcha and gave her a quick hug. "Yes. That is what friends do for one another, and we are friends," she stated firmly.

"There are many in yer clan who may nae like that ye have befriended me. In truth, I'd venture to say most in yer clan will nae like it."

Marion snorted. "I've never been one to let others' opinions sway me, and I will not start now. Besides, most of them will see yer goodness rather quickly."

"I dunnae ken that it truly matters. I'll nae be here long, as I'm certain ye heard the king say that I'm to go with Cameron to track Katherine's murderers. And once we've found them, I imagine the king will nae tarry in using me."

"Well," Marion said, "we cannot know what will come to pass in your future, but I do know this—not long before Broch brought you in here to me, my husband told me that you will be with us for at least a sennight. And so, for this week, I will do my best to help you feel less alone here."

A surge of gratefulness filled Sorcha. "I dunnae want ye to anger yer family. I seem to be doing that with Lena plenty."

"Bah," Marion said. "Lena is more annoying thunder than deadly lightning. She booms her anger and makes all sorts of ruckus, but she will not strike to hurt unless you try to hurt her or someone she loves."

"Aye," Sorcha said. "I recall what ye mentioned about her wishing to protect Cameron as she had been denied being motherly to her brothers. Ye said ye couldn't tell me more then, but can ye now?"

A sad look crossed Marion's face, followed by an angry one. "She was taken from the clan as a child by her uncle, who was vindictive and cruel. She thought for many years that her family was dead, because her uncle told her so, and one day he forced her to marry an abusive man named Findlay Campbell. That is Marsaili's dead brother she spoke of."

The news of Lena's troubles made Sorcha feel immediately more understanding of the woman's unfriendliness.

"Graham, who you have not yet met," Marion continued, "killed Findlay while defending himself after Findlay came after Graham to try to steal his wife, Isobel, from him."

Sorcha gasped and covered her mouth with her hands. "That's awful!"

Marion nodded. "That is not even half of the horrid things the Campbells have done. They are not nice people."

"How did Marsaili's other brother die?"

Marion sighed. "This may make the MacLeods sound rather like murdering fiends, but I vow they are nae. Lachlan killed Colin Campbell after the man stole Bridgette, forced her to marry him, and hurt her very badly."

Sorcha's stomach tightened at Marion's words. "It sounds to me like both Lachlan and Graham are men who truly defend the women they love."

"Aye," Marion said, a smile tugging at her lips. "All the MacLeod brothers are that way. Well, at least I think they are. Cameron is the only one left who is unmarried, but I believe he has the same capacity to love with his whole heart. I was having my doubts, mind you. He has quite the reputation with the lasses. They shame themselves panting after him with the small hope—hope that he certainly doesn't give them—that they might be the lass to change him. And he's always been only too willing to tumble in the hay with anyone who says she understands what he offers is nothing more than just a joining for pleasure."

Jealousy streaked through Sorcha, which she prayed did not show on her face. "Ye said ye were having yer doubts," she asked, embarrassed to be prying and likely seeming so eager to learn about Cameron, but she could not help herself.

"Yes, I was doubting…until you came along."

"Me? But why?" He had kissed her senseless after only knowing her for two days. Maybe he was trying to seduce her. If so, he was going about it in a rather odd way, she thought, though admittedly, she had no experience to rely upon for this conclusion.

Marion held up a fist. "One—" Marion raised a finger "—he kissed you, despite Eolande's prophecy."

Sorcha tilted her head in confusion as unease stirred within her. "Who is Eolande? What prophecy?"

"I'll explain in a moment. First, let me finish my point. Two—" another finger popped up "—he kissed you in spite of promising Iain and Lachlan that he would keep his distance from you."

Sorcha startled at those words. "They dislike me so much that they asked him to keep his distance from me?"

Marion waved a dismissive hand. "No. It's not you. It's the prophecy, and it's the fact that the king has publicly declared that he has intentions for your future. Now, as for the prophecy and Eolande, I can tell you that the MacLeod clan is one that holds a very strong belief in the power of seers and fairies, and Eolande is a well-known seer who is half-fairy. All the prophecies that she has given have come to fruition, though not every part of them, thank God above." Marion squeezed her eyes shut for a moment, then opened them again. "But enough of what she has foretold has come to pass that all the MacLeod brothers—all the

MacLeods, really—are all wary of making choices that will lead to the worst parts of Eolande's prophecies coming true."

Sorcha's pulse kicked up several notches, and a strange, breathless feeling started in her chest. She pressed a hand to her forehead, suddenly feeling overly hot, as well. "I believe," she said, her voice shaky to her own ears, "that ye better tell me of this prophecy now since it apparently involves me."

Marion bit her lip as her gaze swept over Sorcha. "Oh dear. I didn't mean to worry you, Sorcha. Though, now that I think upon it, I don't believe hearing the prophecy will ease your worry. And beyond that, I know Cameron would not want me to tell you, so I should likely have kept it to myself."

Sorcha frowned. "Did he tell ye nae to tell me?"

"Well, no," Marion hedged, "but he did not tell me of the prophecy at all. My husband did, and before he could swear me to secrecy, which I could tell he was about to do, I kissed him senseless." She offered an unapologetic smile. "So you see, I am quite sure neither of them would want me to say anything to you."

"So ye're nae going to tell me?" Sorcha asked, unable to keep the incredulity from her tone.

"Of course I'm going to tell you! We women must lead in matters of the heart because the men may as well be blind and deaf for the way they handle love."

Sorcha sagged with relief, and Marion winked at her. "I just had to make sure you understood I was not *supposed* to be telling you, and I wanted to explain why. This too must stay between us for now."

Sorcha nodded and wiggled forward on her seat as Marion took a deep breath. "I may not remember it exactly—"

"Simply tell me to the best of yer remembrance," Sorcha said, trying desperately to keep the anxiety out of her voice.

Marion nodded, then twined her hands together. "I know you don't recall the first time ye truly met Cameron, but what do ye recall?"

"His hands. A woman staring at me. Daggers."

"Well, apparently you had entered the annual dagger-throwing contest that happens every year at the St. John's Eve festival. You won the contest, besting Cameron, who is known throughout the land as the most skilled with daggers."

Sorcha stared down at her hands in wonder. Her fingers tingled suddenly, and she could practically feel a cool, heavy weight there, but whether it was from a lost memory of throwing daggers or she was feeling these things because of what Marion was revealing, she could not truly say.

"Anyway, that is not the important part," Marion went on. "Cameron ran after you when you fled him, and before he could catch you and learn who you were, the seer stopped him and told him to let you leave. She said that particular night was not the time he was meant to meet you."

"What did she mean by that?" Sorcha asked.

Marion gave her a knowing look. "I do believe he asked the same thing, and Eolande told him that you would come to him once more." She paused a moment, looking contemplative. "I think she said that you would come to him in a battle."

Sorcha hissed in a breath.

Marion nodded. "Yes, I agree. Eolande also said you would be bathed in blood..." Marion's gaze strayed to

Sorcha's injured head. "She also told him you would be marked by a heart."

"My God," Sorcha whispered, her fingers straying to the mark on her body that was shaped like a heart. "How could she ken such things?"

"Because she is a seer," Marion said simply. Her voice had dropped low and held a tinge of awe and wariness.

"What else did she say about me?" Sorcha demanded, her own wariness filling her completely now that she had heard what the seer had gotten correct about her and how she would meet Cameron once again.

Marion worried her lower lip for a minute before answering. "She said he would betray everything he holds dear for you."

"What?" Sorcha exclaimed, her chest tightening.

Marion nodded. "King. Family." Her voice had dropped even lower. "The honor that means so much to him."

"Nay," she cried, horrified. She shook her head almost violently. "I'd nae ever ask him to do these things for me."

"I do not think you would need to ask if he was in love with you," Marion said in a gentle tone.

To be loved so greatly that a man would risk all, betray all, made her feel both hopeful and horrified. She wanted to be fervently loved, but not at the price of a man going against all that meant anything to him. Her blood roared in her ears as she considered what she had just learned. She did not love Cameron. She barely knew him. He did not love her, either. But there was a strange pull between them. She felt it, and he had said he did, as well. And then there was passion so hot it scalded.

"The other prophecies Eolande has foretold to the other brothers… How much of them have come true?" Sorcha asked, her voice trembling.

Marion sucked in her lower lip as an uneasy expression crossed her face. "Well," she started, her words slow, reluctant, "Eolande foretold that Iain's first wife, Catriona, would die young, and she did." Marion gave a little shudder. "She also foretold that the love between Lachlan and Bridgette would drive a dangerous wedge between Graham and Lachlan, and it did."

Sorcha shifted uneasily in her seat at the growing direness of what she was hearing.

Marion gulped in a breath and huffed it out before continuing. "However, she said one of the brothers would die, and both are still alive."

"Well, thank God above for that!" Sorcha exclaimed, relieved for the small sliver of good news.

Marion nodded as if she understood what Sorcha was thinking. "I have not told you all she said about you yet."

"What else?" Sorcha asked, fearful.

"Eolande said that you are the mate of Cameron's heart—and the enemy of his clan."

A wave of powerful queasiness roiled through Sorcha. It was so strong that she covered her mouth quickly for fear she may be sick. After it passed, she slowly lowered her shaky hand. "Oh blessed St. John! I must be guilty of helping to murder Katherine!"

"No, I think not," Marion quickly rebutted, confidence ringing in her tone. "I think either your *clan* is an enemy of ours or what Eolande saw in his future was that some MacLeods saw you as an enemy."

"Perchance," Sorcha mumbled weakly. "Please tell me there is nae any more to reveal."

Undeniable regret settled on Marion's face, which made Sorcha cringe. Marion puffed her cheeks out, then blew out the breath. "One more last thing... Eolande also said that with you comes life or death born of his choices."

"Well," Sorcha said, half in desperation and half-sarcastically, only because if she did not make light of the circumstances she would scream, "I can see now why he became angry with himself when he kissed me."

"Yes," Marion agreed in all seriousness. "I can understand, as well."

"I'm a deadly temptation to him," Sorcha mumbled, moroseness weighing her mind and her words. "I bring destruction and death."

"No," Marion said firmly. "Eolande clearly said you bring life. It's the choices he makes that will be the difference. Perchance they are the choices *both* of you make."

"Then I chose not to lure him to his doom," Sorcha said. Thinking about how that might sound, she added, "not that I think I am so appealing." But the seer had said she was the mate of Cameron's heart. That had to mean he was the same to her. "It's odd, but I feel sad, as if I have lost a great love, yet I don't love him. I barely know him."

"So ye must learn him and let him learn you. Only then can you even know if you are willing to risk the seer's prophecy."

"I dunnae even ken myself! How am I supposed to learn another?" Sorcha demanded, her frustration bursting through her words.

"Word by word. Day by day. Touch by touch," Marion replied firmly. "That is how you learn another, and as you are doing this, I am certain your memories will return."

She wanted to peel back Cameron's layers. Despite the seer's foretelling, she did not want to turn away, but this was folly. "There kinnae ever be hope for us. The king will make certain of that," she said bitterly.

"Yes," Marion agreed. "But what one plots does not always occur as one expects, even for a king. He had plans for Bridgette, as well, and Graham discovered a way around them. Cameron is every bit as cunning as his brother." Marion shrugged. "It is your choice in the end. I only know that if it were me, I'd rather tempt fate. I'd discover the secrets of the man the seer says I'm destined for, and that I know well I am attracted to"—she gave Sorcha a stern look—"than settle for being used by the king and married to a man I may despise."

Sorcha rubbed her aching temples. "How did ye come to be married to Iain?"

Marion smiled, and the fondness of her memories was apparent in the satisfied look on her face. "My father thought to marry me to an evil Englishman so he could attempt to take the throne from King Edward. My king and Iain's king thought to marry me to Iain and stop my father from achieving his goal of becoming King of England. When presented with the choice of an evil knight or a scary Scot, there was no question in my mind. Well, maybe a few." She chuckled. "But I was immediately drawn to Iain, and I knew for certain he was a good man and would never harm me."

"I'm attracted to Cameron," Sorcha said slowly, thinking out loud.

"It is plain to see," Marion said with a sly smile.

Heat crept up Sorcha's neck. "I believe Cameron is a good man, too."

Marion nodded. "He is. I vow it."

"And I dunnae believe he'd ever hurt me physically."

"He'd sooner cut off his own hand than harm you or any other woman."

The fervor in Marion's voice made Sorcha smile. The

woman obviously loved Cameron, as a sister-in-law should. Sorcha's mind raced. "I could do my utmost to keep a wall between us, as he is clearly trying to do."

Marion frowned. "You could," she replied, disapproval evident in her voice and face. "Or you could slowly break down the wall to learn him. You will be forced to travel together, anyway. It would be fairly awkward to travel with a man by your side that you are determined to overlook. Take my word for this. I have tried it, and if you are drawn to the man, it's impossible, truly. A woman's body has a way of defying a mind's wishes when a MacLeod man is involved."

She thought about all she had learned. She knew what her heart wanted to do. "I wish to break through the wall," she said, praying she did not regret the choice.

Marion smiled triumphantly, and Sorcha blinked in surprise. "Do ye ken that ye seem verra innocent, but I see now that ye're rather devious," she teased. "Ye were leading me to this conclusion."

"Yes, I was." Marion stood, stretched, and started toward the door.

"Where are ye away to?" Sorcha asked, springing up.

"*We* are away to find Bridgette. If you are going to lure a man to let down his guard, especially one who fears doing so will lead him to ruin, you need an expert enchantress, and that is Bridgette."

"I dunnae believe Bridgette will be willing to aid me," Sorcha grumbled.

Marion made a derisive noise from her throat. "Once she hears about the prophecy, she'll be wanting to help. Eolande's prophecy for her and Lachlan almost destroyed her chance at happiness with him. I vow to you that nothing will please her more than helping to alter what Eolande has foretold for you and Cameron."

"I pray ye are correct."

"Oh, I'm always correct. I'm the laird's wife," Marion said with a wink.

Nine

Cameron was starving, yet he did not move to fill his plate from the trencher laden with food in front of him. Food was not what he needed. He needed to see Sorcha. He rolled her name around in his mind as he had done at least a hundred times since Marion had casually told him the lass he had called Serene had remembered her name—Sorcha.

It had taken a great deal of self-control not to go to her so he could see her smile when she told him of her recollection. But he had maintained control and kept a purposeful distance. Yet now—*now*—the need to see her clawed at him. He clenched his teeth against the urge. No, he did not *need* to lay his gaze upon her; he *wanted* to. Need was for things one could not live without. One needed air, and food, and drink. One did not need to look upon a woman that made one feel weak. That was want, and want was for men who were not trying to prove they were worthy to stand beside their legendary brothers and represent their clan. To acknowledge the difference meant he could conquer the yearning that had been building in him since he last laid eyes upon her early yesterday.

After he had trained with his men for many grueling hours, he had started to search her out, but the way his pulse had sped at the possibility of seeing her, perchance even touching her as he trained her, made him realize he needed a bit more time to gain full control. Part of him wondered if it had been cowardly to ask Alex to find her this morning and learn what, if anything, she recalled of riding a horse and throwing daggers, but he ignored that part of him that doubted, and instead chose to think he was making wise choices. Men who knew their weaknesses and adapted to overcome them were being prudent, and that's exactly what he was doing.

She was his weakness. It hadn't taken a week or a month for her to seep into his mind and consume it, devil take it. It had taken one kiss. The great hall was full this night, and the hum of voices participating in conversations filled his ears. To his right sat Lena and to his left was Lachlan, both of them eating heartily from their plates. The dais, which was usually occupied by himself, his brothers, and their wives, was unusually empty. Iain had gone to attend to the tenant who had been attacked by a wolf, and Marion and Bridgette had not yet arrived at the great hall for supper. As if his thoughts conjured them, the great hall door opened and the two women entered the room, arms linked and conspiratorial looks upon their faces.

A smile pulled at his lips. His brother's wives were very close and always into some sort of mischief. What would it be like if he had a wife of his own to watch stroll into the hall with a twinkle in her eyes and a grin upon her lips? The errant thought had him reaching for his goblet of wine and taking a long drink. He'd never once pondered what it would be like to have a wife. In truth, the idea had never held any appeal, yet now he could imagine it. He was not such a fool to ignore how the timing of this change within him coincided with meeting Sorcha.

Marion and Bridgette walked down the center of the

great hall, giggling and chatting as they approached the dais. They quickly took their seats, and then Marion leaned around Lena and met Cameron's eyes. "Have you heard about Sorcha?"

His pulse immediately leaped. "Nay. Is something amiss?"

"Not at all," she crooned. "It seems she is even better at archery than at throwing daggers! She bested Alex in every shooting contest they had."

Lachlan whistled, and Bridgette chuckled. "Ye should have seen my brother. He behaved as if he was so superior when he took her out to the woods—"

"The woods?" Cameron asked in a steely voice. "I told Alex to keep her close and to keep a watchful eye on her."

"Oh, he did," Bridgette said with smirk. "He kept her verra close and could hardly wrench his gaze from her. I think he's smitten."

"Ye think Alex wishes to lay a claim upon the lass?" Lachlan asked, surprise clear in his voice.

Bridgette nodded, without looking directly at her husband. Jealousy rushed through Cameron's veins, and he had to fight to keep his fingers from curling into fists. Beside him, Lena drummed her fingers on the table. When he glanced at her, she had an agitated expression on her face, as if the news of Alex and Sorcha bothered her as much as it bothered him. Sometimes he thought his sister cared for Alex but didn't want to, or perchance she simply did not know what to do with the feelings. Given her past and the abuse she had suffered from her first husband, he could well understand this. He set the thoughts aside.

"Where are Alex and Sorcha?" he asked. He was pleased with how indifferent he sounded.

"They should be along any moment," Bridgette responded. "Alex insisted on attending Sorcha to supper."

"Did he now?" Cameron growled, fighting the desire to rise and go fetch Sorcha himself.

When Lachlan shook his head at Cameron, as if reading his private thoughts, he drank another large gulp of wine and shoved some bread in his mouth, though he had lost any hunger he had possessed. As he chewed, the door to the great hall opened once more. Alex and Sorcha entered, heads turned to each other in conversation. As they walked down the center aisle, men paused to gape at Sorcha, but she did not seem to take notice. She walked without a hint of sway to her hips, as if she didn't care to use the curves God had given her to garner attention.

Her seeming innocence appealed to him on a primal level. Had he been the first man to kiss her, to awaken the yearning and desire of her body? His own body grew instantly hard as he imagined schooling her in the wonders of what their bodies could do together, and all the air in his lungs whooshed out as he drank in the sight of her.

Her hair shone like spun gold cascading over her shoulders and hanging down to her waist. Her face glowed as if she had been out in the sun all day, and her eyes were luminous in her delicately sculpted face. His chest squeezed, and he moved his gaze lower to her shoulders. He froze with his goblet halfway to his mouth.

Sorcha was wearing a plaid. The MacLean plaid. Alex's clan's plaid.

Beside him came a strangled cry, but when he looked to his sister, her face was a mask of indifference. Still, he noted her pulse beating furiously in her neck, just as his was beating within him. Alex deposited Sorcha at a table where there was an empty seat beside Broch, who looked only too eager to have her near him, and with a lingering parting glance, Alex made his way to the dais and took the seat beside Lena.

Cameron inhaled a long steadying breath before leaning forward to address Alex. "Why is Sorcha wearing yer plaid?" The words came out calm, though he felt anything but.

Alex, too perceptive for Cameron's liking, narrowed his dark eyes upon Cameron. "I could tell she was feeling as if she dunnae belong, and I had the means to make her feel like part of a clan until she remembers her own. So I did."

"Did ye nae consider how this would seem to others? To the king?" Cameron growled.

"And how does it seem?" Alex snapped.

"It seems ye declared for her," Lena said in a low voice before Cameron could answer.

"Aye, it does," Lachlan agreed, sounding happy about it.

Anger flooded Cameron's veins. He was sure Lachlan was thinking if Alex declared for Sorcha that would end his need to worry about Cameron and Eolande's prophecy.

Cameron turned to glare at Lachlan, and as he did, Alex spoke. "And if I did?" he asked, looking directly at Lena. "Would it matter to anyone sitting on this dais?"

"Nae to me, though why ye would declare for a woman who may well be treacherous does baffle the mind," Lena promptly answered. But as she quickly reached for her goblet of wine, Cameron saw that his sister's hand was shaking. He frowned. Did she truly care for Alex? His gut hollowed at the thought of what his sister had been through and how it continued to affect her, even after her husband's death. He wanted to shield her from things that hurt her, but he could not allow her to be cruel to Sorcha. Yet he feared she may feel he was being disloyal to her if he defended Sorcha from her. It was a problem he needed to solve, but now was not the time.

"I'm glad to ken it dunnae bother ye," Alex muttered, bringing Cameron's attention fully back to him.

"The king has designs for her," Cameron said between clenched teeth.

Alex leaned forward once more to look at Cameron. "If I wished to make the lass mine, I would find a way to change the king's designs, but as it stands, I was simply being kind to her. Nae one MacLeod offered to extend a branch of belonging to a lass who is floating in a sea of lost memories, so I did it. Do ye have a quarrel with that?"

"I dunnae," Lachlan replied in that same annoying happy tone.

Cameron ground his teeth. Yes, devil take it, he had a quarrel with that! If Sorcha was going to wear any plaid, it would be a MacLeod plaid!

"Nay," Cameron bit out instead, shoving food in his mouth to avoid further conversation about the plaid and Sorcha. As he ate, all he could think upon were Alex's words regarding the king and finding a way to change the king's intentions for Sorcha. What if there was a way to persuade the king in his choice of who he married her to? What if—

Cameron cut the thought off. What was he doing? He was sitting here looking for ways to possibly, what? Allow himself to claim her if he wished it? He had to quit this line of thinking. It was dangerous.

"Sorcha is the second-best archer I have ever seen," Alex said, breaking the rather tense silence that had descended upon the dais.

Alex's praise for Sorcha irritated Cameron, though he knew he was being unreasonable. The man could pay Sorcha a compliment if he wished it.

"Who is the best archer ye've ever seen?" Lachlan asked.

Alex tilted his head toward Cameron. "The two of them are oddly matched in their superior skills in dagger throwing and archery." Alex shrugged. "I told her I'd work with her tomorrow again, but in truth, the lass taught me a few things today. To me, it seems wiser if ye work with her, Cameron. Ye're the only one who could do anything to improve her already impressive skills."

"I think that's an outstanding idea," Marion agreed, her gaze landing on Alex and then on Cameron.

"I dunnae," Lachlan said. His words earned him a poke in the side from Bridgette.

"I agree with Marion," Bridgette said. "If the goal is to ensure she has the skills to defend herself in the hunt for the killers, don't ye want to work with her yerself, Cameron, and give her the best chance of survival?"

He did want to work with her—too damn much—which was why he should not, but Bridgette and Alex had good points. By choosing to stay away from her, he could possibly put her at a disadvantage, not to mention that he had to prove to himself and his brothers that he had the self-control to train her without falling under her spell. "I'll work with her tomorrow."

"Excellent," Alex said. "I'll train with ye, Lachlan, if ye can abide it?"

"We can all train together," Lachlan said, giving Cameron a stern look.

Cameron's felt his anger rising. His brother clearly thought him weak. "I dunnae need ye watching over me as I train," he bit out, shoving away from the table just as music started to fill the great hall.

Tables were quickly moved to the sides to make room for dancing, and Cameron, seeing Angus, Neil, and Neil's wife standing with Alanna at the wall by the door, made his way to them. He greeted the others, then asked Alanna, "How fares Rory Mac today?"

"Better," she said with a grin. "He's awake, alert, and grouchy," she finished, chuckling.

Cameron smiled. "Back to his old self!"

Alanna snorted. "Aye and nay."

"What do ye mean nay?" Cameron asked, concerned.

Alanna glanced out at the crowd of people dancing. When her gaze seemed to fasten upon someone, Cameron searched out who she was staring at—Sorcha. "Alex's lass came to visit Rory Mac today."

"Sorcha is nae Alex's lass," Cameron growled.

Alanna smirked. "Then why is she wearing his plaid?"

"She was cold," he snapped. "What did she want with Rory Mac?"

Alanna's face immediately softened, and regret flittered across it. "She wanted to see if he was improving, and she wanted to repent for any hand she may have had in his injuries."

Cameron snapped his jaw shut when he felt himself gaping. "Did she recall something that made her believe she had a part in the attack?" Just asking the question made his chest ache.

When Alanna shook her head, he barely suppressed a sigh of relief. "Nay. She dunnae recall more than her name, but Rory Mac recalled something about her."

"What?" he demanded, his need to know hitting him with the force of a tempest.

"She turned back from fleeing to save him," Alanna announced.

"What? What say ye?"

"Rory Mac says he saw her fleeing on her horse, but she turned around." Alanna's eyes had grown wide, as if her husband's memory still surprised her. "Rory Mac said she may have been looking to see if any of ye were chasing her, or in light of her actions, it's more likely she turned to see if any of the men who must have taken her were chasing her." Alanna cocked her head, a thoughtful expression on her face. "He says when she saw him losing the battle with the enemy, she galloped back to him and struck the man he was battling in the arm with a dagger, just as the man hit Rory Mac. He'd meant to take Rory Mac's head, nae slice his gut!"

"God's teeth," Cameron whispered, his gaze drawn back to Sorcha. Broch twirled her in a fast circle, and she had her head thrown back and a grin on her lips. Cameron wanted to go to her, sweep her into his arms, and kiss her as he had done yesterday.

"I'm ashamed I judged her so," Alanna murmured. "I told her so, and she was verra gracious. Told me if she had been in my place she would have responded the same way. She is nae an enemy of mine."

"Nor of mine," Cameron said, though the words were hard to get out as his throat had tightened with emotion from the simple act of looking at her. The longer he watched her, the greater the desire grew, until he feared he was losing his grip on his control. "I bid ye good evening," he said abruptly. He turned and pushed his way through the crowd, not slowing until he was out the door and striding through the hall.

He was not even certain where he was going until he was halfway down the seagate stairs to the water. When he reached the shore, he discovered Lillianna carrying two buckets of water in each hand. She quickly set them down as she saw him, put her hands on her hips, and pouted at him. "Why have ye nae come to my bed since returning from the king's mission?"

"I'm sorry, lass," he replied. He and Lillianna had been enjoying each other's favors for the last several years. He had made it clear long ago that he didn't want marriage, however, and she had said she was fine with that. She had been forced to wed very young to a man who had treated her cruelly. He was dead now, and she'd told Cameron she had no interest in marrying ever again, so it had been the perfect agreement.

She slid between the buckets to press her body against his. "Help me deliver these buckets to the kitchen, and then I'll help ease the stress I see on yer face."

He should take her offer. If he did, perchance he could get Sorcha out of his mind. Yet he found himself shaking his head. "I'm happy to help ye with the buckets, lass, but I'm in need of an ice-cold swim." It was the only thing that would extinguish the searing yearning that Sorcha had lit in him. Kissing Lillianna would not help that. Though the lass was pretty, and he had surely desired her not long ago, he felt nothing now as he looked at her, except a festering wish to hold Sorcha, kiss her sweet mouth, caress her beautiful body, and help her unlock the secrets of her memories.

"Cameron!" Lillianna snapped, making him aware that he'd been standing there like a clot-heid. "Did ye hear what I said?"

"Nay, lass. I'm sorry."

Her pout grew more pronounced, but then her tongue darted out to lick her lips as she gave him a smoldering look. "I said I'll be more than happy to swim with ye…naked."

"I dunnae believe I'll be taking ye up on the offer tonight. Shall we?" he asked quickly and picked up the buckets before she could offer any more.

She gave him a wicked smile before turning and climbing the steps. Lillianna was a very shapely woman, and she purposely swayed her hips in a manner he knew was meant to entice him. And it would have done exactly that if the damned recesses of his mind weren't filled with thoughts of Sorcha, but her image kept popping into his head. He recalled her plain and purposeful stride that didn't have even a hint of provocativeness it in, as if enticing a man was the very last thing she would ever think to do. Could he make her wish to entice him?

Devil take it! His lack of control over his own thoughts was appalling.

When they reached the courtyard, Lillianna turned around and launched herself at him so quickly that all he had time to do was drop the buckets in order to ensure they both did not fall backward. Just as his hands encircled her waist to keep her on her feet, she twined her fingers in his hair and crushed her mouth to his. As he broke the kiss to set her away, he was instantly aware that they were not alone.

He turned his head to the right and stormy-gray eyes met his. Sorcha stared at him, her lips parted. Beside her, Broch chuckled and said, "I'd like to tell ye that ye dunnae often see such displays around Dunvegan, but when Cameron is afoot and a beautiful lass is near—" Broch winked at Lillianna "—ye'll see such things as ye just saw. But dunnae ye fret, lass," he said, slinging his arm around Sorcha and drawing her firmly to his side. "I'll make sure to keep ye safe from Cameron's advances."

A wave of anger and jealousy rolled over Cameron, but he choked it down with a forceful swallow and bared his teeth in an attempt at a smile. But judging from the way Broch's gaze widened, as did Sorcha's, he was certain he looked more ferocious than friendly. He wanted to close the distance between himself and Broch and pummel the man into the dirt for daring to touch Sorcha. It was that desperate desire that propelled him to pick up the buckets for Lillianna once more, which was preferable to leaving her standing alone in the courtyard after launching herself at him.

"If ye'll excuse us," he said in the general direction of Sorcha and Broch while turning his gaze on Lillianna.

She seemed astonished that he was still accompanying her to the kitchens with the buckets. He followed Lillianna as she walked past Sorcha, intentionally keeping his focus on Lillianna's backside. She worked her hips so hard, he wouldn't doubt if the lass was sore the next day from her attempt to be seductive. Unfortunately for her, the attempt was lost on him. His lust was now apparently only for lasses with blond hair and gray eyes who could well destroy him just by being themselves.

By the time he reached the kitchens with Lillianna he knew two things for certain: he had to make sure Lillianna understood he no longer wanted to dally with her, and he had to keep contact with Sorcha to a minimum when they trained. One touch too long of his body to hers and he feared his control would not hold.

Ten

When Sorcha entered her bedchamber, Marion and Bridgette sprang up from her bed and rushed over to her. "Well?" they demanded in unison before the door was firmly shut behind Sorcha. She pressed a quick finger to her lips to quiet the women, both of whom she still could hardly believe were being so kind to her. Marion had been correct about Bridgette. Once they had found her, and Marion had told her of Eolande's prophecy for Cameron and Sorcha—and of Cameron kissing Sorcha—Bridgette had been eager to help, claiming rather boastfully that she had immediately sensed an attraction between Sorcha and Cameron.

"Shh," Sorcha hushed the women as they giggled like children rather than the wives and mothers they were. She pressed her ear to the door and stilled, listening to Broch's retreating footsteps. When she could hear no more of him in the passageway, she turned slowly to Marion and Bridgette, who were staring at her with expectant faces. She knew they'd want to hear what had happened with Cameron, but she could hardly think past seeing him kissing that woman in the courtyard. It stole her ability to form a proper sentence, making her angry and sad at once.

"Did it work?" Marion asked, interrupting Sorcha's thoughts.

"Of course it worked," Bridgette crowed, and Sorcha bit her lip on contradicting her. "I dunnae ever set a woman on a wrong path to catching a man, now do I?" Bridgette's green gaze glowed as she plunked her hands on her hips and gave her friend a challenging look.

Marion chuckled. "Well, you did aid me with Iain, I suppose."

"Ye suppose?" Bridgette gasped. "The two of ye would nae be happily married if nae for me," she said with a grin.

"I would not go that far," Marion responded. "We were already married when I met you! Though you did have a hand in making us happy." Marion laughed at Bridgette's outraged look, and quickly added, "But I would say that Graham and Isobel are only married because you taught her how to seduce him."

Bridgette nodded with a triumphant look on her face, then turned her gaze to Sorcha once more. "Now that we have established ye can make Cameron jealous—I saw him glaring daggers at Broch and poor Alex in the great hall—I can teach ye how to entice him."

She needed to stop Bridgette and tell her about the kiss she'd just witnessed. "Aye, but—"

"It will only be a matter of time after that until he forgets Eolande's prophecy and gives in to his yearning for ye," Bridgette exclaimed. "Ye'll be a quick learner. That was verra smart of ye to ask Broch to accompany ye into the courtyard. Did ye encounter Cameron?"

Sorcha blew out a long breath. "Aye. I encountered him, to be sure. He—"

"Was Broch with ye?" Bridgette interrupted.

"Aye. He insisted on accompanying me and would nae leave me be." She frowned, recalling the dance that Marion and Bridgette had persuaded her to accept from Broch. He had made her laugh, for certain, but he did not stir attraction in her, and she feared she had led him on. And for what purpose? Cameron was kissing other women. Agitated, she twined a strand of hair around her finger. "I dunnae believe it was wise for me to dance with Broch. I wish only to be his friend, and I fear he now thinks I wish for more."

"Bah," Bridgette said. "Ye told him ye did nae wish his attention. And I watched ye dance. Ye kept a respectable distance, and when he moved his hand too low, ye stepped away. If he refuses to accept that ye wish only to be friends, ye are nae to blame."

"Perchance nae," Sorcha replied, unsure she totally believed that. "But I'll nae be accepting another dance from him, and if he demands to walk me anywhere else, I'm going to have to tell him in a less gentle way that I dunnae desire him."

Bridgette snorted. "Ye'll need to clobber him over the head with a tree trunk. The man is used to lasses falling at his feet, and ye nae wishing to fall presents an irresistible challenge for him, I'm certain."

"Enough about Broch," Sorcha said firmly. "The plot to make Cameron jealous did nae work. I just saw him outside kissing a lass with long, curly, brown hair."

"Lillianna," Bridgette fairly spat out.

"Be kind," Marion chastised.

"I dunnae see why I must. That one is purposeful trouble. She and Cameron have been tumbling in the hay for years, her claiming that she dunnae want anything from him and him being led by an area other than his brain. Tell us exactly what ye saw," Bridgette demanded.

"Well," Sorcha started, hoping she didn't sound as jealous as she felt. "I did see her throw herself at him—"

"Aha!" Bridgette crowed. "I felt certain that's how it came about."

Hope sparked in Sorcha, but was if foolish hope? "However," she said firmly, "it took him quite some time to untangle himself from her. He may have wanted the kiss." The notion that he would kiss her with such abandon and then eagerly kiss Lillianna with passion later made Sorcha ill.

Bridgette shook her head. "It's more probable that she had her talons good and secure into him. What did ye do?"

"Honestly, I believe I gaped."

"What did Broch do?" Marion asked.

"He slung his arm around me in a most annoying manner. I dug my heel into his toe as discreetly as I could, but the man just kept his arm there."

"And how did Cameron look?" Bridgette inquired, though Marion appeared just as eager to know.

"I can hardly say," Sorcha mumbled. "It was as if a mask had been slid over his features. I could have been a window that he was looking through."

"Oh, och!" Bridgette crooned. "That's what the MacLeod brothers all do when they are truly bothered by something."

"It's true," Marion added. "Cameron is very much like his brothers, though I fear he thinks of himself as inferior. As the youngest, their father was hardest on him. Iain feels partly to blame as he says they all coddled him, which made their father angry and fearful that he'd become soft. He wanted only fierce warriors for sons."

"It's getting late," Bridgette said with a yawn. "And I dunnae wish to be so tired when I join my husband in bed that I kinnae enjoy him, so if ye wish me to give ye some pointers on seducing Cameron tomorrow…"

"I dunnae ken that I do now," Sorcha admitted. "If we are truly meant to be, won't it just happen?"

Bridgette shrugged. "It did happen that way with Lachlan and me, in spite of Eolande's foreboding prophecy of our love."

Mention of the prophecy had Sorcha twisting her hands. "Dunnae ye fear helping me will bring about something horrible?"

"I dunnae," Bridgette said with finality. "If I had allowed Eolande's prophecy to make my choices for me, I would nae be happily married, though I have to confess it was Lachlan, nae me, who was first to snub the foretelling. He refused to live without me, and it was that choice and his bravery that enabled us to have a future together." Bridgette took Sorcha's hand in hers and squeezed. "I believe it is exactly as Eolande always says: she can only foretell the future she sees up to the point she touches us, and after that, it is our choices that truly define how the future will play out."

Suddenly, a new idea had Sorcha gasping. "I should visit the seer! She has nae foretold *my* future by touching me! Only Cameron's. Perchance I will hear something that will guide me in what to do."

Marion and Bridgette exchanged a long look before Marion spoke. "Cameron will not like it."

"He'll most likely forbid ye going," Bridgette added, then smirked. "Of course, ye could avoid that."

Sorcha smiled. "Aye, if I go in secret."

Both women nodded. "If ye did so, ye would need to take a warrior to help guard ye, however. There is a man out there still lurking and likely wanting to kill ye."

"Aye, I've nae forgotten," Sorcha muttered.

"I'll join ye," Bridgette declared.

Sorcha startled. "Ye'd do that for me?"

"For ye, for Cameron, to obliterate another of Eolande's prophecies. I vow that seer-fairy dislikes love."

"Well," Marion pronounced, "the two of you cannot go on an adventure like this without me!"

"Iain will be furious if he finds out ye went to the Fairy Pools with an enemy about," Bridgette said.

Marion scowled at Bridgette. "I don't intend him to find out, but lucky for me, if he does, I know how to cool that Scot's temper."

"Will Lachlan nae be furious with ye for going to the Fairy Pools with an enemy about?" Sorcha asked Bridgette.

"Oh, aye. But he expects me to create mischief. I do believe he's resigned himself to it, and he kens that I am well equipped to defend myself."

"How so?" Sorcha asked, intrigued.

Bridgette grinned. "I am verra handy with daggers and swords, and I am a fair shot with the bow, if I do say so. I'd offer to train with ye tomorrow," she said on another yawn, "but Alex says ye're better than I am." She raised skeptical eyebrows. "Also, if ye wish to truly learn the secrets of Cameron's heart, ye best train with him alone. It's hard enough to get a man to open his heart without an audience!" Bridgette moved toward the door, and Marion trailed behind her. "Tomorrow ye train, but the next day, we will find a way to slip away to the Fairy Pools. Marion and I will come up with an excuse. I will ask Broch to accompany us, too, as we need to take a warrior, or even I could nae cool the temper my husband would be in if he discovered I went to the pools without one."

"Nae Broch!" Sorcha protested.

Bridgette quirked her mouth and looked contemplative for a moment. "Ye must set aside yer concerns. Taking him is the best choice. He is a fearsome warrior, and more importantly, I'll be able to compel him to come with us."

"How?" Sorcha asked.

"Ye let me concern myself with that." Bridgette promptly replied, then yawned hard. I'm off to bed."

"As am I," Marion added.

"Sleep well," both women said before departing.

After undressing, Sorcha crawled into bed, certain she would fall immediately asleep from exhaustion. Instead, she lay there for a long time, staring into the moonlit darkness and recalling Cameron's lips on hers, his hands in her hair and gliding over her body, his smell, his taste, and the way he groaned his need. With her own groan, she rolled onto her side and squeezed her eyes shut. After a very long while, she felt the tug of sleep pulling her under, and then the dreams began.

There was a large childlike man near a horse stable. Something was wrong with him, but he didn't frighten her. Actually, she felt a strong need to protect him. The next thing she knew, she awoke with a startled jerk, and his name was on her lips. *Brom.* He needed her. The certainty she felt was chilling. She had to return home for him, because without her protection, his life was at stake. The fear haunted her into the night, and the realization that when she remembered her home it may well be too late dogged her until the wee hours, when sleep finally took her once more.

※

"Show me what ye ken," Cameron commanded as he put away the daggers they had trained with and handed Sorcha a bow and arrows. His voice was purposely gruff, as it had been since they began. His body tingled with awareness of Sorcha, and while there was nothing he could do to control that, he would control his mind. He would control how he proceeded while alone with her.

She gave him a curt nod, moved out of the shadows of the large tree she had been standing under, and raised her arrow to nock it. Her extraordinary eyes met his, making his chest tighten, and as he looked into their depths, the excitement and eagerness that shimmered there filled him with the same excitement and eagerness. A smile pulled at his lips, taking him by surprise. He quickly forced the frown he intended to keep firmly in place while they were alone. He would be cold. He would be gruff.

"What do ye wish me to shoot?" she asked, interrupting his inner monologue.

He pointed to the tree roughly ten feet away, where he had put a target in the wee hours of the morning. He should have been sleeping like everyone else in the castle, except the watch, but sleep had evaded him while memories of the kiss he'd shared with Sorcha had haunted him.

"That target is an affront," she murmured under her breath, angry color blossoming on her cheeks.

It was an affront for anyone who had a small amount of skill with archery. He'd purposely made her first target easy. Alex may think Sorcha was the best archer he'd ever seen next to Cameron, but Cameron wasn't so sure that Alex had not been blinded by Sorcha's beauty. He intended to judge for himself. He crossed his arms over his chest and returned her frustrated stare with a narrowed one. "Then swallow the affront and shoot." His gruff words had their intended effect, though his gut hardened that it was working.

Anger sparked in her gaze, and a line of focus appeared between her eyes. She angled her body toward the target, aligned the arrow, and stared down the length of it. She inhaled a long, breath, and tilted her head slightly to the left. Her golden hair dangled at her waist, and the sun shone down on her, casting her face in a bright glow. She was a sight to behold, so delicate yet filled with steely determination. When she wet her lips, he wanted to groan, but he clenched his teeth instead.

She let loose her arrow, and it whistled through the air before neatly splitting the target fastened to the tree. The shot was perfect. *She* was perfect. She swung toward him, a brilliant smile on her face, eyes alight with a mixture of satisfaction and hopefulness, and the air in his lungs whooshed out of him. "Is that good enough for ye?" she asked innocently, but her knowing expression gave away that she was very aware her shot was perfect.

"Passable," he commented, though the desire to praise her burned his tongue.

The raw hurt that replaced the eagerness in her eyes made him feel nauseated. He felt his resolve to be cold weaken, but he pushed back against the response. He pointed to the next target, some twenty feet away. "Let us see if ye can split that target, Sorcha."

"Ye ken my real name?" she asked with surprise.

"Aye, Marion told me." He wanted to tell her how much he liked it, but instead he said, "'Tis a good sign that ye recalled it. Soon ye should remember more that will hopefully lead us to those responsible for Katherine's murder."

"I hope so," she replied, her words shaky.

"Are ye fearful?" he asked before he could stop himself. He'd intended to keep all talk between them today only about her skills with the bow and arrow, but the possibility that she was afraid rattled his will to be gruff and cold.

She nodded. "Aye, but nae of remembering. I fear remembering too late."

"Too late?"

"I had a dream last night," she said, barely above a whisper, so he closed the distance between them to better hear her.

"What was the dream?" he asked, breathing in her honeysuckle scent.

"I dreamed of a man."

"Someone ye love?" he asked, his tone relatively calm despite the sudden tempest inside of him.

"Aye, I believe so," she replied, her eyes assessing him.

The hand of jealousy squeezed his throat so that he had to choke out his words. "A husband, do ye believe?"

Her eyes widened. "Nay."

"A lover." He was keenly aware that his tone was no longer relatively calm. It vibrated with the anger clawing at him.

Some indefinable emotion sparked in her eyes. "Nay. I dunnae ken exactly who he is to me, but he is nae a man I love like that."

"Ye dunnae need to love a man for him to be yer lover," he growled.

Icy contempt swept across her face. "I would nae ever join with a man I did nae love, unlike ye joining with Lillianna," she growled.

"Perchance I love her," he rebutted, relieved that Sorcha would not easily give herself to a man and pleased that she was jealous of Lillianna.

Devil take it, he had no right to be pleased.

Sorcha bit her lip. "I did nae ken that—That is, I mean to say, I was led to believe your relationship with Lillianna was—" Her words abruptly halted, and she looked away.

"Never mind," she said in a shaky whisper, making the desire to tell her the truth overwhelm him.

"I dunnae love her," he said in a low voice. "And I have nae joined with her since returning to the castle. I find I dunne have interest in dallying with her."

Sorcha slowly turned to look at him once more. "Ye dunnae? Truly?" she asked. The surprised wonder in her voice and the matching look on her face was like a battering ram upon his control.

"Truly," he affirmed. "I find I want only one woman." When her eyes widened, he hastened to add, "but I kinnae act upon my desire. Much prevents it."

A momentary look of sorrow passed over her features, but then her face became inscrutable. "The man I recalled is someone I care for as one would a brother or a sister."

Undeniable relief that he had no right to have poured through him. "I see," was all he allowed himself to say.

"In my memory," she continued, "he is childlike in his mind."

His brow furrowed. "How do you mean?"

"He is innocent like a child. He is a man, but I sensed he did nae have the ability to act like a man. He is kind and in danger, but from whom I kinnae say for certain. It is someone there. He needs my protection. I fear what may be happening to him in my absence."

He stared at her openmouthed, silenced by the admiration he felt for her. She was beautiful, so much so that he knew most any man would want her. But it was the bravery she kept displaying that tempted him so much that he raised his hand and brushed it down the perfect slope of her cheek. "It will be fine," he said gently.

"Ye kinnae ken such a thing," she murmured, pulling back from him. "I ken the king's intentions for me. Even if I remember my home, if it is the king's choice, I will nae ever see it again. I must get back to my home once I recall where it is."

"I vow I'll help ye return there," he said, shocked as the words left his mouth. Still, he did not regret them.

"Truly?" she asked, her astonishment clear in her tone.

"I would leave no innocent to the whims of a cruel, evil person," he replied, choosing to focus on those feelings rather than his overwhelming yearning to keep her safe and happy.

Her face softened, and a gentle, lovely smile pulled at her lips. "Ye are truly a good man."

The need to kiss her as he had before pounded through him. He motioned toward the target. "Shoot," he said in a hoarse voice.

She nodded curtly, withdrew another arrow, and nocked it. He watched intently as she repeated the exact steps she had gone through before. His chest tightened at the familiarity. He liked watching her and learning her habits. What would it be like for her to know him and for him to know her so well that they could anticipate each other's moods, offer comfort in time of need, or laugh at memories only the two of them shared? He'd never wanted that before. His brothers had those sorts of relationships with their wives. They could cheer up their wives or calm their fears with a touch, and they often shared secret smiles or looks. He'd never been jealous of it. In truth, he'd considered his brothers' attachments to and concerns for their wives as a weakness that lessened them as warriors.

Sorcha's arrow flew by him to hit its target true. A grin lit Sorcha's face, and her joy instantly filled him with joy. He almost gasped as he comprehended that this was why his brothers always did everything they could to please their wives.

Sorcha's gaze locked with his. "Is that shot acceptable to ye?"

In order to keep the wall between them, he knew he should offer only a gruff reply, but he could not do it. He could not destroy her happiness. "Aye," he said. "It seems though yer mind has forgotten much, yer body remembers exactly how to shoot. I wonder who taught ye."

"I wish I kenned," she murmured. A twinkle came to her eyes. "I wonder if I could best ye in archery as I did in dagger throwing so long ago?"

"Och." He waved a dismissive hand. "Ye deceived the lot of us."

"I would nae do such a thing!" she teased. "Ye accuse me only to save yer manly pride."

"Perchance," he replied, relenting to her contagious good humor.

"Shall we have a contest, then?" she challenged.

"What would the contest and the prize be?" he asked, intrigued. Besides, he was never one to turn down a contest.

She cocked her head in thought. "We will see who can shoot the truest at an agreed-upon target. If I win, ye will tell me yer fondest childhood memory since I dunnae currently have any of my own. And if ye win—"

"Ye will remove the MacLean plaid that ye're wearing and wear the MacLeod plaid instead," he rushed out. He knew such a thing should not matter to him. She was not his. She was not even a MacLeod. But it mattered very much. He'd not realized just how much until he'd said the words.

She inhaled a sharp breath, then spoke slowly, as if testing how her words would make him respond. "Does it matter to ye?"

"Aye," he admitted, "though I dunnae have the right to ask such a thing of ye."

She nodded. "Ye dunnae, but I'll accept yer terms."

Relief shot through him.

"Do ye have a plaid to give me if ye win?" she asked.

"Aye. Ye can wear mine, and I will get another."

She nodded. "Now, what shall our target be?"

He glanced around the thick wooded area in which they stood. In the distance, well beyond the target she had shot at before, was a low-hanging branch with a large nut hanging from it. He grinned and pointed. "That nut is our target. We will shoot at the same time, and whoever hits it is the winner."

She looked in the direction he was pointing, and her lips parted. For a moment, she simply stared. "Be ready to tell me yer memory."

He snorted as he withdrew his arrow and nocked it while she did the same. "On a count of three."

She nodded but did not look his way. He allowed his gaze to linger for the space of a breath, watching as that same adorable line appeared between her brows again. He wanted to keep watching her and see all the ways he now knew she prepared. But he had no intention of losing, so he returned his attention to his own bow.

"One," they said in unison. "Two. Three."

The arrows released almost simultaneously, but by nature of the fact that he was much larger than she was—therefore could make his bow string tauter for a more forceful release—his arrow sailed past hers, hit the nut, and lodged in the tree.

Grinning, he glanced at her and found her looking intently at his arrow with a smile on her face. He looked back to the tree and laughed. Her arrow had split his down the middle. "Ye forgot to account for my superior strength as a man," he said.

She gave him an amused look. "And ye forgot to account for my superior mind as a woman. I wanted to wear yer plaid, and now ye must honor the contest and give it to me."

Her words left him speechless for a moment, but as he watched her struggle to stop the trembling laughter on her lips, he threw his head back and chuckled until his gut ached. She let her own hearty laughter spill out, and it filled him with joy like he'd never known. As they both caught their breath, his gaze met hers, and the desire he saw reflected back at him battered his self-control.

Wordlessly, he set down his bow and stripped off his plaid, holding her gaze, which had become dark and beckoning. Yearning strummed through him as he moved so near to her that her scent filled his nose like a heady aphrodisiac, and her body heat caressed him. As he put the plaid on her and his fingers touched her silky skin, need exploded within him. He encircled her with his arms, bringing his hand to the small of her back to tug her close. Her soft, womanly curves pressed intimately against his hard, throbbing body, fitting him perfectly, and when she whimpered her need, he captured her lips with his.

Her mouth was velvety, warm, enticing, and not enough. He wanted more. He wanted all of her. He broke the kiss as his desire mounted, and he feathered kisses to her neck where he sucked in her silky skin on a long draw. Her fingers curled into his shoulders, the nails digging in and revealing her own urgency. She pulled him nearer now, twining her hands in his hair and wriggling against him.

Her chest brushed against his hot skin, and he knew that if he did not stop now, he may not be able to stop at all.

Ruthlessly, he discarded the thought, driven by his relentless yearning for her. He took her mouth with his once more, one hand cradling the back of her neck and the other cupping her heavy breast. She shuddered in his hand, and it was all the encouragement he needed. He circled his fingers gently around her hard bud. A guttural moan came from her that nearly drove him mad with wanting.

He broke the kiss to press his mouth to her chest, and her heartbeat pounded in his ear. "What are ye doing to me?" she demanded in voice hoarse with desire.

Her question, so telling in its innocence, caused the reality of what he was doing to crash in on him. He froze, his entire body rebelling against him as he released her and stepped away. When his gaze locked on hers, it took everything within him not to wrench her to him again.

"Jesus," he muttered, disgusted with himself. He'd been a breath away from taking her, and she was likely an innocent. He would never take that from her and not marry her, and to marry her would mean he was choosing to risk that he could change Eolande's prophecy for his future. If it was only his life that hung in the balance, he thought he might just take that chance, but he could not risk putting his family in jeopardy.

"I'm sorry," he said, jerking a hand through his hair.

"Oh nay, Cameron!" She moved toward him, raising her hand as if to touch him. He stepped out of her reach, knowing if he let her touch him, he'd be lost to desire once more. Lines of confusion appeared on her brow. "I liked what ye were doing to me," she said in a quiet but firm voice.

He groaned at her honest admission as it hardened him further with yearning. "I liked it verra much, as well," he replied. "But this—" he motioned between them "—we kinnae do. I should nae have kissed ye. Twice."

The anger that settled on her face shocked him. She crossed her arms over her chest as she narrowed her eyes. "Ye are a coward," she accused.

Maybe she was hurt, and this was her way of showing it?

He frowned. "Ye dunnae ken—"

"Oh, I do!" she snapped, cutting him off. She stepped toward him and poked him in the chest. He felt his jaw slip open. "I ken about the seer's prophecy."

"Ye what?" he bellowed.

She tilted her chin upward, her face the picture of irritated defiance. "I'm quite certain ye heard me. I do ken yer hesitation. I'm hesitant myself to relent to whatever this is"—she mimicked the motion he had just used and swept her hand between them—"between us. I was hesitant the first time ye kissed me, and that was before I even kenned of Eolande's prophecy."

He was so astounded that he simply stood there gaping. By the time he thought to demand who had told her of the foretelling, she was speaking again.

"So dunnae tell me that I dunnae ken," she growled. "I dunnae wish to be the cause of yer betraying yer family or yer king." Her voice had dropped to a hushed whisper, as if just saying the words could make them come true. "I dunnae even ken my own past! I kinnae say for certain why I was in those woods with the men that killed the queen's mistress," she said with such misery that he flinched. "I dunnae blame ye for nae wanting to learn me when I may nae be a good person."

"Ye are," he replied. The conviction he felt about that took him by surprise.

She stilled for a moment, gratefulness flitting across her

face, but then she took a deep, shuddering breath, and lines of contemplation appeared on her forehead. "I ken the king has designs to use me, and I dunnae wish for ye to ever feel ye must defy him because of me. I ken yer thoughts, but now ye must ken mine." Her gaze locked with his, swirling with the gray clouds of her agitation. "Dunnae kiss me again, because each time ye do, ye make me want to ken ye more, and I dunnae wish to be left with such a wanting that I kinnae ever do anything about."

"Sorcha," he started, his voice catching with the raw emotion her words made him feel.

She shook her head while holding up a quieting hand. "Nay, please let me finish. We will part as soon as ye capture the men accountable for Katherine's death, and I will be married or sold to a man I dunnae ken." The reminder of the future the king had planned for her sparked rage within Cameron. His hands curled into fists, and he clenched his jaw to keep quiet as she had asked of him. "I will bear this fate." She bit her lip. "I dunnae remember if I am braw, but I feel I am nae a coward, so I *will* bear it."

His throat tightened almost mercilessly at the courage she unknowingly showed with her words. "Sorcha—"

"I dunnae wish to be haunted by memories of yer lips on mine, yer heat surrounding me, the smell of ye like a poison I crave in my blood," she continued. "And I will be. I will be if ye kiss me again, so dunnae!" She flung out the last of her words, turned around, and raced down the path back to Dunvegan.

For a breath, he stood unmoving, astounded by what she'd said. He thought of the enemy that was possibly still out there somewhere. He quickly gathered his things and hastened to follow her to ensure she was safe. He caught sight of her in moments, staying close enough to keep her safe but not so near that he might accidentally bump into her if she were to cease her flight.

Her words ran through his mind on a loop. It was too late for him, he realized. Memories of her would haunt him forever. He could not imagine yearning for another woman as he yearned for her. He could not imagine allowing her to be married or sold to another man. And it was in his inability to imagine how he could let that fate come to pass that he understood how Eolande's foretelling could come true. He could imagine betraying his king, devil take it, and even his family, to keep her with him.

As they entered the courtyard, she slowed to a walk, so he did, too. When she disappeared into the castle, he let her go without stopping her. From the corner of his eye, he could see Iain approaching, but Cameron continued to stare at where Sorcha had disappeared. A war between what he wanted to do and what he needed to do raged within him. His nostrils flared in a desperate attempt to get air and to calm the tempest that threatened to splinter him.

"What vexes ye?" Iain asked. He was always so perceptive.

"Sorcha," he replied, not looking at his brother. He was ashamed of how weak he felt when it came to her.

Iain gripped Cameron's shoulder. "I ken that look upon yer face, Brother."

Cameron turned to Iain. "What look is that?"

"It's the one that settles upon a man when he kens that he kinnae live without a woman."

"I can live without her," Cameron replied. "Dunnae be silly. I barely ken her."

"I barely kenned Marion when I married her, but I was certain verra quickly upon meeting her that I did nae wish to be without her. What sort of life would it be for ye to ken ye let another man have her, one that may nae treat her well? She is in yer head," Iain said. "And I imagine she is there, too." He pointed to Cameron's heart. "And once a woman is there… Aye, ye can live without her, but it is nae a life I wish for ye. That life is misery."

Cameron's heart quickened at his brother's words. "I kinnae chance Eolande's prophecy coming true."

Iain's gaze grew flinty. "Then dunnae let it, Brother. Ye are strong. Ye will find a way, and Lachlan and I—Graham, too—will help ye. Consider it," he finished.

He squeezed Cameron's shoulder and walked away, leaving Cameron standing there doing just that.

Eleven

It turned out there was no need for Marion and Bridgette to make excuses to their husbands as to where they were going the next day with Sorcha. Both men had been called away to a meeting with Gowan MacDonald, who was the Lord of the Isles and Marion's maternal uncle. The MacDonald's power, as it had been explained to Sorcha by Bridgette, matched that of the kings of England and Scotland. Thus, King David charged Iain with keeping the MacDonald as an ally. All Marion knew about the upcoming meeting was that a messenger had come from Gowan in the middle of the night, requesting an urgent meeting with Iain and Lachlan. Cameron, it seemed, had been sent in Iain's absence to go see a tenant on the outskirts of the MacLeod land who was having problems with his horses being stolen.

Bridgette told Sorcha that Cameron, after arguing with his brothers, had agreed that Broch was best suited to guard her today while he was gone. It seemed Broch held the position of fiercest warrior after the MacLeod brothers, and apparently Lachlan had told Cameron in blunt terms to stop being a clot-heid when Cameron had attempted to assign Angus as her guard. Angus was a fine warrior, but due to his age, he was no match for Broch. Besides, Angus would not have been as easily persuaded as Broch to accompany the ladies to the Fairy Pools.

Sorcha was not exactly sure what Bridgette had said to him to get him to agree, because when Bridgette had returned to the stables where Marion and Sorcha were waiting for her, she had Broch in tow and there was no time to ask her. But the hopeful look Broch cast Sorcha's way made her uneasy and she wondered if Bridgette had lured Broch into keeping the excursion a secret with the false promise that it might gain favor with Sorcha. She appreciated it greatly, but not so much that she could conjure feelings for the man that simply were not there.

Her head and her heart were full of thoughts, longing, and confusion for and about Cameron. On the one hand, he was as changeable in his behavior toward her as the weather, but she understood the reasons behind his behavior. It almost seemed to her that he was fighting his feelings for her, and if that was the case, they had to be strong feelings for him to be so inconsistent, which made her feel more forgiving toward him. Of course, his fury at himself had been so great after their last kiss that perchance he'd never kiss her again. A feeling of loss flowed through her at the thought.

Her suspicions about Broch grew as they started off on the journey to see Eolande and Broch maneuvered his horse close to her. Marion and Bridgette rode behind them, their amicable chatter floating up to Sorcha.

Broch cleared his throat, securing Sorcha's attention. "I overheard Cameron admit to Alex last night at supper that ye were indeed a formidable archer."

Sorcha blinked in pleasant surprise. "I'm astounded that the man praised me since he bested me when we competed."

"I was astounded, as well," Broch admitted. "Cameron

is nae one to easily give praise. He has almost impossible expectations for himself as a warrior, as well as for those of us who are under his command."

Sorcha guided her horse up the hill they were ascending. "Do ye believe him unreasonable?" she inquired, wanting to hear what Broch thought of Cameron. Her gut told her a great deal could be learned about the man from those who served him. If he was a good man and leader, surely they would see that.

Broch shook his head, which filled Sorcha with relief. "Nay, he is nae unreasonable. Simply demanding. But he would nae ever ask anything of us that he would nae ask of himself." A smile split Broch's thoughtful expression. "The problem as I see it is that he asks too much of himself."

"Such as?" she asked slowly.

"Such as forgoing the comfort of settling with one woman," Broch replied, his probing stare landing on her.

She was glad that she had to focus on where to guide the horse over some rocks, for she did not wish Broch to see the dismay she felt in her heart on her face. She focused her attention on the reins as she spoke. "Ye believe he dunnae ever wish to marry?"

"Aye," Broch immediately replied. "He's long said he dunnae wish for one lass, especially a confusing one."

"Shut yer mouth, Broch MacLeod," Bridgette snapped as she drew beside Sorcha on the widening trail. Marion brought her horse up beside Broch and gave him a narrow-eyed look.

"Dunnae fash yerself, Sorcha," Bridgette said soothingly. "Broch's still smarting over Lillianna. He wanted the lass, and she wanted Cameron."

Sorcha tensed, sure Broch would be angry that Bridgette revealed such intimate details of his life, but instead, the man laughed. "I'm nae denying my manly pride was wounded when the lass gave her, er, attention to Cameron, but I was nae overly dismayed. The lass is scheming, and I doubt her schemes include marrying a man who dunnae even ken who his real father is over a man who is the son of a laird."

"Oh, Broch," Marion said in a sympathetic tone. "If a woman is worthy of you, she will not care that you don't know who your real father is. Besides that, I think it would hurt Neil greatly to hear that you did not consider him your father."

The secrets being revealed fascinated Sorcha, so she kept quiet, simply listening as her horse now clopped along at a steady pace.

Broch looked to Sorcha. "I think of Neil as a father. He kens this. He took me in when his sister came to Dunvegan with a bairn and refused to say who the father was. He raised me as his own after my mother died when I was still in swaddling cloth." Broch turned his attention back to Marion. "And I ken that Lillianna was nae meant for me, but that dunnae mean it did nae nick my pride."

Bridgette made a derisive noise from deep in her throat. "Lillianna is nae a lady. I'd nae give her another thought."

Sorcha felt Broch's gaze settle on her. "I dunnae anymore," he replied in a slow, deep tone. "Another lass occupies all my thoughts now."

Heat seared Sorcha's cheeks, and her mind raced with how to respond. Thankfully, she was spared the awkwardness of giving a response that would be a gentle dissuasion, as Marion spoke.

"That's enough talk of your lustful thoughts," Marion chided. "I'm quite certain Sorcha must think us uncouth."

Sorcha opened her mouth to assure Marion she only

had the best thoughts of her, but Marion shot her a warning look. She was trying to turn the conversation, and if Sorcha spoke now, she might bring the talk back to Broch and his feelings for her.

"I'm quite proper, Sorcha, I assure you," Marion said. "I'm half-English."

"Ye used to be," Bridgette corrected. "Ye're full Scot now."

Marion grinned. "That's true. I am. But I was raised to be a lady. I didn't become the mischievous woman you see before you until I befriended Bridgette."

"Ha!" Bridgette snorted. "I befriended ye, and I happen to remember a certain story where a proper English lass feigned her own death to avoid marriage. That dunnae sound like a woman who lacked mischief to me."

Sorcha laughed, but then her laughter froze in her throat as a memory split through her mind.

"Ye're going to tumble into the creek, Sorcha," a dark-haired girl chided.

Sorcha saw herself in a reflection in the water. She was a willowy child, maybe eight summers. She was barefoot, and her arms were thrown out to her sides as she balanced on the edge of some stones and peered into the water. She giggled, turned, and stuck her tongue out at the dark-haired girl, who was not very much older than herself.

"Ye dunnae ever wish me to have any fun," Sorcha complained.

The girl cocked an eyebrow. "I wish ye to stay out of trouble, so that I may, as well. When ye get into mischief, Father always blames me."

Deep regret blanketed Sorcha. "I'm sorry. I will try—"

A scream ripped from her throat as she fell backward off the ledge and plunged deep into the icy-cold water, hitting her head as she fell.

The next thing she knew she was coughing and sputtering as strong hands yanked her from the water. She looked up into the face of the childlike man, and he hugged her to him. "Sorcha hurt?"

She coughed some more and then smiled up at the man. "Nay, Uncle Brom."

"Sorcha!" Bridgette bellowed. Sorcha blinked and the memories disappeared. "Ye almost fell off yer horse," Bridgette added.

When Sorcha glanced down, she realized Broch had a firm grip on her arm. "I had a memory," she said by way of apology.

"Of what?" Marion asked, her eyes wide.

Sorcha told her, and Marion grinned. "This is wonderful! We can send messengers out to some of the larger castles to see if there is a Brom. It will help us locate your family."

"I need to tell Cameron immediately," Broch said. "This might lead us to Katherine's killers."

"My family would nae be part of such a thing," Sorcha protested, though she had to admit she did not know that for certain.

An uneasy silence settled on the party, and then Marion said, "My father was not a good man, Sorcha. He did horrid things, but that did not make me a bad person."

Before Sorcha could comment, Marion told her about her father's plot to take the throne from the King of England. She told of his intention to marry her to an evil knight simply to gain the man's sword arm and fealty and his cruelty to Marion, the people who served him, and Marion's mother. By the time Marion was done relaying her past, the sun was high in the sky and they had been riding for several hours.

They stopped to have a quick meal, and then they gathered their things and mounted their horses once again. For the next couple of hours, the time was filled with Bridgette regaling them with stories of her first hunt, during which Lachlan had first kissed her. She also told of her mother, who was a great fighter and her cousin Archibald, who had betrayed Alex, Bridgette, and the MacLeods by plotting with Marion's father. She went from that serious story to a very amusing, albeit shocking, story of the time Marion had almost died when she fell off a cliff on their way back from secretly visiting a seer near Bridgette's home and how Bridgette had saved her.

Sorcha was so entranced by what Bridgette was saying that she did not even notice what was around her, until Marion said, "We must dismount to hike the trail to the Fairy Pools on foot."

Sorcha blinked, took a look around, and gasped in wonder. A long, winding path of white pebbles slithered up the rolling green hills. On one side of the path was a carpet of green grass, blanketed with vibrant purple and yellow flowers. On the other side of the path was a stream, crystal clear and trickling. They all dismounted, and Broch tethered their horses to some trees before they began to walk along the path.

Her footsteps crunched on the stones, but beside her, Marion's footsteps were muffled by the plush grass. As they moved farther up the path, trees with gnarled trunks lined either side of them, reminding Sorcha of something. She squinted, trying to remember, and then she gasped.

"These trees are like soldiers carved of wood," Sorcha said. "They make me think of the trees that line a trail known as the Marching Oaks."

Broch paused, and when he turned to look at her, his expression was one of hope. "The Marching Oaks is in the Caledonian Forest, where Katherine was murdered. It's where Cameron found ye."

Sorcha shivered.

"Either ye were told the name of that path or ye lived near there," Broch added.

She shrugged, helpless with the loss of most of her memories still.

"If you lived near there, it would make sense that you were taken by the men that attacked the MacLeods," Marion offered in a hopeful voice.

Sorcha gave her a weak smile. It would also make sense that she knew of the trail because she had helped to plan the attack, but all three of them were being kind by not saying so. She felt ill, and she purposely turned her attention to studying her surroundings. Somewhere ahead, water rushed, the sound carried by the wind, which had picked up quite ruthlessly. Her hair flapped against her face in stinging whips. She glanced up at the sky, expecting to see gathering storm clouds, but a bright-blue sky stared back at her.

She frowned. "The wind dunnae make sense."

"Nay. 'Tis always like this in these woods, though," Bridgette assured her.

"Listen," Marion said in a hushed whisper. Sorcha paused as she climbed the steep path. Birds, sounding as if there were hundreds of them from the loudness of their chirping, flew around them for a moment before streaking off.

Fear sent gooseflesh racing across Sorcha's skin. As they climbed ever higher, shadows grew, cast from the rocks that now formed a barrier to block their view of the sky. The sun disappeared, and the temperature grew so warm, she had to fan herself. To the side of the path, brightly colored flowers covered everything and took her breath. She was sure she had never seen such beauty in her life.

The path abruptly halted, and they had to hop from stone to stone across the water to the next hill. They climbed steadily up the jagged terrain, but at the top of the first crest, the rocks seemed to part and the sky shone bright and clear above them once more. She shielded her eyes against the sun. As far as she could see, one peak after another reached toward the sky. To the right was a steep incline that led to a bluish-green body of water, except for the frothy white that came rushing from the waterfall above.

"Eolande lives in a cave down there," Bridgette said, pointing. Sorcha did not miss the tremor of Bridgette's tone.

"If ye fear coming—" Sorcha started.

"Nay," Bridgette rushed out. "I dunnae fear what the seer will say to me. I fear for ye, though. I'll nae lie—her words could make it much worse for ye or much better. Ye won't ken until ye hear them."

Sorcha nodded, grateful for her friend's warning but also aware of her own sudden unease to hear her future. As she made her way carefully down the steep slope behind Broch, she questioned the wisdom in seeking out the seer. What if she said a future between Sorcha and Cameron was unwise? What if Eolande foretold horrors for Sorcha and told her that her family was wicked? Or worse—that *she* was. Sweat trickled down her brow, and she was certain it was not merely from heat but also from her fear.

Once they all reached the bottom, Broch led them along the edge of the water toward a cave that had not been visible from the cliff. As she walked, the bow that was strapped to her back clapped against her skin, and she found herself running her finger along the arrows in the holder at her hip. She was glad she had brought the weapon. It made her feel safer. Broch had his hand on the hilt of his sword and Bridgette had drawn her bow, and Sorcha wondered if both of them felt the same unease that she did. Even Marion had a dagger clutched in her hands, which rather surprised Sorcha, as she had not heard Marion say she had any skill.

They reached the cave and paused as one. Bridgette was the first to speak. "As ye're the one wishing for her future to be foretold, I believe ye must be the one to ask for entry into the cave."

"How do I do that?" Sorcha asked.

"Call her name," Bridgette said. "At least that's what I did. I called her name and then asked to speak to her."

Sorcha nodded, called Eolande's name, and waited. When no response came, she called several more times before saying, "Perchance she is nae there."

"More likely she is ignoring ye," Bridgette said. "I'd say ye have two choices: turn and leave, or go into the cave and demand she speak to ye."

"I'm not sure demanding things from Eolande is a good idea," Marion said, her tone holding a note of warning.

Usually, Sorcha would agree, but without the memories of who she was to guide her, she was feeling desperate. "I'll go in."

"That's what I'd do," Bridgette said.

"You three stay here," Sorcha added, not wishing to bring the seer's ire upon them should she be angered.

"Nay," was the chorused response.

The four of them slowly entered Eolande's domain, and Sorcha's stomach dipped at the astonishing sight before them. A pool of dark-blue water shimmered in the middle of the round cave. On the opposite side, the rocky walls gave way to the outside, allowing sunlight to stream into the space. A waterfall gushed past the opening, and beyond the veil of white mist, sumptuous green trees swayed. Stone steps led up the side of the cave into a dark, shadowed area to the right.

They followed the stairs into a smaller cave. There was nothing in the room but a bed. No clothes, no personal belongings, not even a cup or a scrap of food. Sorcha frowned. "The seer lives here?"

Bridgette shrugged. "As far as I ken, but who can say for certain? She may verra well live in the fairy world and only come here to torment us mere mortals."

A musical laugh suddenly echoed off the cave walls, causing them all to gasp except Broch, who cursed and drew his sword. They turned as one toward the laughter, and Sorcha felt her mouth fall open. Standing there was a beautiful woman dressed in a white gown. Her dark hair cascaded over her shoulders, and on her head, she wore a crown of white flowers. Her pale skin contrasted strikingly with her luminous violet eyes. Those eyes seemed to settle upon Sorcha and peel back the layers of her mind.

"Ye remember me," the seer said. It was not a question but a statement of fact.

"Nay," Sorcha said, pressing a finger to her temple, which suddenly throbbed.

"Ye do," Eolande said forcefully.

A fierce pain bolted through Sorcha's head. Crying out, she clutched at her head as her knees buckled, and she started to fall, only to be caught by Broch.

"What the devil are ye doing, woman?" Broch demanded.

"I'm helping her remember, warrior," the seer bit out. "And unless she wishes me to cease and leave her floundering in the dark, I advise ye set her gently down and wait outside my home."

Biting back pain, Sorcha pushed out of Broch's arms and managed to right herself, though her legs still wobbled underneath her. "I wish her help," Sorcha said, focusing first on Broch, then on Marion and Bridgette, who looked alternately worried and angry.

"Ye're certain?" Bridgette asked, glancing warily between Sorcha and Eolande.

Sorcha nodded, though the slight gesture sent pain spiraling through her head. When all three of her companions remained there with hesitant looks upon their faces, Sorcha said, "Please. I will be fine."

Once they had all departed, albeit hesitantly, Eolande moved closer to Sorcha. "Give me yer hand," she commanded, holding out her own.

Sorcha did, and the moment the seer's icy skin caressed hers, memories flooded her mind.

She was young again and filled with excitement. There was a tent. No, there were hundreds of tents filling a shore, and a shimmering loch, and notes of music, along with the savory smell of meat being cooked.

"Sorcha, stay where ye have been told," her mother had said in a chiding yet loving voice. "Young ladies kinnae wander about at a festival such as this one once night has fallen."

Suddenly, a face appeared in Sorcha's mind. She had Sorcha's gray eyes and light hair—or rather Sorcha had hers.

"Mother," Sorcha found herself whispering as tears filled her closed eyes and leaked out to roll down her cheeks.

Suddenly her memory shifted.

She skipped around tents in the descending darkness,

delighted by the music and the people gathered. To her left was the loch, and to her right, high on the rocks, was a magnificent castle that seemed to rise to the sky. She realized on a sharp intake of breath that this memory was of Dunvegan.

Then her memory shifted again.

Her stomach fluttered as she stood in a line of men and listened to the MacLeod laird—it was Iain!—explain the contest. She took aim, allowing the men to shoot first to gain an advantage. Excitement bubbled, and her heartbeat exploded as a man turned his piercing green eyes on her— Cameron. He smiled, and she felt as if she was melting on the inside, something warm and tingly filled her.

She cried out in dismay when the memory shifted again.

She was running from him and laughing. She wanted him to catch her just to be near him again, but she could not let him do so because she'd be discovered. She whipped around to gaze upon him one last time, for she feared she would never see him again, and her eyes met first his and then a pair of violet eyes that seemed to know her secrets— Eolande.

Sorcha's eyes flew open and locked on Eolande's probing gaze. Sorcha's heart pounded viciously in her chest as she looked at their interlocked hands. "Can ye give me all my memories?" she asked, her voice hoarse.

"Nay," Eolande said. "Only ones that are relevant to ye from when we first met. I am sorry," Eolande said gently. "I would give yer memories back to ye if I could, but dunnae fash yerself, verra soon now ye will remember important things, and once ye start recalling yer life, ye will have choices to make."

Sorcha inhaled a shaky breath. "Ye see that I remember soon?"

Eolande nodded as she curled her fingers tighter around Sorcha's hand. Fighting back the fear of what she might hear, she asked, "What else do ye see?"

Eolande's violet eyes almost glistened as she stared at Sorcha. "I see an attack verra soon that will cause a change. A betrayer whom ye care for and fear. A passion that will nae be denied between ye and Cameron that will either sink with the weight of heavy lies or rise with powerful love. But if the love blooms, many vines will threaten to destroy it. There is a claim upon yer body that will supersede the one upon yer heart, and to free ye, Cameron will forgo his honor."

"Nay!" Sorcha tried to wrench her hand away, but Eolande increased her grip.

"Two deaths," she hissed. "Two deaths will come to pass." Eolande released her suddenly, staggering away from her as Sorcha staggered back, too.

"Whose deaths?" she demanded as she righted herself.

Eolande shook her head. "I did nae see who, but they will break yer heart."

Sorcha felt a sob lodge in her throat. Was it Cameron? Was it someone from her family? "These things ye see," she said urgently, "these things can be changed, aye?"

"Aye," Eolande said, an amused smile coming to her pale face. "As I have always said, I foretell yer future as it comes to me at the moment I touch ye, yet all our futures—mine, as well—can change with our choices."

As the seer started to turn from her, Sorcha gripped Eolande's arm. She swiveled back toward her, surprise etching her face. Sorcha rushed out, "But I dunnae ken what choices to make to ensure the terrible things ye foretold dunnae come true."

"Nay, ye dunnae. Trust yer heart," she said simply, but

then her face clouded and a faraway look came over her. She twisted her hand upward and gripped Sorcha's forearm. "I see a parting of ways between ye and Cameron, and a looming battle. Once parted, ye will nae be reunited—"

"Ye wee *ban-druidh* fairy," Bridgette growled, her footsteps pounding from behind Sorcha. Bridgette must not have left the cave.

Sorcha gasped at Bridgette calling Eolande a witch. She feared what the seer might do, but seconds later, when Bridgette appeared, eyes flashing and a scowl on her face, Eolande gave her an amused smirk, which only served to deepen Bridgette's scowl. "Yer foretelling was the reason I almost lost Lachlan!"

"Nay, Bridgette," Eolande snapped. "Yer fear was the reason ye almost lost him, which was surprising, given how verra braw I ken ye are."

Bridgette stood there, opening and closing her mouth, as if she wanted to argue the seer's words but could not find the proper response.

Eolande waved a dismissive hand. "Make haste back to Dunvegan, but do so with yer weapons drawn."

"Wait!" Sorcha gasped. "What of the parting? We will nae be reunited ever?"

The seer shrugged. "I kinnae say. The link to the foretelling was broken." With that, Eolande turned, strode toward the smaller cave, and disappeared within. As one, Bridgette and Sorcha raced to follow her, but inside the dark cave, they found nothing. No seer and no way to get out of the cave.

Sorcha shivered as gooseflesh prickled her skin. "She's magic," she whispered.

"Aye," Bridgette replied, awe in her voice. "It's fearful and fascinating at once."

Sorcha nodded her agreement as she reached behind her and withdrew her bow. "Where are Marion and Broch?"

"Just outside the cave," Bridgette replied, withdrawing her dagger. "Marion did nae wish to eavesdrop, and Broch could nae verra well leave her alone." Bridgette grinned, making Sorcha realize Bridgette must have foreseen that outcome.

"How much did ye hear?" Sorcha asked warily, already moving toward the exit.

"All of it," Bridgette replied, giving Sorcha an apologetic look. "I am sorry if ye're angry, but I had to be certain Eolande did nae foretell anything that would put Lachlan in harm's way."

"I ken," Sorcha replied, and she truly did. "Then ye heard her say Cameron would relinquish his honor to free me."

"Aye," Bridgette replied. "Dunnae flee."

Sorcha whipped her head toward Bridgette, shocked that it seemed the woman had read her thoughts.

Bridgette smiled with understanding. "I fled Lachlan thinking to save him from me, and all it did was compel him to come after me and prolong our misery of nae being together. I kinnae believe I am saying this, but I feel ye must do as Eolande said and trust yer heart."

Sorcha bit her lip, considering Bridgette's words. "What if my heart is wrong?"

"The heart is nae ever wrong, Sorcha, but that dunnae mean it chooses an easy path. What does yer heart tell ye now?"

"It tells me what awaits me with him could well be the truest thing I'll ever ken, as if I may nae ever care for another the way I could care for him."

Bridgette grinned. "Then ye must stay, and we must

make haste. I fear danger is near."

"Aye," Sorcha agreed, and together they hurried toward the cave entry.

After quickly relaying what Eolande had said about making haste back to Dunvegan with their weapons drawn, they set out without pause. Broch led them to where they had tethered the horses, and once they were mounted, he set a galloping pace toward the castle.

The ride was hard and relentless over the rocky terrain and winding trails. Broch returned them on a different route through the dense part of the forest, so if someone was following them, they would be harder to track. Because of the terrain and the clipped pace, there was no time to move low-hanging branches out of their way, and more than once, a branch snagged Sorcha's hair, gown, and face. Her left sleeve had been almost ripped off when it had gotten caught on a branch, and warm blood trickled down her cheek where a limb had cut her.

She was certain she looked as if she had been in battle because Marion and Bridgette both looked as if they had been, too, with their scraped faces and torn gowns. She prayed they could get inside the castle without being seen, so that coming to see Eolande would not cause trouble for Marion and Bridgette.

As Sorcha's horse galloped onward, closing the distance between the Fairy Pools and Dunvegan at a much faster pace than they had earlier, Sorcha thought on what Eolande had said. Who might betray her? A family member? One of her new friends? She could not imagine it being Cameron, as she did not fear him. The part of the foretelling that had lodged in her stomach like a giant rock was that two people she knew, that she cared for, would die.

Just as she tried to imagine who they might be, an arrow whistled past her ear, swishing through her hair as it went. "Attack!" she yelled before instinctually reaching for her bow and turning her horse toward the thickest part of the woods to try to reach the shelter of the trees. Another arrow came seconds later, this one snagging the skirts of her gown. Whoever was attacking was aiming only for her! Luckily, the archer did not seem to be overly skilled.

Broch raced his destrier toward her, as did Marion and Bridgette. In that moment, fear sliced through Sorcha. Was this the moment that two people she cared for would die, and all because someone was trying to kill her?

"Ye wish to kill me?" she screamed, turning and glancing all around, searching for whoever was shooting at her so that she could aim for them. When a flash of red caught her attention and she knew it was her attacker, she nocked an arrow and aimed, though she knew it was doubtful she'd strike her target. Her enemy had the advantage of cover and could easily kill them all out in the open as they were. She had to do something. She had to save the others.

"If ye wish to kill me, ye must catch me!" she taunted. She bent over her destrier and urged the beast to race toward the clearing in the woods up ahead. If she could reach the wide grassy land, whoever was after her would be drawn out, as well, and Broch or Bridgette could possibly fell them.

Her instincts took over as her body molded to her horse in the best possible way to cut through the wind and give her speed. The trees whizzed by her, and she chanced a glance to her right, gasping at the sight of two men chasing her. One man pulled significantly ahead of the other, but they were both charging without thought toward the rolling hills.

Good. Let them come.

She commanded her horse into a teeth-rattling gallop, looking back briefly to see where Broch, Bridgette, and Marion were. Far, far in the distance she thought she saw Marion, but Broch and Bridgette were nowhere to be seen. She knew full well neither of them would ever abandon Marion, so hopefully they had a plot they were carrying out.

Looking back to her right, alarm shot through her at how near one of the attackers was. She saw his face, carved of determination, his lips set in a grim line. When he yanked his destrier to a halt and withdrew a bow and arrow, she knew a moment of blinding fear. She could not stop to nock another arrow, yet she was close enough for the man to shoot at her. She turned to face forward once more, her only hope to put as much distance between them as possible before he released his arrow.

Her body tensed, expecting the sting of the arrow tip. Yet, when it did not come, she looked over her shoulder and shook with relief. The attacker was lying on the ground, an arrow sticking out of him and his horse racing toward her. She scanned the woods for the other attacker, but instead of finding him, she located Bridgette, high on a rock above with her bow poised to shoot.

A whistle split the air, propelling Bridgette into motion. She scrambled off the rock and disappeared into the woods, only to come out racing beside Broch on their horses. Marion, Broch, and Bridgette reached her as one. But instead of stopping as she thought they would, Broch gave her a murderous look, slapped her horse on its hindquarter, and roared, "Ride hard to Dunvegan."

The journey back was filled with the sound of pounding hooves and nothing more. They were all hunched low on their destriers, and when they finally galloped into the courtyard, Sorcha did not even bring her horse to a complete stop before Broch was off his mount and yanking on the tethers of her destrier to halt the beast.

"What are ye doing?" she cried out when her horse reared back at his handling.

Broch ignored her and clipped a command at the beast, who immediately settled. He reached up and fairly yanked her off her horse. He swung her to face him, his hands gripping her arms tight, his face red with anger. "Are ye mad?" he demanded. "Ye could have been killed!"

Something niggled at the back of her mind. Hands clenching her arms, shaking her, and a desperate feeling to be released overwhelmed her. "Release me," she hissed, trying to fight back the panic.

"Broch!" came a furious roar from across the courtyard.

Sorcha whipped her gaze toward the animalistic sound as Broch obeyed. Her eyes met Cameron's assessing ones, which darted from her head to her feet in a breath. Rage swept over his face, and an icy glare settled on Broch. "I'll kill ye!" Cameron thundered.

"Cameron, nay!" she screamed, but her cry was lost beneath his deafening roar as he barreled across the courtyard and straight into Broch.

Twelve

The sight of Sorcha in a torn gown, with her hair a mess and cuts on her face was difficult enough for Cameron to see, but she was also gripped in Broch's embrace. It made Cameron clench his fists. Then, when Sorcha demanded Broch release her and the man did not, Cameron's anger exploded, and the innate need to keep her safe sent him barreling across the courtyard and straight at Broch.

He crashed into the Scot with a force that sent them both flying backward and to the ground with a hard thud, but the anger pumping through his blood shot him to his feet. Before Broch could gain his, Cameron's fist connected with Broch's nose. Bone cracked and blood gushed, but Broch was not a man to be easily felled. He swiped an arm out, catching Cameron's left leg, and with a jerk, he pulled Cameron to the ground, all his breath whooshing out of his lungs and the courtyard briefly tilting as his thoughts jumbled.

"Cease this foolishness!" Marion bellowed.

Both men ignored her, Cameron rolling to his side as Broch lunged for him and missed. He scrambled to his feet, ducked a punch, and came up with a hard jab to Broch's ribs. The Scot doubled over for a second, then came up swinging, his fist connecting with Cameron's jaw. Pain throbbed through the entire left side of Cameron's face, but he shook it off and hit Broch's chin from underneath. After that, it was one punch after the other, warrior to warrior, rage to retaliation. Cameron's blood roared in his ears, and as he pulled his arm back to hit Broch once more, it was caught from behind. His other arm was yanked up and behind him.

Panting, he turned his head to one side and received a dark scowl from Alex. Turning his head in the other direction, he received a furious glare from Angus. "Let me go," Cameron growled, trying to twist free. Across from him, two of his warriors held Broch in a similar restraining hold.

"Do ye vow to keep yer fists down?" Alex demanded.

Cameron raked his gaze across Broch, and then around him where a crowd had gathered. "I vow," he said in a low voice, "nae to hit him again, but I want him gone from here," he bit out, seething.

Broch cocked an eyebrow at him and spit blood. He looked at Sorcha, who stood trembling between Marion and Bridgette, and back to Cameron. "Ye'd banish me from the clan because ye believe I have somehow hurt this woman?" Broch asked in a voice as low as Cameron's.

"Ye had her gripped in yer hands," he growled.

"Aye," Broch snapped. "I did lose hold of my anger, but only because the lass almost got herself killed by using herself as bait to lead the two men who were shooting arrows at her away from us. She's braw but foolhardy, and I suppose I thought to shake some sense into her head. If ye wish to banish me from Dunvegan for that, then so be it," he said, tilting his chin up in challenge.

The news that someone had once again tried to kill Sorcha had anger battering him. Swift shame followed the anger. He had responded so violently against Broch, a man he had known and trusted for years. Guilt flooded Cameron along with the desire to shake Sorcha for endangering herself. He battled the need to pull her into his arms and press kisses all over her in relief that she had once again escaped unscathed. His emotions reeled so sharply, he felt as if the courtyard was spinning. He took a long breath to calm his heated blood before speaking.

Turning his gaze on Broch once more, he said, "I clearly dunnae ken all that has happened. I thank ye for keeping her alive, and I am sorry for the way I responded." He owed the man that, but he could not leave it there. Fierce, raw possessiveness compelled him to say more. "But hear me now, Broch. If ye ever restrain her again, as ye just did, unless it is to save her life in that moment, ye will regret it. Do ye ken me?"

"I ken ye," Broch clipped. "Bridgette killed one of the attackers, but one is still afoot."

A furious tic began in Cameron's jaw, along with rapidly growing fear. Sorcha had been attacked again, and he'd not been there to protect her. He kept his gaze carefully off her now, fearing that if their eyes locked, he would not be able to stop himself from taking her in his arms, soothing her, and assuring her she would be fine. He had to give orders. Make choices. Be the warrior he was striving to be. But soon, very soon, he would claim her mouth once more. She had almost been taken from him today. The thought sent ice through his veins and clarity into his mind. His heart squeezed tight. It was too late for him to deny her any longer. She was in his head, and likely his heart, just as Iain had said.

He settled his gaze on Marion and then Bridgette, taking care to skip over Sorcha. "Take Sorcha to her bedchamber and stay with her until I come. Can ye do that without getting into any more mischief, or do I need to send a guard with ye?"

Marion grimaced and inclined her head in acceptance, but Bridgette glared and let out a huff. "Aye, we can do that," Bridgette muttered.

He nodded, then finally looked at Sorcha. His heart lurched at how fragile she looked, yet not fearful. The fear was gone. What was that emotion shining in her eyes? When her gaze bore into him and she tilted her chin up, it struck him—defiance and anger. He ground his teeth. "Ye," he growled, "I will speak with shortly."

"Possibly," she snapped. "If I feel like speaking to ye after this"—she waved her hand at him and then Broch—"display!"

"I thought the man was harming ye!" he thundered.

Her eyes popped wide, and her lips parted. "I see," she said very quietly, and he swore a small smile had tugged at the corner of her lips before she quickly got herself under control. "In that case, I'll be willing to talk with ye later."

With that, she turned with her head high and her spine straight as an arrow and walked toward the castle door with Marion and Bridgette trailing behind her.

"What?" he asked, sensing Broch's gaze on him. "I said I'm sorry. What I did was nae acceptable."

"It's already forgotten," Broch replied, and a ghost of a smile touched his face. "I stare because I did nae believe I would see the day that a woman tied ye into knots and caused ye to act crazed."

"I'm nae in knots," he bit out, all too aware of how irrational his denial sounded. He was grateful when Broch simply shrugged. Cameron motioned for Broch to follow him as he moved away from the other men. When they were alone, he said, "Tell me of what occurred today, from start to finish."

Guilt flashed across Broch's face, followed by anger. "It began this morning when Bridgette asked me to accompany her, Marion, and Sorcha to see Eolande."

Cameron's surprise at Broch's words was so great that all he could do was gape at the man. Clenching and then releasing his teeth, he managed to say, "For the love of God, I kinnae imagine how ye allowed yerself to be talked into something ye ken I'd nae approve!"

Broch fidgeted, not answering, and when Cameron's anger sparked again, he was about to demand a reply when the likely answer hit him. His nostrils flared as he stared at his longtime friend. "Ye did it to gain favor with Sorcha."

A flush covered Broch's neck. "Aye. I've no excuse, and I expect to be punished."

And he would be. The man had known Cameron would not agree, but he'd done it anyway. Yet, Cameron did not give the penance immediately. He carefully thought upon what he wanted to say, knowing jealousy was involved on his part. "I must take away yer command of men for a time. Ye ken I would nae have agreed to such an excursion, nor would Iain or Lachlan."

Broch lowered his head. "Aye. The woman enchanted me."

Cameron felt as if Broch had hit him in the jaw once more. He swallowed hard. "Did she...did she give ye reason to believe she welcomed yer attentions?"

"Nay," Broch said with a shrug. "But I'm stubborn, and I'd hoped she would after a time." He lifted his gaze to Cameron's. "I see now that she will nae. I did nae ken ye already had a claim on her heart."

Shock stilled Cameron, and he glanced around swiftly,

relieved to see everyone but he and Broch had dispersed. "Did she say that to ye?"

"She did nae have to. It was in her eyes when she looked at ye. Adoration. Trust. Fear that I had hurt ye. I did nae ever believe I'd wish to be looked upon that way, but I believe now I might desire it verra much."

Cameron knew exactly what Broch meant, but he'd not say it. Instead he said, "Tell me of the seer and the attackers."

As Broch began to talk, Cameron forced himself to focus, though his thoughts kept trying to stray to Sorcha. He would see her soon—after he secured the dead attacker and combed the woods for the one still at large. Once that was done, he would deal with her sneaking away and her recklessness. He had to if he was going to keep her protected. He just prayed he could keep his hands off her long enough to make her understand that she had to take more care with her safety.

Sorcha paced the length of her empty bedchamber, noting the first light of a new day had streaked the sky in a breathtaking display of oranges, reds, and purples. The léine she wore swished against her thighs with her fast, agitated strides. Her head ached, and her eyes stung with lack of sleep. She'd tried to rest—oh, how she'd tried—but the peaceful state had eluded her.

After Marion and Bridgette had departed late in the night, the guard appointed to watch over her from outside her door had told her that Cameron was out with a tracking party looking for her attacker. So she'd waited, tense with anxiety, on the edge of her bed, thinking he would come speak to her when he returned. Thundering horse hooves had filled the courtyard when the moon had nearly departed the sky, and a glance down below had revealed the tracking party had returned, yet still Cameron had not come.

Exhaustion had weighed heavily on her, so she'd stripped off her gown and climbed into the bed, certain that she would fall asleep immediately. Except her mind had raced with a hundred possibilities of why he did not come to her, each tormenting her in its uniqueness and keeping sleep out of her reach. No matter what position she had tried, her head had battered her with questions. Was he furious that she had gone to see Eolande? Was he angry that her journey to the seer had endangered Broch, Marion, and Bridgette, even if accidentally? It could be that he simply did not wish to see her. He may have decided she was entirely too much trouble and was planning to persuade the king to take her off his hands. Or perchance he thought she cared for Broch. Or that she was evil...

The more questions she had, the more irritable she became. She was upset with him. She understood that he likely warred with himself because of the seer's prophecy—and she was pleased he had admitted he'd attacked Broch out of care for her—but she needed him to talk to her so they could determine if they could even cross the divide that lay between them.

She'd abandoned sleep and taken up pacing long ago. As she completed another trip across her room, she paused in front of the window, looking out at the sunlit courtyard and massaging her aching temples. There were no answers, only questions and growing frustration. Cameron had the answers she sought—well, some of them anyway—but perchance he intended to avoid being alone with her ever again. She breathed slowly and evenly, considering what

Eolande had said to her. The attack the seer spoke of had occurred, but what was the change? She skipped over the things the seer had said that she could not comprehend, and she settled on what the woman had said in regard to Cameron. Did they truly share a passion that could not be denied?

Her gut told her that such an attraction as the one that had sparked between them was not a common occurrence. Her mind started to turn to all the obstacles they faced even to have a future, but she shoved the thoughts away. She knew the obstacles well—her memory, the king, the prophecy. Yet, she still wished to learn Cameron. He was the man she wanted to walk with, talk with, train with, and have take her in his arms. But before she could admit all of that to him, she had to tell him what the seer had foretold to her.

Eolande had said their passion would either sink under the weight of heavy lies or rise with powerful love. Who would be the liar? Was it her? She curled her hands into fists. She had no control over the sort of person she had been, but by God, she had full control over whether she had honor or not *now*, and she chose honor.

She sighed as the rest of Eolande's prophecy echoed in her head, especially the part about a claim upon her body that would supersede the one upon her heart. Eolande could have been seeing that the king would force her into a marriage her heart did not want, or possibly someone else would. Either way, Cameron had a right to know since the seer said he would forsake his own honor to free Sorcha.

Fierce determination to see the man and make him look at her and hear her overcame Sorcha. If the stubborn Scot refused to come to her, then she would simply have to go to him. She quickly donned her gown and then marched toward the door and flung it open, coming to a shuddering halt at the sight of Cameron filling the doorway. A thick leather strap that secured his gleaming sword was all that covered his sculpted chest. His hair was pulled back by twine, revealing the harsh but beautiful lines of his jaw. His green eyes appeared almost moss colored in their darkness, and they widened as he raked his gaze over her before meeting her eyes once more. The desire flaming there set her heart to pounding and instantly heated her body.

He stepped toward her without a word but with a predatory look about him. She set her palm to his chest and locked her gaze with his. The rapid beat of his heart thumped against her fingertips, as the heat of his flush singed her. She wanted to relent to him, but he had to be at peace with what he felt for her before she could, and he had to hear what Eolande had said. She opened her mouth to speak, but he pressed a finger to her lips.

"I'm sorry if I've hurt ye," he said, his voice husky. The apology made her heart squeeze. He ran his finger gently over her lips before removing it. They stood face-to-face, very close, but he no longer touched her. "I dunnae want to fight how I feel any longer."

To hear that he had accepted how he felt for her, overwhelmed her. She dropped her palm and pressed her body close to his, bringing her mouth to his ear. "Nor do I," she whispered, allowing herself to forget for the moment what she wanted to tell him of Eolande.

He rubbed his cheek against hers as he set his hands to her waist and lifted her with ease. He carried her into the room and kicked a leg backward, closing the door with a resounding thud. When he set her on her feet again, her chest brushed his, making her loins tighten and her breasts grow immediately heavy. A moan escaped her, and he responded with a growl before his arm slid around her waist once more and his hand fisted in her hair to tilt her head back. He slanted his mouth over hers, stoking the fire that threatened to consume her.

His fast, demanding kisses sang through her veins and made her gasp, but when his mouth suddenly became slow and gentle, almost reverent in its caresses, she wanted to weep at the tenderness he was displaying. It showed her that what was between them had the promise of more than desire, just as Eolande had foretold. As he kissed her, his hands explored her back, her waist, her hips, and then slid up to the neckline of her léine.

Breaking their kiss, he pulled back from her, his gaze boring into her as he tugged her léine down over one shoulder and then the other. Ever so slowly and gently, he inched it along her breasts, exposing the tops but nothing else. He stilled, a questioning look coming to his eyes.

"I'll cease now if ye wish it," he said in a low, gravelly voice.

God, she did not wish it. What she needed to tell him of the seer niggled in her mind, but she shoved it down for one more moment. She wanted him to bare all of her and then set his hands to her burning body, because she was certain he could offer relief to the exquisite ache that had claimed her. "Nae yet," she replied, her voice husky.

Desire darkened his gaze further as he slid her léine over her breasts to her waist. Silently, he stared at her with a look of bold, frank possession. Her blood thickened as he reached out and cupped her breasts, running his thumb over her straining buds. She hissed as her body arched involuntarily toward him, and he caressed her again in slow, teasing circles that made her want to scream with pleasure.

He moved his hand from her breasts, making her

whimper for the loss of his touch, and he cupped her chin and fastened his gaze to hers. "Ye are the most glorious creature I have ever beheld, and I dunnae only mean yer body, though I've nae ever looked upon a lass as beautiful as ye. Ye make me want to drop to my knees and worship ye."

She raked her gaze over his face, thick arms, slabs of his stomach, and muscled legs, locking her eyes to his once more. Intensity shone in the green depths, and his jaw was set, just as it had been the moment she had looked upon him after waking from her injury. She had known then that he had a tight rein on a great amount of power. Was he keeping control for her now? Did he fear releasing it with her? She wanted to see him without his inhibitions, without the shadows of doubt that danced in his eyes. No matter what came for them in the future, this moment was theirs, and it very well could be the only one like this they would ever share. She prayed it was not, even as she reached out with trembling hands and ran them down the length of his chest, glorying in the way his lids grew heavy with the need she was creating in him.

"I want to drop to my knees and worship ye, as well, but first we must talk more," she said, forcing herself to address what she had been putting off regarding Eolande.

"Aye," he agreed, the word full of regret. He bent his head to her chest and brushed a feathery kiss over one breast and then the other before carefully covering her once more. When he held his hand out for her to place hers in his, she could not help but smile at the sweet gesture. She slipped her small hand into his bigger one, his fingers curling tightly around hers, as he led her to the bed. They sat and turned toward each other, but he did not relinquish his hold on her hand. "Why did ye go to see Eolande?"

She hesitated. She wanted to be truthful, but to lay her

heart before someone was a frightful thing. "I wished to hear what her foretelling of my future was," she admitted.

"Why?" His gaze penetrated her to her soul. Even if she had wanted to hide what she was feeling from him, she felt certain he could somehow sense it. "I wanted to see if she would tell me anything of my future that would help me remember my past." She paused. "And I wanted to see if she said anything more about the prophecy for ye and me."

"Because?" he asked in a deceptively calm voice, yet she saw the urgency flash in his eyes.

"Because in spite of my fears, from the moment I awoke here with my memory gone, I knew one thing for certain: I was drawn to ye. I may nae remember what lay behind me, but I feel in my gut that I've nae ever been drawn to a man like I am to ye. I—"

His hand slid to the back of her neck, and he tugged her to him, crushing his mouth to hers. The kiss ravaged her senses and left her panting, and when he pulled back and gave her a look of pure, male triumph, she was glad that she had revealed her heart to him.

"Ye never did tell me who told ye of the prophecy. Was it Marion?" he asked, surprising her.

"How did ye ken?" she blurted, relieved not to have to keep that secret from him. She wanted no secrets between them, but she also didn't want to cause Marion trouble.

"Dunnae fash yerself, lass," he said in a gentle voice. His finger traced a circle over the top of her hand, which brought a flutter to her belly. He looked contemplative, and she thought he might not even realize he was absently comforting her with his touch. "I'm nae cross with Marion. I ken that Iain must have told her, and she, in turn, revealed it to ye, but Marion would only do so out of a wish to help me. I'll nae say anything."

"And do ye feel she helped ye by telling me?" Sorcha asked with a bit of hesitancy.

He squeezed her hand and brought it up to his lips to place a chaste kiss to the top. When his lips brushed her skin, her breath caught, and desire once more tugged at her.

"I do," he said. "If ye had nae gone to see Eolande, then I believe I would have continued to fight what I feel for ye, though I dunnae ken that I would have defeated it."

Her heart hammered so hard, she took a breath to try to slow her racing pulse, but it was to no avail. "What do ye feel for me, Cameron?"

"I am drawn to ye as ye are drawn to me," he said.

Her chest swelled with happiness as he continued. "I feel I have kenned ye for years, though it has been but a few days. To see ye with another man fills me with jealousy. To know someone is trying to kill ye makes me want to kill them. I want to learn the secrets ye keep here—" he splayed his palm over her chest, and she was sure he felt the rapid beat of her heart. His eyes locked with hers, smoldering in their intensity. "I have nae ever wished to ken the secrets of a woman's heart. I did nae believe I would ever wish to, but now I do. Will ye let me learn the secrets that ye recall and share yer memories with me when they come to ye?"

"I want to," she whispered. "I want that verra much. But I must tell ye first what Eolande foretold. I'll nae have ye blind about it."

He nodded and took her hand in his once more, intertwined their fingers, and covered their hands with his other one. She smiled down at their hands. It was the most perfect moment, and she prayed it was but one of a thousand more to come, yet fear twinged within her.

Cameron heard worry in Sorcha's voice, and he found it impossible to remain silent. His need to ease her anxiety flared. "When Eolande foretold my future so many years ago, I scoffed at the idea that that I'd be willing to forsake my honor and betray my family and king for ye," he said. "But mere days after ye came here, I sensed in my bones that I could grow to care for ye so much that I would do these things without hesitation."

"Nay!" she cried out and wrenched her hand from his grasp while springing to her feet. It was most definitely not the response he wanted. She whirled away in a blur. Just as suddenly, she whirled back around to face him. "What I fear more than anything is that these things would come to pass, and then ye would hate me because of what ye felt ye had to do."

He shot to his feet, closed the distance, and pulled her into his arms. It felt like the most natural thing in the world to cradle this woman in her distress, to provide a space where she could always come that would protect her from harm. "I feared that, too. But Iain told me something, and after I thought on it awhile, I kenned it was true."

"What did he say?" she asked.

He brushed a strand of her golden hair out of her face and tucked it behind her shoulder, purposely allowing his fingers to graze the skin near her shoulder bared by her léine. Desire shuddered through him as he felt her tremble, but even greater than the yearning was the intense pleasure he received from the simple act of holding her and touching her so familiarly. "He said that ye were in my head, and ye are."

She smiled slightly, and he could not resist the urge to brush his fingers over her lips. Her sharp intake of breath, and the flush of desire that covered her chest and stained her cheeks made him hard with wanting. He dropped his hand and continued. "He also said that once a woman is in yer heart, though, it's possible to live without her, but it's misery. And he would ken, Sorcha. He endured it when his first wife died."

"Oh," she said with a soft, sad murmur.

He cupped her face in his hands. "I kinnae live with nae giving us a chance to discover what may be. I will regret it, and the regret will eat at me until I am miserable. So what say ye? Do ye wish to chance fate with me?"

"I do," she said, but he read hesitation in her eyes. Before he could ask her about it, she spoke again. "When I went to see Eolande, she told me things I believe ye need to hear before ye decide for certain. I already ken I want to move forward with ye, but I want ye to ken."

Triumph and pride rushed through him. He pressed his lips to her forehead, her cheeks, and settled his mouth tenderly on hers. He didn't know how to say how happy her words had made him, but he hoped his kiss showed her. When he pulled away, she looked utterly bemused and very enticing. "I dunnae need to hear what the seer said. All I needed to hear was that ye wished to move forward. The rest—the prophecy, the king, all of it—we will resolve together."

"Cameron," she said, desperation in her voice and a plea in her gray eyes, "I kinnae be with ye unless I ken ye have heard and accepted everything that could come to pass."

"Tell me, then," he said, understanding deep within that nothing she would reveal would change his mind but also sensing exactly how important it was for her to tell him.

"Might we sit?" she asked, her voice wobbling with what sounded suspiciously like fear.

Silently, he led her to the bed, and when she started to

sit beside him, he pulled her into his lap and encircled her in his arms. She blinked in surprise at him, and a demure smile lit her beautiful face. He studied that smile. Was she shy? He hardly knew. They'd not had time to really learn each other, but he intended to correct that.

"Tell me yer fears," he said, "and I will conquer them for ye."

She ran a hand down his face, her skin a whisper against his. "I believe ye." She took a deep breath. "Eolande told me several things, one of which has already occurred."

He raised his eyebrows questioningly, even as his chest tightened at her words.

"She said she saw an attack coming verra soon, and she warned me that we should make haste to Dunvegan from the Fairy Pools with our weapons drawn."

Unease rippled through him. He did not like that part of Eolande's foretelling for Sorcha had already occurred. "What else did the seer say?"

Fear flittered across Sorcha's face. "She said that two deaths would come to pass that would break my heart." He tensed at the news. "While I was being attacked earlier," she continued, "I thought the deaths she had seen were possibly Marion's, Bridgette's, or Broch's since they were with me as the men were trying to kill me. That is why I raced into the clearing alone. I wanted to draw the men away to keep them safe and give them time to possibly fire on the men instead of being fired upon."

"Ye are verra braw and verra foolish," he admonished. "Ye risked yer life—"

"To save others," she interrupted, her chin lifting into a stubborn tilt and her eyes glittering with defiance.

He had to force himself not to smile at her display of spirit and resolve. He was glad she was brave, but he didn't want her putting her life in danger. "There is a difference," he said evenly, "between being braw and reckless, and being braw and thoughtful."

She frowned and tried to wiggle away, but he refused to let her go. They were learning each other. Didn't she realize it? He did, and he quite liked the process. It was like nothing he had ever experience before.

"What is the difference?" she asked, her words stiff with her irritation.

"Death," he said flatly.

Her eyes narrowed upon him. He likely should have chosen a more delicate way of showing her where she had erred, but he needed her to understand and never forget it. Still, he did not want this to result in an argument. He brought a hand to her shoulder and rubbed it gently, hoping she would soften with his touch. After a breath, her frown disappeared, and the rigidness of her body loosened. It pleased him greatly that his touch could bring her comfort, and a smile pulled at his lips, which caused her to scowl at him.

"I ken what ye just did," she grumbled. "I did nae ken it in the moment ye were doing it, but I ken it now."

He ran his hand from her shoulder into her hair and twined his fingers in the silken strands before drawing her face toward him and brushing his lips over hers. Desire darkened her eyes, which made his body throb to claim her mouth, but now was not the time. "I'm gladdened that ye trust me enough that I can soothe ye with a touch."

"Are ye now?" she teased, even as she blushed. "I wonder," she murmured in a low, voice, "if I can do the same for ye…" She brought her hands to his chest and ran her fingers soft as a feather from his collarbone, over his stomach, to low where his braies sat on his hips. A shudder of yearning coursed through him, and she smiled wickedly.

With a growl, he caught her hands as she started to slide them back up his chest. "If ye dunnae cease that, *bean bhàsail,* I kinnae vow I'll be able to control myself."

She tilted her head, as if thinking seriously about his calling her a temptress. "I believe I like that ye see me as such. I dunnae recall what I was before I woke up here, which makes me feel powerless, but if I'm a dangerous enchantress, then I have power." She grinned, displaying two dimples and the undeniable fact that she truly was a temptress, albeit the most innocent, honest one he'd ever met. Her eyes turned a swirling, sultry gray as she stared at him. "I feel as if we're racing against time and the inevitable, and that we may well lose." She inhaled a shaky breath. "I dunnae wish ye to cease if after hearing all I must reveal, ye dunnae wish it, either."

He pulled her hands against his chest to let her feel what she did to him. Her eyes widened, and her lips parted. "*M'eudail,*" he growled.

"Yer treasure," she repeated, a sigh of happiness escaping her.

God's teeth, her innocent sounds made him want to strip her of her léine and worship her body. "Tell me the rest," he said, his voice hoarse with his need for her.

"Eolande said the attack would cause a change." Sorcha's gaze darted to his and then to her hands. "I do question now if the change she spoke of was this—us—accepting the desire between us."

He nodded, pondering the same. "What else?"

"She said she saw someone who would betray me. Someone I care for and fear. How can I care for someone I fear?"

He thought about that for a moment before responding.

"Perchance ye cared for the person before they made ye fear them. Perchance there are ties that bind ye that make it hard to cease caring, in spite of yer fear. Perchance someone in yer family?" he hazarded.

She shrugged helplessly. "I wish I kenned." She sucked in her lower lip, silent for a breath. "I had another memory come to me. Do ye recall that I told ye of remembering a man who was childlike in his head?"

"Aye," he replied. He had to force his tone to remain even, though he felt suddenly tense.

"He is my uncle, and his name is Brom."

Cameron exhaled a breath of relief. Sorcha arched her eyebrows at him. "I told ye he was nae anyone I cared for in an intimate way."

"I ken ye told me that, but it's nice to have confirmation. I wish to be the only one ye have ever cared for that way," he said, choosing to be completely honest.

She nestled closer to him, making him think his words had pleased her. "In my memory, I was young, and another girl, who was nae much older than me, was chastising me for nae being cautious enough when we were playing by a creek."

"Considering yer actions of yesterday, I dunnae find that hard to believe," he quipped.

She gave him a teasing scowl. "As I was saying, the girl chastised me, and then I fell into the water and my uncle rescued me. I felt safe with him, so I dunnae believe he is the one I care for who frightens me."

Cameron frowned. "Perchance he did nae frighten ye at the time."

"Perchance," she relented, "but I believe I would have felt a tremor of fear in my memory. I felt only happiness toward my uncle. As for the girl in my memory, I referred to our father when I spoke of getting in trouble, so she must be my sister."

He rubbed her back, feeling the tension mount there as her spine stiffened.

"I kinnae believe I dunnae recall my own sister's name," she said incredulously.

"Ye will," he said quietly, unsure how he felt about that. What if the memories she had not recalled made her the wife of another?

"What are ye thinking?" she asked softly, tracing a finger over the length of his brow that he only just realized he had furrowed.

He smoothed it, captured her wrists, and stared into her eyes. "I was considering what I would do if ye recalled that ye are the wife of another man. I nae ever thought I would be the sort of man to take what belongs to another, but if ye did nae love him…"

She put a finger to his lips as alarm and gratefulness warred for a place on her features. "I would nae ever wish ye to sacrifice the honor that makes ye who ye are for me." He opened his mouth to object, but she pressed her finger harder, a silent entreaty for him to let her speak. "I am nae the true wife of any man, Cameron."

His heartbeat quickened at her words. "How do ye ken? Did ye recall something?"

She shook her head. "Nay, but Marion examined me, and she assured me I have nae ever joined with a man."

Gratification blossomed, along with fierce possessiveness. She was his. No other would ever touch her as he would, and though he had not thought it mattered to him, he was glad that it was so. Still, he did not want to say that and make her think he would have wanted her less otherwise, so he said, "It would nae have mattered to me, but I kinnae deny I'm glad to hear it. But only because I feel possessive of ye."

Her lips pressed into a thin line, making him think his words had angered her, but then she smirked. "I feel possessive of ye, as well, but since I ken good and well that ye have joined with many lasses, I will say that if ye wish us to have a true chance and our lives to be intertwined as one, ye will nae ever touch another."

"God's teeth, nay. I'd nae. The idea repulses me," he admitted.

"It does? Truly?" she asked. The hopefulness in her voice revealed her vulnerability.

He leaned close and kissed her neck and then her lips. He could not help it. Having finally allowed himself to freely relent to the desire to touch her, he was finding it near impossible to stop. "Aye, truly. I would nae ever be the sort of man to have more than one woman, and I would expect the same from ye."

"And I will give the same," she replied, huskiness tingeing her voice, "gladly."

Contentment warmed him, even as he knew she likely had more to say. The silence between them remained for several breaths, and he allowed it, savoring the moment, as he suspected she might be doing also. There was much left to discuss, including the king, which he guessed neither of them wanted to speak about. Cameron hadn't mentioned it again purposely, because he was unsure how he was going to handle King David, but he would find a way. He suspected Sorcha left the topic of King David unspoken because she feared discussing it.

"Did Eolande say any more?" he asked.

She gave him an intimate smile. "Aye. She said there is passion between us that will nae be denied."

He leaned in to brush his lips to hers once more, but her small hand came between them and pressed against his chest. Her smile had turned to a frown. "She also said that we will either sink under the weight of lies or rise with the power of love," she whispered, her gaze now averted.

He looked down at her hands, which she had brought to her lap and was currently twisting together. He cupped her chin and turned her face gently to him. "There will be only truth from my lips to yers."

"And from mine to yers," she agreed immediately, making his chest tighten with her ready pledge.

He ran the pad of his thumb over her sweet lips. "Then lies will nae fell us."

She nodded her agreement, yet her hands still twisted with her worry. "Why do ye still fret?" he asked gently.

Her lip trembled, and she bit down on it, stopping the motion. Intense unease sprang within him like a weed.

Her skin grew ashen, making his concern rage. "Tell me," he urged.

"She says"—her voice dropped to a wobbly whisper—"there is a claim upon my body that will supersede the one upon my heart. I fear she refers to King David's plans for me."

"Nay." The word lashed out of him, and she jerked as if he had struck her. There had to be a way to keep Sorcha and not betray the king. He quickly took her hands to reassure her. "I will nae let ye be taken from me as long as ye wish to be by my side. We will find a way to bend the king's mind."

"And if we kinnae?" Sorcha asked, her voice a threadbare tremor. "Eolande said ye would forgo yer honor to free me. That seems to indicate that changing the king's designs for me will be impossible. Vow to me," she implored, the words savage, "vow ye will nae sacrifice yer honor for me."

He wanted to lie. He feared the truth would put a wall between them once again, before they had even had a chance, but he had pledged to tell her only the truth. "I kinnae make such a vow."

She pushed his hand away from her chin and went to rise, but he caught her around the waist and pulled her back down on his lap. "Look at me," he demanded as she had turned her back to him.

"Nay," she choked out.

He twisted her around easily, and when she faced him, the tears streaming down her cheeks made him ache. "I vow to ye that I will find a way to keep ye with me without forsaking my honor."

"Ye vow it?"

"I do," he replied.

She pressed her hands to his cheeks. "Then let us try to change Eolande's foretelling right here in this moment."

"How?" he asked, fascinated by the determination that had swept over her and lit her eyes with a fire.

"Take my body, Cameron."

Unbridled yearning raced through him almost before his mind could respond and keep from tossing her on the bed and taking what she'd offered. It wasn't because he didn't want to. God above, he wanted it so much that his teeth ached. But she was not like any other woman he had ever joined with. She was a woman he wished to wake beside. "Sorcha, ye dunnae mean what ye say," he choked out, fighting the need that whipped at him.

"I do," she insisted. "I ken what I'd be giving ye, but I give it freely. If ye claim my body, then that part of Eolande's foretelling will be forever changed."

"Sorcha—" Disbelief that he was actually trying to

dissuade her from this had him at a loss for words. To join with her like that, he imagined they should be married, and the thought made him break out in a cold sweat.

"Shh," she said softly, leaning into him and brushing her breasts—purposely, he was sure—against his chest. He was going to go mad with desire. She was learning to be a true temptress at an astonishing speed. "Listen. Please," she cajoled. Damned if he could not get his lips to form the word no.

He nodded, desire overcoming reason.

She did not bother to hide her triumphant smile. "Eolande said our choices could change her foretelling, and she said I should trust my heart. My heart tells me to give ye my body. I dunnae care that I've nae kenned ye long. I met ye years ago, and in that moment, I am sure we became tethered to each other."

He nodded again.

"Change the future Eolande saw for me," Sorcha pleaded. "In doing so, ye change yer own. Yer honor will remain yers."

Everything she had said sounded perfect, except that he would nae feel honorable if he took her innocence but did not make her his wife.

"Marry me," he said, shocked at his own words and aware, in that moment, that it would be a betrayal of what the king wanted. But he would fix the betrayal later. He would make it right. Because marrying her was more than right. He could feel it deep within in every beat of his heart: this choice was fate.

Thirteen

"Nay!" she cried out, struck by fear at what he had offered. If he married her, he would go directly against his king's wishes, and that would not have been a choice he would have made if it weren't for her. If he only took her body, she could still be married to another at the king's demand, since her innocence apparently did not matter to him.

Cameron jerked back, a wounded look passing swiftly over his face before a veil dropped in place like a thick fog, leaving his emotions unreadable. Her heart burst with joy that he would ask for her hand, though she realized it was his honor provoking his offer and not love for her. They had not had time to fall in love. He desired her, she knew, with the same all-consuming intensity that she desired him. She would do almost anything to feel his touch—*except* put him in a position of going against his king's wishes.

"Ye find the prospect of marriage to me unpleasant?" he asked, giving her a bland half smile.

"I dunnae ken how I find the prospect until we have spent more time together," she said matter-of-factly. "We have desire, but I dunnae believe a marriage could sustain on desire alone. And beyond those two things, I will nae lead ye to a choice that will cause ye to forsake yer king. The king dunnae care if I'm innocent," she said, her cheeks burning at the blunt conversation. "But ye would directly betray him if ye married me. We could nae even consider such a thing, unless there was a way to convince David that our union benefited him."

Cameron arched his eyebrows at her. "I'll nae take yer innocence without ye becoming my wife. It would be dishonorable."

The man was too stubborn, but she was moved by his honor. Still, she firmly believed that her way had the power to change their future. She would simply have to persuade him to see things her way.

Excitement and caution claimed her as she trailed her fingers down his chest. Unmoving, he gave her a wary look. It touched her deeply that he would deny something she knew he yearned for because he wanted to protect her honor and reputation. Slowly, hoping she correctly remembered the things Bridgette had said about bringing a man to his knees with enticement, she lowered her léine over her breasts, past her waist, and over her hips. Her heart hammered with every movement, but his eyes widened a fraction and his nostrils flared, making triumph rush through her veins. She knew in her heart that she had been no temptress before Cameron, and while she could not have imagined doing this yesterday, in this moment, it felt right and perfect, as if she was changing their future. Or at the very least, she was grabbing the one chance she may ever have to be held in the arms of a man she truly wanted and trusted, a man whose overflowing honor had him rigid with the struggle to maintain his control and protect her.

"If ye can resist me," she said, infusing her voice with a challenge, "then by any means, do so.

"I'll nae take yer innocence," he growled, "until the day ye agree to take my name." Her hopes disappeared, but he reached out and grasped her by the arms. He pulled her roughly to him, and his eyes burned into her as he looked down at her. "There are many ways to claim a woman's body, Sorcha," he said, his voice gliding seductively over her like velvet. "And I'm going to present every one of them to ye."

Heat inflamed her body, and a throbbing commenced very low. Before she knew what was happening, he had her on her back and was hovering over her.

"Wait," she gasped, her heart beating at a dizzying speed.

A knowing, predatory smile curved his lips. "Rethinking yer decision, lass?"

The pompous man! She saw the triumph in his eyes. Did he think his promise to show her the ways of seduction scared her? She trusted him too much to be fearful of him. She allowed a smile to curve her own lips. "Nay, my mind is set. But if I'm to be naked, then so should ye."

His eyes widened considerably. *"Bean bhàsail,"* he accused. "Ye are my nightmare and fantasy in one."

"Good," she whispered, "Ye will nae ever forget me now."

"Lass, I dunnae intend to release ye, so I'm nae fashed that I will forget ye." With that vow, he stood and quickly removed his clothing. His thick, long staff thrust forward from his body, rigid. Awe and fright struck her speechless, and she found it hard to draw her eyes away from his manhood. But when a low chuckle rumbled from his chest, she forced herself to meet his gaze. "Dunnae fash yerself, lass. When we join, I vow to ye that yer body will fit me like a glove."

She nodded absently, aware that a sharp ache had sprung forth in her core. It felt suspiciously as if the only thing that could possibly assuage it would be the joining. She whimpered with the knowledge of what she had begun.

Cameron gave her a look of complete domination, and her heart skipped several beats. He lowered himself to the bed and was looming over her so swiftly that she found herself gasping. His powerful thighs settled on each side of her legs, heat radiating from the burning skin that brushed her. His abdomen rippled as he reached for her hands, caught her wrists, and yanked her arms above her head.

"What are ye doing?" she cried out.

He smiled wolfishly at her as he reached behind him and pulled out the twine that had bound his hair. It fell in a thick, tawny cascade to brush the strong line of his jaw. "I'm assuring I keep control," he said smoothly, quickly binding her wrists and securing them behind her head.

Frowning, she tugged at the binds, but they didn't budge. She arched her eyebrows at him. "Ye're concerned that I'll make ye lose yer control?" she teased.

"Aye," he replied, lowering his head and sealing his lips over hers. As his tongue plunged into her mouth, retreated, and plunged again, scorching desire took her, causing her to moan.

When he pulled away and brought his mouth to her breast, he flicked his tongue around her straining bud, at first gently, then more aggressively. Her back arched upward as her body demanded more. He tantalized and teased until her breasts felt so heavy and achy that she thought she would go mad from desire.

"Cameron, please!" she begged, not caring at all that she was begging.

"Please what, *m'eudail?*" he asked with a lascivious look.

"Quit tormenting me!" she fairly snarled.

"Ah, lass, I have only just begun, but I'll take pity," he

said, lowering his lips to her breast once more and drawing her bud in his warm mouth. He began to suckle, and a scream ripped from her throat as pleasure spiraled through her, accompanied by the razor-sharp pain of need.

 She needed to touch him. She yanked and tugged on her wrists to no avail, and the desire to rake her nails over his back and demand he give her relief could not be assuaged. She tossed her head back and forth, panting from riotous lust coursing through her. He brought his mouth to her other breast and showed it the same sinful attention he had given the other.

 "I kinnae take more!" she gasped.

 He rose up, his leaf-green eyes glittering emerald. "Nay?" he purred.

 She shook her head violently.

 "I assure ye that ye can," he replied as he ran his fingers over the hot, slick skin between her breasts, past her belly, and to the juncture of her legs. His strong hands came to her inner thighs, and rising up and moving back, he spread her legs, even as she fought against it, embarrassed.

 "Cameron," she hissed. "Ye kinnae—"

 He pressed a finger to her lips to silence her. "I vow I can. And I want to. I want to taste ye more than I want to live another day," he said, lowering himself between her legs.

 Suddenly his tongue was on her tender, burning, pulsing flesh. The feel of him there yanked a guttural sob from her chest. Need clawed at her as he repeatedly offered pleasure to a point, then sharply withdrew it. She wanted desperately to scream at him to take her, but she clenched her jaw until it ached. She bucked her hips upward to get nearer to his mouth, and his tongue touched her once more, hitting a spot that made everything inside her clench. Yet just when she could sense release was near, he pulled back again, panting, and came to his knees between her legs, his taut muscles straining beautifully.

"Do ye wish for release?" he demanded.

"God's teeth," she snapped, "ye ken verra well I do."

"Marry me," he demanded.

"Nay," she replied.

"Then I'll nae give ye what ye seek from me," he shot back.

Her lips parted in shock. He had thought to force her to accept his offer of marriage by driving her mad with lust! Tears of frustration sprung to her eyes, and the determined look on his face instantly softened.

"Sorcha—"

She turned her head away as a tear leaked out of her eye. He gently cupped her cheek and coaxed her gaze back to him. Leaning in, he captured her tear with his tongue, then pressed his mouth to hers.

When he pulled back, he said, "This is just the beginning. When we join, ye will ken the most exquisite pleasure of yer life. Yer body is mine," he said savagely.

"Aye," she agreed, knowing his imprint, his claim, could never be erased from her memory or her heart.

He lowered himself between her thighs once more and stroked his tongue up her center to the spot he had touched before. He was gentle at first, but as her need built and her moans increased, his tongue provided greater pressure and the circles around the throbbing spot came faster. She felt strung like a taut bow, and as he suckled on her sensitive flesh, her entire body clenched, then unclenched all the way to her core, as waves of pleasure rippled through her and left her utterly lifeless as a newborn babe.

When he rose up, she forced her heavy eyelids open,

and she could see his staff so rigid that it curled up against his stomach. It seemed to pulse with its own need. "Let me claim yer body. Let me give ye release," she whispered.

Stark relief filled his eyes, making her realize he would have not asked it of her. His every thought was for her. A large lump lodged in her throat. He was stealing her heart like an adept thief. He leaned over her and deftly undid the twine that had bound her wrists. He sat back on his haunches watching her, his eyes seeming to drink in everything about her.

She shifted her body and faced him. She had offered to claim him and give him pleasure, but she had no notion how. "I dunnae ken what to do," she admitted, heat rushing to her cheeks.

A smile tugged at his lips. "Touch me," he replied. "Taste me as I tasted ye, if ye wish to."

She did wish it with everything within her. "Should ye lie back?" she asked.

He grinned. "Do ye wish me to lie back?"

"Aye." It seemed as if she would have more control that way.

He obliged, lying on his back and cradling his head in his arms so that he could watch her. Embarrassment heated her further, but she discarded it as the useless emotion it was. Crawling over him, she settled to one side and placed a hand on his thigh as she curled the other one around his thick staff. He groaned when she did so. Tentatively, she stroked the long length of him, and when another groan escaped him, she understood that he liked what she was doing.

She rounded her hand over the smooth, hot, slightly moist skin and repeated the motion of long strokes until his groans became a moan of need and his eyes grew heavy with lust. The slabs of muscles in his stomach strained, and his thighs muscles jumped with tension. Fresh desire swirled through her, shocking her and prompting her to lower her head to his staff and slide her tongue down one side and up the other before taking the tip into her mouth.

He growled, and his hand came to her hair and fisted it. "More," he demanded, and she was desperate with her own need to comply. She suckled him with long, pulling strokes, and he guided her with his hand, showing her to move faster. She could feel him growing thicker and longer, and then his breathing came in sharp, short breaths.

"Sorcha!" he cried out and yanked her up, claiming her mouth as his chest heaved and he found his release. When he broke the kiss, she was panting, and he flopped back onto the bed, seeming spent.

After a moment, he rolled off the bed, and disappointment filled her as she thought he was going to simply dress, but he went to the bucket and cleaned himself. He brought a cloth back with him once he was finished and motioned for her to lie back, and he gently cleansed her. She stared at him without speaking, drinking in his beauty. He had the body of a warrior, ruthless and merciless, but his heart... Dear God above, his heart was so tender, so giving. When he was done, he returned the cloth, and then came to rest on the bed once more, pulling her into the crook of his arm.

As she laid her head against his chest, his fingers came to her shoulder and stroked her skin. "We have claimed each other in body," he said groggily.

"Aye," she agreed, feeling sleep tug at her, though sunlight streamed in through the window. "In body." And she suspected, for her part, in heart, too.

Fourteen

He awoke to a touch to his arm. His eyes flew open, and his fist shot upward toward the shadow looming over him. But before he could connect, a hand caught his fist in an iron grip. He started to jerk up to escape the hold when a knee came to his chest, and Iain's face appeared a hairsbreadth from Cameron's. It seemed his brothers had finally returned from the MacDonald's.

"Shh. Ye're going to wake the lass," Iain hissed in his ear.

For a moment, his brother's words bewildered him, and then he remembered he was not in his bedchamber but in Sorcha's, and they had fallen asleep after their very active morning in each other's arms. But they had both been naked…

He whipped his gaze to her, relieved to see either she had covered herself while he slept or he had covered her and not even realized it. Tenderness filled him as he looked upon her. Moonlight shone on her, making her look angelic with her golden hair spilling over her shoulders and back, and her face so restful in sleep. She lay on her stomach with one arm raised above her head and the other down by her side, her head turned toward him. So this was how the lass liked to sleep. He put the knowledge away on the shelf in his mind that he intended to fill till it was overflowing.

Every detail about her was precious and worth remembering.

When he turned back to Iain, he found his brother studying him with a mixture of impatience and understanding. Iain inclined his head toward the door, and Cameron nodded, holding up a hand to be given a moment. Once Iain departed, Cameron quickly dressed and kneeled down beside Sorcha. He listened to her deep breathing for a moment and simply watched the rise and fall of her back with each breath and her eyelids fluttering with dreams. He pressed a gentle kiss to the top of her head, secured his sword, and then departed the room to find both Iain and Lachlan waiting for him.

Lachlan gave him a wry look. "I suppose this means peace will nae be coming to Dunvegan anytime soon."

Before Cameron could answer, Iain asked, "Are ye married to the lass?" There was a greater tension to Iain's voice than Cameron had expected, given his brother had all but offered them his support.

"Nay."

Iain and Lachlan exchanged a glance that almost looked like relief. Cameron frowned.

"Did ye ask the lass, er, that is, do ye wish to marry her?" Iain asked.

"I asked, but she will nae marry me—yet."

"'Cause ye have nae kenned each other long?" Iain asked.

Cameron rubbed the back of his neck. "Partly. But 'tis mostly due to Eolande's prophecy for me and the one the seer told her, as well."

At the matching blank looks he received, Cameron realized neither man's wife had informed him of her activities while he had been gone. Cameron quickly told them of the women traveling to see Eolande and the attack. Both men stood still, listening, their faces going from ones of ease to irritation and then anger. "The attacker Bridgette killed is down below," Cameron finished. "I'm going to take Sorcha down to look at him and see if it loosens any memories."

"But ye got sidetracked," Lachlan quipped.

Cameron scowled at him. "Aye," he admitted.

"The lass must marry ye," Iain said firmly. "Ye have taken her innocence."

"Nay," Cameron replied in a low voice. "I have taken all but that." He would not say more. They did not need the private details that were only for Sorcha and himself. He sighed and quickly told them of what Eolande had said to her. "So, ye see, Sorcha is determined that she will nae marry me until she kens me better and until I would nae have to go against the king to do so."

Lachlan and Iain exchanged a knowing look that made disquiet rise in Cameron. "Is there something I should ken?" he demanded, piercing both his brothers with a look.

"Come," Iain replied, his voice grim. "This is a conversation best had in private."

Cameron nodded, and then followed behind Iain to the laird's bedchamber. After the door shut, he rounded on his brother. "Well?"

A distinctive uneasy look came over Iain. "It seems it was David who called us to the MacDonald hold."

Cameron frowned. "Why?"

"A special messenger arrived there and presented him with a resolution from some of his barons, the Earl of March, the Earl of Ross, the Campbells, and the Steward and his sons."

Tension knotted Cameron's stomach and made it

clench tight. "The rebellion has been proclaimed publicly." It was not a question. He knew it, without his brother saying it.

"Aye," Iain replied grimly. "They claim David misused funds levied on the people of Scotland. They say the king led the people to believe he was using the funds to pay his ransom from King Edward of England. But instead, David used the funds to reward his favorite men, such as the commoners who he had presented with land and good marriages to build the support around him that he wishes." Iain took a sharp breath. "The resolution claimed that he rewarded his favorites by knowingly taking money from the good, suffering, poor people of Scotland."

"Lies," Lachlan said hotly.

Both Cameron and Iain nodded their agreement. "It won't matter, though," Cameron said quietly. "If enough people believe it, the people will rebel against the king and—"

"And he will lose his throne. Possibly his life," Iain finished with quiet intensity. "The rebellion must be crushed immediately."

"And he called ye there to gain yer aid?" Cameron asked.

Iain nodded. "Aye, and he also wants ye to go see the Earl of Ross and compel the man to withdraw his name from the resolution."

Cameron let out a derisive chuckle. "I suppose of the four of us MacLeod brothers, I'm the one he'd most willingly put into a position that could well get us killed, given how I failed him."

"Aye," Iain said bluntly. "But he also knows how ye yearn to rectify what happened. And," he added forcefully, "he kens, as well as we all do, that ye are more than capable of bending the Earl of Ross to the king's will, in spite of what happened with Katherine."

"I thank ye for the confidence, Brother," Cameron replied. "What of the king's orders for me to search out Katherine's killers?"

"Ye're to do that still," Iain said, "but the Earl of Ross is to be yer first priority now."

"How in the name of God am I to persuade the Earl of Ross to revoke his support for the resolution when the king has stripped the man of much of his land and made a bitter enemy of him?" Cameron asked.

Iain's lips pressed into a thin line. "The king has a plan. He has decided to give him back Northam Castle and name it as a wedding gift—in addition to a lass the king has chosen to also gift as a wife—to compel the earl to do as David wishes without it seeming as if he is bribing him. That's how ye are to make it seem when ye take the lass the king has chosen to them. They ken none of this yet, of course."

Cameron snorted. The king would give back a castle to a man he knew well was disloyal and dangerous, which was why he'd taken the castle in the first place but he'd never admit it. "So I am to bring some pitiable lass to the earl, as well? Who is the unlucky bride-to-be? I did nae even ken the old clot-heid's wife died."

"She has nae, and the king's plan does nae include the earl being married," Iain explained. "His son, Hugo, is the one the king intends to get the land and the wife."

Cameron made a derisive noise. "So the king takes from the powerful father but gives back to the son, making the son as equally powerful as the father. David is clever to pit father and son against each other. They will turn their attention from him that way. I feel even sorrier for the future bride now, though. Hugo is a grasping, greedy, immoral man." He paused, surprised neither of his brothers had agreed when he knew they felt the same about Hugo. A terrible suspicion struck him. "Dunnae tell me the king wishes us to force Lena to marry Hugo?"

"Nay," Lachlan replied, quickly. "Nae Lena."

When Lachlan darted another uneasy look at Iain, Cameron clenched his jaw against a burst of frustration and worry. "Then who? Who am I to take like a pig to the slaughter?"

Iain clasped Cameron by the shoulder. "His plan is for ye to take Sorcha, Brother. She is the one he intends to present to Hugo."

"Nay," Cameron snarled, the word cutting through the thick tension like a well-honed blade.

"I hear ye, Brother," Iain replied. "But the choice is nae yers."

"What is yer plan," Cameron demanded, sensing his brother had one by his words. Even as he waited for Iain to respond, Cameron's mind began to turn, and he sifted through the ideas firing in his head, hoping to find one that would prevent this nightmare from coming to pass.

"I will nae force Sorcha to marry Hugo if she dunnae wish to. But we must tell her of the king's command, just as I told ye. I'll nae make the choice for her or any other to defy their king." He gave Cameron a long, knowing look.

Fierce rage caused Cameron's blood to surge and throb in his head. "And if she says she dunnae wish to marry Hugo? What then?"

"Then we find another way to get the king what he wants," Iain promptly replied. "I'm certain we can come up with a solution, even if I must compel the earl with land of my own."

Cameron's throat tightened at his brother's selfless

offer. "I dunnae have proper words to thank ye, but I kinnae allow ye to weaken our clan that way. I will find another solution."

Lachlan clasped Cameron's forearm. "We will find it together, Brother."

Cameron gave an absent nod, his thoughts already fully on Sorcha. He feared greatly she would agree to the king's wishes simply to protect him from sacrificing his fealty and honor, and protect his clan from the king's anger. He was contemplating lying and saying he told her and she would not agree, but Iain, who was looking unflinchingly at him, said, "Rouse the lass and bring her to the great hall. We will be with ye when ye relay the information."

"Ye dunnae trust me to tell her?" Cameron demanded, even as guilt that he had considered not doing so needled him.

"If I had been commanded to relinquish Marion to another, I would have done anything to ensure it did nae occur, so nay, I dunnae trust ye, but I dunnae fault ye for that, either. Now make haste. Grant Macaulay arrived while ye were locked away in Sorcha's bedchamber, so ye're set to depart tomorrow for the Earl of Ross's home. Ye will stop at Graham's home first, however, since it is on the way. He needs to be told what has occurred and arm Brigid accordingly. Then depending on what Sorcha wishes for her future"—Cameron tensed but remained silent as Iain spoke—"we will either make our way to the Earl of March's or the Earl of Ross's home next."

"I was to go, nae we," Cameron corrected. "I ken ye wish to help me, but I'll nae leave Dunvegan unprotected by taking ye or Lachlan away." An idea crystallized, one that would be risky but that he felt certain he could make work.

Iain scowled. "There are many fine warriors here to protect our home."

Cameron resolutely shook his head. "Nae like the two of ye." Before Iain or Lachlan could argue, Cameron went on. "I intend to travel to March's home after Graham's and seize March's castle," he said, knowing he had to let his brothers in on the plot that had just come to him.

Both his brothers stared at him with parted mouths. Finally, Iain clamped his jaw shut. "Explain."

"I can gain sway with the king by seizing March's castle. Of March's and Ross's strongholds, March's will be the easiest to breach and seize. I will need a large force, though. I'll ask Alex to gather his men to aid me, and I will ask Graham to send men, as well. He can afford them, given the strength of his castle and the combined forces of his wife's, his, and his wife's father's, given he commands them all."

Iain nodded, as did Lachlan. "All good thoughts."

"But how will seizing March's home gain ye sway with the king?" Lachlan asked.

"The king wishes to compel March and Ross to withdraw their names from the resolution rather than force them and subject the countryside to more war, aye?"

Iain nodded.

Cameron's mind turned as he considered his idea. "But if he kinnae sway them with bribery and talk, he will turn to force, which means we would be fighting anyway. Aye?"

"Aye," Iain and Lachlan said at the same time.

"So if it appears that we have taken the castle on our own, and the king can compel us to return it, he will have great bargaining power with March," Cameron said. "And David will nae forget what I have done for him. He will be much more likely to nae force Sorcha to marry Hugo as the number of betrayers against him will be much smaller."

"Verra clever, Brother," Iain said.

"Ye are strong in body and mind now, Cameron," Lachlan added. "Ye are a fine warrior. I'm proud of ye."

For the first time in his life, Cameron felt like his brothers' equal. His chest tightened with emotion, and he could do no more than nod his acknowledgment.

"Let us pray that this works," Iain finally said, and with that, they parted ways. Iain and Lachlan were no doubt going to chastise their wives for the dangerous trip to the Fairy Pools, and Cameron was going to wake the woman he would wage war for.

※

She'd been awakened by a tender kiss to her forehead, then another to her chin, her nose, and finally, a long, belly-fluttering one to her lips. As she opened her eyes, the edges of a dream she had been trying to hold on to evaporated. She frowned, sensing something in the dream had been important, but when she drank in the sight of the virile man kneeling by the bed, her frown turned to a shy smile.

Sorcha didn't have a single regret about what she and Cameron had done together, but she was slightly embarrassed about how wanton she had been. Did he think her wicked? She eyed him covertly as he brushed his hand gently over her forehead where her cut was almost healed.

He smiled at her. "*Bean bhàsail*, even watching ye sleep tempted me greatly to slide back into the bed beside ye."

She laughed huskily at his admission. "Then why do ye nae?" she teased.

An intense expression settled on his face, and he clasped her hands in his. "Ye trust me, aye?"

She nodded. "Completely."

"I need ye to vow something to me."

The urgency in his words made her catch her breath. "What?"

"Vow to me that in spite of what ye may hear, ye will nae agree to marry anyone yet."

Worry twisted in the pit of her stomach, and confusion blanketed her mind. "I dunnae understand," she murmured. "Has the king returned? I did nae believe it was my choice but his command."

"He has nae returned. He is traveling to his nephew's home from the MacDonald hold. Sorcha—" Cameron glanced quickly behind him toward the door, as if he expected someone would burst through it at any moment. The tension vibrating off him curled around her like a mist, increasing the beat of her heart and the intake of her breaths. "We are on the verge of war between the clans in Scotland. The king means to use ye, and I intend to prevent it." She opened her mouth to protest, but he held up his hand. "Let me finish," he growled. "I dunnae have much time. If we dunnae appear in the great hall shortly, I've nary a doubt that Iain will send someone for us or come himself." He took a deep breath. "What I intend to do will nae risk my honor, and I vow to ye it will nae be considered a betrayal by the king. Ye must trust me. When my brother asks ye shortly if ye are willing to marry by the king's command, tell him ye are nae. King David will nae learn ye refused." He slid his hands into her hair, his strong fingers curling around her head. "If ye truly wish us to have a future, ye must give me yer vow now, or all will most assuredly be lost."

Anxiety tangled inside her as her thoughts raced. She wanted to give him her vow, but she feared making a choice that would endanger him.

A soft knock came at the door, which made Sorcha jump and Cameron spring to his feet.

"I'm sorry to bother you both," came Marion's voice, "but Iain says to tell you that if you do not appear within minutes, he will personally come haul you out, clothed or not. He's truly very unreasonable at the moment."

"A moment, if ye please, Marion," Cameron said.

He picked up Sorcha's léine and gown, which had been discarded on the floor, and motioned to her to come to him. She obliged without thought, and he helped her dress, putting on her léine first, then her gown. He shocked her by thinking to run a comb through her hair, and she knew her answer. She wanted this man in her life, and she hoped he would eventually be her husband.

"I will give ye my vow, but," she said, watching the relieved smile that had come to his face become an instant frown. "But," she repeated, praying for the strength to do what she must, "if there comes a time I fear yer sacrifices too great, I will make it known to all that I have reconsidered and wish to marry as the king commands."

"That time will nae come," he assured her, sealing his mouth over hers in a passionate kiss that stole her breath. He broke the kiss as quickly as it had begun, took her by the hand, and led her out the door to where Marion awaited them.

Sorcha felt all eyes upon her as soon as they entered the great hall. Cameron held her hand and did not release it, for which she was grateful. Upon the dais sat Cameron's brothers, Alex MacLean, Bridgette, and Lena. No one else was present. It didn't surprise Sorcha. The MacLeod laird seemed a very astute man, and the fewer people who knew that he was supporting Cameron in trying to stop the king from using her, the better. She took a deep breath for courage as Cameron led her to the front of the dais. Marion gave her a reassuring glance as she passed her and took her seat beside her husband.

"Sorcha," Iain said, piercing her with probing eyes. "Cameron told ye why ye have been called here?"

She glanced to Cameron, and he gave her a small nod that it was safe to speak truthfully. "He said the king intends to use me and that we are on the verge of a clan war."

Iain motioned her closer, so she released Cameron's hand and stepped nearer to the dais. Iain stood and looked down at her. "Aye, we are on the verge of civil war. Unless we can prevent it, the devastation would be unthinkable. When such things occur, we weaken ourselves and become ripe for someone like King Edward to conquer us. I'll be direct," he said. "Our king has been delivered a resolution by barons, earls, and lairds who are rising up against him. In the resolution, they accuse him of using money that was supposed to go toward the ransom debt that he—and in turn, the people of Scotland—owe King Edward, for his own greedy gain. The truth is, the nobles who signed the resolution dunnae like David's relentless promotion of his favorites, because his favorites dunnae include them but more common men who he considered loyal while he was imprisoned in England."

"Men like ye?" Sorcha asked, wishing to make sure she understood.

"I am one of the king's men," Iain said, his words sounding carefully chosen to her, as if he did not wish to reveal too much, "but the king dunnae promote me. I already had land and wealth when he was released."

"Aye," she agreed, hoping she was not overstepping her boundaries with what she was going to say next, "but kinnae the king take away any man's land if he wishes it and give it to another?"

Something dark and dangerous entered Iain's gaze, but it was gone with a blink. "He has the right," Iain confirmed, his tone one of barely controlled anger, "but he'd need the strength to do so."

She thought she comprehended it now. The king did not have the fighting strength to go against Iain MacLeod, not that the king had wanted to, but if he did, it would take swaying a great many people to join him. So the MacLeod laird held power others did not, but the king left it alone. But why?

"Ye are verra loyal to the king?" she asked.

"Aye," Iain agreed immediately. "I lived near David and grew older with him. He is like a brother to me."

She nodded. "So ye support him, possibly even when ye believe he is nae choosing wisely."

"Ye're verra astute, Sorcha. I support the king always, kenning that sometimes it is the best choice to support the king while offering my opinion and counsel, which I pray to God he takes."

"And what has the king chosen for me?" she blurted, wanting to get it over with. Her stomach was in knots, and sweat trickled down her back.

Iain surprised her by descending the dais and coming to stand in front of her. He studied her for a long moment before speaking. "David wishes to use ye because it is convenient. He dunnae have to go through the hassle of bargaining with yer father, who may well be a lord, because ye dunnae recall who yer father is."

She nodded, not overly shocked by this news.

Iain's nostrils flared a bit, hinting at his suppressed anger, but that was the only clue he was unhappy with the king. "He wishes to marry ye to one of the lord's sons who signed the petition against him because, in doing so, he can use it as an excuse to give ye a dowry since ye dunnae have anyone else to do so."

She frowned. "How does giving me a dowry help the king?"

"It aids him because he will give back the land he had previously taken from the lord under the guise of yer dowry, *if* the lord withdraws his support from the rebellion against the king."

"So he wishes to marry me to this lord? What is his name?" Her throat tightened, thinking of the possibility of being married to some nameless, faceless, older stranger, as opposed to the possibility of having a future with Cameron.

"The lord who signed the resolution is the Earl of Ross."

Fear sliced through Sorcha, causing her scalp to prickle. She didn't know why, but something about the name tugged at her memory.

"Ye're nae to marry the earl, though," Iain continued, unaware of how his words had affected her. "Ye're to marry his son. The king cleverly planned to give ye as bride to the son, with Northam Castle as yer dowry. What was the father's will become the son's."

She inhaled a sharp breath, understanding starting to dawn.

"Thereby both father and son will be occupied with their quarrels over the castle," Iain went on, "and trying to best each other to gain the king's favor and attain the land."

She nodded. "What is the son's name?"

"Hugo," Cameron said, coming to her side and taking her hand. "Hugo."

Such strong fright gripped her that she found herself clutching onto Cameron. "What is it?" he asked, concern etched on his forehead.

She searched her memory, her frustration rising that she could not say why the name had struck her so. "I dunnae ken," she choked out, the words hard to get past her tight throat. Her free hand fluttered to the column of her neck, and her fingers brushed against her skin where her pulse raced. "I—" she faltered, wishing she could put to words exactly why she was fearful, because she sensed in her gut that it held great importance. "I sense I ken the man, and that I dunnae like him. Dread has knotted my belly and tightened my chest."

Cameron took her hand with his, offering silent strength, which she appreciated. "Perchance ye met Hugo the time ye were here for the St. John's Eve celebration. He threw daggers in the same contest ye did. He tried to goad Bridgette into an argument by taunting her."

"I did nae ken that," Lachlan said suddenly from the dais. "I should cut off Hugo's tongue for daring to talk to ye that way," he added, looking at his wife.

Bridgette gave him an indulgent smile. "It was years ago, Husband. He'd nae dare to speak to me that way now or I'd cut out his tongue myself."

Lachlan's response to his wife was to pull her to him and kiss her soundly. Sorcha felt the slightest twinge of jealousy about how settled and sure Lachlan and Bridgette's life together seemed, but Sorcha reminded herself that they had been through much to get there.

Bridgette looked at Sorcha. "I agree with Cameron that ye likely remember Hugo from the St. John's Eve festival. He was verra obnoxious, and if I were told I was to marry that man after such a meeting, dread would settle in my belly, too. Of course, I truly ken Hugo, so if ye told me I was to marry him now, I'd disappear."

At first, relief had Sorcha nodding her head vigorously in agreement with Bridgette—she'd likely met Hugo at the festival—but as Bridgette continued to talk about what she would do if she were told to marry Hugo, Sorcha's relief fled. There may be no choice but to marry this man she feared but did not remember. She stole a glance at Cameron's profile. Tension was evident in the clench of his jaw and his narrowed eyes.

Iain cleared his throat pointedly at Bridgette, whose words trailed off as her cheeks promptly turned red. When all was silent, Iain said, "I wish to hear what ye desire, Sorcha, and I will do my best to honor it."

Cameron's fingers curled tighter around hers, but when she glanced at him, thinking it was purposeful, he seemed completely absorbed with scowling at his eldest brother, who glared back. She loved that Cameron was so close with his brothers, and that they seemed to be able to express themselves without too much animosity. She had a sudden yearning to be part of this close family where the wives spoke their minds and challenged their husbands, and the husbands not only accepted it but seemed to take a measure of pride in the fact that their wives were so bold.

Cameron did not seem much different from his brothers in that regard. She had seen smiles tug at his lips when she responded boldly to him, and he had listened to her thoughts on things with real attention. Suddenly realizing that taut silence had descended upon the great hall and that everyone was staring at her, she cleared her throat. "I dunnae wish to marry Hugo, but I will willingly submit to the king's wishes before causing strife for Cameron or any of ye."

"Let us hope it will nae come to that," Iain said.

Cameron tugged her close so that the length of her

body was pressed against the length of his. "I welcome strife," he growled, "if it means I'm keeping ye safe."

His words brought her comfort but also fear. She did not want Cameron to put himself in harm's way to protect her, and she worried that despite what he had said, he would be putting himself and his family in grave danger. What if he lived to regret it?

Her thoughts were brought abruptly back to the moment as Iain strode to door of the great hall, opened it, and accompanied a tall man with a long scar down his right cheek and eyes so blue they almost did not seem real, into the room. He had black hair shorn close to his head and dark stubble covering his chin and lower cheeks. "Sorcha, this is Grant Macaulay, a trusted and loyal friend."

Grant flashed a smile at her and winked, before saying in a low, silken voice, "Cameron and I have a long-standing competition when it comes to wooing away whatever pretty lass the other is currently interested in."

"Grant!" Bridgette and Marion said as one.

"Our competition is over," Cameron said, his tone harsh. "And if ye so much as look at Sorcha in a covetous way, I'll be forced to teach ye a brutal lesson."

Sorcha rather liked that Cameron was protective of her, and she was not overly concerned that he would actually execute that threat, given he ended his sentence with a smile, even if it did look a bit more like a wolf baring its teeth than a man offering a show of pleasantry.

Grant chuckled as he shook his head. "It seems I will be the last man standing, which suits me fine."

She didn't know what that meant, but Cameron seemed to as he nodded. "Likely ye will," he said, "and I've nary a doubt ye'll fare well in the position."

Grunts of agreement came from all the men, and then

Iain spoke. "Relay the plan that ye told us of earlier, Cameron."

Sorcha looked to Cameron. She was not surprised he had devised a scheme, since he had told her to trust him. Though worry knotted her stomach, she had vowed to trust him, and that was exactly what she intended to do, unless his plan was too great of a risk for him.

"'Tis quite simple. I intend to seize March's castle and inhabit it to give the king bargaining power with March. Once I am in the castle, I'll send a special messenger to the king telling him what I've done, and then he may meet with March and negotiate with him. It will appear that the king has either compelled or ordered me to return the castle to March, but the king will only do so if March agrees to withdraw his name and support from the petition. In return, I will ask the king to consider my request that Sorcha nae be forced to marry Hugo."

"Why do ye care if this woman is forced to marry Hugo?" Lena spat.

Sorcha could not help but glance at Cameron. What would he say? He desired her with the same ravenous hunger with which she desired him, and she knew well he felt the same pull to her that she did to him. Still, they had not spent enough time together for anything deeper to form, even though she could not imagine a future without him in it.

His jaw twitched with suppressed irritation, but he offered his sister a sympathetic smile, as if he somehow understood and forgave her anger. Sorcha knew Lena had endured a terrible past, and perchance everyone gave her greater leeway for her behavior because of it. Cameron squeezed Sorcha's hand and then said, "Because she is important to me. Just as ye are, Sister."

Lena's scowl deepened. "Ye ken what Eolande said. This woman will bring ye trouble."

"Lena," Cameron said. His voice was seemingly calm, but Sorcha heard the tension that vibrated in it. "I dunnae need ye to tell me what the seer said. I'm old enough to keep my own counsel, and ye should stop eavesdropping and listening to conversations ye have nae been invited into."

"Ye'll forgive me for caring about ye and wishing to keep ye safe! I was denied the opportunity to do so when we were younger, and I see clearly that none of ye need me now," she growled and stormed from the great hall.

The door slammed and silence fell, broken after a moment when Marion said, "I'll go talk to her."

Cameron nodded. "Make sure she understands," he said, his voice low and full of emotion, "that I'd nae ever forsake her."

Marion patted Cameron on the arm. "She knows this, Cameron, deep within."

As Marion departed, Sorcha glanced toward the dais to Bridgette, but instead, Alex MacLean's face caught her attention. Pain twisted it, and something else... Longing perchance? Sorcha was unsure, and when Alex's eyes fell on her and he realized she'd been watching him, whatever emotion had been there disappeared, as if extinguished by an iron will.

Iain cleared his throat, then spoke. "Once ye seize the castle, I advise ye go straight to Ross's home. Leave men to defend the castle and send a messenger to me, as well as to the king. Include in yer message to the king that ye desire for Sorcha nae to marry Hugo. That way, if the king dunnae agree, ye will be far away. That will give ye more time to come up with a new solution, yet ye will still appear as if ye're obeying."

"And when he gets to the Earl of Ross's?" Lachlan asked. "What if the king denies the request? Cameron would be at Ross's, and the king will expect the lass to be offered in marriage in exchange for Ross yielding to his wishes."

"I will find another way to compel the Earl of Ross," Cameron said, his tone unfalteringly confident.

"And if ye dunnae?" Lachlan persisted.

"I will do what I must," Cameron replied, giving his brother a dark, warning look. Worry spiraled through her at what he had left unsaid. She feared he'd not expanded because he did not want her to hear.

"The question is," Cameron said, "can I rely upon yer support, Alex and Grant? I need warriors but also yer silence. If it is asking too much, there will nae be anger on my part."

"Ye have my unwavering support, my friend," Alex replied immediately. "Ye ken I stand with the MacLeods as if we were brothers."

"As do I," Grant replied. "But what of yer original message to me? What of finding Katherine's killers in the midst of all this?"

"I've till the leaves turn to find who was responsible," Cameron replied, matter-of-fact. "After that, I forfeit my life to the king."

"Nay," Lachlan and Iain said together.

"If ye have nae located who was responsible," Lachlan said, "ye will flee."

"Nay, I—"

"Will flee," Iain interrupted Cameron's attempt to object, which made Sorcha exhale with relief. "That is an order as yer laird and a plea as yer brother."

Cameron opened his mouth as if to argue more but then snapped it shut. But Sorcha knew with absolute certainty that he'd never flee. He would not put his family in danger like that. She was both proud and fearful at once. Moreover, she was determined to help him. She had to get back her memory somehow. If she could recall the details of the night Katherine was killed, she was sure that she could help Cameron find the woman's murderers.

Fifteen

Two days later, Cameron, Sorcha, Broch, Grant, Alex, and Lena set out with fifty MacLeod warriors for Brigid Castle. Cameron had been reluctant to bring Lena along, but he relented to Marion's advice since Lena had skill in the healing arts and desperately wished to feel needed—and because his guilt at making Lena feel she was being forsaken was plaguing him. Cameron pushed the guilt aside and focused on what was to come, desperately hoping that Graham would offer men to support the attack on the Earl of March's home.

The journey to Brigid would usually only be one day, but now that they were accompanied by Sorcha and Lena, he did not want to tire them, so they would do it in two days. He was also well aware that stopping halfway gave him time to be alone with Sorcha. That would be harder to find at his brother's home. They would be at Graham's for several days, as they would be waiting on Alex's men to meet with them, but there would be no solitude to be found at Brigid, though the castle was large.

With all of this in his thoughts, he located a suitable place to stop that had lush, soft grass to sleep on and many trees to hide them, along with a rushing stream that ran along a winding path. He called for his men to halt.

He helped Sorcha down from her horse, soaking in the

chance to touch her. Every time his skin met hers, his body set to flame. He'd spent much of the early part of the journey replaying the intimate night they had spent together, so that now, with his hands curled around her waist, all he could think of was sliding them lower to the soft, silky skin he knew to be between her thighs. Of course, he could not, surrounded as they were by his men and his sister, which is why when she said, "I'm going to attend to my needs," he allowed her to disappear before barking orders to his men to set up camp. He hurried into the woods after her.

He spotted her before she was aware of him. She stood in the center of a circle of trees with the last rays of the day's sunlight shimmering down on her. Her head was tilted back, her hair grazing the top of her perfectly rounded bottom, and her eyes closed. Her lips parted slightly as she inhaled a deep breath, then exhaled with obvious enjoyment. It was the most innocent yet erotically alluring thing he had ever seen. She was the picture of beauty, made perfect by her ability to enjoy such a simple thing as warmth upon her face. He'd known many women intimately, but he had never taken the time to know a woman truly. All he wanted now was time to learn the woman before him.

"Sorcha," he said, wincing at the catch in his voice caused by a swell of emotion only she could cause.

She whipped her gaze to his, and a flirty smile twisted her lips. "Couldn't resist following me, I see," she teased.

"Someone needs to guard ye," he said smoothly.

She snorted at that. "The only person I need guarding from is ye," she replied with a laugh.

"The enemy could be about," he reminded her gently, though he had taken great pains to ensure no one was following them.

Her eyes widened a bit. "Do ye truly believe so?" she asked, glancing around the woods.

"Likely nae," he replied, closing the distance between them. He slipped his arm around her waist. "But I will nae risk yer life." He yanked her against his chest, and her soft body crashed into his, her breath whooshing out and her eyes widening. She slid her hand to the base of his neck and twined her fingers in his hair. "Do ye ken what I want more than anything in this moment, Cameron MacLeod?" she asked in a throaty voice.

His body hardened at her tempting question. "I've a thousand wicked replies, and I pray each one of them is on yer mind, lass, but I invite ye to show me, instead of my guessing. Of course, if ye wish me to guess by actions…" He allowed his words to trail off as he brushed his mouth teasingly over her plump lips.

She smacked him playfully on the arm. "Dunnae ye fear ye will give in to my wish for ye to claim my body if ye touch me as ye did last night?" she asked, seeming so innocent now.

"I'll manage somehow," he growled.

Quirking a finger at him, she abruptly turned in his arms and skittered away from him, forcing him to chase her deeper into the woods. He overcame her at the stream, and when he grabbed her by the waist and hauled her backside against him, she laughed and leaned her head back onto his chest. His breath snagged with contentment.

"Isn't it beautiful?" she whispered, raising her head to look at the glistening stream.

"Aye," he replied, sparing a momentary glance at it but then settling his attention back on her. "It is, but it dunnae compare to ye."

She twisted in his arms toward him and deftly tied her

thick, golden hair into a knot high upon her head, exposing the long, slender column of her neck. He could not resist the temptation to press his lips to her skin. He kissed along the creamy length of her neck, relishing the way his touch made her pulse beat so rapidly. When she moaned, he took it as an indication that she wanted him to continue, and he was more than happy to do so. He trailed a path of kisses to her breasts, but her hands suddenly threaded in his hair and tugged his face to hers.

"Lie down with me," she demanded, her voice a velvet tone of persuasion.

He nodded, stripping off his plaid and laying it on the ground for them. Bright-yellow flowers covered the ground all around her, and her hair trailed off the plaid, becoming lost among the flowers that matched its color. She settled on her back and grinned up at him, so trusting and secure in his presence. Every doubt he had about himself and every worry about whether or not others saw him as worthy dissipated in her adoring gaze. She made him feel unconquerable. Something deep in his chest jolted and tightened as if someone had just squeezed his heart in their fist.

A frown appeared between her brows. "Are ye nae going to join me?"

Silently, he kneeled beside her. For a moment, he considered looming over her, but then chose to settle on his back next to her. He took his hand in hers as he stared up at the slit of orange sky visible between the canopy of trees. For many breaths, he lay there, enjoying the soft sound of her deep, steady breath, the enticing scent that swirled from her skin every time the wind blew, and the feel of her warm hand resting in his. This moment, though not intimate in the way last night had been, offered a different sort of happiness, one he had never known. This, he suspected, was a hint of what it was like to be with a woman one truly knew. He'd thought the greatest thing he would ever achieve was to become a renowned warrior like his brothers, but now he wondered if perchance the greatest achievement was to learn a woman's heart and her mind.

"Do ye want to ken what I wish for ye to do?" she whispered.

He turned his head slowly toward her, and the emotion that struck him made it hard to speak. "Aye," he forced out on a whisper.

She rolled to her side, bending her right arm, and cradling her head in her hand. Her gray eyes clung to him, searching for what, he was not certain, but he knew he wanted to give it to her. "I wish ye to fill in the voids in my memory with ones of yer own. Tell me of yer childhood, of ye as a young lad, of what drives ye so relentlessly to be a strong warrior."

He'd never had an open, honest conversation about himself with any lass, much less another person at all. His brothers probably realized better than anyone what pushed him to act the way he did, but what they did know, they had deduced. He'd never told them bluntly. It had seemed a secret to be kept hidden, one that made him somehow vulnerable, but with her, he did not feel the need to appear more than human. He could show her who he was, and perchance she would accept him, weaknesses and all.

He slung his arm behind his head to prop it up so he could see her as he talked. "My childhood was nae a bad one," he started, trying to decide how to put into words what he wanted to say.

She reached out and caressed his cheek. "Saying it was nae bad is nae saying it was good. Tell me," she prompted, "I'm listening."

It was as if she had the key to unlock what he'd held in for so long. "It was hard. My da was a harsh man. He loved me, dunnae misunderstand, but he made sure I kenned I was nae close to the warriors my brothers were. I ken now that he pushed me so I would become a better warrior, but it did the opposite for a verra long time. Instead of focusing only on training, as I felt it was futile, I chased the lasses much more than I should have."

He glanced up from his hand, which he'd been staring at, sure he would see judgment in her eyes, but all he saw was understanding and compassion. It humbled him.

"Tell me more," she prodded. "I ken ye were still chasing the lasses when I met ye..."

He grimaced. "Nay, I was nae. I have nae chased the lasses since I was fifteen summers. That dunnae mean I have nae enjoyed the lasses, but I did nae chase them. I mostly trained, truth be known, but since the lasses seemed to like me—" he gave her a sheepish smile "—I developed a reputation."

She chuckled. "I can see how that could happen. So at fifteen summers ye had decided nae to try to be a great warrior anymore? What made ye do so?"

"My father died, for one, so I did nae have him in my ear all the time anymore, telling me I was nae equal to my brothers. And actually, Graham gave me a strong speech on nae giving up and on being seen as an equal. He told me Iain was testing me, and my reckless pursuit of the lasses was dividing my attention too greatly and causing me to fail." He shrugged. "Graham's words jiggled my mind, and what he said made sense, likely meeting ye that night helped to drive his words into my heart."

"Truly? Ye think meeting me had something to do with it?"

"Aye, I do. I did nae really ken it then, but looking back now, I ken it to my bones. I decided I had to be more focused if I wanted to show everyone I was strong and worthy to fight by my brothers' sides."

"And ye have shown it!" she exclaimed.

"Nay." He shook his head. "Nae as I hoped. I have the physical strength to fight now, but I have failed to prove myself a worthy leader when I failed to defend Katherine. That was the most important task I have ever been given, and I failed. My brothers never would have allowed that to happen."

"Ye kinnae say that," she protested. "Yer brothers are nae faultless, and from what I have heard, Katherine disobeyed ye."

"I let her. I was weak."

"Nay," Sorcha said, her face fierce with indignation for him that made his heart tug. "Ye are kind. There is a difference between kindness and weakness. How did Katherine's death occur?"

He told her quickly about the trail and the lady talking after he had told her not to, which allowed the enemy to determine her location even though it was dark.

"Ye could nae have kenned she was going to make noise," Sorcha said. "Yer brothers could nae have kenned it, either, if they had been there," she added, a confident look upon her face. "That dunnae make ye weak. It makes ye human." Her tone was so emphatic it gave him pause.

"Perchance," he relented, thinking about what she had said.

She snuggled close to him, wrapping her arm around his waist and laying her head on his chest. "Is this agreeable to ye?"

"Ye in my arms is more than agreeable, *bean bhàsail*. It is perfect."

She smirked up at him. "I bet ye said that to every lass ye joined with."

"Nay," he growled. "Ye are the first lass I have ever held in my arms. It is something I nae ever wished for, something I thought I would nae ever desire, but then ye appeared, and with ye, it is different. I am different."

"Ye nae ever held the lasses that ye joined with in yer arms?" she asked, incredulity in her voice.

"Nay," he replied.

She frowned. "I imagine that made them feel as if ye did nae care about them."

Her words struck him to his core. He had not cared about the lasses, not as he already cared for Sorcha, and he did feel guilty thinking upon that. "I did nae offer any hope for a future with me, and I made sure they understood there was nae going to be one. But that dunnae excuse how I behaved. I dunnae have excuses. All I can say is that until I held ye in my arms, I had nae ever wanted to. I had nae ever wanted to allow someone that close to me."

She quirked her mouth. "It dunnae make ye weak to let a woman close, ye ken."

Her words stilled him. How had she known the thoughts he had not voiced? It was astonishing to him and a gift he would defend with his life. "I ken it now," he said gruffly, holding her tighter and running his hand through her silken hair.

They lay head to head, body to body, their hearts seemingly beating as one. When Sorcha let out a sigh, he glanced at her. Her brows dipped together in a frown. "What's the matter, lass?"

She bit her lip, then released it and spoke. "I'm so happy, and I fear it will nae last. I feel as if our time together is borrowed."

His fingers curled reflexively around her arm. "Dunnae fash yerself," he said fiercely. "I vow to ye that this is just the beginning, nae the path to the end."

She took a deep breath, as if she was going to argue something, but she released it on a whoosh. "How pretty the stars are tonight. So bright and beautiful."

He pointed to the sky with his free hand. "Do ye see the star that shines the brightest? It looks like an eye?"

He studied her as her face became a mask of intense focus. "Aye! I see it," she said in a breathless whisper.

He grinned, her excitement contagious. "My da always said that was the eye of the first MacLeod laird watching all his descendants and judging whether they were worthy or nae. It seemed every time I was out at night with him I saw that star, and he would say it was because I had much improvement yet to make. It got so I feared the night, which made my da furious. Once he forced me to accompany him and my brothers on a hunt in the darkest hour of the night, and when he realized I was too scairt to walk alone in the woods, he ordered all of them to leave me and ride back to Dunvegan. I was nae allowed to return until I caught the wild pig we were hunting."

"How old were ye?" she asked, her words vibrating with anger.

He had to cast his mind back, as it had been many years since he'd thought of the night he'd shamed himself so. "Seven summers," he replied, then shook his head. "Nay, six summers."

"Yer father was a beast," she gasped.

"Nay," he said. "Harsh, but only because he wanted us to be fierce warriors."

She suddenly shifted and climbed atop him, resting her

chin on her folded hands upon his chest. Their faces were a hairsbreadth apart. "Is that how ye would train yer sons?"

"Nay," he replied. He stilled, realizing she had made her point without him even knowing what she was doing.

She grinned. "I'm pleased to hear it."

His body stirred with awareness of her pressed so firmly against him. God's teeth, he needed to touch her. Thankfully, he knew no one would come for them; his men knew better than to intrude. And even if someone was foolish enough to search them out, they were well hidden, and he would hear them before he and Sorcha were seen. With a wolfish smile, he slid his hands to her back, running his fingers up and down the perfect curve that ran from the top of her bottom to the base of her neck. She shivered and moaned, and her breath quickened. An ache sprang to life in his gut, a pulsing longing to flip her onto her back, spread her legs gently, and claim her body as she had begged him to do so recently. To feel her that way, to be so deep inside her... He groaned with the painful need.

"I want ye," he bit out, his voice husky and ragged.

She reached behind her with both her hands and brought them to the top of his, which now rested near the base of her spine. She grasped them firmly and led his hands over the delicious curve of her bottom to just below where her legs began. Pressing her hands firmly atop his, she leaned toward him and brushed her lips against his ear. "Then take me."

He squeezed her flesh hard, flipped her onto her back as he had yearned to do, spread her legs in a deft move with his knee, and settled between her thighs. Leaning on his right hand, he used his left to tug down her bodice until her creamy, full breasts spilled out. He brought his mouth to her nipple and suckled it with one long, exquisite pull, lashing and teasing the taut bud with his tongue.

She hissed and bucked upward, arching her chest into his mouth, letting him know she liked what he was doing very much. Her hands fisted in his hair and pushed his head harder toward her chest. He chuckled, released her right bud, and showed her left bud the same attention. His blood roared in his ears, and his heart beat furiously as he settled his mouth between her thighs, and gained access to the core of what made her a woman. He lingered over her, torturing himself and her, by tasting her and teasing her into such a frenzy that she had to cover her mouth on a scream of need before he took her over the edge and offered her release.

When she lay quiet and panting, and he had put her gown back in order for her, she quirked an eyebrow at him. "That was nae what I meant when I said take me."

"I ken," he replied, coming to settle beside her once more. "But when I join with ye, Sorcha, it will nae be on the forest floor and things between us will be settled in a permanent way." He didn't want to mention marriage again, not until he was certain she would agree and until he understood fully what this woman meant to him. She was a drug. A temptress. A light in the darkness he had dwelled in, and when he looked at her or thought about her, his heart ached. But what did that mean? He sensed he'd need to know how to persuade her to be his wife if agreeing to do so still meant that he may have to go against the king.

She rolled to her knees, her hair enticingly tousled, her lips swollen and rosy from his kisses, and her eyes heavy with her own desire. "I think it only fair I give ye the same torment and release ye just gave me."

"Ye dunnae need to convince me," he assured her with a grin.

Her hands came to his thighs, and she gained her own

access to him as he had to her. As she lowered her mouth to his staff, he could not contain the groan of pleasure that tore from deep within. She was true to her word about offering him the same exquisite torture he had given her. She took him deep within her warm mouth with hard pulls and then withdrew, stroking greedily down one side of his staff and then the other. She was tireless in her attempt to treat him as he had her, bringing him to the very edge and pulling back repeatedly with a wicked laugh.

The next time she did it, he growled, "I ken ye're trying to break me. It will nae work. I'll nae be joining with ye this night, but I will be finding my own release in a breath if ye dunnae give it to me. I'm dying."

Her answer was to take him once more into her mouth and offer him pleasure unlike any he had ever known. When she was done, he gathered the little remaining strength he had and pulled her up onto his chest, then nestled her back at his side. "There is nae a doubt left in my mind that ye are truly a *bean bhàsail*."

She frowned. "I ken it, as well, but I ken in my heart that ye bring it out in me."

"It better be only me," he growled and kissed her soundly on her pretty mouth. "I have nae ever been jealous over a lass, but with ye, it is different. Ye are mine. I'd kill any man who dared to touch ye."

"I am nae yers yet," she teased, but the shadows of worry flickering in her eyes told him it was not so light-hearted as she would have him believe.

He grasped her chin gently. "Ye are mine."

"For now," she conceded, settling back beside him.

He lay perfectly still, listening to her breathe and thinking about what she had said. Her words reinforced what he'd thought earlier. She would need utter surrender from him, all his heart and soul, to make her trust him completely and give hers in return. Was he prepared to surrender to her fully? For so long, he had kept his heart shielded and allowed no one in—as he had believed it was what he wanted—no, needed—to do to become the warrior he intended to be. And now? What did he need to do to protect her, keep her, and still be worthy of the MacLeod name?

His brothers all had wives they had surrendered to, and they were still fierce warriors. Of course, he was not his brothers and never had been. Maybe that was the problem, or maybe it was the answer? The truth evaded him, and after a while, he realized Sorcha's breathing had grown deep and steady. He glanced at her to find her eyes shut and her face peaceful with slumber. As much as he wanted to sleep here with her, it was safer to return to the others, so he gathered her and his plaid in his arms as carefully as he could, pleased he managed to do so without waking her. She had to truly trust him with her safety to sleep so soundly.

He walked slowly into camp with her nestled in his protective embrace. A fire burned in the middle of multiple rings made of his men. The inner circle, the one closest to the fire, included Lena, Alex, Broch, and two empty spaces that Cameron knew had been left for Sorcha and himself. He nodded to the guards who'd been assigned the first watch as he weaved toward the inner circle. Lena lay between Broch, who was facing her, and Alex, whose back was to her. Lena, Cameron realized with a start, was awake and staring intently at Alex's back. She seemed to have no notion that Cameron even approached so focused was she upon Alex.

Cameron knew the moment she noticed him. Her gaze skittered from Alex, and a scowl came to her face, followed by a disapproving frown.

He could feel her eyes on him as he laid out his plaid, settled Sorcha onto it, and then went searching for a blanket to cover her. Once he had it tucked under her chin and at her sides, he started to lie down, as well.

"I dunnae like that ye are growing so close to this woman," Lena said.

He straightened and looked at his sister, who had sat up and had her knees drawn to her chest. Her long russet hair fell over her knees, reaching all the way to her ankles. She looked fragile, as if she had been broken and put back together but left with great cracks.

Her blue eyes were narrowed upon him, hinting at her displeasure. "We dunnae even ken her past. She may well have plotted to kill Katherine," Lena hissed.

He ground his teeth in an effort to stamp out his rising temper. He knew his sister meant well, even if she was showing it poorly. "She did nae," he said firmly.

"Ye dunnae ken that for certain," Lena snapped. "What if when she recalls exactly who she is and realizes she is our enemy, she tries to kill ye or, at the verra least, warns whoever she plotted with that ye are after them?"

"She will nae," he insisted.

"Are ye sure?" Lena whispered ferociously. "Would ye risk my life on it? The king's? Alex's? The safety of the MacLeod clan? It could be—" Lena scrambled over to him and clutched him "—that her family was involved in the plot to kill Katherine. It could be that her family is one of the ones rebelling against the king. Use yer brain, Cameron," Lena urged, her voice rising.

He opened his mouth to argue, but his sister's words had sent doubt slithering through his mind. Furious with himself for allowing any uncertainty in, he growled, "I would gladly risk my life on her nae hurting me or any of ye."

Lena's eyes narrowed further. "And mine? Yer family's? Dunnae ye see that Eolande's prophecy is coming true? Ye are forsaking yer family and yer king for this woman!"

He set a hand to his sister's arm. "Have faith in me, Lena. I will nae ever forsake ye or our brothers. Ye are my family."

"We shall see," Lena muttered and went back to her place, lay down, and turned her back to him.

Grunting with frustration, he lay down, too, knowing he needed sleep, but when he rolled onto his side, he froze.

Sorcha stared back at him, tears streaming down her face. His gut twisted with her pain, and fury at his sister heated his blood. "Sorcha," he murmured, reaching for her, but she shook her head while swiping at her tears.

"I'll nae be the thing that separates ye from yer family," she said vehemently. With that promise, she turned away from him. He brushed his fingertips against her shoulder, but she shifted farther away from him, placing her almost against Broch. Left with no choice but to cease trying to grasp her or see her practically lying on top of Broch, he pulled back and settled for staring at her.

He could not say how long he watched her, waiting to see her breathing deepen and know she had succumbed to sleep, but eventually her back rose and fell in long breaths, her tense posture relaxed, and she rolled onto her back, her face tilting toward him.

Moonlight streamed over Sorcha's face, highlighting her beauty while tightening Cameron's chest and quickening his breath. The need to touch her strummed through him, keeping sleep out of his reach. How ironic that he'd never before ached to hold a woman with the intent of nothing more than tenderness or cared to sleep the night with a woman by his side, and now he could not sleep because the desire to do both those things with Sorcha was battering him. When he decided it was safe to attempt to touch her once more, he moved toward her and slipped his arm across her waist. With her eyelids still closed in heavy sleep, she released a contented sigh that made him smile. She turned on her side again, but this time, instead of trying to put distance between them, she wiggled her backside against his groin.

The overwhelming need to protect and shelter her flowed through him. He tugged her as close as he could get her, closed his eyes, and enjoyed the simple exquisiteness of her heat against his skin, the soft exhalations of her breath, and the lush womanly curves nestled trustingly in his arms. He turned his focus to the weeks ahead, his stomach tightening at the thought of all that was at stake—his family, his honor, his life, and most certainly his heart. Before he could think much upon it, sleep finally, mercifully, claimed him.

Sixteen

Sorcha may have awoken in Cameron's arms, but she had done her best not to touch him all day, and it was about to kill her. She had also tried not to ride at the front of the caravan by his side, but he'd flat out refused her request to allow her to ride in the back of the line with the rest of the warriors. As determined as she was not to come between Cameron and his family, he was just as determined to keep her next to him, which literally put her between him and his sister for the day-long journey.

Sorcha suspected he had done it on purpose to prove a point to his sister. As much as she hated to be that point he was trying to prove, she could not deny that his desire to be with her and his commitment to what he wanted inspired awe and an equivalent desire to stick by his side. But worry was there, too. Lena stayed next to them the entire day, as if she needed to protect Cameron from Sorcha, and when they turned onto the long, narrow bridge that led to Brigid Castle and Cameron rode forward to speak with the guards, Lena grasped Sorcha by the arm as the entire party drew to a stop.

"I will be keeping a watch on ye," Lena hissed. "Ye have fooled my brother, but ye have nae fooled me. I dunnae believe ye kinnae remember who ye are."

"I kinnae," Sorcha replied, forcing herself to keep a civil

tone.

Lena snorted. "Seems a verra convenient memory loss to me, given ye were seen with the party of men who killed the king's mistress."

"Lena," Alex growled from the other side of her, "Cameron is a grown man."

"One blinded by lust," Lena snapped, glaring at Sorcha. "As ye have blinded my brother, I will be his eyes so that he will nae destroy himself."

Lena's words struck too near Sorcha's fears of hurting Cameron. She jerked her arm out of the woman's hold, and just as she did so, Cameron came thundering toward them, a man and a woman riding beside him. He pulled to a stop in front of Sorcha, giving Lena a reproachful look as the man and woman also came to a stop.

The man swept his golden-brown gaze over Sorcha. She thought she noted a gleam of interest and caution there, but when his gaze settled on Lena, it turned friendly and filled with obvious love. "Sister," he said, "it's verra good to see ye well."

"Aye," the pretty brown-haired woman by his side said as she urged her horse forward toward Lena's. "I have so longed for ye to come for a visit, Lena. I'm so glad ye are here!" The woman turned to Sorcha next and smiled. "Ye must be Sorcha," she said. "Cameron tells us that ye are here with him by the king's edict."

"Aye," Sorcha replied, wondering if Cameron had told them anything else yet.

"I'll explain all shortly," Cameron interrupted, giving her a reassuring look.

She started to smile at him when Lena said, "Perchance ye should explain now, Brother, that ye bring trouble to their door."

"Lena," Cameron growled, even as his brother's eyebrows quirked upward.

"Is there something of importance we should ken?" Graham demanded.

Cameron nodded. "I'll tell ye when we are alone."

"That can be now," Graham said, turning his horse and starting back toward the castle. He glanced behind him with an expectant look at Cameron.

"Sorcha—" Cameron said, a question in his voice.

"Of course," she insisted. "Speak with yer brother. I'll be fine."

"I'm here," Alex assured Cameron, moving his horse to Sorcha's side, which garnered and almost murderous look from Lena.

As soon as Cameron rode off, Lena said, "Come, Isobel. Let us see what has come to pass with each other as we ride to the castle."

The woman, Isobel, nodded to Lena, then looked to Sorcha. "Would ye care to ride with us?" she asked.

Sorcha shook her head. Even if she had wanted to, she feared it would only worsen matters with Lena, who clearly did not want her around. "I'm sure there is much the two of ye wish to speak of in private."

"Nonsense," Isobel replied, clearly unaware of Lena's hostility toward Sorcha.

"Actually," Lena said, "I do have some private matters to discuss. Shall we?" She turned her horse away from Sorcha as Isobel gave her an apologetic look.

As the women rode away, Sorcha felt suddenly more alone than she had since she had awoken that first day at Dunvegan. Lena's accusations were false, but her worry was well placed. Sorcha could well lead Cameron to his ruin and not mean to do so at all.

"It's nae ye she hates," Alex said. His words mirrored the ones Marion had told her before, yet the agony in Alex's voice made Sorcha's breath catch. She glanced at him. He looked as pained as he sounded, his gaze firmly on Lena's back as she rode away.

"It certainly seems that she hates me," Sorcha replied, not even sure Alex would hear her, but he turned his gaze upon her.

"She hates herself. Iain told me she had conquered the feelings when Isobel helped her face her past, but I was with her a short time when we had to travel together and she did things that made me suspect she had simply learned to suppress her anger. And since I've been at Dunvegan for a spell, I see that my instinct was right. She still harbors great anger, and I believe she is searching for a way to gain the control over her life that was taken from her."

"How does turning her anger upon me help her gain control?" Sorcha asked.

"Let us ride to the castle and I'll tell ye my thoughts."

She nodded, and as they started to move, all the men a distance behind them did so, too. She realized then, rather embarrassed, that they had been waiting on them to ride. "Were they waiting on ye?" she asked.

Alex chuckled. "Nay, they waited for ye. Cameron made each of them pledge to guard ye with his life."

Her lips parted in shock as she looked toward the castle that Cameron was likely now inside.

Alex took a deep breath. "She could nae prevent what happened to her, but she feels she can prevent anything terrible from happening to Cameron. Therefore, her purpose is to be his protector at a time when she otherwise feels she has none. What she came home to is nae at all what she remembered. Be patient, if ye can. She has a good heart."

Sorcha nodded. She believed Alex's words, as she had Marion's, but that did not change the fact that right now Lena hated her, and it was fueling Sorcha's own doubts about herself and her past. "What if she's correct about me? What if Cameron indeed needs to be protected from me?"

Alex stared at her for a long moment before answering. "I'd be more concerned if ye had nae ever voiced that worry. Besides," he added with a sudden faraway look, "ye dunnae strike me as a lass who is hiding demons."

"And do ye truly believe ye'd be able to tell?" she asked, her worry churning in her belly.

"Oh, aye."

"How?" she demanded.

"I've hidden my own demons long enough that it dunnae take but a breath to recognize another attempting to do the same. And ye," he said, spearing her with a keen look, "are nae hiding anything, at least nae purposely."

Alex moved away without looking back as Isobel greeted them, and a flurry of activity to get the guests situated began.

Sorcha awoke the next morning to a knock on the door and Isobel's voice. Disappointment filled her instantly that the night had come and gone and she had not seen Cameron. He, Graham, Alex, Broch, and Grant had been absent from supper last night, and all Sorcha knew was what Isobel had told her, and that was that the men were in the laird's solar devising a plot for the attack upon March's castle. Sorcha had not wanted to question her, as Isobel's face had a distinctly wary look upon it, making Sorcha think Lena had painted her in an unflattering light.

"Enter," Sorcha called after she had hurried to dress.

Isobel poked her head into the room. "I wish to beg forgiveness," she said, looking chagrined.

Sorcha frowned. "Whatever for?"

"Well," Isobel said on a breath, "I started to judge ye based on things I heard, and my husband told me again in bed last night that I was once judged so, and I did nae find it to my liking. I'm here to see if we can start anew."

Sorcha nodded, though her thoughts were on why Cameron had not come to see her if talks had broken up last night.

Isobel smiled gently. "Cameron apparently had his men training most of the night. He's relentless that way."

Sorcha tried not to sigh out her relief. "I suppose he and his men are sleeping now?"

Isobel shook her head. "Oh nay. They got a few hours of sleep, and then they were all up at dawn to ready the castle for any attacks that may come. Cameron is overseeing the chains."

"The chains?" Sorcha asked.

"Aye, my grandmother devised them. She's quite brilliant. Ye will meet her today if she's feeling well. She's been sickly this last week and in her bed. Anyway, since our castle stands between land and the Minch, the only safe passage to the Isles is to travel by water in front of Brigid. We simply keep chains raised to stop enemy ships from going by, but we like to test them every once in a while by having one of our own ships try to go through."

"Is that nae dangerous?"

"Aye," Isobel replied. "But it would be more dangerous to presume they still work properly. The men will be at it all day, and I thought I could show ye around the castle grounds."

"I'd like that," Sorcha replied with a smile.

"Perfect. Lena is waiting for us in the great hall," Isobel added, turning to go out the door.

Sorcha's stomach twisted. "Does Lena ken ye were asking me to come with ye, as well?"

Isobel slowly faced Sorcha once more. "She dunnae."

"I dunnae believe she will wish me to be there," Sorcha said flatly as she stopped to gather her bow and arrows, and secure them.

Isobel chuckled. "Ye dunnae need yer weapon. I'll keep ye safe from Lena." She teased.

Sorcha eyed the dainty woman and thought her no match for the stubborn, angry Lena, though Lena was not really her concern. The weapon was simply to make her feel safe. "I dunnae fear Lena but who may hunt me."

Isobel frowned. "Graham told me a bit about that, but ye're perfectly safe here."

"I'll keep my bow with me, if ye dunnae mind."

"I dunnae," Isobel assured her.

Not long later, Sorcha's doubt that Isobel could handle Lena was erased rather quickly. She'd not have believed it if she hadn't seen it, but after Isobel led them to the hall and hauled Lena off by the arm to speak with her privately, as Isobel had put it, Isobel came back into the room with Lena trailing behind her. They quickly had a bite to eat, with Isobel doing all the talking, and then the three of them set off with Isobel to see the bakehouse and the brewhouse.

They spent the morning in the bakehouse learning to bake bread and eating their fill of it. At one point, Lena actually smiled, recalling a sudden memory of learning to bake bread with her mother. "She was a terrible baker, mind ye," she said with a laugh, finishing a story about their father getting ill after eating some bread their mother had baked. "She had no desire for feminine accomplishments as far as I can recall. What I remember most about her," Lena continued in a soft, musing voice, "is that she was fierce, and I wanted to be strong like she was to make her proud."

Her smile faded, and she turned away from all the women in the bakehouse who had been raptly listening to her story. "I thank the Lord she is nae alive to see how far short I fell from her glory," Lena mumbled under her breath.

Sorcha glanced at Isobel to see if she would say something comforting to Lena, but Isobel was talking to a guard who had just entered the bakehouse. The other women had already gone back to their work, for they had to have bread ready for supper tonight, which left only Sorcha to ease Lena.

Taking a deep breath, Sorcha moved to Lena's side. She started kneading the dough alongside Cameron's sister, and after a few moments, she finally said, "I think ye are verra braw, Lena, if ye dunnae mind me saying."

Lena stilled, her hands suspended in air, but she did not look at Sorcha. "Ye dunnae ken me," she said in a forceful yet soft voice. "Ye dunnae ken if I'm braw or nae."

"Well," Sorcha said slowly, "I ken that ye were seized as a young girl and that ye faced many horrors and lived through them with yer mind intact. Some women may have lost their wits in similar circumstances or taken their lives."

Lena looked at her, her eyes burning bright. "What makes ye think my wits are intact?"

The question startled Sorcha, but she could see Lena's fingers working the dough nervously, and she suspected the woman was putting up a barrier to keep Sorcha at a distance. Lena may have purposely done the same with most people because she feared letting them close.

Wanting to try to build some sort of friendship or at least peace between them, Sorcha decided to be honest, even if it irritated Lena. "Because it takes a woman with a keen mind to decide her brother needs protecting and then make a persuasive argument to the woman she wishes to drive off."

Lena's mouth fell open. "Did I—" She paused, took her hands from the dough, and wiped them on her skirts, leaving a trail of white flour. "Have ye decided that ye should leave Cameron be?"

"Ye made me question myself, certainly. I truly kinnae recall most of my past, and that makes me fear greatly that I will hurt Cameron or lead him to destruction, as ye said."

Lena bit her lip and gazed silently at Sorcha for a long moment. "Isobel reminded me that I almost drove her off from Graham when she first came to Dunvegan. It seems I have a habit of negatively judging women my brothers may love."

Sorcha gasped. "Cameron dunnae love me."

Lena gave Sorcha an indulgent smile. "I believe he does, Sorcha, and I believe ye may well love him, too, but neither of ye are quite ready to admit it. I have no words to excuse myself; I am simply jealous and feel adrift."

Lena's words about love swirled in Sorcha's head. She wanted to focus on them and examine them, but she needed to set her wants aside for the moment and be as selfless as Cameron was. Her heart squeezed just thinking about him. "I feel adrift, as well," she divulged. "I'd verra much like to be friends with ye, and if I truly am the enemy or related to the enemy, I vow I will tell Cameron and nae lead him to harm."

"Sorcha, Lena," Isobel called from across the room, interrupting their talk. "I have to go back to the castle. My grandmother is nae feeling well. Do the two of ye want to come with me? Or ye could follow the stone path to the brewhouse and take it just a bit farther to the west side of the loch. The shore is verra beautiful over there, and the water is warm for swimming."

Lena looked to Sorcha. "I love to swim," she said, her smile seeming hopeful.

Sorcha grinned. "I dunnae ken if I even can, but I'm willing to learn."

"Excellent! Then it's settled," Lena announced. "We'll come back to the castle this afternoon."

A triumphant look flitted across Isobel's face. Was her grandmother even ill, or had Isobel planned all this simply to give Sorcha and Lena time to resolve their differences? Either way, Sorcha needed to thank her later.

They followed Isobel out, and the three women paused outside the closed door. "Just return to the castle before dark. It's perfectly safe, mind ye. Nae a soul gets on this island without having to pass by the guards at the bridge, but Graham, worrier that he is, still dunnae like me to wonder about after dark. I'm certain Cameron will feel the same way."

Both ladies nodded, then parted ways with Isobel as she headed toward the castle and they took the path to the brewery. They walked in companionable silence, Sorcha thinking upon Lena's memory of her mother. Something about the memory had tugged at her mind, but she could not quite part the fog in her head to understand why.

"Alex's men have arrived," Lena murmured, pulling Sorcha's thoughts back to the moment.

She glanced through the trees, down to the bridge that

connected the castle on the island to the land. A long line of men on horses had halted, and as Sorcha and Lena watched, it did indeed appear that each man was only allowed to pass through the heavily secured towers after personally being spoken to by the guards.

A knot of tension that Sorcha had not even realized was in her stomach seemed to loosen. They were certainly quite safe on this island. It was too bad they could not stay here forever. It was by a look of silent agreement toward the brewhouse that they continued on their way and spent a few hours laughing and speaking with the men who worked the house as they sampled a good bit of brew. It was only later, as they made their way to the loch Isobel had told them of, did Sorcha realize how lightheaded she felt, much the way she had felt after imbibing in too much wine back at Dunvegan.

She groaned. "I fear I drank too much ale."

Lena chuckled. "I feel most excellent, but then, my husband forced me to drink exceeding amounts of wine and ale because he said it took the fight out of me."

"Oh, Lena—"

"Dunnae," Lena bit out. "I kinnae stand the pity."

Sorcha nodded, understanding. As they came to the shore, they exclaimed in unison as they looked out at the sparkling water and sat down.

After kicking off their shoes and moving close enough to the water that it washed over their feet in cool, rippling laps, Sorcha closed her eyes, tilted her head to the sun, and soaked in the heat. When Lena cleared her throat, Sorcha opened her eyes and turned to look at the woman. A soft breeze blew a few curling strands of Lena's long, russet hair across her face. Sorcha's breath caught as the woman lifted a trembling hand to push the locks behind her ear.

"It might help to tell someone about some of the things that are in yer memory," Sorcha said. "It seems to me that it would give them less power to haunt ye."

"My head kens ye're right," Lena said in a trembling tone, "as it did help ease the pain a bit to speak of my marriage a bit before to Isobel. But my stomach knots and my throat tightens when I even consider telling all the horrid details of how weak and groveling I became. I tried to seem braw when I was rescued, but it was nae real."

"I understand," Sorcha assured Lena. "I've a great fear of what I might learn about myself, but I try to be braw every day."

Lena's eyes widened, and she gave a nod of recognition. "He'd make me drink until I lost my accounts," she said suddenly, looking down at the ground as she swirled her finger in the dirt. "He'd put his hand on my neck and choke me until I drank, and then—" A violent shudder racked her body. "Once the room swayed and all the fight had left me, he'd tear off my clothes and do things that my body rebelled against. I simply did nae have the strength at that point to stop him."

Sorcha kept absolutely quiet, not wanting to disrupt Lena, yet she did curl her fingers hard into the dirt as rage for the woman coursed through her.

"I've wished many a night, I had nae lived through his treatment."

"Lena, nay!" Sorcha burst out. "If ye had nae lived, then ye would nae have a chance to find happiness now."

Lena turned sad eyes to Sorcha. "I dunnae believe I will ever find happiness."

"I believe ye will. Ye will marry, and—"

"Nay," Lena said harshly. "I will nae ever submit to marriage again. I'd rather be dead." Sorcha bit her lip but held her words, feeling they would only be seen as pity as before. Lena drew her knees to her chest. "I dunnae ken what I should do quite yet. I thought at first I would stay at Dunvegan and be with my brothers, but they are all married and dunnae really need me."

"Cameron is nae married," Sorcha protested.

Lena smiled. "Nae yet," she said in a teasing voice.

"Just because yer brothers have taken wives, dunnae mean ye dunnae have a place, though," Sorcha said, choosing to leave Lena's comment alone.

"Oh aye, it does. Unless I want to be the sad, unmarried, angry sister for the rest of my life—or worse, they have to defy the king as they almost did afore to protect me from a forced marriage. Nay." She shook her head. "I must take hold of my future. I am simply nae quite certain how yet."

"Ye might change yer mind about marriage," Sorcha said hopefully, thinking upon seeing Lena and Alex each give the other looks of longing when they thought no one was observing them.

"I'll nae be changing my thoughts about that," Lena insisted. "However—" she gave Sorcha a shy look "—I do wonder sometimes in my bed at night what it would be like to be kissed by a man I did nae fear. But I grow tense even thinking of a man's lips on mine. Do ye see the problem for me? Even with a want to discover the tenderness of a gentle kiss, I fear submitting to it too much to ever allow it."

"Perchance ye simply have yet to meet the man who will be able to make ye long for his kiss more than ye fear it."

"Nay," Lena said with ringing certainty. "I—That is, there is a man who I long to kiss, but it is nae enough. The longing is nae enough," she finished quietly, her voice sad.

Impetuously, Sorcha reached over and hugged her.

Lena tensed at first, but then she relaxed. "It is nae enough *yet*," Sorcha insisted. "Give it time. I feel certain it will be. And now," she said cheerily, certain the mood needed to be lightened, "let us see if I can swim!"

Laughing, they both stood. Sorcha took off her bow and set it and her arrows down under the tree. She walked back to the shore, stripped to her léine as Lena had done, and they both waded into the water. Sorcha's heart began to pound as the water crept up her legs, past her thighs, and to her stomach. She paused, but Lena nudged her.

"I'm here for ye, if ye need me," Lena assured her. "I'm a verra good swimmer, and I'll nae let ye drown."

Sorcha nodded and moved with slow, tentative steps farther into the water. It passed her chest, then her neck, and when it got to her nose, she glanced to Lena. Sorcha stood on her tiptoes, breath held and heart speeding.

"Submerge yerself!" Lena urged. "I vow I'm here."

Taking a deep breath, Sorcha dipped her head all the way under the water and pushed off from the ground. Suddenly, her body took over and her fear abated. Her arms and legs moved instinctively from memory, and such exhilaration filled her that when she broke the surface, she let out a whoop.

When she looked to her right, Lena was there beside her, grinning. "Ye swim as well as a fish!" she praised.

"Thank ye," Sorcha replied, laughing. "And thank ye for staying with me. Ye made me feel safe, as if—" the truth of her feelings in the moment hit her "—as if ye took the place of my sister who is nae here."

Lena's lips parted, and she slowly smiled. "Thank ye, Sorcha," she replied, her voice trembling with emotion.

They whiled the rest of the afternoon away, swimming, eating, and then swimming some more. When the sky became orange with the first hint of dusk, they decided it was time to return to the castle.

"Care to race?" Sorcha challenged.

Lena answered with a grin and a dive under the water. She shot past Sorcha in the clear water. Chuckling, Sorcha gulped in a deep breath and dove under to catch up, not coming up for air until she saw the ground appear beneath her in the water, so that she knew she was very near shore.

She broke the surface with a whoop, stood, and rubbed the water out of her eyes. "Did I win?" she asked breathlessly as she blinked her eyes open.

Her breath solidified in her throat when she saw Lena, lying unmoving on the shore, her face turned toward Sorcha but her body twisted the other way, as if she had tried to fend off someone but had been caught unawares. Blood streamed down her forehead, and her eyes were closed.

Sorcha's gaze flew to the face of the man looming over her. She squinted up at him, struggling to really see him as the setting sun was in her eyes. He held a dagger in his hand and had a savage smile on his face, but his features were blurry.

"Hello, Sorcha," he said in an eerily pleasant tone, as if greeting an old friend.

Something in his voice made her gasp. She knew that voice. Happiness and dread flooded her at once, and as the man bent down to his haunches and his face came into view, her stomach knotted in recognition as memories flooded her mind. "Finn," she choked out, looking into the face that so mirrored her own. Silver-gray eyes the exact color as her own stared back at her with cold dispassion.

Finn ran his blade across his now-bearded face, as if he needed to scratch an itch. "Ye've caused me much trouble,

Sorcha, and wasted an immense amount of my time, but here we finally are."

"Ye came to retrieve me?" she asked, her voice betraying her fear, despite her effort to sound nonplussed.

Finn frowned. "Nay. I've come to kill ye," he stated without a hint of emotion.

She responded at the same moment he lunged for her. Lurching backward, she ducked under the water, frantically clawing at it in hopes of escape. His strong hand locked around her ankle as she kicked, and it yanked hard, pulling her back toward the shore she had been trying to get away from. She was dragged, sputtering and gulping in mouthfuls of water, onto the shore, past Lena's still form, and across the rocky land. She dug her nails into the ground, trying to gain purchase, but to no avail.

"Finn!" she screamed, as he hauled her toward the edge of the stone path she and Lena had come down earlier.

He stopped directly beside the tree where she had left her bow and arrows. When he flipped her onto her back, he stared down at her with an expression of hatred that made her shiver. "For years," he spat at her, "I had to endure Father berating me, telling me I was weak and unworthy, shaming me in front of others, but I withstood it because I kenned that one day Blair Castle would be mine and I could finally be free of Father. But ye ruined that as ye ruin everything!"

Her heart slammed painfully against her ribs as she stared at her brother. All the while, she was trying to discreetly judge if she could reach her bow and have any hope of nocking an arrow and aiming before Finn stopped her. She was unsure. She had to get closer, had to keep him talking.

"How do I ruin everything?" she asked, even as memories filtered in that made her think she partly knew.

"I was Uncle Brom's favorite," he growled, "then ye stole his love."

"Ye were cruel to him," she countered, trying to edge a bit toward her bow.

"Cruel?" Finn scoffed. "He almost drowned ye. He deserved the beating I gave him."

"Nay." She shook her head, the memory of the day she had fallen into the water coming back to her even more clearly now. Brom had saved her, but Finn had appeared, taken her from Brom, and started to shake her for being careless. Finn undoubtedly had known, just as her sister, Constance, had, that Father would blame them for Sorcha's carelessness. Age-old guilt besieged her, yet it was edged with the awareness that her brother's heart had been twisted into an ugly thing. Still, he was her brother.

"Finn," she said, softening her tone, "ye made Brom fear ye. That is nae my fault."

"I had to beat him because of ye," Finn accused. "I had to lie to Father to protect myself because of ye," he shouted. "So aye—" he narrowed his eyes "—it is yer fault."

Tears filled her eyes. "I'm sorry," she said simply, knowing her impetuousness as a child, combined with her father's quick temper and harsh treatment of Finn, had led to this moment.

Her twin shook his head almost violently. "*Sorry* will nae suffice. Father will give my castle to that bastard Hugo if he learns ye still live."

Sorcha gaped at her brother for a long moment, as she soaked in what he had just said and sifted through her memories. She recalled in quick flashes the night she had heard her father plotting Katherine's death, and she knew Finn's words to be true. She and the castle were the prizes offered to Hugo for his deed.

She swallowed hard, horrified. She truly *was* related to the enemy. But there was no time to consider what it meant now. "Why does Father think me dead?"

"Because I led him and Hugo to believe I saw ye killed. Did ye think I was coming to rescue ye?" he jeered.

She didn't bother to tell him she'd had no memory of who she was until a moment ago. "Finn," she said in a broken whisper. "I dunnae wish to marry Hugo or have yer castle. If ye will just let me speak with Father, I may be able to compel him to allow me to marry another." She thought immediately of Cameron. What if she used what she knew her father had done to try to coax him into letting her marry as she wished? It was a risk, but she saw no other option. "I'll go with ye this day to speak to him!"

"Nay!" he yelled.

When he pulled his arm back as if to strike her, she rolled toward her bow and arrows, grabbed them, and scrambled to her feet as Finn brought the blade down near her leg, grazing her skin. For one breath, she stared in astonishment at the blood trickling down her leg before she whipped up her bow and aimed it at Finn's heart.

"Dunnae move," she said, her voice steady and cold, though her heart raced wildly. "I will shoot ye, and ye ken I will nae miss." The memory of her brother's jealousy over her skill with daggers, with the bow, and on a horse rushed back to her. Each recollection of the hostility he had for her made her flinch and die a little inside.

Finn's nostrils flared, but his lips pressed into a smirk. "Ye dunnae have the fortitude to kill me. Ye love me." He spat the last sentence with dripping scorn. She understood well why. Father had made Finn believe that soft emotions—love—was for the weak and the foolish.

"I'll find the strength," she vowed, unsure if it was so. As the words left her mouth, Finn surged forward, and she released the arrow, aiming for his shoulder instead of his heart. He stumbled backward and dropped his dagger, which she kicked well out of his reach.

"Ye shot me," he roared, yanking the arrow out of his shoulder with a curse. Blood immediately began to pulse from the wound, turning Sorcha's stomach with dismay and sorrow. "Ye shot me," Finn said again, but this time his voice was a bewildered mumble. His gaze caught hers, hurt flashing across his face as he swayed a bit. "I did nae truly believe ye would shoot me. Ye're my sister."

She sucked in sharp breath at his words, at his obvious pain. More memories flooded her of a time when he had not been twisted by jealousy and hatred. They used to play a hiding game from their parents, and Finn had always found them the best hiding places. And she, Finn, and Constance would climb trees, and he would always help her into the tree and go down before her to ensure she didn't fall. Finn used to catch light bugs in his hands for her, so she could make wishes on them, and he'd shown her how to fish. Her throat tightened painfully. What should she do?

"Shoot me," Finn demanded suddenly.

"What?" she asked in horror.

"If ye take me to the MacLeods, the king will have me executed for helping to kill Katherine. That death will be slow and painful, but ye can kill me quickly."

"I kinnae kill ye, Finn." She trembled with the mere thought of it.

"Ye will be sentencing me to death when ye hand me to the MacLeods, and possibly Father, too. I kinnae vow if they torment me that I'll nae tell that Father was involved in the plotting to kill King David's mistress, so it's best if ye shoot me. Do it here," Finn growled, ripped open his shirt, and poked a finger at his heart.

From somewhere behind her, Lena moaned, making Sorcha jerk. Finn's gaze skittered past her to where Lena had been left. "She's waking. Ye have little time to shoot me. Do it now."

Sorcha shook her head, tears already leaking down her face. She could not kill her brother. It had been one thing to defend herself when he was trying to kill her, but she could not kill him as he was asking. Nor could she set him free and be responsible for Cameron's possible death if he did not catch him. A bitter, sour taste filled her mouth as Lena moaned again. Sorcha stared at her brother. She could not be responsible for sending him to his death. What was she to do?

Queasiness turned in her stomach as Lena moaned again. Sorcha stared at Finn, her heart feeling as if a hand had gripped it in a merciless hold, and her mind registered that he had on a MacLean plaid. "My God," she gasped. "Finn, did ye kill a MacLean to gain access to the island?"

He narrowed his eyes. "What if I did? What difference does it make? I tried to kill ye," he said, his voice breaking and tears leaking out of his eyes now, too. She saw then what she had known, why she was standing here still. Finn was broken. His shoulders suddenly slumped, his hand came to his face, and he buried it in his palm. "I'm sorry, Sorcha. So sorry. I'll nae ask yer forgiveness."

Flashes of memory hit her.

Beatings. So many beatings Finn had taken at Father's hands for not being stronger, more ferocious, a better swordsman, shooter, rider. And through many of them, Father had taunted Finn that she had more skill, a woman, his sister, than he did.

"Oh, Finn," she sobbed.

He flinched, jerking his hand down. "I'd rather die by yer hand. 'Tis fitting."

She shook her head. "I kinnae." Maybe Cameron would keep this secret and let Finn flee? No! Despair clawed at her. How could she even ask it of him? Ask him to relinquish his honor and lie for her?

"Make haste." Her own voice startled her. "Make yer way to Aunt Blanche. Dunnae return to Father, Finn. I'm going to tell the MacLeods what he has done, but I'll keep yer part to myself. They'll capture Father and take him to the king, and if ye are there, I'll nae be able to stop them from taking ye, too."

"Sorcha?" she heard Lena call, her voice full of fear.

Sorcha turned for a breath to ensure Lena could not see her, and when she twisted back around, Finn was fleeing into the woods. Her body shook violently with awareness of the lies she would now tell to protect her brother. Lies that, according to Eolande, would destroy any love that may blossom between Sorcha and Cameron.

Cameron. Every moment they had spent together filled her head—his words, gestures, kindness, gentleness, passion, and honor. She pulled her bow close to her and wrapped her arms around herself as she turned to go to Lena. Love had taken root, and she had not realized it until now. She allowed herself one brief moment of happiness before overwhelming sadness washed over her. Better to destroy her happiness and the possibility of Cameron loving her in return than to destroy the man she loved.

Yes, he would take her father, Ross, and Hugo to the king, and the king would spare his life for Katherine's death. He would survive.

Seventeen

Cameron, Alex, Graham, and Grant made their way from the water, where they had toiled and trained the entire day. Bone weariness had claimed him long ago, but now, with the thought of seeing Sorcha, his body stirred to life once more. When they came up the seagate stairs from the shore and rounded into the courtyard to find it full of men on the verge of riding out armed for battle, Cameron's first thought was of Sorcha. Trepidation filled him as he caught sight of Broch at the front of his men.

"Broch!" Cameron boomed. He strode with the others toward Broch and grabbed at his horse's reins to stop the man's departure.

Broch glanced sharply down at him, his tense face relaxing when he realized it was Cameron. "Lena and Sorcha were attacked on the other side of the island."

Dark fear swept through him. "Have they been harmed?"

Broch nodded. "Aye, but nae fatally. Lena took a cut to the head, and Sorcha one to the leg—"

"Where are they?" he demanded, his voice mingling with Alex's, who demanded the same.

Broch looked at the two of them. "In the healing room with Isobel."

"Wait here for my return," Cameron ordered. "I'll ride

out with ye."

"We all will," Alex added, turning toward the castle entry with Cameron.

"Dunnae tarry!" Graham called. They paused and looked back at him. "Whoever gained access to this island could have only done so under disguise, which means they've likely already left the way they came." His grim voice displayed his anger. "I'll meet ye back here and ride to the other side of the island with ye after I speak with the guards. Make haste."

Cameron and Alex both nodded as they turned toward the castle door and hurried inside in silence.

It didn't take long to reach the healing room, and when they entered, they parted, Alex going toward Lena, who was lying on a bed with Isobel huddled over her, and Cameron going to Sorcha, who stood by the window with her back to the door. She turned as he approached, happiness flooding her face, then disappearing in the same instant, replaced by a stark wariness that stopped him. Unease gripped him as he started once more toward her, pulled her into his arms, and ran his hands over her head, shoulders, back, hips, and kneeled at her feet to gently lift her gown and expose her legs.

"What are ye doing?" she asked, her voice a breathy whisper.

He traced a finger gently down her leg where her wound had been dressed. Slowly, he unwrapped the bandage, feeling her eyes upon him as he did so. He inhaled sharply at the long, angry cut on her leg, and as fury flowed through his veins, he tilted his head up to look at her face. "I will nae sleep until I find who has been hunting ye. I'll kill them. I vow it."

The fear that flashed in her eyes confused him, but as he

stood and pulled her into his arms, she clung to him and he thought that the fear must be for him. He brushed a hand through her hair. "Dunnae fash yerself, *mo chridhe*. I'll be verra stealthy, so I'll nae be in danger."

She pulled back and met his eyes. That same look was in her eyes—stark, vivid fear—but now wariness accompanied it.

Apprehension flickered through him. "What is it?"

"*Mo chridhe?*" she whispered.

He frowned. "Ye dunnae wish to be 'my heart'?" He intended his voice to be steady, yet he heard it wobble.

"What? Nay!" she said in a low, rushed tone, as she pressed her lips to his.

When she started to draw away, he locked his arms around her back and held her prisoner as she was holding his heart prisoner. She had his heart. She'd taken it, likely just as his brother had warned—from the very first kiss. He slanted his mouth over hers, tasting her, feeling her, tormenting them both with a kiss that stirred their passion but must be stopped for what lay ahead. She pulled away before he could manage to gather the will. Her hand came to rest on his heart, and her gaze, burning bright with worry, locked with his.

Unease blanketed him once more. "What is it?" he demanded.

"I've remembered my past," she whispered, her voice laden with misery.

His gut twisted at the obvious fear in her tone. "Ye ken who ye are?" he asked quietly as he drew her to the far side of the room, away from Isobel and Lena. He was aware Isobel had stilled in her ministrations to Lena.

Near the window overlooking the courtyard they faced each other. She stared out the window as she spoke. "My father is the Earl of Angus."

Her words cut through him like an icy wind on the coldest winter day. He winced and inhaled sharply. The Earl of Angus had once been one of David's allies. He'd had the king's favor and had believed that David would never make a choice that would lessen the earl's wealth. But the king would abide no man who attempted to tell him how to rule, and all who had tried—like the Earl of Angus had—had ended up having land taken from them and given to someone who was truly loyal. Thus, the earl's power and wealth had been greatly diminished, thanks to David.

Cameron swallowed the bitter taste in his mouth. She was the daughter of an enemy of his king and his family, yet she had his heart. Eolande's prophecy rang in his ears as he asked Sorcha, "Why were ye in the woods the day Katherine was killed?" His heart thudded as he waited for her to answer. It seemed an eternity before she spoke, yet he knew it had taken only two breaths.

"My father, the Earl of Ross, and the Earl of March learned that Katherine would be traveling through the woods near our home." Sorcha had a faraway look on her face and a crease between her brows. She swallowed audibly. "They decided to kill her to send a message to the king that he could nae control the nobles," she said, biting down on her lip, her distress obvious. "And that if he tried, there would be grave effects. Hugo offered to kill Katherine in exchange for my hand in marriage."

A tremor coursed through her, and he squeezed her tighter. Disgust coursed through him. Both her father and King David had been willing to barter her away to a loathsome man like Hugo simply to keep their power.

Cameron had to stop it.

"Father also offered Hugo the castle my brother was

supposed to inherit—Blair Castle." Sorcha paused again, and a dark look overcame her. She took a deep shaky breath. "I overheard the exchange and tried to beat Hugo, his men, and my father's men to yer party to warn ye, but I was overcome by Hugo."

Cameron nodded, rage pounding through his veins for Katherine's murder, for the betrayal of the king, for Sorcha.

"I'm sorry, Cameron," she said with a shake of her head. "I understand if ye wish to turn from me—"

"Nay!" he growled, yanking her to him and circling his arms around her waist. "Ye are a victim of yer father as much as Katherine was. But ye ken the king will nae be merciful to yer family."

She nodded, sadness twisting her features. She disentangled herself from his hold, wrapped her arms around herself, and stared out the window. "My brother, Finn—we were born at the same time and look alike—he's gone. He fled."

"Are ye saying he was nae involved with killing Katherine?" Cameron asked.

"He did not kill her," she replied woodenly. "Hugo killed Katherine."

Cameron frowned. She had answered his question, but she had not. Coupling that with her avoiding his gaze, he was sure Sorcha was lying. But why lie now after revealing so much? Unless her brother was involved, and she was trying to protect him... Anger and understanding warred within him. If his own brothers or sisters had done such a thing, he would do everything in his power to protect them, yet if she would lie to him about this, how could he trust her? Sorcha's relaying of Eolande's prophecy came instantly to him: *We will either sink under the weight of lies or rise with the power of love.*

Graham suddenly appeared in the doorway and motioned for Cameron to join him. "We have to ride out," Graham growled. "If we are to catch the people responsible for attacking Sorcha and Lena, we kinnae waste any more time."

Cameron gave a quick nod and turned his gaze to Sorcha once more, staring hard at her face for signs of truth or lies. "Can ye tell me who we are looking for?"

"Nay," she said in such a soft tone that he would have missed hearing the word if he'd not been watching her lips.

He clenched his teeth in vexation. "We kinnae live happily together without truth," he said simply, letting her know her lies were apparent. "I kinnae do what I must to help ye if ye are nae honest with me."

When she still did not look at him, his simmering temper began to boil. He cupped her chin and turned her face to his. The wariness he saw there stole his breath. The old voice that had long made him uncertain of himself grew loud. "Dunnae ye have faith in me?" he asked.

"I have complete faith in ye, Cameron," she cried out. "I've never kenned a man as braw as ye. That's the problem!" she sobbed.

"Cameron," Graham pressed. "We must give chase *now!*"

Frustrated with the lack of time and with her untruth, he released her. "We'll speak more on this when I return," he muttered, stalking from the room and not looking back.

※

Many hours later, as he and the rest of the hunting party were searching the area where Sorcha and Lena had been attacked, Cameron noticed the moonlight glittering off what appeared to be a blade. His heart thumped as he kneeled down and brushed the dirt from the blade, revealing a dagger. He picked it up and brought it close, seeing the House of Angus's emblem with the initials *FA* carved into the handle. Those were Sorcha's brother's initials.

God's bones! Had her brother been the one to attack her? Was he the one who had been trying to end her life? If so, why? And why had she lied? Was it to protect her brother? Or was it to protect him from having to lie for her brother along with her?

Cameron slammed the point of the dagger down into the dirt.

"Cameron!" Graham called from a few feet away. "Have ye found anything?"

Eolande's prophecy came to him, making him shudder. *Ye will betray yer king, yer family, the very honor ye hold dear.*

"Cameron?" Graham called again.

"Nay," Cameron replied, forcing his breath to become even, his heart to slow, and his mind to quiet. One thought became loud, one purpose clear. He refused to believe she had lied to him for any reason other than to protect him, and he refused to live without her. Therefore, he needed to be so cunning and so ferocious that he could outmaneuver whatever person or force tried to separate him from Sorcha. Methodically, he thought of each of their enemies and what he would do if he were them, as well as what it would take to change the course of those choices. He considered the king and the conspirators against the king—Hugo, Finn, their fathers, March, even Sorcha.

The fear of Eolande's foretelling slipped away from him, and fierce determination replaced it, along with the certainty that he was strong enough, shrewd enough, to handle what may come, but with his brothers and his sister by his side, he would be unstoppable. The majority of his life he had avoided leaning on anyone, but no more.

Suddenly, a realization struck him that stole his breath: he did not lose his honor by protecting Sorcha. It was honorable to do so. She was innocent.

"Graham," Cameron called, standing and motioning his brother over, "I've found something." A plan was forming in his mind that involved marrying Sorcha without her realizing it. If she knew what was happening, she'd refuse in order to protect him from making choices that would cause Eolande's foretelling to come true. He intended to propose his unfolding plan to the king, but if the king did not agree to it, then the only thing preventing Sorcha from still being used as a pawn would be their marriage. When Graham came near, Cameron handed the dagger to him. "This is Sorcha's brother's dagger. I'm certain of it."

Graham frowned as he ran a finger over the initials. "And?" he asked. The question of why Sorcha's brother had tried to kill her had not been voiced, but it was clear what Graham wanted to know, given his incredulous look.

Cameron sighed. He quickly told Graham what Sorcha had shared about her father, Hugo and his father, and the Earl of March, and how she had said her brother had fled and not killed Katherine.

Graham shook his head when Cameron paused. "Those men have no honor. To have killed Katherine to strike at the king is a coward's move," Graham spat.

"Aye," Cameron agreed.

Graham's eyebrows dipped together. "Tell me yer thoughts on why her brother would be trying to kill her and why she would lie to ye about it."

"I believe," Cameron said slowly, "her brother likely

knew she would tell us what had happened, and he and the others would be accountable to the king. Perchance he intended to try to prevent it, or if they thought the king would lose the throne, perchance he did nae care and he simply wanted to ensure she died so Hugo would nae inherit the castle her brother was meant to receive." He shrugged. "I dunnae ken the why of it for certain, but I do ken this for certain: Sorcha's heart is big. She loved her brother, and even if she discovered he had intended to kill her, I believe she might have let him flee to keep him safe from harm."

"Then she lied to ye," Graham said flatly.

Cameron nodded. "Aye, but she did tell me the entire truth of her father and the others. I believe she lied to me so I would nae have to lie, too. Would ye nae do all in yer power to keep me from death, even if ye kenned I was nae a good person?"

"I would," Graham said begrudgingly. "What is it ye wish to do?" he asked, surprising Cameron by not questioning and arguing.

"Ye trust me to make the correct choices?" Cameron asked, his chest tight.

"Aye, Brother. I have trusted ye to make the correct choices for a long time now," he said. "Ye were just blind to the fact."

"Aye," Cameron agreed. "I was." He cleared his throat. "I want to call Lachlan and Iain here and have a meeting with them, ye, Lena, Marsaili, Bridgette, Marion, and Isobel. I wish to get Sorcha to declare in front of yer priest that she intends to marry me in the future, but her statement must be gained in such a way that she dunnae realize she has given the first part of what is required for a man and wife to be married."

Graham's eyes widened. "And after she has shared her intent in front of my priest, what then?"

"Then," Cameron said slowly, "I will acquire the second part of what is required to make her my wife by the law of church and man. I will join our bodies." Though Sorcha simply would think he had finally given in to his desire. "I must defend her against all that may occur, and I fear the cunning of Hugo and his father. If there is a way to get the king's pardon, they will think of it, and if they gain it, Hugo will still want Sorcha as his wife to get her castle. I must prevent this."

Graham nodded. "Aye, I agree." He studied Cameron for a long moment. "In truth, 'tis a good thing ye wish to marry her."

"Aye," Cameron agreed. "It is."

※

They returned to the castle near dawn, and Cameron went straight to Sorcha's bedchamber. He didn't care what anyone might say. If things went according to the plan he had outlined for Graham not long ago, she would be his wife very soon. He knocked on her door, not wishing to simply barge in, and before he could take a breath, the door swung open. His chest tightened with relief at what her face revealed.

Her eyes brimmed with warmth and happiness. She closed the distance between them and threw herself into his arms, circling her own around his waist and laying her cheek against his chest. "I was scairt ye would nae come to me."

He kissed the top of her silky head while trailing his fingers along her bare arms. "From this day forward, I will always come to ye," he assured her.

She looked up at him. "Ye may nae always feel that way," she replied, guilt soaking her tone. She was too guileless in her heart to successfully hide the part of the truth she had attempted to keep from him, but he'd not point that out now.

He tipped her face farther up and, leaning down, brushed his lips to her soft ones. "I will always feel that way."

"What…what if," she hedged, and he tensed with hope that she would reveal something that would give him further proof of what he believed she hid and why, "I hid something from ye so ye would nae get hurt? What if I lied to ye? Would ye still care for me?"

The need to tell her that he loved her burned through him, but he held it back. He didn't fear that she would not want to hear it, he feared what further lengths she would go to with her efforts to protect him if she understood just what lengths he would go to in order to protect her. "I would still care for ye, Sorcha." He brushed the back of his hand over the delicate slope of her cheekbone, savoring the raw pleasure such a simple thing gave him.

A strong ache to pick her up, carry her to the bed, and love her overwhelmed him, but he could not give in to the temptation—not yet. He needed to uncover as much information as he could to guide his course of action to safeguard their future together. He took her hand and led her to a chair in the corner of her bedchamber. He sat down and pulled her into his lap. "Tell me of yer family."

She frowned. "I already told ye what my father did." She bit her lip. "I take it ye did nae find my attacker?" Her voice sounded as if it were strung as tight as a bow.

He shook his head, hating to lie but knowing the truth

may well push her to flee. He was extremely grateful that he no longer had such a lack of faith in himself that he could now understand that when someone tried to protect him, it did not mean they did not have faith in him. It meant they cared.

A knot formed in his throat. "Nay," he finally replied, watching her worried face relax, "we did nae capture yer attacker." He slipped his hand up her back to press her closer. "Tell me of yer sister?" he asked, beginning his probe.

She shook her head. "My father married Constance off to a man four times her age, despite her protest and dismay. I imagine he'd do the same to me if he got the chance."

Anger at her father simmered. "He'll nae get the opportunity."

"Nay, he'll not," she agreed, but something in her eyes, a sudden wariness, told him that she did not expect her marriage to be one of her choosing. Had she resigned herself, then, to the fate of the king's whim? Or did she think Cameron would not want her to be his wife once he learned she had hidden the truth from him? He squeezed her arm gently, offering silent comfort for that which he could not yet chance putting into words.

"Are ye close to yer sister?" he asked instead.

Sorcha nodded. "Aye. We still write. Or we did… She is verra unhappy, but I dunnae see what can be done now that she is wed."

"I have to agree," he replied, thinking of his own plan. "It is much harder to undo a marriage than to stop a marriage from ever happening. What of yer brother?"

She glanced down at her lap, twisting the material of her gown. "We were close once," she whispered. "He used to be so loving and kind. He looked after me and Constance. He was gentle, nae a warrior, and my father did nae let him forget it for a minute. Father twisted him so much I hardly could believe what he had become, the betrayal he was capable of. It breaks—er, *broke*—my heart," she continued, still looking down. "I was better than he was with daggers, at archery, and riding horses. He became jealous and bitter, and he developed a terrible cruel streak. Still, I have hope for him," she said vehemently. "He has seen the horrible error of his ways and fled to—" She abruptly stopped speaking. "He's fled away from Father and vowed to go somewhere safe to redeem himself."

He grasped her hand in his, moved by the sorrow and naive hope in her voice, and just as his fingers curled around her slender ones, a tear splashed against his hand. He had to clench his teeth against responding, for fear she'd quit speaking. He wanted to kill her brother, and he was almost certain that was one of the things she feared, one of the things that had driven her to help him and lie about it.

"The king," Cameron said carefully, "may believe yer brother was involved in the plot to kill Katherine. He may order yer brother to be hunted."

Her gaze flew to his, fear etched on her own. "Ye dunnae believe he would still demand yer life if ye dunnae bring him my brother, do ye? Surely, he will be happy with securing my father and the others who actually devised the plot, and Hugo who shot Katherine."

"I think he will be well pleased, and my life will be safe," he replied and watched as her shoulders sagged with visible relief. "But I believe he may order me to find yer brother." He left unsaid that he suspected greatly that her brother had not fled. He believed Finn had said what he needed to in order to get away, and that the man's true intention was to go to one of the men involved in the plot. Finn would warn them that Sorcha was alive and would likely reveal what they had done. He'd failed to kill her, so Finn probably hoped one of them would. Her brother would want to make the best deal he could to save himself and the castle he'd been willing to kill his own sister for. That sort of twisted heart was too far gone to change, and it hurt Cameron to his core that Sorcha's hopes would be crushed and her spirit take a blow when she learned her brother had betrayed her yet again.

There was a part of him that hoped he was wrong about Finn and that the man was innocent of involvement in the conspiracy. Yet he did not think Sorcha would have lied to him if that was the truth of the matter.

"Come," he said, his voice gruff. He tugged her by the hand to the bed.

Her eyes widened in surprise, and he pulled her to the bed and tugged her into the folds of his arms, tight against his chest, then murmured, "I want to hold ye as I sleep. I want to see ye when I wake. If I have but these two things every day for the rest of my life, I will be the most blessed of men."

She twisted back to look at him, wonder dancing in her eyes. "Cameron, I love ye. I do. I love ye with all my heart."

He could not hold the words back. He needed to for the sake of care until all was sorted, but they would not be contained. "I love ye, too, *m'eudail.*" He kissed her forehead. "Now." He pressed his lips to her nose. "Tomorrow." He brushed her lips across hers. "Always. Ye are mine."

"I want to be yers," she whispered with fierceness.

"So ye shall be," he promised and willed it to be so.

Eighteen

Two nights later, Cameron stood in Graham's solar in a circle with his brothers and their wives, his sisters, and Alex MacLean. Iain, Marion, Lachlan, Bridgette, and Marsaili had arrived from Dunvegan just moments before, under cover of night for their secret meeting. Bridgette and Marion had just entered the room after settling their children into bed.

"I asked ye all here for yer help," Cameron started, noting Iain's eyebrows shoot up and Lachlan twitch with surprise. Stepping toward the table in the middle of the circle, Cameron set the dagger on the table that he had found two nights before. "This dagger belongs to Finn Stewart, the Earl of Angus's son," he said to remind the others who Finn was.

"How did ye come to have this dagger, and how do ye ken it's his?" Lachlan asked, his confusion obvious in his voice.

"It has the Angus crest upon it and Finn's initials carved into it. I came to be in possession of it because Lena and Sorcha were attacked two days ago by a man who had this dagger."

Marion's brow knitted. "Why would the Earl of Angus's son come to this island to attack Lena and Sor—" Marion gasped. "Do you think he is one of the men who has been trying to kill Sorcha?"

Cameron nodded. "Aye. And he's her brother."

The shocked looks that swept through the group didn't bother him, not as much as the suddenly tense expression Iain wore. Likely, Iain already suspected that the Earl of Angus might be involved in the plot to take the throne from David.

"Did Sorcha's memory return?" Iain demanded.

"Aye," Cameron said, struggling and failing to keep the grimness from his voice.

A frown appeared on Iain's face, and Lachlan's eyes narrowed. Graham, who already knew all that Cameron was about to relay, gave him a look of encouragement. Just as Cameron was about to continue, Bridgette spoke.

"I dunnae comprehend why her brother would be trying to kill her," she said. Before Cameron could answer that question, she blurted another one, her face twisting into a frown. "And where is Sorcha? Why is she nae at this meeting? Why did ye demand we come under cover of night?"

"She's nae here," Cameron said, "because she dunnae ken that I found her brother's dagger." He quickly told them about his conversation with Sorcha, and how she had revealed that her father, the Earl of March, and the Earl of Ross were not only involved in the conspiracy to take the throne from David but they had been the ones to plot Katherine's murder. He also told them about how Sorcha's father had offered Hugo her hand in marriage, along with her brother's inheritance of Blair Castle, if Hugo killed Katherine.

"So ye believe, what?" Iain asked. "That her brother kenned she was still alive after they fled and that he wanted her dead so he'd nae lose his castle?"

"Aye." He told them what she had relayed to him of her brother—how he had once been kind and how their father's criticism and Finn's jealousy had twisted his heart. "I feel," he said, taking a deep breath, "that when Finn came for her himself this time, instead of sending others, she saw him and her memories returned. Kenning her and her quickness and skill with the bow, I've nary a doubt she managed to get the bow and put him at a disadvantage, but he must have convinced her that he was sorry and that he would flee."

"And ye suppose she let him go because of her love for him?" Bridgette asked softly.

Cameron nodded, tensing with the expectation that Bridgette would be the first to discredit his theory, but that was why he had called them all here. He staked much on what he *thought* had happened and what he should do based on what he *believed* would happen. It was a great risk, but one he was willing to take for Sorcha. Yet, he did not have the right to take the risk for his brothers and their wives. If they wanted to put distance between themselves and the situation, he would give them that chance.

"If I was faced with the knowledge that Alex had betrayed me, tried to kill me, even," Bridgette said slowly, "and I kenned the why of it and he vowed to flee, I'd do exactly as ye believe Sorcha did. I'd find it worse to offer up my own brother, who I had seen good in at one time, for certain death than to risk myself and lie by releasing him. Beyond that, she *did* tell ye of her father's part in the plot, and to me, it means much that she did. She must ken there is nae any hope of redemption for her father. I kinnae imagine how hard that must have been for her to accept and then tell ye of his wrongdoing."

"Neither can I," Cameron replied, relieved that Bridgette agreed with him. She was a keen woman and not one to be easily swayed.

Lena cleared her throat. "I believe ye have assessed the circumstances correctly, as well."

"As do I," Marion interjected, giving him a reassuring smile.

"I agree, also," Marsaili said with a definitive nod.

"Ye already ken I agree with what ye think happened, what ye foresee will occur, and the course of action *we* should take," Graham said. It was not lost on Cameron that his brother had stressed the word *we*, and his chest tightened in appreciation.

He glanced at Lachlan and Iain. Of everyone in the room, he expected the two of them to be the people who would disagree or show Cameron where his thinking involved too much hope and not enough logic.

"I dunnae like that she lied to ye," Iain began, making the knots in Cameron's shoulders grow tighter. "But," he said, glancing swiftly at Marion, then back to Cameron, "kenning women as well as I now do they will do all sorts of illogical things to defend the men who have won their affections."

"Aye," Lachlan agreed, his gaze resting fondly on his wife. "Now that we all agree with yer assessment of what has likely occurred up to this point, why don't ye tell us what ye think will happen next and what ye believe we should do?"

Cameron released a long breath and took a second to appreciate this moment of feeling close to all his brothers and sisters. "I asked myself what I would do if I were Finn," he began. "He kens she is going to reveal the plot against David and who killed Katherine, which will implicate him. So Finn will search out the best person to create an alliance with. As the Ross family is the strongest and Hugo has the most to lose by killing Katherine, I believe Finn will go to them."

"Agreed," Lachlan and Iain replied.

Lachlan scrubbed a hand across his face, looking contemplative for a moment. "If I were Finn, I'd go to Ross and Hugo and tell them Sorcha would betray them all."

"Aye," Iain said. "I was thinking the same thing. I'd try to strike a bargain with them, proposing that they all name the Earl of Angus as Katherine's killer. Someone has to pay with his life."

"That was my thought," Graham said. "In doing this, Finn dunnae need Sorcha's castle anymore because he could gain his father's land upon his death."

A grim silence fell upon the room, broken only when Iain cleared his throat and said, "The Earl of Ross is cunning, as is his son. They will think upon every possible outcome and set plans in motion for each to come out in his own favor. Even as they make it seem they have agreed to unite with Finn, so that they can ensure he will nae tell anyone of their part in Katherine's death, they'll likely send word to King David immediately without Finn's knowledge—"

"Begging forgiveness for their support of the petition and telling the king that they wish to withdraw their support of it," Cameron finished, having made the same assumption as Iain.

"Aye," came a chorus of agreements.

Lachlan made a derisive noise from deep in his throat. "Hugo will still want Blair Castle, though, so he will still wish to marry Sorcha. They will propose this to the king, likely even advise that Finn should be killed, as well as his father, for Katherine's death. The betrayal will be unknown to Finn until the last possible moment, in case something went wrong. Hugo and his father would nae wish to alienate a possible ally."

Cameron's hands curled into fists, hearing what he believed to be true affirmed by his brother. "Exactly. They'll believe the king will agree, simply to stop the petition, and if the king does agree, I must marry Sorcha now. If she is married to me, she kinnae be made wife of another."

"Aye," Iain said. "And I suppose ye are relying upon what they will nae ken so they will nae expect that we will have taken March's castle and gained his withdrawal from the petition already, therefore weakening the rebellion." He locked eyes with Cameron. "Ye will propose this to the king at the start, which will make him more likely to accept yer marriage to Sorcha. David is wise. He should see that ye—a man he can trust who fights against those who have shown themselves disloyal—marrying Sorcha is a greater benefit than agreeing to unite her with Hugo." Iain's gaze grew flinty, as it often did when he was plotting. "Ye are certain ye wish to marry Sorcha?"

"I'm certain," Cameron replied. "I'm also certain she'll nae agree to wed me because she wants to keep me safe from Eolande's prophecy."

"Damned seer," Lachlan growled to grunts of agreement.

Marion tilted her head, a cunning smile twisting her lips. "Then wed her without her kenning it."

Cameron grinned, relieved to hear that a woman he trusted had come up with the same idea he had. When it had first occurred to him two days ago, he'd had a moment of worry that she'd resent him for tricking her into getting married. But in the face of her life and their future being at risk, and armed with the certainty that she *did* want him for husband, he set the fear aside. "That's exactly what I intend to do."

Bridgette grinned. "It should be fairly easy to get her relent to the truth of wishing to marry ye in front of the priest."

"Aye," he agreed. "The difficult part will be for her to state an *intention* to do so in the future. Without that—"

"And without a joining," Iain interrupted, leering at his wife, "it will nae be a binding marriage."

"If ye all can help me with getting her to say the right words, I'll do the rest," he said with a wink.

Alex, who had been silent and only nodding his agreement up until this point, met Cameron's gaze. "If ye are wrong," he said, "ye will be bound for life to a woman who has betrayed ye."

Cameron exhaled slowly. "I will take that chance for Sorcha, though I dunnae believe I'm wrong. But I'll nae ask ye to take it with me. I intend to send Broch to the king tonight with what I ken, as well as with word that I have married Sorcha. I anticipate the king's first response will be anger—he dunnae like being thwarted—but he is wise, as ye say. And he will be less angered when he realizes my plan will gain him all he desires. He'll gain the withdrawal of the Earl of March and the Earl of Angus from the petition, but will still keep the Earl of Ross as somewhat of an ally, even if it's merely a deceit. The king will also have the deaths of two of the men who plotted to kill Katherine."

"Aye," Iain said, clapping Cameron on the shoulder. "Well done, Brother. Where shall we start?"

Cameron gave a tight smile. "First, I'll propose that the king continue to seem agreeable to the marriage of Sorcha to Hugo to keep the Earl of Ross happy. This gains me time and ensures the king dunnae lose an ally. And as I said, I believe Hugo, Finn, and the Earl of Ross will ask the king to allow them to formally come to him to beg his forgiveness for signing the petition."

Everyone nodded, and Iain gestured for him to continue. "I'm going to advise to the king that he go to them instead, under the guise of traveling to see his lands," Cameron said. "I'll also advise meeting them at the Falls of Friar, which is close to the Ross stronghold. The valleys and cliffs around the Falls will offer good cover for me, which I will need as the plot proceeds. If the king is nae to look like he has betrayed his word to the Earl of Ross, then I must appear to have gone against the king's command regarding Sorcha."

"Do ye intend to let Hugo actually take Sorcha?" Iain asked.

Cameron's chest squeezed at the thought, and he barely managed to get out a reply. "Aye," he said. He paused to clear his throat. "But only briefly. Only long enough for it to look like my desire for her drove me to rebel against the king. Yet David will know what I intend, and he will know I have already taken March's castle to aid his cause. I'll also have given him the names of the men responsible for Katherine's death and delivered Sorcha's father to him. And I will have done all of this while allowing him to gain the Earl of Ross back as an ally."

"This is verra dangerous, this game ye must play," Iain said.

"Aye," Cameron agreed.

"What next, Brother?" Lachlan asked.

Cameron swallowed, his throat growing dry from so much conversation. "Hugo will be forced to travel back to his castle from the Falls to wed Sorcha, so I will ken exactly where to wait to ambush him and take Sorcha back."

"And what about that bastard Hugo?" Bridgette spat.

"What will ye do with him?"

"Hugo will die in the ambush, thereby giving the king the death of the man who killed Katherine. The Earl of Ross will nae blame the king, either, because he will nae ken that the king knew I was going to kill his son." He took a deep breath. "Anyway, I get ahead of myself. After we take March's castle, I'll ride to the Falls with Sorcha to deliver her to the king, as he's commanded. Once there, I will protest her being given to Hugo, thus forcing the king to demand I leave."

"Ah, and then ye will have time to hide so you can ambush Hugo," Isobel said. Cameron smiled grimly, his emotions warring inside him. He was filled with comfort that his entire family was supporting him and offering their aid, yet he did not want to risk any of them, nor risk Sorcha.

"With Hugo dead, I dunnae doubt that the king will want Finn dealt with, as well," Iain said.

Cameron nodded. "I'm going to request he spare Finn's life and hand him over to me to punish in the king's stead." He inhaled a shuddering breath. "I dunnae ken that he will, however, and it weighs heavy on me. I dunnae want to hurt Sorcha more than she already has been."

Lachlan clasped Cameron's shoulder. "Brother, ye kinnae control everything. Yer plot is wise, and ye are doing all that ye can."

"I agree," Iain echoed.

"As do I," Graham added.

Cameron nodded, his throat tight with gratitude for his brothers and their counsel. He prayed that Finn's life would be spared for Sorcha's sake, though he was not certain Finn really deserved to be spared. He'd plotted to kill an innocent woman, stood by and allowed it to happen, and had actively tried to murder his own sister. If it were not for Sorcha's feelings, Cameron would likely kill the man himself.

He clenched his jaw on a fresh wave of anger at Finn. He inhaled a calming breath as he knew everyone was waiting for him to finish explaining. "I have asked Broch to make it seem as if he is betraying me when I protest the king's marriage of Sorcha and Hugo at the Falls. I will draw my sword, and Broch will stop me. The king will then have a believable reason to order Broch to accompany Hugo and Sorcha to his home. That way, Broch will be there to defend Sorcha for the short time I am not with her. I would nae be able to allow her to ride off with Hugo otherwise."

"It will also allow the king to appear as if he has upheld his agreement with the Earl of Ross so he does nae join the petition again and will reveal who else is behind the uprising," Graham added. "Verra clever."

Cameron merely nodded, suddenly overcome with worry. He would be deceiving Sorcha, and he despised that. And if anything should go wrong... He shook the thought away.

"Ye have my full support," Iain said.

Lachlan gripped Iain's and Cameron's forearms. "And mine. Divided we are weak, but together—"

Graham came closer, clasping their forearms, as well. "We are strong."

Cameron nodded and swallowed past the thick emotion that was clogging his throat. "Aye. Together we are strong," he repeated, thanking God that he truly understood that now.

Soon Lena, Marsaili, Bridgette, Marion, and Alex joined them in their huddle.

After they broke apart, Cameron said, "The one question I've nae come up with the proper answer to is when I should tell Sorcha that she is my wife."

He looked to Marion, Bridgette, Marsaili, and Lena for counsel. Marion sucked in her bottom lip, Bridgette cocked her head, Marsaili appeared utterly befuddled, and Lena quirked her mouth.

Finally, Marion released her lip and said, "When all is done."

"Aye," Bridgette agreed. "Otherwise, she may do something foolish to try to defend ye."

He nodded, though the thought of lying to her made his gut ache. "How long do ye believe it will take her to forgive me for lying to her?" he asked the women.

They all grinned, and Marion answered—and by the look shared among the four of them, Marion spoke for them all. "About as long as it took you to forgive her. Love is quite odd that way, Cameron."

He prayed they were right. "We will leave," he said, looking to Graham and Alex, "as soon as Broch returns from delivering my plan to the king. I'll need confirmation from Broch if the king has agreed to this plot."

"He will agree," Iain said in a confident tone. "He kens that to name ye an enemy would be to name the MacLeods an enemy, and he will nae do that. Ye have a good plan."

They all nodded their agreement, and Marion clapped her hands. "Now we must determine the best way to get Sorcha to confess her intent to marry you in front of the priest."

"That," Cameron said, "sounds like an excellent idea."

Everyone was acting so oddly tonight at supper, but then again, Sorcha thought the past several days had been strange. She was not about to voice her concern, however.

The longer Cameron chose to linger at his brother's home instead of heading for the Earl of March's castle, the more time she had with him. Each moment was precious, and not just because she feared the moments were numbered.

In the past few days, Cameron had spent a great deal of time with her, perfecting her ability to defend herself; showing her how to work with iron, wood, and other metals to make swords, daggers, even a shield; swimming with her; and talking with her about their childhoods. Each night, they danced in the great hall, and afterward took long walks in the moonlight. And at the end of every evening, he'd come to her bedchamber with her, worshipping her body in ways that took them both just to the edge of losing control, but not over, never over. She would fall asleep in the safety of his arms with him singing softly to her. He had one of the most beautiful voices she'd ever heard. She could have been utterly happy, except for her lie. It gnawed at her, and the need to tell Cameron pulsed within her. Yet she could not chance revealing the truth and putting him in a position to choose between her and the king.

Sorcha felt eyes upon her, so she looked up from the trencher she'd been staring down at to find Lena smiling at her. The smile looked suspiciously as if Lena knew a secret. Lena took a long drink from her goblet and set it down, giving Sorcha a hard look. To Sorcha's left, the young priest she had met earlier accidentally knocked over his goblet of wine.

"I beg yer pardon, my lady," Father Blackstone said, his cheeks turning red.

Cameron had told her the man was rather new to his brother's castle and had earned a reputation as somewhat of a clumsy man. Sorcha quickly helped him clean up the mess, and when she was done, Father Blackstone thanked her profusely. He leaned close to her, a twinkle in his light-brown eyes. "My predecessor told me the best way to gain the confidence of yer flock is to show them ye are human. How am I doing?"

Sorcha felt her eyes widen. "Ye mean ye're doing these things—" she motioned to the table where the wine had been spilled "—on purpose?"

"Aye," he replied, a look of guilt flashing across his face. "I've been here since winter and nae a soul has come to confess to me. The last couple that got married even sent word to the old priest and had him journey here to perform the ceremony. It seems my age makes people believe I'm nae ready to lead them."

He gave her an expectant look, as if she had a reply that would make him feel better. She cleared her throat and said, "I have faith in ye."

"Do ye?"

She nodded.

He grinned. "Ye may be the only one." He turned and glanced at Cameron, who sat on the other side of him. Cameron took no note, as he was engaged in conversation with Isobel, but Isobel smiled sweetly at the priest and then gave Sorcha a look. It seemed a strange mixture of happiness and secretiveness, almost like Lena's had been.

Sorcha frowned, but when the priest patted her on the hand, she focused on him once more. He leaned in again, as if he had something private to say. "Do ye intend to marry Cameron if he asks ye?"

His question shocked her, but she assumed he was asking because he wanted her to say he could perform the ceremony. "I'd like to," she whispered.

Suddenly, she felt someone hovering over her, and when she glanced up, Cameron stood there, looking down at her, an expression of utter possession gleaming in his eyes. Had he heard what she'd said? Embarrassment had her stuttering for words. "I...I did nae mean—"

"Do ye intend to marry this woman?" Father Blackstone asked Cameron.

"Aye," Cameron replied. Her heart fluttered in both happiness and wariness.

"Excellent," the priest replied, suddenly standing and moving from the bench. "When ye are in need of me to perform the official ceremony, I'll be here."

As the priest left, Cameron held out his hand to her. She took it, suddenly aware that everyone sitting on the dais was staring at them. She skimmed her gaze over Lena, Alex, Isobel, Graham, and Isobel's grandmother. What must they think after hearing her say she'd like to marry Cameron? Did they think a marriage would soon occur? Did Lena worry that Sorcha had forgotten the prophecy?

"If ye'll excuse us," Cameron said, cutting into the whirling noise of worry in her head.

Once they had quit the great hall and were walking toward her bedchamber, she paused and turned to Cameron. "Please dunnae feel ye must ask me to marry ye this day," she murmured, her embarrassment so acute that her entire body felt singed. She tensed, prepared for Graham to argue.

"Dunnae fash yerself," he said, a smile hovering at the corners of his mouth, as if he found her embarrassment—the whole situation, really—amusing. "I dunnae feel that way in the least. I ken how ye feel about marrying me. Everything happens when it is time," he added, his tone almost...what was it? Resigned? Had he resigned himself to the fact that she had thus far refused his marriage proposal? Would he not ask again? But no, he'd said he would. Yet, her stomach turned with sudden worry that he might give up so easily on her. She was being unreasonable. That's what she was—utterly unreasonable. She could not demand blind devotion when she was not giving it.

Biting her lip so she'd not voice the absurd thoughts in her head, she followed him into her bedchamber, half expecting him to decide not to sleep with her tonight. He closed the door as he ushered her in, and she found herself suddenly agitated and unsure what to say or do. She turned from him, toward the window, and strolled to it, feigning interest in the stars so he'd not see the emotions on her face.

She felt his presence before he touched her. When he moved, the air crackled with his power and intensity. His warm hands came to rest gently on her shoulders, and the heat of his body enveloped her. Unable to resist the pull of her body to his, she pressed her back against what felt like iron but she knew was his body, carved of almost pure muscle.

"I've nae ever seen a more beautiful sight," he whispered, his breath fanning her neck and making her shiver.

"Aye, the sky is lovely tonight," she replied, staring in wonder at the bright-white stars dotting the dark sky and feeling somewhat calmed by his touch.

"Nae the sky, *mo ghraidh*," he said, his voice a balm to her worries.

His love.

She committed to memory how the endearment sounded coming from his lips. Whether they were married in this life or not, she would always know he had loved her and remember this moment.

She turned suddenly in his arms, slid her hands up his chest and around his neck, and pressed her chest to his, her pelvis to the proof of his hard desire for her. "Cameron, I want ye," she said simply, infusing the four words with a silent, desperate plea. When he didn't immediately remind her that he'd not join with her until they were married, she pushed forward. "All of ye. I want to ken ye as I nae ever have." As she might never get the chance to again...

The tenderness that filled his burning gaze as he brushed his hand over her cheek made her stomach clench in hopeful anticipation. The hand that had touched her skin slid to cradle the nape of her neck, and suddenly, he pulled her to him and slanted his mouth over hers in a kiss that began gentle but quickly became demanding. She came to her tiptoes, desperate to meet his need and fulfill her own. Her heart pounded, and her hands shook as she moved them back over his chest to tug at his clothes.

She felt the rough slide of his own hands as his fingers hooked under the shoulders of her gown, and he divested her of it and her léine before she had managed to rid him of his clothing. She gasped when the cool bedchamber air hit her bare skin.

Cameron pulled away, his gaze now filled with unbridled yearning. "Ye'll nae be cold long," he assured her, the silken promise in his voice making her belly tighten.

Kicking out of his plaid, he swept her into his arms as his mouth captured hers once again. The greedy kiss sent her senses reeling, so that when the soft bed came under her back she blinked in surprise that he had laid her down and she'd not even realized it. His lips left hers to trace a burning path to her full, aching breast. Without hesitation, he sucked her nipple into his mouth in a long, luxurious pull that forced a ragged moan from her as she arched her back toward him. His tongue flicked deliciously over her hard bud, teasing her and tormenting her.

She dug her nails hard into his back in a silent demand

for more. He broke the contact with her breast only to move to the other and give it the same treatment, except this time, he gently swirled his tongue around the bud before taking her breast into his mouth. When he finally suckled her, her insides quivered with sweet need. "Cameron, please," she begged, not caring at all what she sounded like.

His answer was to swiftly come between her thighs, delve his hands under her bottom, and slide his tongue up the center of what made her a woman. "Cameron!" she sobbed in pleasure and pain. His tongue lavished her with wicked strokes that made her pulse race ever faster and her blood roar. She clenched her hands against the bed, then his shoulders as she thrashed her head back and forth. She was going to die of wanting him. "I kinnae take any more!" she pleaded, and that's when his tongue touched a spot she'd not known existed.

Pure pleasure spiked through her as he sucked that pulsing spot into his warm mouth, but she needed something more. Her impatience was becoming explosive. His hands came to either side of her thighs, which he spread wider, and when his fingers came to the spot he'd revealed to her and rubbed in a frenzied circle, hot liquid poured through her, and she shattered into a million glowing stars to match the ones in the sky.

Suddenly, he released her, and she opened her eyes to find him above her, strain and wanting warring on his beautiful face. "Now ye're ready," he said huskily.

"There's more?" she teased, though she did wonder how she could possibly take any more. She felt utterly spent.

But in the slide of his hand between her breasts, then around one bud and then the other, her pulse, which had just begun to abate, sped up again, and deep in her core, desire sprang to life once more. "Show me," she invited, sensing he was waiting for her to give him a sign that she was ready. "Show me this *more*," she purred.

"I'll show ye, my *bean bhàsail*. Over and over again, I'll show ye until neither of us can speak or move."

※ ※ ※

She grinned up at him, the picture of an unrepentant temptress, and his heart squeezed so hard that he had to clench his teeth against the wave of love he felt for her. In moments, their union, which had begun with the priest securing each of their intents to marry the other in the future, would be complete when they joined their bodies. The knowledge made him tremble with gratitude and awe.

He ran his hands over the silken skin of her flat stomach to her round, proud breasts. He trailed a path down her shapely legs and back up over her lush, womanly hips only to move his hands back to her inner thighs, where he spread her a little wider to prepare her for him.

She watched him with the slanted eyes of a cat who was lounging in the sun and appeared the picture of contentment. He parted her at her core and slid his fingers slowly down her center. She was ready for him. "It will hurt—"

She pressed a finger against his lips. "I ken. I've seen horses breed, ye ken."

He chuckled at that. "'Tis nae like horses breeding."

She smirked at him. "Well, I ken that, but if it hurts for a giant mare when a stallion enters her, then I presumed it would be the same for a man and a woman."

"I'm nae quite as big as a stallion," he teased. He pressed his mouth to hers as his fingers found the spot that he knew would make her more than ready.

He watched the need for him grow on her face and through her body as she began to thrash, then buck, and finally claw at him. His own need was a wild storm within him that he kept contained as long as he could, wanting her to experience as much pleasure as possible. When his body prevailed over his will, he touched the tip of his staff to her entrance and shuddered with desire. There was no hope to prevent the moment of pain for her, so he quickly thrust into her and stilled, clenching his teeth against the battering need to move. But she was hot and tight and ready based on her sudden glare and demand that he move *now*.

He pulled out slowly and slid back in, memorizing the way he felt inside her, his *bean bhàsail*. Being with her was unlike anything he'd ever known. It was more, so much more, and the ache that filled him was one of happiness and love. He released the hold he had over himself as he knew he never had, as he'd never been able to. With her, he did not feel the need to protect himself. He began to move faster, the age-old rhythm of mating taking over. The pressure inside him grew until it was a living thing that would not be contained. Yet he waited, sweat slicking his skin and his muscles burning. The moment her back arched, she threw her head back, and her core pulsed around him, washing hot liquid over his rigid staff, he released his last restraints on himself and filled her with his seed, making her his forever.

Nineteen

Sorcha much preferred to wake as she had this morning at Brigid Castle—in Cameron's arms after he had joined with her in a soft bed—as opposed to being jarred awake on the back of a horse. She instantly felt the protective, warm embrace of Cameron's arm's encircling her waist, though, and she smiled. As the bleariness of sleep cleared from her eyes and her thoughts sharpened, the Earl of March's castle became visible in the moonlight. Suddenly, dread seized her. She knew the plan to attack the earl's castle and force him to take his name off the petition against the king, but that did not stop fear from blossoming in her belly.

The massive castle sat atop a hill and seemed to be made up of several adjacent stone structures, as well as one structure that was set apart from the others. She attempted to breathe in a deep, calming breath, but she furrowed her brow at the brackish air that filled her nose. Cameron brought his destrier to a halt, and behind them, she could hear a collective *whoosh* as the army of men who had come with Cameron to seize the castle halted, as well.

A shiver coursed through her, and her thoughts swirled in her mind. Would they have to swim through water to reach the castle? She could swim well enough, but something about swimming at night had always given her a fright. "Cameron, is the castle surrounded by water?" she asked.

"Nay, the harbor is on but two sides."

She sighed. "Oh, good. Night swimming is nae my favorite. I'm nae scairt, mind ye," she fibbed, not wanting him to perceive her as weak.

"Dunnae fash yerself, Sorcha. Neither ye or Lena will be coming with us to attack the castle," he replied matter-of-factly.

Before she could protest, he gripped her around the waist and set her on the ground. Around her, men and Lena dismounted and a flurry of activity began. Broch started to tug her away from Cameron, who was only just getting down from his horse, but she twisted free and stepped toward Cameron, placing her hand on his arm to gain his attention, as he was turned to speak to Graham.

Cameron looked to her at once, his eyebrows quirked up with annoyance. His face softened immediately as his eyes locked with hers. "Broch will make ye and Lena a bed, and I'll say farewell before we depart to attack the castle."

"I'm coming with ye," she said, letting him hear the resolve in her voice.

"Nay." The reply was but a word, yet it had the ring of finality.

Her temper flared. "I'll nae slow ye down. I'm faster than most of yer men on horseback, I'd venture to say."

"I'm inclined to agree with ye, *bean bhàsail*—"

"Ye're trying to sway me to do as ye wish," she accused.

He gave her a wicked grin, which she could just make out in the moonlight. "Always." The word danced with merriment.

"How can ye be so lighthearted when ye're about to go into battle?" she asked, exasperated.

He cupped her face and pressed his lips to hers before pulling away. "Because I've nary a doubt that we will triumph. It should nae take overly long to take the castle. Ye sleep, and I vow I'll return before light even breaks the night sky."

"Nay," she growled. "I will ride with ye."

"We are nae riding in, Sorcha. We'll climb the rock and take the castle by stealth."

Around them, the men had moved away, and she could see most of them tethering their horses and preparing their weapons. Her heart quickened with real fear of being left behind. Her gut tightened with worry as she recalled Eolande foretelling that if they parted, they'd not be reunited. If only Sorcha knew the rest of Eolande's sentence! She did not want to part with Cameron in a time of strife. She did not wish to part with him ever, but to do so now made her heart beat furiously and her palms sweat.

"Eolande said if we part, we will nae be reunited." She didn't bother to tell him that the seer's foretelling had been interrupted. She wanted him to relent and allow her to accompany him.

"Eolande is wrong," he said in a hard voice. "We will always be reunited, Sorcha." He tugged her to him and folded her in his arms. "Even if I had to spend the rest of my life searching for ye, I would find ye. Ye are my air, my food, the shelter for my soul."

"And ye are the same for me," she murmured into his chest, giving him a squeeze. "Which is why I must accompany ye. I kinnae bear the thought of ye going into battle and me staying behind."

He pulled back and stared at her. "Listen to me," he said, his voice gentle. "If ye accompany me, I will nae be as focused as I need to be. Do ye ken what I'm saying?"

"Ye're saying I'm a weakness for ye," she mumbled, feeling miserable because she understood but did not want to.

"Aye." He kissed her soundly. "In the best sort of way. Ye are a weakness because yer life means more to me that winning the battle, but ye are also my greatest strength. I will win the battle kenning it will allow us to spend our lives together."

"I'll stay," she agreed quietly, her gut wrenching at the thought of the upcoming separation.

"And I'll return," he vowed.

"Before daybreak?" she asked hopefully.

"Aye," he said. "Before daybreak."

"Ye two need to sleep," Broch said. He sat on a rock a few feet away from where he and the other four men left to guard Sorcha and Lena had made beds for the two women.

"I kinnae," Sorcha replied as she paced, Lena by her side.

"Nor I," Lena agreed.

"'Tis almost day," Broch continued. "Ye'll be very weary tomorrow, and I feel certain Cameron will ride us on toward the Earl of Ross's home, which means fitful sleep on the horses at best."

Almost day. Sorcha stared off toward the castle. Where was he? He'd promised to return before the sun broke the sky, and the sky was now lightening with the dawn. Eolande's prophecy grew to a deafening roar in Sorcha's ears. She swung around and marched toward the nearest horse. "I'm going to the castle," she blurted as she started to untie the black destrier.

"Nay! Cameron will kill me if I let ye put yerself in harm's way," Broch said. "Look!"

Triumph filled his voice, and she swiveled around to see what he meant. Her heart leaped with joy and filled with relief, as on the horizon, a large group of men approached. As they came closer, Cameron's tall, powerful build and light hair made it easy to identify him. She did not hesitate. Racing forward, she quickly closed the distance between them and flung herself into his arms.

"Are ye hurt?" she asked breathlessly, pulling back to run her hands over his chest and sweeping her gaze over his legs, arms, trunk, and face.

He pulled her against his side and slid his arm around her waist. "I'm nae harmed, and we've gained the castle." Cameron released her and tugged out a piece of foolscap. "March has withdrawn his support of the petition and pledged his undying fealty to the king." At those words, Cameron and Graham both paused to spit at the ground, as she had noticed they always did when speaking of disloyal men.

"He's nae trustworthy," Cameron explained, "but he's fearful, and he wishes to keep his castle."

Lena had walked up as Cameron was talking and now touched her brother on the arm. "Where is Alex?" she asked. Sorcha saw the unbridled worry on her face.

"He's staying here with his men and some of ours. He'll hold the castle in the king's name until David gives word to return it."

Lena bit her lip. "Was he unharmed, as well?"

"Aye," Cameron said.

Lena's shoulders visibly relaxed, and while Cameron had already turned his attention to speaking with Graham, Sorcha studied Lena for a moment. The woman evidently cared a great deal for Alex, but it seemed she did not want anyone, including Alex, to know. Or it could be that she didn't want to care but could not seem to help it.

"We have to ride out now," Cameron announced, squeezing Sorcha close and scrutinizing her. "Did ye sleep?" he asked, concern lacing his tone.

"Nay," Broch replied, answering for her.

She glared at Broch. She had not intended to tell Cameron that she had been awake all night because she knew he'd worry. At the concern that swept across Cameron's face, she held up her palm to cease him from speaking. "Dunnae even try to leave me here and ride off. I vow I'll follow ye."

She saw the beginning of a smile tug at his lips, which he quickly mastered. He gave a curt nod before leaning toward her and whispering, "Ye need to be tamed."

His words held a seductive, teasing promise that made her belly clench with longing. "What is next?" she asked, greatly relieved he would not argue against her accompanying him.

He darted his gaze away for a moment, then settled it on her. A strange look flickered in his eyes, almost as if something was bothering him. Was he worried about what was to come? She gripped his hand tightly to offer silent support, to which he gave her a strained smile. "I go simply to do as the king bids," he replied, his words stilted, as if saying them was somehow almost uncomfortable to him.

He was acting odd, indeed, but she suspected it was because he did not want her to be concerned. She stood on her tiptoes and pressed her lips to his ear. "I have faith in ye."

"I hope so," he replied, a grim look skittering across his face.

Cameron was unaccustomed to lying. It did not sit well with him, even though he knew it was to protect Sorcha and to ensure they would have the future together that they wanted. He reminded himself of this again and again during the long, grueling ride to the Falls.

What should have taken three days had been done in one so that they would arrive in time to meet with the king. Sorcha was sleeping the sleep of the dead as they rode through the thickening woods toward the Falls. Up ahead, he saw the king's banner fluttering in the wind. Cameron's heart pounded for what was likely to come and the idea of parting with her, even if only temporarily.

He paused and glanced to his left to meet his brother's gaze. "Are ye ready?" Graham asked.

Cameron nodded, keenly aware of the soft, warm woman sleeping so trustingly in his arms. His wife, and she did not yet even know it. He loved her so much it was a physical ache. He looked to Broch. "Are ye ready for what ye must do?"

Broch gave an easy nod. "I'm always ready to die for ye, Cameron. Feigning to betray ye will be an easy task," he said, clearly trying to lessen the tension. "I'll simply recall the times ye angered me." He grinned, and then his face got very serious. "I will guard Sorcha with my life. I vow no harm will come to her while breath is in my body."

Cameron nodded, for his throat was too tight with emotion to speak. Signaling his men forward, they entered the pathway of trees and continued until they were almost upon the group, which Cameron could now see contained the king, Hugo, Finn, and the Earl of Ross. Sorcha's father was notably absent.

Slowing his horse to a near stop once more, Cameron gently woke her. After a minute, she sat up straight, and seconds later, her body stiffened in his arms. "God's teeth," she muttered, and he was certain she had seen her brother. "That's Finn," she whispered, her tone full of torment. "Cameron—" she turned toward him, fear blanketing her lovely face "—I must tell ye something."

The urgency in her tone shook his resolve. "Later," he said, knowing she likely wanted to confess that she had lied to him. "Ye can tell me later. Now, ye must trust me."

"But Cameron, ye dunnae understand—"

"Cameron and Graham!" the king bellowed, the timing near perfect to what Cameron had imagined in his mind when he had thought this day through. "Bring the lass forward with ye now." Even though it was all as Cameron had planned, he found himself suddenly loath to do as the king bid.

"It is but temporary," Graham reminded him in a reassuring tone.

Aye. Temporary.

He signaled to his horse and moved them directly in front of the king. Once there, he quickly dismounted, helped Sorcha down, and they both paid their proper respects to the king while waiting silently for his brother and Broch to do so. Behind him, the collective tension of his men pressed against his back like a wave of heat. All they knew was that no matter what came to pass, they were not to take action without his orders.

Beside him, Sorcha's tense face was twisted with pain as she stared at her brother, whose dispassionate face made Cameron want to rip out the man's black heart.

"Sorcha Stewart, come forward," King David commanded.

It took Cameron a moment to force his fingers to uncurl from hers. He watched her walk forward, head held high, back straight, and her shoulders thrust back. He'd never been so proud in his life, nor so grateful that she was his. She was his wife by God's law, which the king knew.

The king pressed his lips into a thin white line before he finally spoke. "I'm verra pained to hear that yer father betrayed me so grievously," the king spat.

Inside, Cameron winced for Sorcha as her eyes widened and fastened accusingly on her brother. She had no idea of the plan, and he could well imagine her fear of what was happening. "Yer Grace, my father was nae the only one to betray ye. My brother and—"

The king held up a silencing hand. "I ken my betrayers well, Sorcha. In time, all will get what they deserve, even if at first they seem to escape justice."

"My lord," Sorcha's brother whined. "I did nae betray ye, I vow it. She simply wants my castle."

Sorcha gasped. "Nay!"

"Finn Stewart," the king said in a voice so cold it felt as if an icy wind blasted Cameron, "ye've been named traitor to me and murderer of Katherine Mortimer—"

"I did nae kill Lady Mortimer!" Finn shouted. "Sorcha! Sorcha, Sister, tell the king that I did nae kill Lady Mortimer. I beg ye."

Cameron trained his gaze on Hugo, who was barely controlling the gleeful smile on his face. Cameron would kill the arrogant man this day. He'd kill him for murdering Katherine and betraying the king, but more so, he would kill the man because he intended to make Sorcha his wife to gain the castle that was now hers. Her father, no doubt, would soon die in prison, the Earl of Ross and his son obviously having done exactly as Cameron had suspected.

They'd taken their names from the petition, pledged renewed fealty to the king, and given the names of Sorcha's father and brother as the murderers. And in exchange, they expected Hugo to marry Sorcha and inherit Blair Castle.

"Hugo shot Lady Mortimer," Sorcha said quietly, "but my brother and father did willingly aid Hugo and the Earl of Ross. They plotted against ye, Sire."

"Hush, lass," the king ordered. "It is honorable of ye to try to defend yer brother and father, but dunnae do so with lies."

Sorcha's eyes widened. "But, Yer Grace!"

"Sorcha Stewart," the king declared, and Cameron braced himself for what he knew was coming, "I hereby transfer yer care over to Hugo and give my consent for him to wed ye."

"Nay!" Cameron thundered, the words bursting from his chest. The situation felt so real that his stomach turned.

As Hugo's men moved to seize Sorcha, Cameron withdrew his sword, and Broch stepped in front of him with his own sword drawn. "Ye dare to defy yer king?" Broch roared.

To his left, Sorcha was crying, and when he glanced her way and saw that Hugo now grasped one of her arms with a look of possession on his face, Cameron forgot for a moment that things were occurring as he himself had planned. He lunged toward Hugo, only to find the point of Broch's sword digging into his chest.

"Shall I kill him, Sire?" Broch asked.

For one breath, the king looked as if he were actually contemplating it.

"Yer Grace," Graham said calmly, "I'm sure ye dunnae wish to do such a thing." He had withdrawn his own sword, and suddenly the swish of hundreds of swords being drawn behind him filled the tense silence. His brother's support and fealty humbled Cameron.

"Of course nae," the king finally answered. "We've all lost reason over a woman before. Take yer brother and ride home. Ye," the king said, motioning to Broch, "go with the lass and ensure she is treated well."

"Yer Grace," Hugo protested, but he fell silent at the king's quelling look.

Graham tugged on Cameron's arm to get him to move. He knew he was supposed to go; he'd devised it all exactly this way. Depart. Hide. Wait for Hugo to ride past with Sorcha on the way to his home. Then Cameron would take her back. Yet, he could not leave. He had something else to do for Sorcha. "Sire, I request ye give the discipline of Finn Stewart over to me."

"Nay," the king said in a tone that brooked no argument and rang with the finality of all his rage against those who had killed Katherine or stood by and let it happen. Cameron wanted to argue for Sorcha, but to do so would be folly and possibly destroy his carefully laid-out plan.

"Away, now!" Sorcha sobbed at him. "Away before ye get yerself killed! I'm yers," she continued, her sobs racking her body. "I will always be yers."

Graham had to drag Cameron away, and when he got to his horse, he stood there until Graham hissed, "Mount the damned beast and let us away. Ye have planned this, and I ken it's gutting ye, but it is going exactly as ye said it would. Dunnae lose faith in yerself now, Brother."

Cameron nodded grimly, mounted his destrier, and rode away. He didn't look back. He feared if he did, he'd change his mind and ruin everything.

Twenty

Sorcha's entire body was wrapped in weariness and despair. Sitting on a horse behind Hugo and beside Broch, waiting helplessly for them to depart, she tried to think of something she could do, yet she could not seem to rip her focus from what had just occurred. She stared off in the direction Cameron had disappeared, both relieved that he'd left and was not killed, and shocked that he had actually departed. He was gone.

Betrayal and abandonment enveloped her, yet she shoved back at the emotions. She'd told him to go, wanted him to do so. If he'd stayed and fought for her, he would have lost his life. The thought of a life hanging in the balance brought Finn to mind. What could she do to aid him? She glanced behind her to where he was being held, and as she did, his scream ripped through the air. A scream tore from her own lungs as her brother grabbed a sword from the hands of the startled warrior to his right. The warrior to Finn's left, one of Hugo's men, responded lightning-quick, plunging his sword into Finn's heart. Sorcha watched in mute disbelief as Finn crumpled to the ground.

She started to slide off the horse to go to him, but Broch jerked her back on. "Ye kinnae help yer brother now."

Blood poured from Finn's wound onto the ground, and she knew it to be the truth. Her heart wrenched, and she turned to Broch for comfort, only to remember he had betrayed Cameron by drawing his sword against him. She knew in her head that Broch likely felt he had to first be true to the king, but her heart hated Broch at this moment. "I despise ye," she hissed.

"Good," he growled. "I'd be disappointed if ye did nae."

She frowned at the statement, but there was no time to contemplate it, as Hugo had ordered them to depart. It seemed as if they rode forever, with nothing more than the clopping of horses to break the silence. They departed the woods and turned toward twin cliffs. She recognized them; they were near her home. It made her think of her father.

"What will happen to my father?" she demanded of Hugo.

The man stopped his horse and turned to her. "He is dead, Sorcha."

She flinched at the news, and despite everything her father had done, sadness weighed on her heavily.

"We feared he would try to plot further against our beloved king, so we were forced to kill him," Hugo finished.

"Ye're a hideous beast," she spat.

He offered a twisted smile. "That's what yer uncle said when I told him what I had planned for ye. He vowed to hunt me down, but the poor devil dunnae have a very astute mind. I simply led him into the cellar and locked him in. I suspect he'll be getting quite hungry and thirsty verra soon. Now, if ye are an obedient lass and marry me quickly and without trouble, I'll save him for ye. I ken he is special to ye."

She gritted her teeth. "I'll nae marry ye until I see ye release my uncle and give him time to get away from ye."

"I could beat ye till ye submit," Hugo threatened.

Sorcha saw Broch stiffen beside her. She supposed it

was something, at least, that he disliked Hugo's threatening to hurt her, though Broch's response did not make her forgive him for betraying Cameron.

"I'd prefer death than marriage to ye," she said sweetly, "so if ye wish to beat me to try to get me to do as ye bid, ye best be ready to end my life. Will the king still grant ye Blair Castle, do ye ken?"

She saw the doubt her words caused flicker across Hugo's face.

"Damn ye!" he bit out. He jerked his horse off the path toward the right. "We ride to the Stewarts' home!" he yelled back to his men.

"Dunnae fash yerself with defending me, Broch," she muttered. The man looked even more worried now than he had a moment ago when Hugo had threatened to beat her. "I can defend myself."

Riding into the eerily quiet courtyard of the home in which she had grown up, memories flooded Sorcha's head. In her mind's eye, she saw herself racing her brother and sister across the courtyard. They all collapsed in a laughing heap of arms and legs. She recalled long walks near dark with her mother, revealing her hopes, dreams, and fears. Her chest tightened with the memory of waiting in the courtyard with her mother for Finn to return from the first battle to which Father had sent him. Finn had come home, defeated and shamed.

These were but a few of her memories, and though they were both good and bad, she had to blink back the tears at her happiness to have them returned. In the end, they made her who she was and had brought her to

Cameron, who had given her, if but for the briefest time, extraordinary love.

She glanced around her abandoned home. No doubt the servants had fled in fear, and she imagined her father's men had been dispersed to other lords' commands. When Hugo started shouting orders at his men, her attention was brought harshly back to the moment and the very real need to save her uncle. Hugo yanked his destrier to a halt and dismounted, and before she had time to think of a plan, he jerked her from her destrier and set her hard upon her feet, fairly dragging her toward the very cellar in which he had told her they had locked Brom.

Her uncle's animal cries hit her halfway across the courtyard, and rage surged. She tried to twist out of Hugo's hold to race to the cellar, but his grip became so tight that she hissed in pain.

Broch, who had fallen into step beside her, narrowed his eyes on Hugo. "The lady is stubborn," Broch said, his voice vibrating with what sounded to Sorcha like barely controlled anger. "If ye treat her thusly, she may refuse to marry ye, the king's edict be damned."

Hugo bared his teeth at her and Broch. "Do ye intend to stop me, as the king commanded ye to see she is treated well?"

"Nay," Broch said, though he did sound reluctant to Sorcha.

Hugo grunted his amusement. "Excellent. I imagine she will relent if I beat her long enough, or perchance I'll beat her uncle."

Sorcha flinched at Hugo's threat. No matter what, she somehow had to get Brom away. So loud were Brom's cries that Sorcha had to curl her hands into fists in an effort not to pummel Hugo for what he had done. However, she feared a show of her anger toward him would worsen his treatment of Brom. When the cellar door was finally opened, Brom came barreling out, bellowing and swinging his fists in front of him, his face twisted in rage. For one breath, Sorcha wondered if he could escape, and she considered not calling his name—he was too wrought with emotion to have noticed her otherwise—but when Hugo raised his sword as if to strike Brom, she feared what Hugo would do.

"Brom!" she called. The swinging of his fists slowed a bit, but as Hugo's men started to encircle him, he became frenzied once more. "Brom!" she yelled again and broke out of Hugo's hold. When he reached for her as if to stop her, Broch gripped Hugo by the forearm.

"Let her try to calm the man, so that yer own men are nae injured," Broch said.

Hugo jerked his head in a nod, and that small relenting gave her hope. "Call yer men back, please," she begged, as an idea finally came to her.

"Fall back," Hugo barked.

The moment they did, she moved slowly toward Brom, who was still swinging his arms. His eyes held a wild look, darting to and fro, but she called to him over and over until his gaze came slowly to her and recognition dawned in his eyes. Some of the fear ebbed, and a genuine smile lit his face. "Brom's Sorcha," he said in a voice filled with happiness. He held out his arms, and she went to her uncle and gave him a hug, pressing her lips to his ear.

"Let's play a game," she said to him, her voice a threadbare whisper. She could not tell him the truth; he'd never run if he thought she was in danger. The only way she could possibly save him was to lie to him.

He nodded, and she took his hand in hers and led him,

under Hugo's watchful gaze, some feet away to take a seat on a log. Brom was big but fast, and he knew these woods well. If she could give him a lead, even if only a breath of one, maybe he could escape. It was his only chance.

She patted Brom on his big hand. "You hide, and I'll come find ye. Just like I used to," she whispered, recalling the time it had taken her an entire day to find him.

She'd feared what would happen if she could not find him because she realized he was not going to come out from where he had hidden. He would wait, with his childlike trust, for her to come to him.

Brom nodded enthusiastically. "I hide," he whispered back.

"Aye, Brom. Ye hide. And dunnae come out until I find ye." Her gut twisted with the knowledge that the time may not come.

She stood with him, pushed him in front of her so that she would at least be partially blocking him should Hugo order his men to shoot, and moved him toward the woods, ignoring Hugo's calls for her not to venture so far. She shoved Brom with more urgency, and when footsteps pounded behind her, she whispered, "Away with ye! Hide with the speed of an eagle."

Brom laughed and dashed off into the thick woods. When one of Hugo's men started past her in pursuit, she stuck out her foot and smiled with grim satisfaction as he fell to his knees. Suddenly, she was yanked around, and Hugo loomed over her, glaring at her menacingly.

"That was verra foolish," he hissed as men streamed past them to go after Brom.

Hugo gave her a hard tug and started dragging her toward the castle. "And what do ye intend to do, Hugo?" she demanded, allowing her rage to pour out of her. She gave a derisive laugh. "Ye kinnae marry me. My home is abandoned. There is nae a priest," she said triumphantly.

Hugo stopped midstride and gripped her chin. "I left the priest, my sweet." He grinned evilly before jerking her behind him and continuing toward the castle. Except, when he passed the castle entry, she realized that he was headed to the chapel.

She dug in her heels, but it was pointless. Before she knew it, she was inside the chapel and standing in front of Father Grayson, the half-blind, half-deaf, sometimes-moral priest of her childhood home. Hugo held out a coin purse to Father Grayson, and the horrendous traitor took it without even glancing her way.

Broch came to her side, and when she looked at him, she saw that lines of tension creased his forehead and his brows were dipped together in a scowl. As the priest began the ceremony and Hugo said his vows, Sorcha found herself watching Broch and not the priest. The man seemed agitated, shifting from foot to foot, and she could tell he was clenching his teeth by the pulse that appeared at his jawline every few breaths.

"Say yer vows," Hugo demanded, snapping her attention to him.

"Nay," she replied calmly, conjuring up a picture of Cameron in her mind to give her strength. "As I told ye, I'd rather be dead than married to ye."

Rage swept over Hugo's face, and he whipped toward her and pulled his arm back. Her instincts sent her scuttling backward right into Broch, who shoved her behind him, and said, "Dunnae lay a hand on the lass."

His deadly voice sent a tremor through her, along with a wave of gratefulness. Whatever anger she had against him for not standing by Cameron's side lessened in the moment he tried to aid her. But the slow smile that spread across Hugo's face made her fear what was to come.

"I'm glad to see ye will actually be of use to me," Hugo said cheerily. He flicked his hand toward his men, and they descended on Broch to seize him.

As Broch fought them, Hugo turned to her. "Either ye marry me now, or I'll kill him."

Biting her lip, she glanced toward Broch and cried out at the sight of him, restrained on either side by Hugo's men with another of Hugo's guards standing in front of Broch, hitting him repeatedly in the face. Blood spurted from his nose, and his head started to fall forward.

"Fine, I'll marry ye," she spat, unable to stand the thought of Broch forfeiting his life because of her.

<hr />

Something was wrong. Night was descending and the time for Hugo to have ridden this way with Sorcha had long passed. "We ride," Cameron barked, not waiting to even check with his brother. Cameron had his destrier at a full gallop before Graham overcame him.

"Where are we heading?" Graham asked.

"Back," Cameron said simply. "Something is amiss." His chest tightened almost unbearably with worry.

"Let me lead," Graham offered.

Cameron wanted to deny the request, but he knew well that Graham was the best tracker. He gave his brother a curt nod and fell slightly behind him, never more grateful than at this moment that he was no longer the fool who would not take help from his brothers.

They rode hard through the dark night, back past the Falls, now abandoned, and just as they paused for Graham to decide which way they should go, sticks snapped to Cameron's left. He and Graham drew their weapons at the same time a large man emerged from the woods, blubbering and half stumbling.

"My Sorcha," he cried. "My Sorcha, my Sorcha."

Cameron felt like he was drowning in sudden fear. He remembered Sorcha's stories about her uncle, and dismounting his horse, he stepped into the giant's path. "Brom?"

The man stopped and turned his childlike gaze on Cameron. "Me Brom."

Cameron almost laughed with gratefulness. "Brom, I'm Sorcha's husband. Lead me to her. I'm here to save her."

"My Sorcha? Sorcha at chapel. Bad man, evil man, marry her."

The tic in Cameron's jaw sprang to life. "Nay, Brom. Hugo Ross kinnae marry her. He can try, but Sorcha is my wife. Lead me to her now."

Brom nodded. "Brom take ye to her. Ye take her away and keep my Sorcha safe."

"Aye, Brom," Cameron said. "I vow it."

Sorcha could hardly believe she was wife to Hugo. Her mind denied it, but when Hugo turned to her, leered, and said, "Time for the joining," she could not hide from the truth.

She glanced toward Broch, who was lying unmoving on the ground after the beating he'd taken, and she was not sorry she had saved him. But now that she had bought him time, she had to escape. As Hugo turned to grab her, she brought her knee into his groin as Cameron had taught her.

She raced past his doubled-over form, slung open the chapel door, and stepped out into the courtyard. She had every intention of fleeing and not looking back, but the sight that greeted her shocked her to a stop.

Cameron sat on his horse, and her uncle was seated behind Graham on his horse beside Cameron. His warriors stood ready for battle behind them. The baleful grimness of his face, highlighted by the fact that his hair was pulled back, was both a welcome and worrisome surprise.

"What are ye doing here?" she gasped.

"I told ye," he replied in a calm voice as he dismounted, "I will always come for ye."

She raced toward him, even as the door behind her banged open and Hugo bellowed after her. Cameron closed the distance between them, jerked her to him, and shoved her behind him as he brought up his sword.

"Give me back my wife," Hugo snarled. As Hugo's men poured out of the chapel, Cameron's, who far outnumbered them, came forward with their weapons drawn. Hugo's men looked to him for orders, but Cameron spoke first.

"She kinnae be yer wife, Hugo, as she is mine." Cameron's words, though calm, held an undercurrent of deadly intention.

Sorcha frowned. Was Cameron trying to trick Hugo?

"I married her at my brother's castle over a sennight ago," Cameron went on, "and we were most assuredly joined. Ask her if ye dunnae believe me."

Cameron turned to her, and she saw the plea in his eyes for her to trust him. She took a deep breath and nodded. "I am his wife." Even if it wasn't exactly true, she was his wife in her heart.

"I'll kill ye!" Hugo roared.

He charged Cameron, but Cameron was ready, fierce,

and fast. He moved in a blur, swinging his sword high and plunging it straight through Hugo's heart. The man fell to his knees and then crashed forward, landing with his face in the dirt, hunched over the hilt of the sword with the blade protruding from his back. Cameron's men advanced past him to push Hugo's men back, while Cameron rolled Hugo over with the tip of his boot. He spat in the dirt near Hugo and, with a grunt, jerked his weapon from the dead man.

She trembled as Cameron came to her and encircled her in his arms. "It's over," he said soothingly in her ear.

She shook her head and pressed her palm to his pounding heart. "Nay," she said on a sob. "Broch is hurt."

"Nay, lass," came Broch's voice as he staggered from the chapel. The sight of his battered face made her gasp, but he managed a grin. "It will take more than that to kill me." He looked to Cameron. "I'm sorry I failed ye."

Sorcha frowned as Cameron said, "Ye did nae fail me, Broch."

Then Cameron wrapped his arm around her waist and led her a distance from his men and sister, who she only just saw well in the back out of harm's way. "It *is* over," he said emphatically.

"Ye have betrayed the king because of me and—"

He kissed her soundly to loud cheers from his men. "Nay, *bean bhàsail*. I plotted this scheme to save ye and us. The king was aware and part of the deception."

She listened in growing shock and wonder as he told her all he had plotted, from their marriage, to the joining, to her thinking he had left her. His brow creased as he held her around the waist. "Say something. Say ye hate me, yell at me, anything. I kinnae stand yer silence."

"We're truly married?" she asked in amazement.

"Aye," he said. The obvious joy in his voice warmed her

entire body. He brushed his hand over her cheek. "I'm sorry for the deception. I had to keep ye safe. Are ye cross?"

She thought for a moment before answering. He had risked everything for her and so had his family. Was she cross?

"Nay!" she assured him, kissing him as soundly as he had kissed her moments before. "I've nae ever been so glad to be deceived in my life. I only wish I'd kenned I was getting married. Lasses dream of that moment, ye ken?"

"Do they?" he asked, his surprise quite evident. "Then we will marry again so that this time it will be exactly as ye dreamed it."

"Ye would marry me again?" She was so touched tears welled in her eyes.

"*Bean bhàsail*, I would marry ye again every day for the rest of my life if ye wished it. I love ye that much."

She shook her head in disbelief, a smile curving her lips. "And I love ye, Cameron MacLeod. Now kiss me again, my fierce warrior."

Epilogue

Sorcha wanted her second time marrying Cameron to be the perfect memory, but as the day arrived, she found herself wishing things had happened differently. Even though she was surrounded by his wonderful family, who had embraced her as one of their own, and her Uncle Brom, who was now living at Dunvegan, she could not shake the sadness that shrouded her that her father and brother were gone. She really had no other family to stand here with her, no one that truly understood what this day, this joining with Cameron, meant.

So when she walked into the gardens and the first two people she saw were her sister Constance and her Aunt Blanche, she knew without a doubt that Cameron was responsible for getting her sister and aunt to Dunvegan for her wedding. She blinked back the tears that suddenly blurred her vision, made her way to her husband, and standing on her tiptoes, kissed him on the lips, not caring about the many eyes upon them.

Cheers arose from his family, her aunt and sister, and even Father Murdock, who waited patiently to begin the short ceremony. It did not take long to be formally married, but knowing what she knew now, knowing how important memories were, she embraced this one for every precious second. Never would she forget the way Cameron took her hand and squeezed it reassuringly in his, or the way he stared at her, his eyes so full of love, or the kiss he gave her at the end of the ceremony that curled her toes and heated her blood.

When the ceremony was complete, she made her way to Brom as Cameron's brothers beckoned him to them and surrounded him in what appeared to be a private meeting. They all wore smiles and whispered, and she could imagine they may well be teasing him, as the brothers seemed to do to one another. When she reached her uncle, he hugged her so hard it stole her breath.

"Brom's Sorcha," he said.

She kissed him on the cheek and was about to say something to him, when Angus—who Brom had decided was his new favorite person—called to Brom and her uncle went running like an excited child to an adult with a sweet treat. And then she saw that Angus did give Brom something, which he popped in his mouth with a happy grin.

Sorcha felt a grin on her own face to see her uncle so welcomed and happy. Suddenly her sister and Aunt Blanche were before her, and all three of them were exclaiming their joy.

"It is so good to see you both!" Sorcha cried, hugging her sister and then her aunt. Though Cameron had explained in his notes to them both all that had happened to her, apparently his explanation had been very brief. She took the time to fill them in on the details of all that had occurred, and glanced to Constance, who looked surprisingly happy for one who had always written to Sorcha of her constant misery in her marriage.

"Constance, it seems yer marriage is agreeing with ye more now," Sorcha tried to gently probe.

"Nay," Constance assured her with a shudder, "it nae

ever agreed with me at all, but my husband was killed in a hunt and I'm nae married any longer."

"Ye can come live here," Sorcha proposed, certain Cameron would nae mind.

Constance grinned. "Actually, yer husband already offered, but Aunt Blanche has offered, as well, and I have a desire to see England. If it's acceptable, I'd like to go to England for a spell and then come back to Dunvegan, possibly around Hogmanay?"

Sorcha nodded, glad that her sister was no longer tied to a man who treated her terribly. "You may return here anytime, to live or to visit."

She was about to ask her aunt how her husband was faring when King David strode into the gardens with a dozen men behind him, all armed for battle. Sorcha's stomach dropped as she watched the king approach Cameron, his brothers, and Alex MacLean, who must have joined them while she wasn't looking.

She watched Cameron's face, and though his expression was serious, he did not seem overly concerned. The king spoke for a few moments, waving his hands in the air, and when he departed, Alex and Iain went with him.

"I beg yer leave for a moment," Sorcha said to her sister and aunt, who both nodded.

She hurried over to Cameron and his brothers, arriving at the same time Lena did. She and Lena exchanged a worried look.

"What did the king say?" Sorcha asked.

Cameron slid his arm around her waist. "He offered his praise for how I handled the matter with March and Ross, and made plain that he considered my debt paid."

"Why did Alex and Iain go with the king?" Lena demanded.

Cameron shrugged. "I dunnae, Sister. He asked to speak with them in private."

Lena's face grew tight, but she did not say more.

Cameron squeezed Sorcha's waist and pressed his lips to her ear. "Come," he said, his voice husky.

"Where are ye taking me?" she demanded, laughing as he had already started to turn her away from the group.

"To bed," he said in a low, teasing voice. "Ye must have a proper joining." The look of pure desire he gave her made her shiver with anticipation.

"I like getting married," she replied with a giggle.

"So do I, *mo chridhe*, so do I."

As they started away, Sorcha felt a hand come to her arm. She turned to see Lena standing there.

Lena embraced Sorcha and hugged her tightly before letting go. "I'm glad to have a new sister," she said in a shy voice.

"As am I," Sorcha promised her.

As Sorcha and Cameron made their way out of the garden, Eolande appeared at the edge of the woods, staring at them. Sorcha paused. "Cameron, do ye see her?"

"Aye," he replied. "I sent her word of our wedding, and she told me she was coming to whisper a blessing upon our union for many children."

At that moment, the wind began to swirl, and Sorcha could see Eolande's lips moving. "How many children do ye suppose she is blessing us with?"

"Many," he replied with a grin, "so we best get started making them."

"I kinnae wait to make that memory," she teased.

He grinned wickedly. "I dunnae doubt it, *bean bhàsail*."

Dear Readers,

I hope you enjoyed the book. I invite you to leave a review for it, and to try the first chapter of My Fair Duchess, A Once Upon a Rogue novel, Book 1.

Prologue

The Year of Our Lord 1795
St. Ives, Cambridgeshire, England

The day Colin Sinclair, the Marquess of Nortingham and the future Duke of Aversley, entered the world, he brought nothing but havoc with him.

The Duchess of Aversley's birthing screams filled Waverly House, accompanied by the relentless pattering of rain that beat against the large glass window of Alexander Sinclair's study. The current Duke of Aversley gripped the edge of his desk, the wood digging into his palms. He did not know how much more he could take or how much longer he could acquiesce to his wife's refusal of his request to be present in the birthing room. He knew his wish was unusual and that she feared what he saw would dampen his desire for her, but nothing would ever do that.

Camilla's hoarse voice sliced through the silence again and fed the festering fear that filled him. She might die from this.

The possibility made him tremble. Why hadn't he controlled his lust? After six failed attempts to give him a child, Camilla's body was weak. He'd known the truth but had chosen to ignore it. Moisture dampened his silk shirt, and Camilla screeched once more. He shook his head, trying to ward off the sound.

He reached across his desk, and with a pounding heart and trembling hand, he slid the crystal decanter toward him. If he did not do something to calm his nerves, he would bolt straight out of this room and barge into their bedchamber. The last thing he wanted to do was cause Camilla undue anxiety. The Scotch lapped over the edge of the tumbler as he poured it, dripping small droplets of liquor on the contracts he had been blindly staring at for the last four hours.

He did not make a move to rescue the papers as the ink blurred. He did not give a goddamn about the papers. All he cared about was Camilla. The physician's previous words of warning that the duchess should not try for an heir again played repeatedly through Alexander's mind. The words grew in volume as the storm raged outside and his wife's shrieks tore through the mansion.

Alexander could have lived a thousand lifetimes without an heir, but he was a weak fool. He craved Camilla, body and soul. His desire, along with his pompous certainty that everything would eventually turn out all right for them because he was the duke, had caused him to ignore the physician and eagerly yield to his wife's fervent wish to have a child.

As Camilla's high, keening wails vibrated the air around him, he gripped his glass a fraction harder. The crystal cracked, cutting his hand with razor-like precision. He yanked off his cravat and wrapped it around his bleeding hand. Lightning split the shadows in the room with bright, blinding light, followed by his study door crashing open and Camilla's sister, Jane, flying through the entrance. Her red hair streamed out behind her, tears running down her face.

"The physician says come now. Camilla's—" Jane's voice cracked. She dashed a hand across her wet cheeks and moved across the room and around the desk to stand behind his chair. She placed a hand on his shoulder. "Camilla is dying. The doctor needs you to tell him whether to try to save her or the baby."

Pain, the likes of which the duke had never experienced, sliced through his chest and curled in his belly. A fierce cramp immediately seized him. "What sort of choice is that?" he cried as he stood.

Jane nodded sympathetically, then simply turned and motioned him to follow her. With effort, he forced his numb legs to move up the stairs toward his wife's moans. With every step, his heartbeat increased until he was certain it would pound out of his chest. He could not live without her, yet he knew she would not want to live without the babe. If he told the doctor to save her over their child, she would hate him, and misery would continue to plague her and chafe as it had done every time she had lost a babe these past six years.

He could not cause her such pain, but he could not pick the child over her. Outside the bedchamber door, Jane paused and turned to him, her face splotchy. "What are you going to do? I must know to prepare myself."

Alexander had never been a praying man, despite the fact that his mother had been a devout believer and had tried to get him to be one, as well. His father and grandfather had always said Aversley dukes made their own fates and only weak men looked to a higher power to grant them favors and exceptions. Alexander stiffened. He was a stupid fool who had thought himself more powerful than God. The day his mother had died, she had told him that one day, he would have to pay for this sin.

Was today the day? Alexander drew in a long, shuddering breath, mind racing. What could he do? He would renounce every conviction he held dear to keep his wife and child.

Squeezing his eyes shut, he made a vow to God. If He would save Camilla and the babe, he would pray every day and seek God's wisdom in all things. Surely, this penance would suffice.

A blood-curdling scream split the silence. Alexander's heart exploded as he shoved past Jane and threw the door open. The cream-colored sheets of their bed, now soaked crimson, lay scattered on the dark hardwood floor. Camilla, appearing incredibly small, twisted and whimpered in the center of the gigantic four-poster. Her once-white lacy gown was bunched at her waist to expose her slender legs, and Alexander winced at the blood smeared across her normally olive skin.

Moving toward her, his world tilted. His wife, his Camilla, stared at him with glazed eyes and cracked lips. A deathly pallor had replaced the healthy flush her face usually held. Blue veins pulsed along the base of her neck, giving her skin a thin, papery appearance. The sour stench of death filled the heavy air.

Only seconds had passed, yet it seemed like much longer. The physician swung toward Alexander. He appeared aged since coming through the door hours before; deep lines marked his forehead, the sides of his eyes, and around his mouth. Normally an impeccably kept man, his hair dangled over his right eye, and his shirt, stained dark red, hung out from his trousers. Shoving his hair out of his eye, the physician asked, "Who do you want me to try to save, Your Grace?"

Alexander curled his hands into fists by his sides, hissing at the throbbing pain the movement caused his cut palm. His mother's last words echoed in his head: *Great sins require great penance.*

The duke glanced at his wife's face, then slowly slid his gaze to her swollen belly. "Both of them," he responded. Fresh sweat broke out across his forehead as the doctor shook his head.

"The babe is twisted the wrong way. Even if I can get it out, Her Grace will be ripped beyond repair. She'll likely bleed out."

Anger coursed through Alexander's veins. "Both of them," he repeated, his voice shaking.

"If she lives, I'm certain she'll be barren. You are sure?"

"Positive," he snapped, seized by a wave of nausea and a certainty that he had failed to give up enough to save them both. Rushing to Camilla's side, he kneeled and gripped her hand as her back formed a perfect arch and another cry broke past her lips—the loudest scream yet.

Alexander closed his eyes and fervently vowed to God never to touch his wife again if only she and his babe would be allowed to live. He would do this and would keep his sacrifice between God and himself for as long as he drew breath and never tell a living soul of his penance. This time he would heed his mother's warnings. Her threadbare voice filled his head as he murmured her words. "True atonement is between the sinner and God or else it is not true, and the day of reckoning will come more terrible and shattering than imaginable."

Alexander repeated the oath, coldness gripping him and

burrowing into his bones.

Moments later, his throat burned, and he could not stop the tears of happiness and relief that rolled down his face as he cradled his healthy son in his arms.

Then in a faint but happy voice Camilla called out to him. "Alex, come to me," Camilla murmured, gazing at him with shining eyes and raising a willowy arm to beckon him. He froze where he stood and curled his fingers tighter around his swaddled son, desperate to hold on to the joy of seconds ago, and yet the elation slipped away when realizing the promise he had made to God.

That vow had saved his wife and child. As much as he wanted to tell Camilla of it now, as her forehead wrinkled and uncertainty filled her eyes, fear stilled his tongue. What if he told her, and then she died? Or the babe died?

"You've done well, Camilla," he said in a cool tone. The words felt ripped from his gut. Inside, he throbbed, raw and broken.

He handed the babe to Jane and then turned on his heel and quit the room. At the stairs, he gripped the banister for support as he summoned the butler and gave the orders to remove his belongings from the bedchamber he had shared with Camilla since the day they had married.

As he feared, as soon as Camilla was able to, she came to him, desperate and pleading for explanations. Her words seared his heart and branded him with misery. He trembled every time he sent her away from him, and her broken-hearted sobs rang through the halls. The pain that stole her smile and the gleam that had once filled her eyes made him fear for her and for them, but the dreams that dogged him of her death or their son's death should the vow be broken frightened him more. Sleeplessness plagued him, and he took to creeping into his son's nursery, where he would send the nanny away and rock his boy until the wee hours of the morning, pouring all his love into his child.

Days slid into months that turned to the first year and then the second. As his bond with Camilla weakened, his tie to his heir strengthened. Laughter filled Waverly House, but it was only the child's laughter and Alexander's. It seemed to him, the closer he became to his child and the more attention he lavished on him, the larger the wall became between him and Camilla until she reminded him of an angry queen reigning in her mountainous tower of ice. Yet, it was his fault she was there with no hope of rescue.

The night she quit coming to his bedchamber, Alexander thanked God and prayed she would now turn the love he knew was in her to their son, whom she seemed to blame for Alexander's abandonment. He awoke in the morning, and when the nanny brought Colin to Alexander, he decided to carry his son with him to break his fast, in hopes that Camilla would want to hold him. As he entered the room with Colin, she did not smile. Her lips thinned with obvious anger as she excused herself, and he was caught between the wish to cry and the urge to rage at her.

Still, his fingers burned to hold her hand and itched to caress the gentle slope of her cheekbone. Eventually, his skin became cold. His fingers curiously numb. Then one day, sitting across from him at dinner in the silent dining room, Camilla looked at him and he recoiled at the sharp thorns of revenge shining in her eyes.

The following week the Season began, and he dutifully escorted her to the first ball. Knots of tension made his shoulders ache as they walked down the staircase, side by side, so close yet a thousand ballrooms apart. After they were announced, she turned to him and he prepared himself to decline her request to dance.

She raised one eyebrow, her lips curling into a thinly veiled smile of contempt. "Quit cringing, Alexander. You may go to the card room. My dances are all taken, I assure you."

Within moments, she twirled onto the dance floor, first with one gentleman and then another and another until the night faded near to morning. Alexander stood in the shadows, leaning against a column and never moving, aware of the curious looks people cast his way. He was helplessly sure his wife was trying to hurt him, and he silently started to pray she would finally turn all her wrath at how he had changed to him and begin to love the child she had longed for…and for whom she had almost died.

Series by Julie Johnstone

Scottish Medieval Romance Books:

Highlander Vows: Entangled Hearts Series
When a Laird Loves a Lady, Book 1
Wicked Highland Wishes, Book 2
Christmas in the Scot's Arms, Book 3
When a Highlander Loses His Heart, Book 4
How a Scot Surrenders to a Lady, Book 5

Regency Romance Books:

A Whisper of Scandal Series
Bargaining with a Rake, Book 1
Conspiring with a Rogue, Book 2
Dancing with a Devil, Book 3
After Forever, Book 4
The Dangerous Duke of Dinnisfree, Book 5

A Once Upon A Rogue Series
My Fair Duchess, Book 1
My Seductive Innocent, Book 2
My Enchanting Hoyden, Book 3

Lords of Deception Series
What a Rogue Wants, Book 1

Danby Regency Christmas Novellas
The Redemption of a Dissolute Earl, Book 1
Season For Surrender, Book 2
It's in the Duke's Kiss, Book 3

Regency Anthologies
A Summons from the Duke of Danby (Regency Christmas Summons Book 2)
Thwarting the Duke (When the Duke Comes to Town, Book 2)

Regency Romance Box Sets
Dukes, Duchesses & Dashing Noblemen (A Once Upon a Rogue Regency Novels, Books 1-3)

Paranormal Books:

The Siren Saga
Echoes in the Silence, Book 1

About the Author

As a little girl I loved to create fantasy worlds and then give all my friends roles to play. Of course, I was always the heroine! Books have always been an escape for me and brought me so much pleasure, but it didn't occur to me that I could possibly be a writer for a living until I was in a career that was not my passion. One day, I decided I wanted to craft stories like the ones I loved, and with a great leap of faith I quit my day job and decided to try to make my dream come true. I discovered my passion, and I have never looked back. I feel incredibly blessed and fortunate that I have been able to make a career out of sharing the stories that are in my head! I write Scottish Medieval Romance, Regency Romance, and I have even written a Paranormal Romance book. And because I have the best readers in the world, I have hit the USA Today bestseller list several times.

If you love me, I hope you do!, you can follow me on Bookbub, and they will send you notices whenever I have a sale or a new release. You can follow me here: bookbub.com/authors/julie-johnstone

You can also join my newsletter to get great prizes and inside scoops!

Join here:
www.juliejohnstoneauthor.com

I really want to hear from you! It makes my day!
Email me here:
juliejohnstoneauthor@gmail.com

I'm on Facebook a great deal chatting about books and life.
If you want to follow me, you can do so here:
facebook.com/authorjuliejohnstone

Can't get enough of me? Well, good! Come see me here:
Twitter:
@juliejohnstone
Goodreads:
https://goo.gl/T57MTA

Made in the USA
Middletown, DE
14 January 2018